Lessons in Duck Shooting

JAYNE BUXTON

arrow books

Published by Arrow Books in 2006

1 3 5 7 9 10 8 6 4 2

Permission for the quote on page vii has been generously granted by Brian Tracy, *The Psychology of Selling*.

Permission for the quote on page vii has been generously granted by the Association Chaplin.

Marmalade facts are from C. Anne Wilson, *The Book of Marmalade*, Prospect Books, 1999.

Arrow Books
The Random House Group Limited
20 Vauxhall Bridge Road, London, SW1V 2SA

Random House Australia (Pty) Limited
20 Alfred Street, Milsons Point, Sydney,
New South Wales 2061, Australia

Random House New Zealand Limited
18 Poland Road, Glenfield
Auckland 10, New Zealand

Random House South Africa (Pty) Limited
Isle of Houghton, Corner Boundary Road & Carse O'Gowrie,
Houghton 2198, South Africa

Random House Group Limited Reg. No. 954009

www.randomhouse.co.uk

A CIP catalogue record for this book
is available from the British Library

Papers used by Random House
are natural, recyclable products made from wood grown in sustainable forests. The manufacturing processes conform to the environmental regulations of the country of origin

ISBN 0 09 949242 3

Typeset by Palimpsest Book Production Limited, Polmont, Stirlingshire
Printed and bound in Great Britain by Bookmarque Ltd, Croydon, Surrey

For Cal.

Acknowledgements

Thanks first to Euan Thorneycroft at Curtis Brown, without whose guidance and insights this story would almost certainly never had made its way into print; to Kate Cooper at Curtis Brown for her tireless efforts on my behalf; and to Kate Elton and Nikola Scott and their team at Arrow Books for their unbridled support, warmth and editorial expertise.

Thanks also to Justine Horsman for invaluable advice about necklaces and romantic heroes. To Olivia, Joely and Matt, thank you for your for tolerance and graciousness in the face of an almost permanently empty fridge and bouts of bad humour too frequent to mention. A special mention for Matt, the inspiration for a certain five-year old cowboy. And finally, thanks to Patrick, who has the whole business of being tirelessly supportive and enthusiastic completely taped.

Luck is quite predictable. If you want more luck, take more chances. Be more active. Show up more often.

BRIAN TRACY

It takes courage to make a fool of yourself

CHARLIE CHAPLIN

Part 1

Chapter 1
Are You Raising Children on Your Own?

The queue in the post office is twelve people deep. Having expected to sail straight up to the counter, I am reduced to making frenzied calculations about just how late I will be if I wait. Twelve people times approximately one and a half minutes each, divided by three counter assistants – no, wait, one has just closed her window so that makes two. I'll be here for at least six minutes. Probably ten.

I decide that, on balance, it is worth being a few minutes late at the school gates rather than another entire week late with my nephew's birthday gift (which is what will surely be the case if I miss this opportunity). So I shift from foot to foot and try to pass the time without appearing overly irritated.

To my left is a shelf full of brightly coloured leaflets. Their titles are difficult to decipher, as someone has obviously disturbed them and replaced them in a great hurry, and with complete disregard for the original leaflet-stacker's carefully considered system. I can see *The Family Tax Credit Made Simple*, and a pile of what look to be motoring-related documents. At the far end of the shelf, partially obscured by some leaflets on housing benefit, I spot one that asks, rather nosily I think, *Are you raising children on your own?*

Casting a sideways glance to make sure that no one is paying particular attention, I reach out to take the leaflet for single parents, grabbing one on tax discs at the same time to put any casual observers off the scent. Leaflet safely in hand, I take a second to regain my composure, avoiding the eyes of the filth-splattered builder ahead of me, who has turned round to identify the source of all the rustling.

On the cover of the leaflet is a photo of a family, I suppose, though it's not like any family I've ever seen. There is a youngish woman surrounded by four children, each one from a different racial background, all beaming into the camera in apparent delight at the political correctness of their multiracial single-parent family. Boy, she must have been busy, I think, looking for some sign in the woman's eyes. Tired yet determined. Resigned. Desperate for a lie-in. Anything would do really, other than the bright-as-a-button smile she actually proffers.

With five people still ahead of me in the queue, I open the leaflet to find a series of headings. I can see immediately that the most important ones are missing. A quick scan reveals that there is plenty of advice about what money is available, and how to collect it, but where, for instance, is the bit about how to adjust to the sudden, vast emptiness of your bed? And the long, hollow days of every second weekend? Where does it tell you how to train yourself not to reach out for that hand you've held a thousand times, or about all the different ways you're going to have to find to say to your children *this is not your fault*? And where's the advice about how to fix a blocked shower drain or a malfunctioning waste disposal unit once the person who used to do these things has left home?

But the most glaring omission is the section about how you ever find another man. Where's that one? Nowhere, that's where. Because you're not going to find one. Unless you are Elizabeth Hurley, with best mates like Elton and David, you're not going to be invited to parties heaving with handsome men seeking out the singular charms of a single mother. And even Liz didn't have too easy a time of it at first, if the pages of *Hello!* are anything to go by.

No. Once a divorced mother of two, likely always a divorced mother of two. I fold the leaflet in half and stuff it into my bag, just as the bespectacled woman at the counter beckons to me. I would have put it back on the shelf where it belongs, but I don't want anyone to take me for a desperate single mother on the make.

Chapter 2
Wake-Up Call

The familiar strident beep brings an abrupt halt to my early morning dream, erasing any shred of memory I might have had of it. In exhausted disbelief (can it really be ten to seven?) I roll over to check the time, reaffirming my long-standing commitment to replacing the greying plastic digital clock with something with a sleeker look and a less intrusive sound.

I push the snooze button and lie back on my pillow trying to take in the day through the tiny slits in the shutters. I listen for rain, but hear nothing. Good, no need for an umbrella, which is just as well as the chances of finding one anywhere in the house are practically non-existent.

My body longs to linger. Seeking to justify my lethargy,

I remember the foxes. Their eerie howls, like the wails of cats being strangled, had persisted for what seemed like hours in the street directly below my bedroom window during the night. Knowing little about the habits of foxes, I'm not sure if they are carrying on in the name of lust or battle, but I do know that they are becoming louder with every passing night. Dad says I ought to write to the council and ask to have them relocated, but that particular task seems destined to remain on the lower rungs of my mental to-do list, somewhere above the note about fixing the cracked tile in the hallway, but well below the reminder to clean out the tumble dryer filter once a week lest it overheat and explode.

The door squeaks, and Jack pads into the room in full cowboy regalia, as is his habit. Immediately he wakes, he springs out of bed and dons hat, vest, chaps, holster and guns before coming in to see me. He insists on remaining in this outfit until a few minutes before we leave for school, at which point I have to cajole or occasionally wrestle him into his school uniform. David says I make life hard on myself by not being tougher with Jack, that I should insist on the uniform from the word go. I think the reason I let Jack get away with it is that I sympathise with what I see as his mini-protest. He doesn't see why he should have to put on a tie and blue trousers and go to school for six hours every day at the age of five; much of the time, neither do I.

Jack sits beside me in the bed making 'pching poing' noises and taking aim at the photo of the smiling couple with two small children on the dresser.

'Mummy, do I have to go to school today?' he whines.

'It's sooo long before you pick me up. Do you know how many worksheets they make me do? Do you?'

'Jack honey, you have to go to school. Everyone has to go to school. It's the law. And anyway, it won't be too long before I see you,' I say somewhat disingenuously, knowing full well that today is one of the days I have to work, and that he will be collected by Jill, our babysitter.

'Ohhh,' Jack moans. 'Archie's mummy lets him have a day off when he doesn't feel well. I don't feel well.'

'You can have a day off if you're really ill,' I say. 'But today you don't look particularly ill to me, so you're going to school. Now, come here and give me a big cuddle before I have my shower.'

Jack relents and sinks into the pillow beside me, his honeyed sleep-breath warming my cheek. For an instant I am completely in the moment, drinking in the plump softness of the tiny hand clutching its prized pistol, without a thought for the rest of life. Then the thing I have been trying not to remember rushes to the forefront of my mind. Now that it's here, I can't shift it. Not even the gloriousness of this little man beside me can banish it.

Today is Thursday. Tomorrow the children's teachers have an INSET day (a challenge periodically thrown out to working mothers by the educational establishment), so tonight David is coming to collect Jack and Millie for the weekend. They are going to meet David's girlfriend, Chantal, and I am going to spend the weekend more or less alone.

David is my ex-husband of two years and three months precisely. Chantal is David's girlfriend of four months, give or take a week. Clearly, Chantal is not the woman

David left me for. Caroline was the woman he left me for. Though she and David were only together for three months, in my mind she will forever be the woman responsible for breaking up my marriage.

In between Caroline and Chantal there have been too many women to count, and more than one or two inappropriately young girls. I heard about a Madison (American), a Suzanne (Scottish) and a Jessica (perfect English Rose, apparently). I think there was also a Cynthia, though she was spoken of so fleetingly that I can't be sure she was anything more than a mere rumour.

The fact that David seems to have successfully shagged his way through the past twenty-seven months while I have been out with just two men has ceased to bother me. That's not strictly true, but after the initial sting of the separation, the gruesomeness of the divorce and the strange hollowness of the first few months after it, learning of David's romp across the London singles landscape began to lack impact. I soon became accustomed to it.

In a funny way, thinking of David hurtling from one woman to another has been vaguely comforting. I have chosen to see it as a sign of just how misguided and rootless he is, and perhaps even of how regretful he might eventually become. Not that there is the slightest chance of my ever accepting him back, after what he has put me through. But I have drawn some solace from the fact that having thoughtlessly discarded someone he once referred to as his 'forever girl' he has so far not succeeded in finding a suitable replacement.

But Chantal is different. Chantal has lasted beyond the customary eight weeks, and is now well into her fourth month. She looks suspiciously as if she might stay. David speaks in warm, admiring tones about her, mostly to our friends and very occasionally to me, suggesting that he thinks of her as something more than a means of whiling away the hours between midnight and seven a.m. Worst of all, though, is the fact that David wants her to meet the children.

None of his other women ever met Jack and Millie. It was never even suggested. David would see Jack and Millie at my house (formerly our house) while I disappeared for a few hours, or take them for supper at Pizza Express, or a weekend at his parents. If they went to his flat, he assured me that his girlfriends were never there. I think that even at the height of his self-centred self-indulgence (from which it is arguable that he has not yet descended), he knew that they were never going to be permanent fixtures, and that it would be cruel to allow Jack and Millie to become attached to them.

I am saved from my thoughts by the sight of Millie peeping around the door. Jack hears her and pops his head and shoulders up from the pillow, delivering a swift blow to my eye with his elbow in the process. I resist the urge to scream, managing to hold myself to a restrained grimace.

'Hello, darling. Did you sleep well?' I say, patting the empty space in the bed. The upside of having been left by your husband is that your bed can accommodate at least two children without becoming intolerably uncomfortable for all concerned.

'Mummy, I had a bad dream,' says Millie quietly as she crawls into bed beside Jack.

'Really, darling, what about?'

''Bout a witch. She kept banging on my window. She looked like Mrs Williamson.'

Mrs Williamson is the resident battleaxe at Millie and Jack's school. Millie is normally quite adept at avoiding her steely glare, but has recently had a nasty run-in with her over an incident involving four seven-year-old girls, some missing hairclips and one unduly irate mother. I'm absolutely sure that Millie had nothing to do with the theft of the hairclips, but Witch Williamson seems to have decided that it is better to cover all bases and apportion blame evenly rather than seek out the true culprit. Millie and the two other suspects were forced to spend break-time writing 'I will respect the property of others' two dozen times while their classmates were happily cavorting in the playground.

'Well don't worry, sweetheart, there's no witch going to get in through your window, not even one who looks like Mrs Williamson. The windows in this house are completely witchproof,' I reassure her. 'Anyway,' I attempt brightly, 'guess what today is?'

'What?' Jack and Millie ask in unison. 'Half day at school?' adds Jack hopefully.

'No, better than that.' I say, with now heroic levels of cheer. 'Daddy is coming to collect you for the weekend after tea tonight. You're going to stay with Papa and Gran, and visit Barwell Zoo on Saturday. And best of all you're going to meet Daddy's friend, Chantal. She's going to go with you to the zoo.'

'I don't bemember Chantal. I never heard of that name,' says Jack.

'What kind of a name is Chantal?' asks Millie

'Chantal is a French name, and you have heard of her, Jack. I told you about her last week, remember? She is Daddy's very good friend, and she really wants to meet you, because you are the most important things in Daddy's life.' I got this little number from *Divorce With Grace: Helping Your Children Deal With Marriage Breakdown*, a book at which I had loudly scoffed before finding myself repeatedly referring to it.

'I hope I like Daddy's friend,' says Jack warily.

'I'm sure you will, sweetheart. You love Daddy, and Daddy wouldn't like anyone horrid.'

Thus satisfactorily fobbed off, Jack bounds out of bed, guns in hand, and runs to his room. Millie and I lie still for a minute or two, listening to the 'pching, poing' noises emanating from the other side of the hall. Then she sighs, and in her most concerned voice asks, 'What will you do without us, Mummy?'

I could have told you this was coming. Even after more than two years' worth of weekends spent with her father, Millie never fails to express a touching concern about leaving me behind. Initially I might have been guilty of inviting this worry, having been unable to muster the appropriate levels of mature nonchalance required of me in the early days. But I was pretty sure that I had managed, for the better part of the past year, to feign just about the right amount of delight at the prospect of my solitary weekends. But Millie refuses to be fooled. She has always been the kind of child who can spot fear, sadness or weakness at fifty paces. The community midwife who visited me in the weeks after she was born used to insist that Millie had an unusually acute ability to pick up on people's hidden feelings, and that if I wanted a calmer baby I was going to have to do a better imitation of tranquility myself.

'I will miss you, Millie, you know that. But because you're not here, I've organised a really nice weekend. I'll see Mel and Clara tomorrow night, and have my hair cut on Saturday – you know how much I love those head massages that George gives – and probably see a movie on Saturday night. I will be fine, Millie. You forget about me and enjoy yourself.'

'Don't see *The Lost Princess*, will you, Mummy. I really want to see that with you.'

'Deal.' I say, sensing her cross-examination mercifully drawing to a close. 'I'll see something you absolutely do not want to see. Now, we need to get going. Scat,' I say, pulling back the duvet and nudging her gently.

Millie scampers to her room just as the alarm goes off for the second time. I roll out of bed, knowing that my favourite moments of the day have just gone. It's all one big sprint from here.

'Come on, Jack,' I snap with more than a little impatience. 'It's eight thirty and we have to leave five minutes ago. You can put your holster back on when you get home tonight and wear it all weekend if you like.' David will kill me for this, but being up against the clock I've no other option.

Jack grudgingly removes his holster and tucks his shirt into his blue school trousers with a painstaking slowness that makes me long to do it for him. I pull his red sweat-shirt over his head, hurriedly combing his hair with my fingers as the top of his head emerges. I cannot remember the last time I actually used a brush or comb on Jack's hair. The only times I remember, or have time to do it, there isn't a hair implement in sight.

Millie stands ready by the door, blue coat buttoned up neatly, red school bag firmly in hand. How did I spawn such a sensible and organised creature?

'Mummy, you're making us late,' she chastises as she watches me apply lip gloss in the hall mirror. I can hardly see my refection for all the smudges on the glass, which seem to have multiplied overnight. Ever since I let Rita go, in an attempt to economise, all the mirrors in the house have been disgracefully cloudy. Mirrors seem to be one thing I cannot keep up with, along with bookshelves and the fridge. I am, I have to add in my defence, very strong on counter tops, floors and loos, which seem to put themselves forward for a regular scrubbing in a way that cannot be ignored. The prospect of visitors peering disapprovingly at a sludge-brown ring around the bottom of one of the loos is enough to galvanise me into dropping a toilet duck into each of them once a week.

If I were to make a list of all the ways in which my life has changed since David left, the state of the house would feature pretty high up on it. Not, you understand, because David ever did any housework. No, the reason the house has been a relative shambles since he left is because when we were together I could afford to pay Rita to keep the ironing basket in check and the filth at bay. Once it became clear that I would not be in regular receipt of Ivana Trump-like alimony payments and that I faced paying the mortgage single-handedly, Rita became an unaffordable luxury. So I do my best to clean my own house, meaning that the bookshelves are thick with dust and the fridge shelves are thick with congealed Ribena. There is only one category of people with less time for housework than working mothers, and that is working single mothers.

I am tempted to use my pashmina to wipe the worst of the fug from the mirror, but remind myself that it is the palest of creams and decide against it.

'Right, everybody, ready?' I ask, stretching out my hand to take Jack's. Millie opens the door, and we are off. I have already decided against walking to school, which we can only ever do when we are unusually organised. So we pile into the car, all of us having to negotiate for our seats with casually strewn mental-maths quiz sheets and empty juice cartons.

Horrid Henry helps us pass the ten-minute drive to school. I'm never entirely sure I'm doing the right thing in letting the children listen to this tape when, without too much effort, I could retrieve *Wind in the Willows* or *Alice in Wonderland* from the depths of the glove compartment. Millie is all right; she seems to rise above it. But I worry that Jack will learn too much from Henry. All the raspberry blowing is bad enough, but more worrying is that Jack might emulate Henry's constant and highly successful campaign to breach every single rule set down by his long-suffering parents. Still, Henry does make us all laugh. Jack positively chortles his way to school, and by the time we arrive he has forgotten that he'd rather have stayed home playing cowboys all day.

We manage to park just outside the gates (one of the great advantages of being on the late side: others have long since moved off by the time you arrive), and tumble from the car, falling into line with all the other small red and blue figures running towards the front doors. We walk up the front steps and into the comforting smells of freshly sharpened pencils and damp school-shoe leather and I kiss the tops of the children's heads and send them off with pats on their bottoms. Millie hesitates at the top of the stairs, and turns round to wave goodbye. I detect just the slightest quiver of her bottom lip, which must mean she has remembered Mrs Williamson and the hairclip incident and fears another day of hard stares. I blow her a kiss and she turns to face the music.

Jack, meanwhile, is dragging himself upstairs unenthusiastically. *Horrid Henry* is now a thing of the past, and an entire day of phonics worksheets, sitting still and possibly even eating broccoli looms ahead. I duck out as quickly as possible, knowing that if he turns round he's liable to run back down and beg to be taken home. And today that is positively not an option as I am due to meet Paul Delaney from the agency. Faced with the challenge of getting the car back home and myself into the office in under forty minutes, I haven't got time to do more than throw a concerned backwards glance in his direction.

On my way out of the schoolyard I hear a high-pitched shriek behind me. I turn around to see Sally Chambers's mum (is it Helen or Harriet?) tottering towards me in what look to be a pair of open-toed sandals (in February for God's sake).

'Ally, I'm glad I caught you. You know the spring fête is coming up, and you said you'd be prepared to help on one of the stalls? Well, I've put you down for the tombola. I hope that's all right.'

'Oh, sure. That's fine.'

What's a tombola again?

'Excellent. We've decided that this year we should fill the jars with small items, Woolworth-type things. I should think we'll need three hundred or so. But you've got a couple of months to get them together. And I'm sure everyone will be more than willing to help. That OK?'

Now I remember what a tombola is. Shorthand for an awful lot of effort by a lot of mothers leading to the raising of a very small amount of money. Still, the kids love it, and it's not rocket science. I must be able to manage it.

'Fine. I'll get on to it right away. Sorry, but I have to go now. I'm late for a meeting.'

'Do let me know if you need any help,' gushes Sally's mum (Hilary? Hannah?) as I rush away from her.

It's only now that I can pay attention to the day that lies ahead of me. And it doesn't look pretty. Pushing marmalade is not as easy as you might think. The day's schedule is full-to-overflowing with production meetings, negotiations with suppliers, phone calls to chase late publicity shots and budget discussions too tedious to contemplate in advance

And at the end of it, all I have to look forward to is a six o'clock rendezvous that will serve to remind me of just one thing: that my ex-husband is moving on with nary a backwards glance, while I am frozen in a life consisting of every other weekend spent alone and absolutely no prospects of a romantic attachment within five thousand miles.

Chapter 3
Handover

True to my New Year's resolution, I walk up the three floors to my illustrious cubicle at Cottage Garden Foods. I always used to think that when I'd climbed the ranks to Product Manager I'd be given my own office complete with deep, squashy sofa. But by the time I got there, offices were out of vogue and open plan was the thing. Now I'm Group Product Manager, in charge of marketing an entire range of marmalades, but I have to work at a desk located within spitting distance of the water cooler with nothing more than a five-foot-high screen to protect me. I suppose I should count myself lucky that Cottage Garden Foods hasn't yet cottoned onto hot-desking.

In my inbox, intermingled with worthy emails pertaining to ad campaigns, planning meetings and budget over-runs, are thirteen invitations to try one or another form of viagra, five solicitations to partake of penis enlargement, and two offers to roll up my debt into one easily manageable package. My colleague Lisa, who is to chutneys what I am to marmalades, insists that I must have responded to one of these types of messages in the past, thereby emboldening whomever sends them, but I swear I've done nothing to invite this daily bombardment.

There are also two messages from Mel. Feeling rather fragile, I decide to go to hers first.

From: mel.atkinson@me.com
To: ally.james@cottage.garden.foods.co.uk

Are we still on for Friday night? Copy going better than anticipated, so could be with you by 5:30. How bout it?

By the way, need your help with something. Could even help you find your next husband. Will bring details on Friday.

From: mel.atkinson@me.com
To: ally.james@cottage.garden.foods.co.uk

You do still plan on having a next husband don't you?

From: ally.james@cottage.garden.foods.co.uk
To: mel.atkinson@me.com

Definitely still on for Friday. Will need intravenous supply of gin to commence, as will have made acquaintance of leggy French bird who will be worming her way into my children's hearts all weekend.

Will be glad to help. What is it this time? Need a quote for a piece on women who've found life after divorce, or one from woman who can't get over divorce? Or perhaps one from woman who wants divorce but can't get one? Will try to dream up adequate soundbite. Will also confirm with Clara.

Mel is a staff writer with *Me* magazine, a monthly devoted to the modern thirty-something woman who has a lot going on in her life. They don't use the word 'juggle' (so outdated) but it's nevertheless there, playing a behind-the-scenes role in every issue. Mel writes about what it's like to have a brilliant career that keeps you away from your children, what happens when your career outshines that of your partner and what to do when the career goes down the toilet and you've still got mouths to feed. That sort of thing. Every piece has an upbeat tone – she always seems to find examples of women who've managed to find solutions that 'work for them'. After all, a magazine whose mantra is 'celebrate and inspire' cannot afford to feature too many articles of the shocking and depressing variety. *Me* is not *Marie Claire*, nor ever wants to be.

Like most feature writers, Mel is often short of interesting interviewees, and the time in which to seek them out. So she comes to me quite regularly, asking if I know 'someone who . . .'. On occasion, I've been declared a suitable example myself, and have provided quotes directly, though always using a pseudonym. I'm not the kind of person who wants to see her name emblazoned on the cover of a magazine.

Mel and I go back almost eighteen years. We met in our second year of university, and must have shared five different flats in our twenties. The last time we lived together our flat was directly above Clara and Jonathon's. Once we overcame the initial noise issue and worked out how to accommodate Jonathon's almost constant presence, we became more or less inseparable.

Clara is a tall New Yorker with a mass of thick blonde hair that swings just above her broad, confident shoulders. She is a partner in the management consulting firm Peters and Young, where she has worked since joining them as an astonishingly clever but lowly analyst at the age of twenty-four. She earns a minor fortune, as partners in these sorts of enterprises invariably do.

Where Clara is tall, blonde and formidable looking, Mel is tiny, with long dark hair that seems to swill capriciously around her face, especially when she's angry. Where Clara is fearsomely clever and logical, Mel is highly-strung and emotional, you could say bordering on the wacky. Where Clara earns a six-figure salary bossing around stout, big-bellied men in expensive suits, Mel has scraped together a living writing for magazines.

But both of them have ended up with slightly offbeat, gentle kinds of partners. (We have, in our baser and more inebriated moments, bemoaned the fact that not one of us fell for a rich investment banker who might have allowed us to live out our days in the manner to which we could easily have become accustomed.) Mel has been living with Dominique, the owner of a small music shop who moonlights as a piano and clarinet teacher, for six years. They haven't got around to getting married or having babies, but they are as tight as two people can be. Jonathon, who married Clara despite the fact that she seemed to come with a couple of female appendages, is an illustrator who sometimes has three projects on the go and other times has none. He's quiet and unassuming when you first meet him, but he has a razor sharp wit and an intensity that takes you by surprise. For all her professional indomitableness, Clara would be lost without him.

It's thanks to Mel and Clara that I survived my divorce. They were also the ones who supported me when I swapped the glamour of marketing lipsticks for Chanel in Knightsbridge for the rather more humdrum business of promoting marmalade for a food conglomerate just off Hammersmith roundabout. After the divorce, I needed to increase my salary and reduce my working hours, always a tricky combination. Cottage Garden Foods were rather chuffed at being able to lure someone from the world of prestige product marketing out to their distinctly unfashionable offices near the M4, so were persuaded to raise my previous salary by ten per cent for a four-day week.

So here I sit, on what the Americans once called the Mommy Track. I'm not sure what they call it now, but here we know it simply as trading a potentially brilliant career for a do-able job. Whatever it is, it is all I can handle. Friday is my sanity saver. The day when I can do the Tesco run, pay the bills, whip round with the Hoover and replenish the stores of emotional strength required to be the mother of two children under eight.

But now is not the time to ponder the blessings of a part-time career. I have to scope out an innovative promotion plan for Cottage Garden Food's most recent innovation: Seville Sunset, a marmalade of Seville oranges with crushed redcurrants. It is due to be launched in March just after National Marmalade Day, and I am currently trying to engineer a jam-packed week of radio discussions (one, about Literary References to Marmalade, is already in the bag), in-store tastings and the sponsorship of an exhibit on Edwardian Life at the V&A. The thing that is giving me most grief at the moment is the print ad campaign the agency has been working on for several months, with very little of any merit to show for their efforts.

I can see the Head of Marketing, Anna Wyatt, meandering through the sea of desks towards me. She is practising her management-by-walking-about bit, smiling graciously at her underlings while expressing sincere interest in their latest project. I have nothing against her really. True, she is overtly and quite combatively ambitious (which begs the question as to why she traded Manhattan for West London), but she's straight and fair, and nothing like the monumental idiot who might have become my boss, and who currently sits ten feet away from me grinning into his coffee in anticipation of a desk visit from Anna.

The only problem with Anna has to do with children. She hasn't got any, doesn't want any. I suspect she doesn't even like them. Being a part-timer with two of the vile little creatures is something of a blot on my copybook as far as she is concerned, so I generally have a lot of making up to do. Most of the time, this means that I endeavour to do an impression of a keen and committed twenty-eight-year-old, much as I did at Chanel. I do not have pictures of Jack and Millie on my desk. I do not say I have to leave early because the babysitter is ill. I do not decline drinks invitations because I have to get home to make a Greek goddess costume from an old sheet. I spend a great deal of time lying, or, as my mother would say, being appropriately economical with the truth. It's an essential skill. Most working mothers have it.

Anna is getting closer now. What shall I say when she asks me how the promotion plan for Seville Sunset is going? I certainly won't tell her that it's not done because Millie has had a project on rivers and lakes to complete this week, and Jack has developed a new habit of appearing on the stairs demanding some life-critical resource (water; a tissue; Frank the Bear) every ten minutes for an hour and a half after I put him to bed every evening, both of which have rendered me incapable of doing anything other than gaping at *Celebrity Big Brother* once I have finally settled everyone down. No, I won't say any of this. Ever so economically, I'll tell Anna about the unbelievable arrogance of the few key retailers who are still dragging their heels regarding the in-store tasting schedule. I expect them to get back to me by Friday afternoon, and the plan will be on Anna's desk by Monday.

As it turns out, Anna never made it to my desk. She was sidetracked by an urgent call (something to do with a printing error on the chutney labels), and never resumed her tour. My budget meeting was also cancelled, because the finance director had gone home with a stomach complaint (or could it be the babysitter?). So I was able to spend two hours on the Seville Sunset master plan, which means I won't have to spend the entire weekend doing it. Perhaps, this weekend, I will take the time to pamper myself a little. I'll get the groceries done early on Friday, and maybe even make a trip to the gym.

Walking to the Tube, I am struck by a better plan. I'll pamper myself right now. I will not rush home, arriving in a bedraggled heap to find my ex-husband and his impeccably groomed girlfriend having tea on the sofa with Millie and Jack. I will, instead, steal half an hour to visit the nail and facial bar on Angel Street, and arrive home with glowing cheeks, French-manicured nails, and, with any luck, some semblance of inner calm. Jill can entertain them until I return, and David will just have to wait before embarking on his weekend getaway.

The nail and facial bar is, it being Thursday evening, rather packed. Not with mothers like me in need of a quick tarting up, but with an array of young things preparing for a night out, on this the first clubbing night of the weekend. It is twenty-five minutes before I'm even called to the chair, and I then face a decision about how late I can afford to be. Do I stay and risk David and the children's ire when I arrive home very late? Or walk out now and arrive home more or less as planned, but decidedly scruffy and definitely unequal to the challenge of meeting a French babe?

I compromise with myself, opting for the buff and shine rather than the full French manicure (saving: 10 minutes) and the mini-facial rather then the complete works with the neck massage (saving: 12 minutes). With any luck, I'll be out of here within twenty minutes, and no one will even notice how late I am. With even more luck, David will arrive late as well, and Jill will insist on bringing him up to date on Jack and Millie's latest exploits. I consider then quickly discard the idea of ringing home to let them all know my whereabouts. I can't possibly risk the ridicule, and, besides, Sally has started on my nails and would be most upset if I ruined them by digging into my bag for my phone. I'm almost certain I detected the beep of the battery dying earlier, so it probably isn't even working.

As I succumb to Sally's pliant fingers, making an almighty effort to draw as much relaxation and rejuvenation from the experience as I can, I am also willing her to speed up. It all seems to be taking longer than the promised 25 minutes. At one point I want to implore Sally to get on with it, to be a little less thorough, but I know this will be unforgivably rude. I close my eyes and my to-do list pops up in front of them where the blank canvas of the truly tranquil should be. Tombola jars, unarranged dental check-ups and unmade phone calls to plumbers, ballet teachers and the Inland Revenue are suddenly swimming in front of my eyes, and I can feel the tension rising to the place on my forehead into which Sally is resolutely massaging deep-penetrating vitamin E cream.

Finally, it is over. I thank Sally, press a twenty-pound note into the hands of the receptionist – taking care not to chip my newly buffed and shined nails – and rush out of the salon with one sleeve of my coat dangling. I am subjected to a disapproving stare from an incoming customer, for whom I have failed to hold open the door long enough, but I cannot worry about this. I am late, and there is no time for niceties. I am a woman on a mission.

Miraculously, the trains are running with some efficiency. I run from the station as fast as my two-inch heels will allow, slowing down to a mere speed-walk about a hundred feet from the house. Time to gather the sense of calm confidence that will be required of me once I open the front door. As I turn the key in the lock I admire my immaculately groomed nails, glowing gently under the porch light.

'Hello, I'm home,' I shout cheerily. 'Sorry I'm so late. Anna Wyatt caught me just as I was leaving the building, and I thought she was going to go on for ever. Hope you've all been having a nice time.'

I sling my coat on one of the hooks by the door, deposit my bag near the radiator, and walk back to the kitchen, peering into the sitting room on my way past. The house is eerily quiet. There is no one in the sitting room, and, I discover, no one in the kitchen either. I spot three pieces of notepaper laid out side by side on the kitchen table in front of the fruit bowl, in which a single, miserable-looking pear is quietly disintegrating.

Moving closer, I can see that they are all in different handwriting. The first I recognise as Millie's big, rounded letters.

Dear Mummy,

Sorry we couldn't wait. Daddy said we had to leave. I will miss you. Here are some kisses from me. XoXoXoX

Millie

The second note is from David.

Ally,

Where were you? Tried to call but your phone was off. Had to leave, as traffic is terrible and we'll be late as it is. Sorry. See you Sunday night.

David

I sit down heavily on the nearest chair, suddenly overwhelmed by nausea. I've missed them. I've missed saying goodbye to my babies, and all in the name of vanity. Millie will be distraught. She hates not being able to say goodbye properly. And without my being there to check, Jack has probably gone off without something essential to his Wild West ensemble. What kind of ridiculous idea was it to try to make myself look glamorous for some French woman I've never met and a man who is probably so enamoured of her that he wouldn't have noticed me anyway?

I read the third note, which I now see is from Jill.

Ally,

Sorry. Had to leave. Hope I did the right thing letting David take the kids. Thought you would understand.

See you next week,

Jill

P.S. Chantal is quite stunning so I was afraid she wouldn't be very nice, but she seems great. Brought gifts for the kids. Hope that makes you feel better.

Then, scrawled across the bottom of the note in a different coloured pen:

By the way, you are out of milk.

Chapter 4
Proposition

I am perched precariously on the edge of a bar stool waiting to spring upon a nearby sofa the minute it is vacated by its occupants. I watch them closely, wary of missing my one opportunity to secure a comfortable seat and table somewhat off the beaten track of the bar area, which is filling up with alarming rapidity. Sitting on a cosy sofa in a bar with my girlfriends on a Friday night is an experience I can embrace, but hovering on a metal bar stool amidst hoards of over-confident, drunk twenty-somethings is another matter altogether.

The couple who have been canoodling on the sofa rise in unison, he helping her on with her coat with a tenderness that only couples who have not yet entered their third week of dating can muster. I slip in behind them as they leave, plonking my white wine firmly on the table to mark my territory. I have only been seated a few minutes when I see Clara's blonde head making its way through the crowd. Being five foot ten, she doesn't disappear into the sea of jackets as I would, but rather cuts a clean path straight through it. Mel will, of course, be late.

'Ally, you're here first for a change. You must have been desperate to get out!' she jokes, removing her coat (a sumptuous black cashmere number with fur collar that I covet) and parking herself beside me. We hug, as always, rather than resorting to the two-cheeked air-kiss we have both agreed should be reserved for mere acquaintances.

'So, sweetie. Tell me how you are. Is she really as gorgeous as you feared?' she asks, simultaneously pointing at my wine glass and gesticulating to the waitress.

'I'm guessing so,' I say. 'Only I don't really know, because I didn't actually see her. I arrived home late, and they had already gone. But Jill left me a note confirming my worst fears.'

'So Jill thinks she's gorgeous. That doesn't mean a thing. A lot of French women look gorgeous when they're all done up, but without the Chanel they are very ordinary. Anyway, Jill could be wrong.'

'Doubt it,' I respond dejectedly. 'You know, it's not just the fact that she might be pretty that bothers me. It's the fact that she might be pretty, and nice, and intelligent and that Millie and Jack will grow up admiring her. Am I really going to have to go through life hearing Millie say things like *Chantal would never wear that* or, *I wish I could be elegant like Chantal*? Because if I am, frankly, I'm not sure I'm up to it.'

'Don't be ridiculous,' scoffs Clara. 'Children always love their mothers best. You know as well as I do that you could go around in a high-necked Crimplene blouse and a kilt and Millie would still think you were the epitome of style.'

Just then Mel appears, looking hot and flustered. 'Hi, you two,' she says, unwinding her eight-foot-long scarf and dropping her satchel to the floor with a thud. 'Sorry I'm late. Hell of a day.'

There isn't a spare chair in sight, so we are forced to squeeze three to the sofa, with Clara and Mel on either side of me. This makes for quite a lot of tiring head action for me.

Mel tells us why her day has been hellish (editor's idea for mini-feature sprung upon her during mid-morning coffee, followed by train getting stuck in tunnel on way to critical interview for piece due on Monday, topped off with Charlie the cat throwing up all over two pieces from Dom's collection of rare sheet music). Clara has her own tale of woe.

'Do you know that after all the business I've brought in this year, and all the effort I've put into developing the MBA recruitment programme, Harrison passed me over for that position on the main board in favour of that PowerPoint wanker Jeremy Thistle.'

'That's outrageous! You'd been more or less promised that position. What are you going to do?'

'Nothing to do, for now. I've just got to bide my time, wait for everyone else to discover that Thistle is nothing but a set of PowerPoint presentations and beg me to take his place. It won't take long. He's absolutely useless, and the only reason they've put him there is because they bought his company and have to pretend that he's an important part of the deal.'

'I don't know how you can be so philosophical. I'd be spitting blood.'

'I've already done that, in the privacy of my own bathroom. You should see the white tiles now,' replies Clara, smiling.

There's something forced about Clara's smile. Losing the position on the board will have been a real blow. Clara is one of those people who really wants success. She knows she's smart enough, and strong enough to withstand the pressure of working fifteen-hour days. And Lord knows she's sacrificed enough for it. Jonathon has wanted children for years but she's always resisted, saying the time isn't right, that her career would never recover from the maternity leave let alone the inevitable juggling that would follow it. Just over a year ago she relented and they started trying for a baby. With every passing month she seemed to grow more enamoured of the idea of becoming a mother, even talking in practical terms about how she would manage to fit it in with her career, which made it all the more difficult when the months passed without any sign of a pregnancy. To lose the much coveted board position now, when it seems that she may have sacrificed so much to get it, must be a bitter pill to swallow.

We rarely dwell on the question of whether or not Clara is pregnant. For the first few months after she announced to us that she and Jonathon were ready to try we would receive a monthly report on the results of their efforts. After a while the reports stopped, and Clara made it clear that she wasn't up for detailed discussions about her cycle or Jonathon's sperm count, or any of the other reasons they might not be conceiving. Things just went silent, and a shadow seemed to fall over Clara. You would never describe her as deflated, or sad; she's far too vibrant and strong willed for that. But there's definitely something different about her. Every now and then you catch her flinching, as if she's been stabbed by her own thoughts. Then she's back again, livening up the conversation, giving everyone else the benefit of all her certainty.

'Well here's to Friday and no more of that kind of nonsense for two whole days,' says Mel, raising her glass.

Suddenly I remember that Mel needs my help with something. 'What's this thing you need help with, Mel? Some article to do with husbands, wasn't it?'

'Oohh. Thanks for reminding me,' says Mel, leaning to fish something out of her satchel. She retrieves a crumpled but still shiny brochure and begins smoothing it out on her lap.

'Okay, here's the deal,' she begins. 'You know this trip to New York I went on a couple of weeks ago, to do the research for that piece on the dating habits of American women? Well, I came across this woman, Marina Boyd, who's from Atlanta, apparently, but is the talk of the town all across the states. She's this . . . dating guru, I guess you'd call it, who runs seminars for single women.'

'Oh, I know who you mean,' I interrupt. 'Is she the one who thinks we should be spending our days lounging around in kitten heels and bikinis like proper Southern belles?'

'Not exactly,' continues Mel. 'Quite the opposite, in fact. Her theory is that women need to take charge and "manage" their search for the perfect partner, the way they'd manage a business project. You know, set targets, write action plans, that sort of thing. Apply business principles.'

I take a large gulp of my wine, still unclear where all this is going.

'Anyway, she's running a series of seminars over here starting next week, and I've been asked to cover the whole thing. My editor wants a piece on this Marina person's whole approach and how it actually plays out in the UK. She wants me to get the inside story by following one woman and documenting her experience.'

I'm somewhat clearer about where this is going.

'Unfortunately, Ms Boyd will not allow this kind of intrusion into people's privacy under any circumstances.' Mel stretches out the *Ms* disdainfully and rolls her eyes heavenwards. 'The most she'll allow is one visit to one of her seminars. So I'm rather stuck for a real live person who'll help me generate some genuine insights.'

It's clear as a bell now. I can almost lip sync the words that come out of Mel's mouth next.

'So, Ally, this is where you come in. I mean, obviously I can't go undercover, cos I'm with Dom. And Clara is with Jonathon. So I wondered . . .'

'No, Mel. Absolutely not. It's one thing to give you a few quotes, but quite another to actually have to go through some charade involving attending God knows how many seminars about how to snag a husband.'

'Ally, wait. Before you say no, let me explain a bit more. You could use another name. No one would ever know it was you. And it might be fun. I heard this person on the radio while I was in New York, and you know a lot of her ideas made sense.'

I look at Clara, hoping for some moral support. I can see immediately I'm not going to get any.

'You know, it's quite a cool concept actually,' she starts. 'It's obvious that times have changed, and maybe women do need to look at different ways of finding the right man. It's not that crazy an idea to manage the situation a bit.'

I might have known this would appeal to Clara. She is always going on about business principles, and how they could transform aspects of life that she has deemed shambolic. I'm sure she dreamt up the idea of patient-driven funding for the NHS long before Margaret Thatcher. She is constantly berating her clients for their foggy, undisciplined thinking. Her role as a management consultant, she says, is to impart clarity where there is confusion, to force people to make disciplined choices rather than blindly following the path of business as usual.

Mel picks up on Clara's receptiveness. 'I agree. Times really have changed. I mean, Esther Rantzen has even done a primetime show that's supposed to help her find a mate! And what about all those speed-dating clubs? People don't want to waste time sitting around waiting for someone to come along. They want to make it happen.'

I pick up the brochure as if it were something rather nasty destined for the bin. On the front cover is a picture of Marina Boyd, and just below this a list of all the benefits of attending her series of seminars:

* *Learn how to take action to find a partner instead of waiting around for it to happen.*

* *Discover exactly what you want in a man; and what you have to offer.*
* *Experience the fantastic feeling of being in charge!*
* *Fall in love within one year!*

Inside, there are the Eight Essentials of the Proactive Partnership Programs, all beginning with P. Planning includes a section called 'Get Rid of Your Baggage'; Product includes 'Be Proud of Your Brand' and Promotion is followed by the urge to 'Go to Market!' At the bottom of the second page, written in extra-large capitals, is an exhortation as scary as any I have seen in a long while: IF YOU ARE OVER THIRTY YOU HAVE NO TIME TO LOSE. TAKE ACTION NOW. Blimey. This woman is serious. She's making me nervous. Suddenly, finding a partner is no longer something I can lazily wish for to enhance my otherwise quite full life, but a matter requiring urgent action.

I shake my head, beckoning to the waitress. I feel the need for some sustenance. Some hummus and crudités. Perhaps a portion of giant sized chips with Thai mayonnaise.

Mel has a strange, manic look in her eyes. 'Ally, this woman's talking your language. All this stuff about the four Ps of marketing has got to make sense to you.'

'Actually, its all the Ps that worry me. It's totally ridiculous, Mel, surely you of all people can see that! The idea of marketing a person in the way you might market a soap powder or a marmalade is just mad. No, it's more than mad, it's insulting. I couldn't possibly take anything like this seriously.'

I look at them both incredulously, unable to fathom quite how two such normal women, women I've called friends for almost two decades, could be taken in by such utter claptrap.

'You don't have to take it seriously,' perseveres Clara. 'Just think of it as an interesting experience. But you never know, you just might pick up some good ideas. It's not as if you've anything to lose.'

Clara is right about that. I've not had a tremendous amount of romantic success in the past two years. I've not looked for it, but I wouldn't have turned it away if it had appeared on my doorstep. But is hasn't appeared, on my doorstep or anywhere in the vicinity.

Di from the accounts department says that since she got divorced she's become a target for the inappropriate affections of inappropriate men, including her girlfriends' husbands and their incorrigible bachelor friends. I've not received inappropriate attention from married men, or indeed from many men at all. Quite the opposite in fact. I think I've become invisible.

Perhaps the invisibility has something to do with age. Perhaps when your children are in their teens, like Di's, and you're deemed to be footloose and fancy free, you have the appeal of a nubile young creature, but with twice the experience. We've all read the literature about women in their forties being in their prime. When you're in your mid-thirties with two young children, maybe you fall into the category of 'too much like hard work with not enough pay off'.

Of course it's possible that the invisibility is self-inflicted. When you're over thirty, single and surrounded by couples, you're an automatic object of suspicion. People can't help but see you that way. So you spend an awful lot of time keeping your eyes down and your hands to yourself in case anyone should interpret you as a threat. In mixed company, flirting is simply out of the question. Invisibility is by far the safest option.

Mel makes one last-ditch effort to persuade me. 'Look, Clara's right. I think it might be an interesting experience, as well as helping me out. I don't know much about this Marina woman, and I have to admit some of her ideas sound pretty outlandish. But another part of me thinks she might be on to something. I mean, finding someone you like when you're in your mid-thirties is a whole lot different from finding someone when you're at college, or when you're twenty-five and going out with your friends every night of the week. These women I met in New York certainly know that. My God, they are incredible.'

'I'll think about it,' I concede disingenuously, anxious to get us off the topic and move on. 'Tell you what. I'll read the brochure over the weekend and let you know what I think. In the meantime, can we please stop talking about it. We're all intelligent working women. Surely we've got better things to talk about.'

Just at that moment, a man of indefinable age with a helmet of salt-and-pepper hair appears at the side of our table. The kind of men you meet in bars inevitably being the wrong kind, I look at him with an expression that I hope communicates the right balance between politeness and sod off.

'Excuse me, ladies,' he gushes. 'I notice you're not using your ashtray. Would you mind if I borrowed it?'

In fact, I have nothing to fear from this man, and my carefully considered expression is lost on him. While reaching for the ashtray, he is doing his best to seduce Clara with his orthodontic smile.

Clara is not oblivious, but she is uninterested. And she clearly doesn't think this bloke is worth tossing to me as leftovers, either, since she dismisses him with a 'Sure' and a wave of her hand. He takes his ashtray back to the bar, shoulders drooping discernibly.

'Come on,' says Clara. 'Let's go and find some dinner. I've had enough of this place.'

We pay the waitress and put on our coats. I've had enough of this place as well. Suddenly, it is no longer full of inappropriate types I'd rather not talk to, but of vaguely attractive sorts with great potential who would rather hit on Clara. It would be very bad for morale to stay.

Chapter 5
Meeting Francesca

I was never supposed to be here. I never dreamt that David would leave me with two small children and the mortgage on a three-bedroom terrace to live out his romantic impulses in the arms of other women. It was the furthest thing from my mind when we said our vows in the tiny church in Bishops Sutton, surrounded by forty people who wished us nothing but unending happiness. It was inconceivable as I lay in the maternity ward with a newborn Millie in my arms and watched tears welling up in David's eyes. I can't say that it ever entered my mind even when I first tumbled into bed with the dangerously handsome man with the loose dark curls that everyone had warned me about.

Being divorced was never something I factored into my

life plan. My parents have a chocolate-box kind of marriage that has endured more than forty years. My older brother Nick is a funny, kind and, as far as I know, utterly faithful husband who showed me what a proper marriage could be like years before I contemplated it. All my life I have been surrounded by shining examples of marital bliss, and I never had any reason to doubt that I could manage to secure some of it for myself.

Apparently there's this psychologist who's devised a mathematical model that can predict which couples will divorce on the basis of the first few minutes of a discussion about some disputed issue. According to this Dr Gottman, a couple's attitudes during an argument are directly linked to their propensity to get divorced. Those with a high 'bitterness rating' are doomed almost from the first conversation.

Well, even Dr Gottman wouldn't have predicted the fate of my marriage based on his formula. David and I always argued well, incorporating lots of the teasing, laughing and other signs of affection that Dr Gottman links with successful partnerships. In fact, my ability to engage David in debates about controversial topics was one of the things that drew him to me, if you believe his account of the courtship.

The problem with David and me was much simpler than Gottman's formula would suggest. David loves women, in the way that French men love women. In the plural sense of the word. He can't resist a flirting opportunity, and can be counted on to be found engrossed in conversation with the only female in the room when all the other men are staring goggle eyed at the football. He not only loves women, but he loves the whole business of loving women. I just happened to be a woman that he loved a bit more at one time in his life, and we both mistook it for the real thing. When I discovered that I was pregnant at the age of twenty-nine after knowing David just ten months, we both wanted to believe that David could love me for ever, and that he wouldn't need to love women any more.

I felt no sense of shame in being unmarried and pregnant. Having been a good girl all my life, I found it exciting. I felt it gave me character, made me unpredictable where I had always been the master of the expected. And in the face of friends' astonishment at the news that the pregnancy had enticed David to commit to marriage, I felt newly powerful, and flagrantly optimistic.

And, besides, I had no choice in the matter. I loved everything about him. And I loved what he loved about me. Amidst a sea of bronzed, gazelle-like beauties on a shoot for a new range of sun-kissed lipsticks, he chose the slightly stroppy five-foot-five-inch woman sitting next to the director with a clipboard on her lap. My brains and determination made me stand out, he said. Models were two a penny, but how often do you meet someone who's challenging and totally shaggable at the same time?

I'll never make that mistake again. There is good reason why people talk about leopards never changing their spots. David was never cruel, heartless or demeaning. It's just that his love of women could not be stifled. After three brief dalliances, one while I was pregnant with Jack, he decided to come clean. He didn't want a marriage full of lies any more than I did. Neither did he want to be trapped inside the life of a committed family man. He walked out when Jack was twenty months old.

I wonder what Dr Gottman would have to say on the subject of professions as predictors of divorce. I hate to succumb to the power of the cliché, but I can't help being drawn to the theory that David's being a photographer might have been a warning to me. Of course, when you are twenty-nine, ripe for settling down, and lying next to a dark-haired creative genius whose very being promises to imbue your life with magic, the profession is part of the attraction. Later on, the attraction pales. All you can see is the unsociable hours, the unpredictable income and the fact that your husband is frequently in the company of young goddesses with legs rising up to meet the bottom of their skimpy belly-tops.

Suddenly remembering the leaflet that has been stuffed into my bag, I wonder what Marina Boyd would have to say about such matters. Would she have advised me to go out with David all those years ago, then marry him? Or would she have known it would never work?

Still squinting from sleep, I look over to the chair beside my bed, where I can see a corner of Mel's leaflet peaking out from my bag, willing me to pick it up. I reach out and extract it, dropping a lip gloss and a plastic replica of Scooby Doo on to the floor in the process. I open it to the list of action steps I'd perused yesterday evening.

Step #1: Planning
Step #2: Product
Step #3: Packaging
Step #4: Prospecting

Step #5: Promotion
Step #6: Place
Step #7: Props
Step #8: Perseverance

Packaging. Promotion. Place. These words are all so familiar to me. I've lived and breathed them every working day since I first landed the junior marketing assistant role at Chanel after graduation. When I was sent on my first marketing course I was immediately drawn to the apparent science of it all. I'd always loved a good theory, and now here was a theory that made sense of creams and lipsticks and powder and blushers and all the reasons women bought them. The first marketing plan I ever produced filled me with an enormous sense of mastery. Full of predictions and promises about share of market and sales, and exciting ideas for point-of-sale promotion, it made me feel a bit like a conductor – as though I really could orchestrate anything I'd set my mind to.

Reality soon set in, of course, and I quickly realised that sales predictions were a lot easier to make than actual sales. But I was still a little in awe of the discipline of it all. Combined with the heady atmosphere of the luxury cosmetics world it made for a pretty interesting working life.

I've never really regained my enthusiasm since leaving Chanel. Perhaps I've never overcome my reluctant departure from Coco's world for the saner but far less exciting world of packaged food. Or perhaps I just tired of dealing in the language of marketing, stopped believing in it quite so much. Whatever it is, I've felt for a long while as though I'm just going through the motions.

I can see that Marina has expanded the original four Ps of marketing to eight, but it's not immediately clear to me what any of them have to do with romance. Translating 'Packaging' into the dating arena is something I can just about manage; after all, with makeovers gracing the pages of every woman's magazine on the news-stand, the notion of making the most of your physical attributes isn't so foreign.

But promotion and props? What do these have to do with finding a soulmate? How on earth would you promote yourself, even if you were inclined to do so? The idea of advertising your attributes like you would advertise a household cleaning product is just repugnant.

I am forced to abandon contemplation of this weighty matter when I realise that it is ten a.m. and I have to be at the hairdresser in three quarters of an hour. I shower and dress hurriedly, gulp down some juice and a half a muffin abandoned by Jack two days ago, and manage to get myself into the car in under twenty minutes. Moving at this pace, I succeed in relegating Mel's challenge to the recesses of my mind.

With new salons opening up every other week, I could easily have settled on a hairdresser within walking distance of home. But I've been with George for ten years, and couldn't possibly surrender him now. He has seen me through at least three versions of the ubiquitous (and always fashionable) bob, one very short cut, the traumatic growing out of the short cut, and four shades of the blonde highlights I have been faithfully applying since the age of twenty-one. I would feel unsafe in anyone else's hands. So about every six weeks I endure a drive to the other side of the city to get to George at *The Strand Hair Design*.

This morning I am in luck, my journey being timed to coincide with the nine-to-noon talk show with Julia Stone on City Talk Radio, usually featuring an interesting guest in the studio combined with calls from listeners about interesting guest. I'm just in time to hear the guest responding to a caller's question, in a velvety American accent.

'Well the fact is that the method I've developed can work for anyone. I've helped women who are twenty-five and sixty-five, women who have never been married and women divorced for the third time. It really is a matter of saying to yourself "I am serious about finding a lifetime partner" and devoting the time and energy to the essential steps of marketing. I believe there are eight of them. What I call the eight Ps of Proactive Partnership.'

My God, it's her. It's Marina Boyd. I turn up the volume, noticing absent-mindedly that Thursday's buff and polish is not holding up particularly well.

'So tell us all, Marina, because we are dying to know. What is the secret of the eight Ps? And let me tell you, listeners, that this lady sitting with me in the studio is charming and lovely, and just happens to be very happily married, so it might just be worth taking her advice.'

Marina's voice is smooth as honey. I can almost see her perfect, fixed half smile. 'The secret to this approach is to apply some tried and tested principles that have been proven in the business world many times over. After thirty, the stakes are raised and the territory gets more challenging, so you have to get serious if you want to find a husband. These principles are practically foolproof.'

Julia asks Marina to elaborate and she's off. Totally

unstoppable. Julia takes the odd call from a listener to lighten the proceedings, but the next fifteen minutes are essentially a monologue. Marina begins by describing the eight Ps in detail, starting with the importance of good packaging (*Basic rule number one: wear your hair as long as you can manage. Men prefer longer hair*) and goes on to explain how the different aspects of promotion, such as direct mail, advertising and telesales are important tools for the woman seeking a partner today.

'But the underlying secret of my approach,' she says, conspiratorially, 'is the combination of method and moral support. I think of it as the Weight Watchers of the romance world. Weight Watchers works because it gives people a method to follow. By counting points they can be assured of losing weight. It also works because it offers moral support to people. They can go to meetings, get weighed in, get a pat on the back, find out how their friends are doing. These things improve the chances of success. It's the same in the dating game. People need a method to follow and plenty of moral support along the way. My seminars offer that.'

Then Marina's voice softens a little, and she stops talking about her method and begins telling stories about real people. Women who have bucked seemingly insurmountable odds to find lifelong soulmates using the Boyd method.

And the funny thing is, the more I listen, the less I dislike this Marina. The more she talks in ordinary terms about 'making the best of yourself' and 'opening your mind to different sorts of people' and 'getting out more rather than expecting Mr Perfect to just knock on your door', the more I am taken in. Behind the jargon, there's a glimmer of common sense.

Just the faintest glimmer, mind you. Marina might be charming and articulate, but she can't disguise the fact that she's asking grown women to attend seminars that espouse the application of eight Ps to something as unmanageable and indefinable as love. It's still a load of nonsense.

'Well, that's all we have time for. But let me tell you, tickets for Marina's first series of London seminars are selling like hotcakes. There are only a few left. Keep calling, because we have one ticket worth £500 to give away to the woman who can persuade us that she needs it more than anyone else. In the meantime, thank you, Marina, for being with us. Now, coming up, Hattie Jacob will be telling us how she survived a year on a bicycle in Africa.'

I arrive at The Strand and never get to hear Hattie Jacob's story. My mind is buzzing with Marina Boyd's advice despite its better judgement, and this unnerves me. I can't decide whether I've lost the plot or seen the light. Even George notices that something is up.

'Hello, darling,' he gushes, kissing me on both cheeks. 'My goodness, you look flushed today. I hope it ees for something nice!'

'Must be the extra shot in the cappuccino,' I lie, recovering myself.

'Come, come over here,' says George solicitously, ushering me towards the sink. 'I am ready for you. You are going to feel marvellous when I've finished with you.'

George is the only hairdresser I know who washes his clients' hair himself. He has made it an art form. It's all part of the deal of being flattered, pampered and indulged for an hour – or three if there are highlights involved. I've never heard George pop the much-dreaded question 'and where are you going on holiday?' Instead he regales his clients with stories of his own holidays, which, George being a sixty-year-old, single, gay Chilean of aristocratic heritage, are always adventures. Once George runs out of stories, we switch to tittering at the ghastly outfits and badly executed plastic surgery on display in the pages of the latest *Hello!* or *OK!*, an activity that always passes the remaining time quite nicely. We did once have a three-way conversation (with another woman having a cut and blow-dry) about the Hutton Report, but that was quite exceptional.

Today I find it hard to concentrate on George's tale. My mind keeps drifting back to Marina Boyd and her seminars. I am intrigued. And repelled. And not entirely sure what to say to Mel.

As George's story comes to a close, and he wraps my hair in a turban before shepherding me over to the bank of mirrors on the opposite side of the room, I take the opportunity to jump in.

'George, do you know any women who are looking for husbands?'

George is slightly taken aback by this question. It doesn't fit the usual pattern. But he copes with it. 'Well, of course, darling. There are lots of beautiful women I know who should be married. They just haven't found the right man yet.'

'Yes, but are any of them actually *looking* for a husband. You know, really working at it?'

'Let me think about that one, darling.' This he does while combing out my hair. 'Most of the ladies I know are just hoping a prince will fall out of the sky one day. But there is this one woman; she ees fantastic. So full of life. Her name ees Francesca. Her husband divorced her three years ago, and she has made it no secret that she weell not be left to seet in a dark room the rest of her life. She ees a shameless flirt. And she goes out all the time. Has a really good time. In fact, I think she ees having a better time than when she was married. She always says that she will find herself another husband before she ees feefty.'

'Perhaps I should be a bit more like that,' I proffer. 'What do you think?'

'I theenk it would be fantastic, darling. You are too beautiful to seet in a dark room the rest of your life also. Now, what are we doing with your hair today?'

My hair has been bothering me lately. It seems to fall lankly into my face all the time when I don't blow-dry it. And blow-drying makes me hot and bad tempered. I've been thinking I should cut it quite short.

'Let's go for much shorter today. Sort of short and shaggy, a bit like Lulu a year ago,' I say.

'Lulu it is,' says George. 'That will be quite nice.' George has clipped up one half of my hair and is brandishing his scissors when something makes me stop him.

'Wait,' I shout. 'I've changed my mind. Let's go for long and slightly shaggy. Sort of like Lulu now.'

'Fantastic, darling. I think that ees much better. Between you and me, I theenk men always prefer longer hair.'

Chapter 6
Signs

I leave George with my this-year's-Lulu hair and a burgeoning desire to be more like Francesca, with all her zest for life and unflaggable romantic enthusiasm. But more mundane things await me; I need to make a couple of pit stops on the way home. I'm still debating with myself about going to the seminar as I pull into the Tesco car park, just missing out on a space near the door. I don't begrudge the loss of the space until I notice the bright yellow 'Baby on Board' sticker pasted to the back window of the car that has nipped in ahead of me. Why people bother with these twee little stickers is an unending mystery to me. What do they think, that cars without babies on board are targets for every tail-bumping maniac on the M4? That the lorry driver about to accidentally slam into the back of your car will suddenly find himself able to stop once he realises a small child's life is at risk? (I once saw a Ford Ventura with a 'Twins on Board' sticker on its rear window, which only goes to prove that these stickers have morphed from health and safety aides to family advertisements.)

Successfully parked about a mile from the door, I make a mental note of the necessary purchases as I admire my new hair in the rear-view mirror. Resenting Saturday grocery shopping with a not uncommon passion, I then race round the aisles like a woman possessed. I've taken a basket rather than a trolley so that I can safely scoot up the inside lane marked 'fifteen items or less'. When I reach the cash desk, I notice a row of books with green and white covers arrayed on the best-seller racks below Victoria Beckham's autobiography and above a shelf full of bodice rippers. It's called *Finding a Mate for Life* and it doesn't take a mathematician to spot that it has been allocated double the rack space of the other books. Perhaps Clara and Mel are right. Maybe in today's fast-paced, fragmented world it really isn't enough simply to hope to meet the right person. Maybe the whole of Britain, or at the very least everyone who shops at Tesco, is waking up to the fact that you need to work at it.

Next stop is the library, where I must return five overdue children's books and explain that the sixth, *Whose Bottom?*, cannot be found. The librarians are usually pretty forgiving, having heard a variation on this story from me several times already. Their customary stance is to renew the book in good faith, and reassure me that it will probably turn up during the next spring clean (which, I infer, is no longer just a spring-time activity in most civilised English homes).

As I hand over the books to the librarian and begin my rehearsed and humble apology about the missing *Whose Bottom?*, I glance over her shoulder to the 'Books of the Month' table and cannot believe my eyes. You guessed it. It is awash with books about finding love. *Getting Ready for Love*, *Taking Charge of Your Love Life*, and at least half a dozen others are arranged artfully on the table, offering hope and succour to the single and lonely amongst the patrons of the local library.

This is ridiculous. If books like these have made it on to the 'Book of the Month' shelves in semi-suburban libraries, the topic of husband-hunting must have achieved the status of the solidly acceptable. Last month it was Carol Shields on that shelf, for God's sake, and before that Joanna Trollope. What is happening to the English? Perhaps they are not as stuffy about self-help as I thought. Perhaps they are a whole lot more American than they ever thought.

I am still musing on the unexpected popularity of these books urging us to be assertive in our search for soul-mates as I unlock the front door. I make a dash for the phone, which sounds to me as if it's on its fifth or sixth ring, picking up to hear Millie's sweet voice.

'Hi, Mummy, it's Millie,' she says, as if I could ever mistake her for anyone else.

'Hi, darling. How are you? Are you having a lovely time with Daddy and Papa and Gran?'

'I'm having the best time,' she sings. I feel relieved, and just a little resentful.

'So, tell me. What have you been doing?' I ask generously.

'Well last night we got to stay up late and watch *Finding Nemo* on video. Jack fell asleep, but he did see quite a lot of it. Then this morning we went to the zoo. We just got back. I saw a rare Mongolian bison. Chantal bought me a book about it. Do you want to talk to Jack?'

There it is. It's started. That woman is going to compete with me on the 'best presents' front on top of everything else.

'That's great, sweetheart. Yes, put Jack on for a minute.'

'Hi, Mummy. I've got a new gun. Chantal bought it for me,' says Jack. I can picture him with his cowboy hat tipped slightly forward, cradling the new weapon.

'Well, aren't you the lucky one,' I say, now rather weary. These sorts of conversations are always a little unsatisfactory, small children being immensely self-centred and not yet having mastered the fine art of telephone diplomacy.

'AND, this afternoon Dad and I are going to play soccer in the garden, AND Papa is going to build a boat with me. Bye, Mummy. I love you.'

And then he is gone, no doubt having left the phone dangling. I wait for a few seconds to see if an adult is going to rescue the receiver and fill me in on any crucial details about arrangements, but no one does. Finally, Millie comes back on.

'Bye, Mummy. I can't wait to see you tomorrow. You didn't see *The Lost Princess* did you?'

'Absolutely not. I'm saving that for you. Now, give my love to everyone and have this big kiss from me.' I give the receiver an enormous smooch, and listen for the one that comes back. Then I hang up. It never does to prolong the goodbye bit.

I spend the afternoon getting to grips with some household tasks I've been putting off for months. These are the sorts of things I can't really do with the children around, so today is an opportunity not to be missed. I sort out old clothes from the backs of cupboards to make room for neat stacks of sweaters like those in Ikea catalogues; I find and then screw on three knobs that have been missing from Millie's drawers for at least six months; and I finish the afternoon by applying a rich, cherry-coloured wood-stain to the shabby, greying step below the doors to the back garden. The truth is I quite like these sorts of jobs, when I've got the time and the mental space in which to complete them. The worse truth is, sometimes when the children are with me I'd rather be doing these sorts of jobs than playing Guess Who? or Operation for the umpteenth time, or shivering in an unbearably crowded and noisy public swimming pool.

It's a terrible thing to admit: that you'd rather spend the afternoon with a paintbrush and a tin of wood-stain than playing with your children. It's particularly terrible when you don't have your children with you every weekend. I feel as though I ought to cherish every moment spent with Jack and Millie on my weekends. But of course that is the trouble. Every moment *is* spent with the children on my weekends. It's all or nothing. There's no popping down to the shops while your husband builds a Lego tower with them, or lying in bed while he takes them swimming. Everything's up to you, from the minute they wake up until the moment they choose to close their eyes. There's no light relief, no grown-up with whom you can share a joke or a moan. No one to whom you can turn and say 'Wasn't Jack clever to swim to the other side like that?' or 'Millie's behaving rather strangely. What do you suppose it is?'

Early on, I remember feeling so guilty about not wanting to spend all my time with my children that I went into the chatroom of a website called mumsworld.com. I didn't really have anyone else to talk to about these sorts of things as I was the first of my close friends to have children. But once I confessed to mumsworld I discovered a vast community of women who admitted that they didn't feel the way you were supposed to feel. With the anonymity of the chatroom to protect them, these women weren't afraid to divulge that hanging around children's playgrounds filled them with quiet despair, or that they found the stretch of time between *Teletubbies* and tea interminable, and could never think of enough ways to fill it. Or that when they were with their children they often drifted off into a reverie, or made complicated mental plans for something, rather than suffer the peculiar kind of insanity than can come with the endless building of Lego towers with a two-year-old. I haven't really used chatrooms since, but if I ever had a serious question I might. For a few short weeks, mumsworld was something of a lifeline to me. Made me feel I wasn't such a bad mother after all.

Annoyingly, all through the afternoon the question of Marina Boyd's seminars keeps reasserting itself. Applying the third and final coat of the cherry stain, I'm struggling to establish what it is, exactly, that makes me want to reject the concept outright. After all, taking advice from someone standing on a podium wouldn't be all that different from taking it from a book. And I've done that plenty of times. There was the time Clara thrust *Divorce With Grace* into my hands two years ago, insisting that if I overlooked the psychobabble and the chronic American over-optimism, I would find a few gems that would save my life. Actually, she was right. The gems were very, very hard to find, but once found they proved to be indispensable.

Glancing up from my crouched position over the back step, I can just make out the dark green cover of *Divorce With Grace* on the bookshelf next to the fridge. It is squeezed in between a well-thumbed copy of *Cooking for Toddlers* and *Siblings Without Rivalry*, the latter also given to me by Clara in response to my complaints that Jack and Millie were tearing chunks out of each other. I remember how it immediately improved my outlook, being full of examples of squabbling siblings far worse than my own, and of mothers confessing to wanting to strangle their offspring for some peace and quiet.

Clara has never purchased a self-help book for herself, and none graces her shelves. Instead, she scours the bookshops for titles that she can offer, like throat lozenges retrieved from the depths of a handbag just as a sore throat becomes unbearable, to her struggling friends. I am not the only one to benefit from her largesse. Her sister has been sent books by the dozen, and even Jonathon received one in his Christmas stocking the year he decided to make a career change and start illustrating full time: *What Colour is your Parachute?: A Practical Manual for Job Hunters and Career Changers*. Everything is so clear to Clara. Perhaps this is the best way she can think of to make things clear for the rest of us. It must be all those years she has spent in management consulting, finding the solutions to seemingly intractable client problems in two-by-two matrices and glossy PowerPoint presentations.

No, the idea of taking advice, from a book or a seminar, doesn't strike me as odd. The thing that fills me with more trepidation, I think, is the thought of sharing the experience with people. I'm not that big on group moral support; I'd much rather struggle away at things on my own, which is why Weight Watchers never really worked for me. My mum has always sworn by Weight Watchers. Insists it is the only sane way to lose weight in a world awash with diets that forbid fruit, or banish meat, or punish you for eating fruit and meat in the same twenty-four hour period. At her instigation I started the programme six months after Millie was born, hoping to shed the ten pounds that seemed to be clinging resolutely to my stomach and hips. But I only ever managed one meeting. Everything about it put me off, from the elderly woman with thick Wheatabix-coloured knee-highs collapsing around her ankles who weighed me in, to the group leader's talk about the cooking of winter squash without oils and the importance of planning ahead for bikini season.

But the thing I found most unbearable was the ra-ra, we're-all-in-this-togetherness of it all. I didn't want to share my weight-loss successes and failures with people I hardly knew, or get pats on the back from a room full of fellow fatties. The rolls hidden under my sweater were, I felt, a matter for me and my mother to know about. No one else. Not even David, if I could suck in my stomach sufficiently at crucial moments.

All that public struggling just isn't for me. Mel's going to have to find another guinea pig for her underhand little plan. I'll ring her and tell her tomorrow. In the meantime, with sweaters stacked, handles in place and a step robbed of its filthy greyness, I feel I deserve a treat. It's already dark, so I know exactly what it will be.

After putting away the tin of cherry stain and running the brush under the tap I go to the fridge and fish out the bottle of Pinot Grigio from the back. It's two thirds full, which is perfect. Then I empty a tin of tuna on to a plate, sprinkle it with pepper and encircle it with the entire contents of a family-sized bag of cheese-flavoured tortilla chips. I take the whole feast into the sitting room, where I root around in the cupboard under the TV where the videos live until I find the cover for *Sleepless in Seattle*. It takes a few more minutes to locate the actual video, but once I have found it, I put it in the machine and settle comfortably into the sofa, the Pinot Grigio located within easy reaching distance.

I might not be up for a course in husband-hunting with a hundred classmates, but I can still dream.

Chapter 7
Blind Date

On Sunday morning I am woken by a call from my brother.

'Ally, it's Nick. Did I wake you?'

'Of course you woke me, it's eight o'clock,' I reply, only a little gruffly. He is my brother after all.

'Sorry. It's just that I wanted to catch you before you went out anywhere.' And where might that be on a Sunday morning when I don't have the kids and I do have a chance to lie in?

'Kate and I were just thinking, we're having a small lunch party today, and as you're on your own, if you're not doing anything, why don't you pop up and join us?'

'Up' means to Belsize Park, North London.

'Uhmm. Let me think,' I mumble. Do I have anything

I need to do today? Can I be bothered to drive up to North London for lunch?

Then one of Marina Boyd's little gems from yesterday's radio interview suddenly pops into my head: *Home is a four-letter word. You're never going to meet anyone there*. I might not be a candidate for one of Marina's seminars, but it doesn't mean I have to ignore such obviously sensible advice.

'That would be lovely,' I decide. 'What time should I be there?'

'Oh, you know. Noonish. Give us time for a G&T before lunch,' says Nick.

'Noon it is,' I say, now wide awake and able to be chirpy.

The day now mapped out, I sit up in bed and muse upon what to wear. Of course, it's a pretty academic question until I determine what is actually clean, as opposed to lying squashed at the bottom of the overflowing linen basket. Needing to shed some light on the crucial task of outfit selection, I go to the window and open the shutters. Peeping out into the morning light (dull, grey, typical February), I spot a man walking by the house pushing a small child in a pushchair in that unmistakably nonchalant way men have. You know. Walking slightly to one side of the offending vehicle, pushing it with one hand as if to say, 'I am not really doing this. I am actually stepping out to do something incredibly masculine and this pushchair insisted on coming along for the ride.'

Poor bloke, I think. Fancy having to be out with a baby and a pushchair at this hour.

After fifteen minutes flitting back and forth between my closet and the linen basket, I ascertain that the best option open to me is the jeans with the black V-neck Max Mara sweater with the jagged sleeves (purchased in the sale, of course). This I put on after showering, all the while trying not to ruin the remnants of yesterday's cut and blowdry with either water or static electricity. As it's still only eight forty-five and I have heaps of time before I have to leave, I reluctantly decide that some laundry must be done.

Of all the god-forsaken domestic tasks in the world, the worst has got to be sorting socks freshly scrambled by a tumble dryer. I am not expecting to have to face this particular task this morning, but there is a surprise lying in wait for me. I open the washing machine, ready to stuff in the great pile of whites I have heaved downstairs, and discover that the machine is full of wet clothes. To make matters infinitely worse, I open the dryer to put the wet clothes in and discover that it, too, is full, of socks and underwear. Three people's worth of socks and underwear all tangled together. I am incensed that, having planned to simply throw a few clothes in the washing machine, I now have to pair up socks before I can even begin.

This whole episode puts me in a foul mood, which I remedy by eating a bacon sandwich in front of *Frost on Sunday* followed by the last ten minutes of a *Will and Grace* rerun. Thus revitalised and renewed, I feel able to tackle the pile of bills that have been staring at me accusingly all week, and before I know it it's time to set off for Belsize Park, land of the luvvies, the intellectuals and the bohemians. I'm just about to walk out the door when the phone rings.

'Ally?' It's Clara, but it doesn't really sound like Clara.

My Clara's voice is strong and sure. This Clara sounds decidedly shaky.

'Clara, what is it?'

'I got my period this morning.'

'Oh, Clara. I'm so sorry. It must be so hard to go through this every month. To tell you the truth I wasn't really sure that you were still trying. I thought maybe you'd decided to wait until, you know, the time was better or something.'

There's a brief silence, then the unmistakable beginnings of sobbing, which goes from contained to gutteral within seconds.

'I just don't think I can take this any more. I know people do, lots of people. But I can't. I want a baby!'

'Honey, I know. Is Jonathon with you?'

'He's just gone out to get some papers. I don't think he can take any more either. The awful thing is, I'm afraid he blames me. All those years he spent saying we should have a baby and I kept saying no. Now look what's happened!' She blows her nose before adding 'I'm thirty-eight years old, Ally! I have old eggs!'

'What about IVF. Have you thought about that?'

'Yes. And no. We've decided that's not for us. All that torturous business and a very low likelihood of a baby even then. We don't want to go through all that.'

I listen to Clara's sobbing for a minute or so, offering rather lame counsel like 'The important thing is not to give up' and 'It will be all right, you'll see,' then the slam of a door signals Jonathon's return, so Clara blows her nose again and says she should go, before I have time to say anything really helpful. I'm not really sure what I would say, in any case. I can imagine the awful combination of heartache and regret that Clara must be feeling. Maybe she has left it too late.

Or maybe her situation requires more dramatic action than whatever it is they're doing at the moment. Surely there are other things she could be doing before having to resort to IVF?

Nick and Kate live in a wonderful double-fronted house full of bare oak floorboards and stainless-steel appliances. Theirs is the kind of home I'd aspire to if I thought I could ever afford it. It helps that Nick is an architect, and manages builders for a living. When he and Kate found this house eight years ago he knew immediately how to transform it from wreck to *Wallpaper* heaven on a budget.

Letting myself in the front door, I am immediately accosted by the glorious smells of Moroccan lamb (a speciality of Kate's; I've had it before) and the bodies of two boys. I am used to Jack hurling himself at me unexpectedly, so I don't mind when Will and Ollie do it. I squeeze them both, just missing in my attempt to plant a kiss on each of their heads as they escape from under my arms.

'Hey, Will, you're ten now! Did you get my present?' I shout after them.

'Yeah, it was great thanks. I loved it,' Will yells back as he disappears around the corner.

Kate rushes to greet me, oven gloves in hand.

'Ally, come in. How wonderful that you could come at such short notice. How are you?'

'Fine, fine,' I tell her. 'How are you guys?'

'We're all great. Now come into the kitchen and meet everyone. As usual, we are all squashed in there, sweating away, and the sitting room is practically empty. I don't know why we have one.'

I follow Kate through the hall (which is blissfully square and spacious, rather than long and narrow like my own). When we reach the kitchen I can see Nick wrestling with a corkscrew, and another couple hovering by the central island with their wineglasses. Gosh, this really is a small lunch party, I think, a little disappointed.

Nick gives me his speciality big-brother wink. 'Ally, come in. Let me introduce you. Phil and Jackie this is my little sister, Ally. Ally, these are our friends from down the road, Phil and Jackie. Phil, Ally works in advertising too.'

Of course, I don't work in advertising at all. Advertising is like the high-gloss world of luxury cosmetics that I left. It is full of bright, slick, fast-talking creative types who mostly work in W1. I, on the other hand, manage marmalade brands from a place that is practically the suburbs. Since leaving Chanel I've never fully reconciled myself to the contrast between my old world and my new one. But I feel I must come clean now before I'm made to look a fool in front of Phil.

'Nick, I'm not in advertising and you know it. I'm a product manager for Cottage Garden Foods,' I say.

'Excuse me,' says Kate. 'Group Product Manager.' She thrusts a gin and tonic into my hands.

'Whatever. Nothing like the world you're in,' I say, turning to Phil. He seems nice enough. Open face, friendly eyes. Definitely nothing like the worst of that breed.

'Really, what products?' Phil asks generously.

'Marmalades, actually. Ordinary marmalades, luxury marmalades. All types.'

'Oh, I adore marmalade,' pipes up Jackie. 'So much nicer than jam.'

I can't tell you how often this happens. My job may not be the world's most exciting, but people never fail to express an opinion about marmalade. There's the jam versus marmalade debate, the 'how thick do you spread your marmalade?' question, and the 'thick cut versus thin' conundrum. Occasionally, someone will mention Paddington Bear and his marmalade habit. Marmalade can keep most groups going for at least a few minutes. Today we manage almost six minutes before moving on to asylum-seekers.

Eventually, sensing a lull in the conversation, Kate breaks away, grabbing me by the arm. 'Come into the sitting room,' she whispers.

I follow her into the sitting room, wondering what secret she is going to share with me. Another baby? She's going back to work? As we pass through the doors, I see the secret, kneeling on the floor with his head stuck in the fireplace.

'Alan. Get out of there. You are officially relieved of responsibility for that fire. Nick will have to sort it out later. Come and meet Ally.'

Alan backs out of the fireplace on hands and knees, and stands up to face me. He has a black smudge across his forehead, but is otherwise very presentable. About five feet ten or eleven. A little on the heavy side maybe. Beige cords. Pale-blue shirt. The habitual attire of the middle-aged, middle-class British man.

'Very pleased to meet you, Ally,' he says, extending his hand. His voice is dripping with lineage.

'Alan is a whiz with gas fires,' interrupts Kate, gesturing to Alan to wipe his forehead. 'He owns that gorgeous fireplace shop on the New Kings Road. You know the one, Ally?'

'Yes, I think so,' I say, only half lying. There must be half a dozen fireplace shops on the New Kings Road, so I'm bound to have seen Alan's at one time or another.

'All Nick's clients have fires from Alan,' continues Kate, as if reciting a CV.

'Must be lucrative,' I say to Alan.

His forehead now wiped clean, Alan recounts the story of a house with eight fireplaces that he once did for Nick. He is nice. Not stunning, not even what you would call good looking. But pleasant enough.

Kate leaves the room, and Alan and I pass a few minutes talking about fireplaces (mine; his; Nick's, and why it isn't working). I begin to think that Alan's line of work is almost as useful as mine as a catalyst for small talk.

As we talk I am not really concentrating. My mind keeps drifting off to consider the possibilities presented by today's lunch. Not the lamb, or the pavlova I'd spied on Kate's counter, but the possibility that I might possibly fancy this man, that the barren days might be headed for some sort of temporary hiatus. Who needs a seminar series when I've got my brother looking out for me?

Eventually, Kate comes back and announces that lunch is ready. We all shuffle to the dining room, and Will and Ollie are beckoned from the garden. A boy and a girl, who look to be about five and seven and presumably belong to Phil and Jackie, follow them.

Lunch is delicious, as always when Kate is cooking. The

children poke at their food, and disappear back into the garden about six minutes after sitting down. The adults begin by debating the war in Iraq and end up in a discussion about schools and house prices, via a few minutes of light-hearted wrangling about whether or not Nicole Kidman has had something done to her forehead.

All through the lunch, I'm aware of Alan watching me. His watching intensifies as the meal progresses. I know that he's recently divorced, with two nearly teenage girls who attend a very smart but overly precious school near Sloane Square, and an ex-wife who has apparently fleeced him. (This last part I gleaned not from him, but through one of Kate's whispered asides.) He seems a kind man. A good man. A man who can sort out a fireplace. But I'm not interested, which disappoints me more than it should. I've gone from high hopes to disillusionment all in the space of an hour and a half's lunch. Actually, the journey probably took less time than that. I'd realised there was nothing there before the pavlova even arrived.

The trouble is, Alan appears to be interested in me. I am not so out of touch that I can't pick up on these things. I suppose I ought to be grateful after my years in the wilderness, but I'm just uncomfortable. I start to send off 'politely uninterested' vibes to make it absolutely clear that there is to be no exchange of telephone numbers at the end of this meal.

As Nick serves the coffee, I suddenly become the focus of the conversation. It's natural, I suppose, as I haven't shared much about myself during the lunch beyond the fact that I'm in marmalade. I know that they must all have been briefed about my situation before I arrived. But I am still surprised when Phil says, with a boldness fuelled by three quarters of a bottle of red wine, 'So, Ally, how do you handle the whole-single parent thing? Do you find it hard being on your own?'

I'm momentarily stuck for words. I could reply that I've found it tough, that I'm not cut out for being on my own, that I'm not ready to resign myself to the scrapheap and wish I could think how to meet someone else. I could say that if you want to know the worst thing about being a single parent, it's a toss up between having no one to share in the delights and dramas of raising small children and inhumanly long periods of celibacy. But I'm wary of giving Alan an opening. As it is, he has pushed his pavlova plate to one side and is leaning on the table, staring at me with a disturbing intensity.

'Actually, I'm pretty content with my life, and busy. Sooo busy you wouldn't believe it. The kids take up so much time, and then there's work, and my charity work, and my parents. I really can't think how I could fit anything else in.'

I know none of this will actually put him off, but it will give me a ready-made excuse to decline the inevitable request for my phone number while allowing him to save face. It will not be about him; it will be about not wanting to be in a relationship.

I've heard that one before. 'I just can't be married,' David had said, with the self-importance of someone who's discovered some self-evident and laudable character trait.

I am grateful for the opportunity to help Kate with the dishes while everyone else slumps in front of the malfunctioning fireplace. Once this has been accomplished, I make noises about having to get back for the kids, and plan my escape. I venture into the sitting room to say goodbye to everyone, taking care not to set in motion a round of cheek kissing that could get me into trouble. Amidst 'nice to meet yous', I give friendly waves to people, which seems acceptable given that I am already wearing my coat and the air of someone in a hurry.

Freedom secured, I make the journey back to the safety of South London. I arrive home an hour and a half before Jack and Millie are due back, which gives me just enough time to make the house feel warm and inviting, as if someone has been in it all day. I turn on the heat and run around turning on lights and plumping up the pillows on their beds. I take out the whites from the washing machine, and replace them with a pile of darks (mostly school uniforms). I have just finished putting the lovingly sorted socks into drawers when I hear the doorbell.

When I open the door, Millie jumps in and hugs my legs, leaving David standing there with Jack slumped on his shoulder. Thankfully, Chantal is nowhere in sight. I had kept on my Max Mara sweater just in case.

'Fell asleep ten minutes ago,' he whispers. 'Busy weekend.'

There is nothing quite so appealing as a sleeping five-year-old boy. His cheeks are pink and squashed against David's shoulder, and his mouth wide open like a choirboy's.

'Could you take him straight up?' I whisper back. David tiptoes up the stairs with Jack while I help Millie with her bag.

'It's lovely to see you, darling. We'll have some tea and you can tell me all about it. How does cheesy pasta sound?'

'Great,' yawns Millie.

'Come on then. Lets go in the kitchen.'

I put some water on to boil as David comes into the kitchen. This is something that still makes me uncomfortable. Somehow it is bearable to see him at the front door, in the sitting room, or somewhere else entirely. But here, standing in the kitchen stirring cheesy pasta sauce, it is too difficult. It's like a scrap of false intimacy in an otherwise cool and businesslike relationship.

'How was your weekend?' he asks.

'Fine. Good. Were the kids good?' I reply.

'Great. Really great. I'll be going then. I may have to call you about the next time. I've got some complicated work things coming up, so we might have to reorganise the dates a little. We'll see.' Then he turns to Millie. 'Goodbye, gorgeous. Thank you for a lovely weekend. Give me a hug that will last me till next time.'

Mille obliges, pressing her head deep into his stomach. This is even worse than David watching me make cheesy pasta. I concentrate on opening the spaghetti packet.

When the hug is over I walk David to the door. 'Bye then. Let me know what you want to do,' I say as he opens the door and disappears into the black.

'Will do,' he shouts back from the pavement. 'See you.'

And that is it. Short. Sharp. A fairly typical handover. Maybe one day we will have learned to sit together for an hour discussing the children, the weekend, the rest of our lives. But for now this is the best we can do. We are much better on the phone.

Millie is so droopy she can hardly eat her pasta. I sit with her in front of *Sleeping Beauty* for half an hour after tea, but I can see that she won't last long. At eight I lead her up to bed and she's gone within two minutes.

I'm pretty tired myself, though it can't be from an over-abundance of physical activity. I put it down to the red wine consumed at lunch and all the sock sorting. After drying and folding the uniforms and watching the *Antiques Roadshow*, I'm desperate to go to bed with a good book and the rest of yesterday's *Observer*. Halfway up the stairs I remember Clara and decide to check in with her first.

'Clara? Hi, it's me. How are you feeling?'

Clara is no longer shaking and sobbing but there's an unmistakable greyness in her voice. 'Oh, I'm all right. Better than this morning. We went out for lunch and drank two bottles of bordeaux, so that helped. Now I'm trying to sober up sufficiently to make sense of this wretched report about the future of the telecoms industry.'

'Did you and Jonathon work anything out?'

'What is there to work out? I'm not pregnant. I'm probably not going to get pregnant, but we'll keep trying I guess. He says how am I ever going to get pregnant when I'm in Zurich or Paris half the time when I'm ovulating, and that maybe I'm subconsciously running away from getting pregnant! Which is a bit rich don't you think? It's not as if I can do anything about that. Travel goes with my job. What am I going to say when the chief executive of the largest telco in Europe asks me to a board meeting? "Sorry, I can't, I'm ovulating that day". And I don't hear Jonathon volunteering to live on his illustrator's earnings.'

I'm not sure how to respond to this, as she's clearly not in the mood for a lecture about cutting back or travelling less. Anyway, perhaps my role is to help her stay light and optimistic. I'm sure her conversations with Jonathon are weighty enough.

'Anyway, you wouldn't be the only one who's running away. I think I just ran away from a man. And it wasn't even subconscious.'

Lying in bed, I scan the paper but can't find much of interest. Some days it is like that. The news is just plain un-newsworthy. I am about to discard the paper and pick up my book when I spot a headline on the 'Private Lives' page.

> *I'm a 45-year-old divorcee. I have a good job and three great children, but I'm terrified I'll never meet another man.*

Then, in the body of the letter:

> *I have not had a relationship in the nine years since my marriage ended. I never seem to meet anyone, and can't see how I ever will. Friends think I have a good life, but I'm saddened by the thought that I will never be part of a relationship again. I just don't want to be alone.*

There are four letters from other readers offering advice. *Just remember*, says the last one, who apparently spent fifteen years dating a depressed alcoholic followed by a man who lived hundreds of miles away before finding at the age of 47, the love of her life. *It's never too late. Try not to feel too desperate – it will show. Be happy and you will be a magnet.*

So I'm not alone. It is not weird or pathetic to want to

find someone. But I'll be damned if I'm going to wait fifteen years and make do with a depressed alcoholic and a no-hope long-distance affair in the interim. And I refuse to believe that a series of husband-hunting seminars designed for overly assertive New Yorkers represents my only alternative.

Chapter 8
Entrapment

Sometimes I worry about Jack. Can a fascination with guns, swords and handcuffs be healthy for a five-year-old? Shouldn't he be kicking toilet rolls around the kitchen like a young Johnny Wilkinson?

At this moment he is having a fight with himself. This involves repeatedly hurling himself to the ground having been punched by an imaginary enemy, each time emitting an 'uuhhhh' to rival Yul Brynner's guttural outbursts in *The Magnificent Seven*. To the side of him sits an enormous stuffed Father Christmas (an item that seems somehow to have escaped the ritual packing away of the decorations in early January) that has been handcuffed to the banisters. And all this before eight fifteen in the morning. There is something unnatural about the whole thing, and I am grateful for the absence of curious bystanders.

It is now time for Jack to leave the OK Corral and put on his school shoes. I begin with the best of intentions, deploying all the persuasive powers available to me at this time in the morning. When this fails to register with Jack, I am forced to remove the handcuffs from Father Christmas and go through the one-two-three routine: if Jack's shoes are not on by the time I get to three the handcuffs will be mine for a week. He scrapes home just in time, aided and abetted by my deliberately slow counting and the introduction of two and three quarters into the number sequence. This is expressly forbidden by *Toddler Taming*, the source of the counting trick, but I cannot see how a child of Jack's nature would manage anything within three counts without being granted some sort of leeway.

Once Jack's shoes are on the rest is a piece of cake, since Millie is already standing waiting by the door. We pile into the car in a hurry to escape the lashing rain, and *Horrid Henry* greets us with his customary raspberry. Just as I am about to pull away from the curb I spot a man with a pushchair coming towards us. It's the same man I saw at the weekend, only this time he's unable to feign quite the same degree of casual disregard for the pushchair. Today the rain and the wind are just too strong, and a two-hands-on-the-handle, head-down sort of determination is required.

School drop-off completed and car safely deposited back at home I make my way into work, all the while running through the calls and meetings that await me: *Meet with Anna to discuss Seville Sunset plan (help! Not ready yet); harangue two retailers remaining stubbornly opposed to tasting schedule; talk to Andy in production re reported Pure Gold zest clumping problem (new. Why is this happening?); schedule grove visits to bond with suppliers (when will have time to do this? Who will look after Jack and Millie? Send Nicki instead?); call Paul at agency re new idea for Seville ads (despise suggested shot of sarong-clad couple on beach enjoying view of sunset while tiny jars of marmalade dangle from hooks above beach-side bar as amusing rum substitute).*

As if this isn't enough I know I'll have to deal with two dilemmas on the personal front. Nick has wasted no time in presenting me with the first one.

From: Nick@JamesThorntonArchitects.co.uk
To: ally.james@cottage.garden.foods.co.uk

Ally, great to see you yesterday. Alan wondered if he could have your phone number. Shall I give it to him?

I decide to ignore Nick's email (how long can one wait before replying to an email from one's brother without crossing the line between 'understandably busy' and 'rude'? One day? Two?). I cannot do the same with Mel's. She's pushier than Nick, and if I don't reply she'll be on the phone by noon.

From: mel.atkinson@me.com
To: ally.james@cottage.garden.foods.co.uk

Ally, hope you had a good weekend. Mine spent entertaining Dom's mum and dad. Threatened to leave home when Elaine embarked on her usual lecture about how much money I could save if I stopped buying M&S ready meals.

Come on. Put me out of my misery. Are you going to do it or not?

The trouble is I'm truly torn. I veer irrationally between being convinced it's pure madness to think about attending a seminar run by an American relationship guru and the panicked conclusion that unless I take some sort of proactive control over my love life I'll end up like the lonely divorcee in the *Observer*.

I'm mid-vacillation when the phone rings. It's Mel, and it isn't even noon.

'Hey, Ally,' she announces cheerfully. 'What have you decided? Are you going to help me out and have some fun in the process?'

The moment of truth has arrived. 'No. I'm afraid I'm not,' I say with what I hope is Herculean firmness.

'Oh, Ally, why not?' moans Mel.

'Why not? Because I don't think romance can be engineered using clever marketing tactics. Because I hate the idea of being in a room full of people so lonely and despairing that they'll resort to a group seminar to help them find someone. Because I'm just not that desperate. I'm really not.'

'Whoa. I never said you had to take it so seriously. In fact you don't have to take it seriously at all. You could just go along for interest's sake, like me. Listen to what she has to say, try out a few of her suggestions, have a laugh. And provide me with some fodder for a good story.'

I guess I never thought of that. All weekend I've been

agonising about whether or not to subject myself to this modern form of romantic torture, when, in fact, I could just go along for a laugh and see what happens.

'Well, if you put it that way, it doesn't sound quite so bad,' I say, chewing on my biro.

'Not only do I put it that way, but I'll put my money where my mouth is. The magazine are willing to put up £1000 in "investment money" for things like beauty treatments and clothes. It's all part of the deal.'

Now that's tempting. £1000, to spend on myself? I am badly in need of a new spring coat, and a top to toe waxing for that matter. £1000 would certainly come in handy.

'Is there a catch? With the money, I mean?' I ask, making one last-ditch effort at a considered rejection of the whole idea.

'No. None at all. The only thing you have to do is spend it on "investment" items specified by this Marina person. But as these are all things like manicures and silk underwear, that shouldn't be too much of a hardship.'

I consider the proposition for a few moments. The end of the biro comes off in my mouth and I can feel little plastic filaments on my tongue.

Mel hates silences. She must be worried that this one means I'm going to let her down. 'So, what do you think?'

One thousand pounds notwithstanding, I still think it's a bad idea. 'Mel, I just can't. I would hate it.'

Then the dam bursts. 'Ally, you have to! You can't say no.' The desperation in Mel's voice is palpable. I'm so surprised by it that I don't say anything for a moment.

Mel's voice goes from desperate to quietly pleading. 'Look, Al, I wasn't entirely honest with you on Friday.

And I've felt really terrible about it ever since.'

'What do you mean you weren't entirely honest?' I say, now thoroughly alarmed and conjuring up a vision of the seminars that's even scarier than the one I've been carrying around in my head for three days.

'Well, what I didn't tell you was that I really need you to do this. I mean REALLY. It could make the difference between me keeping my job and not.'

Suddenly I'm the one who feels guilty. Here I've been feeling feeble and put upon while my best friend appears to be having a minor crisis.

'How can that be, Mel? You've been at *Me* for ever. Cynthia loves you.' Cynthia is editor-in-chief of *Me*, and Mel's rather formidable boss.

'That's the point. I've been there for ever, and I'm getting a little stale, allegedly. Cynthia says she wants to see me regain the fire in my belly. Come up with more creative ideas for stories, and more creative angles on the stuff I write.'

Mel's sigh is heavy and laden with anxiety. 'Al, I'm thirty-seven, and there are all these young journalists pecking at my heels. They're practically fucking teenagers, bursting with bright ideas and energy. It's a nightmare trying to stay ahead of them. And I really should be an editor by now. I sort of need to make that commitment, to really go for it. I'm hoping this piece will convince Cynthia I'm up to it. She was thrilled by the idea of it. So that's why I wanted you to do this so badly. Even though it is kind of, you know, weird.'

Listening to her now, I'm finding it hard to get really angry. I can tell she's expended a lot of angst on this. If my friend needs me to help her reignite her career, surely I should help her.

'Oh, all right. I'll do it. For you and the sodding £1000. But if I really hate it, I'm not going to see it through. Two meetings. That's all I'm promising.'

'Oh, Al, you're a star!' she whoops. 'And I don't think it will be as bad as you think. I think we're going to have fun with it. The first seminar is Tuesday night, tomorrow. Can you get a babysitter?'

No wonder she was pressuring me.

'I'll see if Jill can stay on a bit later,' I say resignedly. 'Remember, you owe me.'

'You never know, Ally. You might just end up owing me.'

Chapter 9
Confession

The rest of Monday was eaten up by what seemed like an endless series of unsatisfactory meetings. When I'd finished with Mel it was time to meet Anna for the monthly product review. Then the conversation with Paul at the agency took an age (I think he was a little hurt at my rejection of the dangling marmalade jar idea. Perhaps it was his) and the clumping-zest problem proved to be more complicated than I'd expected (apparently being something to do with the new machinery, purchased with the express purpose of speeding up production and reducing unit costs, but currently having just the opposite effect. Unless Andy can sort it out I may end up having to round up volunteers for rotating shifts of hand-zesting).

So I never did do anything about Nick's email. Today I'm

staring at another one, which is crying out for a response.

From: Nick@JamesThorntonArchitects.co.uk
To: ally.james@cottage.garden.foods.co.uk

Ally, where are you? Did you get my last message about Alan? He called again – I told him you were probably off with some orange growers but don't want to put him off much longer.

Damn. I don't want to insult Nick by telling him his favourite fireplace man and good friend is not fanciable, but I don't want to go out with Alan either. My every instinct is telling me that a recently divorced, very earnest man with a thick middle and two children approaching their teens will be more trouble than he's worth.

From: ally.james@cottage.garden.foods.co.uk
To: Nick@JamesThorntonArchitects.co.uk

Sorry, Nick. Have had dreadful week so far. Am having MAJOR bloody problems with clumping bloody marmalade, and agency is not coming up with goods for new ads. On top of this, Millie not very happy at school.

With all this going on, am not sure I'm in right frame of mind to go out with Alan. Am not very good company. It's not him, you understand. It's me. Can you plse explain?

I'm perfectly capable of feeling guilty about this for the whole day, even the whole week. I know what it's like to have your feelings hurt, and I hate doing it to someone else. But I don't have time to dwell on this today. I've hours of blind tastings ahead, followed by an evening in the company of a bunch of desperate singles. Set against the ignominy likely to be on offer at the Savoy this evening, the slight bruising of one man's ego hardly seems worth a second thought.

Jill was happy to stay and babysit tonight. She's always saying that I should get out more, and probably thinks that my caginess about where, exactly, I am going this evening is indication of a hot love affair requiring a discreet cover-up. Millie and Jack have been promised later bedtimes as compensation for my absence, so even they are not too put out.

It would appear that I am the only one who is put out. I want to help Mel, but I'd be lying if I said I was anticipating this evening with anything but dread. All kinds of awful scenarios are unfolding in my mind: group confessions about why we are all single; rows and rows of pale, overweight, unattractive sorts linking arms in a mutual commitment to finding the perfect partner; obligatory 'practice run' dates with the bachelor brothers of fellow seminar attendees. And to top it all off, there will be me regurgitating my feelings about the whole experience for Mel's article.

Mel and I have decided to meet in a pub close to the Savoy for a drink beforehand. We'll have to take care not to be spotted together as we enter the hotel, as she's supposed to be an independent reporter who knows no one at the seminar. My ticket was purchased by Mel's sister to ensure the seminar organisers wouldn't be able to trace it back to *Me* magazine.

At six o'clock I make my way to the back of the Coach and Horses (which, being in the middle of the Strand, is nothing like the quaint country inn conjured up by its name), where I find Mel cradling a beer. She's ordered me a white wine. She looks tense. I can't think why. I'm the one who's going to have to do all the pretending. All she has to do is write about it.

'Hi. Can't believe how nervous I feel. I've never gone "undercover" before,' she says.

'For God's sake, Mel, you're not going undercover. You're going as you, writing an article about my experience. I'm the one who's actually got to endure the experience. Surely I should be the one who's nervous.'

'Oh, I know. I'm nervous for you. It's a bit weird, after all.'

'I thought you said it was an "interesting concept", something that "everyone is doing these days". I thought you said I might find it pretty enlightening!'

'Well, that's all true. I'm sure it will be interesting once we're in there. But from here I have to admit it does look a little, well, contrived. The whole idea of creating a business strategy for catching a husband.'

'Well, like you said, it's not as if either of us is going to take it seriously. I mean, I certainly don't need the advice of some smooth-talking American love guru to find someone to spend my life with. I'm doing this for you. And you are doing it for a good story. So let's get on with it,' I say, raising my glass.

Mel clinks my glass and down a huge gulp of beer. 'I really appreciate this, Ally. Honestly. Now, what would you like to be called in the article? You can be anyone you like.'

I don't have to think for long before replying, 'You can call me Francesca.'

Chapter 10
Undercover Operation

Entering the high-ceilinged, chandelier-adorned Wessex Room, where the seminar is to take place, I can see Mel already seated near the front. There are only about fifty other people in the room, scattered amongst the hundred and fifty or so chairs arranged in rows of ten. (Clearly, the £500 fee for a series of three seminars is beyond the pockets of most people, even those desperate to find a man.) I decide upon a seat in the seventh row. I make my way towards it, squeezing past a thin woman in a dark suit sitting ramrod straight with the seminar brochure folded under her hands on her lap, and a smaller, rounder, far friendlier looking type wearing a cream sweater set with black trousers and loafers. We are all seated a chair's distance from one another. Unless this room fills up, I think, it's going to be a bit of a stretch for us all to hold hands in a show of heartaching unity.

I look around the room, trying to take in the other attendees. I'm genuinely curious about just what sort of woman would come here of her own volition. Twisting my neck round to stare at those seated behind me would be massively indiscreet, so I can only evaluate those in front of me. At first glance they all look remarkably normal. There are a few bad outfits, and a couple of suspect hairdos (the worst of which, I decide, is the shoulder-length perm sported by the freckled redhead sitting directly in front of me), but aside from this there is nothing particularly abhorrent. I don't know what I expected (outward signs of desperation? the physical marks of repeated romantic failure?) but it certainly wasn't this.

There is a woman in the third row I would describe as extremely attractive. Beautiful, even. She has short, dark hair and glorious skin. Not the brown skin of the sunbed or a short break in the Maldives, but the deep olive complexion of the Spanish or Italians. She's wearing a simple black polo neck and a pair of jeans, and a pair of slim, black-framed glasses on her nose. Why on earth would some one like that need to come to a seminar like this? She must have men falling at her feet everywhere she goes. I conclude that she must be a journalist for a rival magazine to *Me*. Come to think of it, half of these people could be undercover journalists.

As I scan the room I am making superhuman efforts not to catch Mel's eye. I needn't worry. She is staring at her notebook, no doubt even more conscious than I about the need to keep up the pretence that we are strangers to one another. I allow myself one turn of the head to the back of the room, less to examine the attendees than to establish just how full the room is. I am shocked at what I see. In the five minutes I've been sitting here, almost all of the back rows have been filled. Women are sitting side by side, and there is the gentle murmur of polite introductions; ours is one of just a few silent rows with awkward looking spaces between seated attendees.

Conscious of appearing unapproachable, I lean across the chasm represented by the chair between myself and the woman in the cream twinset. 'So, what made you decide to come here?' I ask.

The woman relaxes appreciably. Perhaps she has also been aware of looking like the seminar equivalent of a wallflower.

'Oh, well my sister lives in the States and has heard Marina Boyd speak. She says she is just fantastic, and that these seminars have changed the lives of some of her friends. So I thought, what the heck, I'll give it a try. I'm not having much luck otherwise!'

Ah. So that is the connection. These women must all be linked to America in some way, through brothers, sisters, friends or colleagues. Perhaps some of them are American themselves. How else to explain the popularity of seminars like these in a country of people dedicated to the maintenance of decorum and the stiff upper lip?

'How about you?' ventures my neighbour. She has rosy cheeks and eyes that smile out from beneath the fringe of her thick, sandy-coloured bob.

What am I going to say now? I've not thought carefully enough about this. I've asked a seemingly innocuous question and inadvertently trapped myself into having to reveal things I'd not planned on revealing. How much of the truth – about me, and David, and the past two and a half years – am I prepared to bare?

Not much, as it transpires. 'Me? A friend of mine bought me the ticket and practically forced me to come. I'm just here to see really.'

My twinsetted friend looks a little crestfallen at this answer. I realise that I've managed to insult her already by insinuating that this is all a joke to me. It's clearly not a joke to her, or she wouldn't have spent £500 on a ticket. I'll have to watch myself, or I'll have made a room full of enemies before the coffee break.

Suddenly the murmurs die down and a hush descends upon the room. Bottoms wiggle on seats to get comfortable, and backs are straightened in anticipation of the appearance of our speaker on the podium. I'm not aware of what has signalled to everyone else that the show is about to begin, until I notice an officious-looking woman who must be Marina Boyd's assistant struggling to lower the microphone.

Then Marina Boyd appears from behind one of the two screens at the front of the room, and the room erupts into spontaneous applause. I am caught off-guard by this, not having realised that I would be in the presence of such perceived greatness (which I can only assume is the result of a lengthy feature interview on Oprah), so it's a few seconds before I join in. Marina basks in the warmth of the applause for a moment or two, then raises and lowers her hands to quieten it down.

Marina then embarks on her introductory monologue.

It's much the same speech she gave on the radio, but one hundred times more impactful because of her presence. She is tall and slim, and perfectly groomed, as you would expect. Her thick, blonde hair falls elegantly below her shoulders like expensive velvet, and complements the velvet collar and cuffs of her chocolate brown cashmere sweater dress. Her brilliant white smile radiates success and confidence, and, through some well-practised delivery technique, seems to be directed specifically at me, along with each and every other woman in the room. We British just don't do women like her.

'So, there are three secrets to the success of The Proactive Partnership Program,' Marina is saying to a rapt audience. 'The first is disciplined adherence to a method – and my method is based on the trusty four P's of marketing success – Product, Packaging, Place and Promotion – plus four more I've added. The second is moral support, the support that I'm going to give you, and that you are all going to give each other. But the third secret is perhaps the most important of all, and it is sitting right in front of me . . .'

We all crane our necks to look at the carpet in front of the podium, trying to identify the third critical success factor for the Proactive Partnership Program.

Marina continues. 'And that secret is you. Each and every one of you. You have all come here this evening because you genuinely want to make a difference to your life. You are tired of being alone, and you have very cleverly come to the conclusion that once you reach a certain age in today's world, you need to take considered action if you're going to find someone to spend your life with.

You are not looking for ordinary dinner dates, or casual sex. You are looking for Mr Right. And I'm going to help you find him.'

The room erupts into applause for the second time. It's all so horribly un-English, but I find myself unable to sit back in a dignified manner while everyone else is engaging with Marina so enthusiastically, so I join in on the second wave of clapping.

Again, Marina calms us all with a refined raising and lowering of her hands. It's such a subtle movement that you couldn't even really accuse her of imperiousness. 'Now, we have some work to do this evening, ladies. I want us all to emerge from this first seminar with some clear action steps to do with refining the product and its packaging – that's you – and prospecting – that's practising. But before we can do any of this, we need to do some planning. Planning is all about making this Proactive Partnership Program a priority and clearing the path for its success – what I call Dumping the Baggage.'

Then Marina descends from the podium and moves towards the first row. 'What I'd like you to do now is to gather together in small groups of five at the round tables you see all around the room. That's right, you five from this row get together and go to table one, and so on. Then I want you to sit for thirty minutes as a group, each of you telling your table mates why you came here tonight, and how you are going to demonstrate that this programme is truly a top priority in your life.'

Christ, I knew it would come to this, but I hadn't thought it would come so soon. As the room becomes a jumble of bodies shuffling this way and that towards empty tables, I catch Mel's eye, trying to roll my own eyes towards the heavens with sufficient subtlety that no one else notices.

Predictably, I find myself seated at a table with the woman in the cream twinset and the scary rail-thin one. Additions to our group from further down the row are an athletic-looking woman with cropped blonde hair, and a rather overweight, dark-haired woman in an ill-fitting rust-coloured suit (that will have to go, for a start). Much to my surprise, and delight, we are joined at the last moment by the olive-skinned beauty with the trendy glasses. She must have found herself stranded as the rest of her row scattered to fill seats at available tables. Now at least this will be interesting, I think. I'm dying to know what a woman like her is doing in a place like this.

It's all rather awkward at the beginning. We sit smiling gormlessly at one another, occasionally looking around at other tables to see if they have started. Eventually, Marina taps cream twin-set on the shoulders and says, 'Come on, ladies. What are you waiting for? You can't find Mr Right if you can't get the basics right.'

So we begin. The kindly one in the twinset, whose name is Angie, starts us off, recounting a tale of years spent working in the office of her brother's building firm to support her two daughters, never meeting anyone of any consequence, and wondering to herself, 'Is this really all there is?' She tells the others what she had earlier told me: that her sister who lives in New York knows many American women who've been successful with the help of Marina's programme, so she saved up her pennies to give it a try.

The rail-thin Katherine is a forty-one-year-old actuary

and has never been married. She figures the Proactive Partnership Program is her last chance at finding a partner with whom she can have a child. Nancy with the short blonde hair came out as a lesbian two years ago, but has no idea about how to meet women. A friend of hers had seen a segment about Marina on Oprah (I knew it), and suggested she give it a go. The plump Louise is a mere child at twenty-nine. But she has never had a relationship. She doesn't know if it's her weight or her breath, but she's beginning to worry. Her godmother sent her to this seminar.

Then it's time for the olive-skinned one to speak. Her name is Claudia, and she is, as I had guessed, of Spanish origin. 'I am thirty-nine years old,' she says, 'and I am fed up with waiting for the right man to come along. I was married in my twenties, but that was a disaster. I am a translator and work on my own so I rarely have the chance to meet men. And I don't know that many people here in England, so my chances of just happening upon the right person are very remote. So I thought, Fuck it! I am going to take matters into my own hands. I am too good to be going to waste. I am going to find a gorgeous, sexy man before I am forty!'

Wow. What can you say to that? This is George's Francesca all over again. Gutsy, exotic, beautiful. And no way going to seet in a dark room for the rest of her life. I am lost in admiration of her strength of feeling and her thoroughly un-self-pitying attitude when I realise that all eyes have turned to me. I am the last one, and must fess up.

I stare at the crisp white tablecloth, twirling the slim, silver hotel-supplied pencil over in my fingers like a baton, waiting for inspiration.

I can't possibly repeat the line about having been dragged here by a friend; it went down so badly with Angie the last time. And I decide that inventing a completely new persona for myself will be too complicated. It will tie me up in knots and I will surely blow my cover at some stage (particularly as I have noticed that the coffee break is actually one with wine and canapés). Mel can call me Francesca for her story, and change a few details, but I am going to have to be myself.

'My name is Ally,' I begin. 'Alexandra James. I have two children, a boy and a girl. My husband and I were divorced over two years ago and I have only been out with two men since. These dates were such categorical disasters that I hardly dared answer the phone for months afterwards. Since then it seems that I just don't meet men. Or not the right types, anyway. For quite a long time I didn't mind. But now I mind.' And then I add, because someone is surely going to ask me why, suddenly, I mind, 'My ex-husband has met someone he's quite serious about, and I'm afraid he's going to marry her.'

Angie flinches in sympathy. 'My ex married the month after our divorce came through. It was horrible,' she says.

Claudia touches my arm and announces to the group, 'My ex has been married for ten years. The men always get remarried first, you know. Personally I think it's a sign of weakness. They can't stand being on their own. Look at Paul McCartney and how quickly he got hitched to that Heather woman. When the love of his life had been gone hardly a year.'

'We'd better move on to the next topic,' interjects Katherine, who's clearly something of a stickler for a smoothly run process. 'We've only got ten minutes left.'

So we move on to topic two: how are we going to demonstrate that the Proactive Partnership Program is a priority for us? Personally, I'm not sure how anyone with any obligations, such as represented by a couple of children, could possibly rank such a programme as their highest priority. But for some reason they are all looking at me, and it's clear I will have to go first. It's also clear that I'll have to demonstrate more commitment than I gave Mel before I agreed to come; now that I'm here, remaining completely detached seems somehow churlish, like a betrayal of everyone else in the room. So I solemnly promise to attend *all* the seminars and slavishly read my notes afterwards.

I can see that this impresses no one. Louise vows to devote five hours per week to the programme; Katherine pledges ten per cent of her income for six months; Claudia announces that she's going to make sure she goes out in the evening at least twice a week, even if it means eating in restaurants alone. Biting her lip as she considers these testimonials to commitment, Angie undertakes to dedicate an hour of every day to the tasks spelled out by the Proactive Partnership Program. That's quite something for someone who returns home from working full time in a construction office every day to a second shift cooking meals and doing laundry for two pre-pubescent girls.

Marina delivers me from too much cross-examination by gently placing her hand on Claudia's shoulder and asking us all to return to our seats. Once we are all settled she asks one of the groups to volunteer the contents of their round table for plenary consumption. Thankfully, no one from my group puts up their hand, and Marina chooses a group from row four, who (quite proudly, I think) move up to the front to tell their stories. These women are not all that different from the ones in my group, in the end: a couple afraid of eternal spinsterhood and three determined to bounce back from divorces; some with children, some without. But one, whose name is Caroline, makes a demonstration of commitment that rather shocks us all: she is going to give up her job for six months in order to follow the programme religiously and devote all of her time to finding the perfect mate.

When we break for wine the room is abuzz with conversation. In the small group in which I'm huddled (comprising Claudia, Angie and myself, Katherine and Louise having temporarily attached themselves to another group, perhaps in registration of their disgust at my paltry offering earlier), the conversation is about Caroline. We can't agree on whether she is mad or courageous. She's clearly of independent means, or very good at saving. But will her gamble pay off? Is it the right thing to do anyway? Any man who gets wind of the fact that a woman is hunting him down on a full-time basis will surely run a mile. Won't he?

As we ponder the sagacity of Caroline's decision, I spot Mel in a group of four on the other side of the room. She's in full interview mode, looking earnestly into the eyes of a very tall woman, lapping up every word. Every now and again she scribbles something in her scrappy little notebook, then lifts her head in readiness for further gripping confessions.

When we have each consumed a couple of glasses of chardonnay and several vol-au-vents, we are asked to take our seats for a small lecture on baggage. Marina tells us what baggage is; basically, it's anything that gets in the way of our thinking we can find a partner. It could be a long-held worry about being too fat, or a fear of relationships resulting from having been brutally bruised by the last one. She explains that before she met her husband she used to fear that she was too clever and bookish to be attractive to men (apparently, Marina has a doctorate in behavioural psychology *and* a law degree); it wasn't until she 'owned' her brains, and dumped the baggage associated with them, that she was open enough to have a relationship with the man who turned out to be her husband. As Marina recounts this story, I happen to glance at Katherine, who is nodding with her mouth slightly agape, as if she's had an epiphany.

Predictably, Marina asks if anyone would like to volunteer their baggage for our inspection. I'm almost certain that Katherine will raise her hand, but she keeps it firmly in her lap, and in the end we hear from Louise and the woman with the unsightly red perm I spotted earlier. Louise says that she thinks her weight, or rather how she feels about her weight, might be her baggage. Marina responds to this confession by offering a short anecdote about an overweight woman who attended her seminars in Washington, and who managed to hook up with a delightful – if slightly older and less socially mobile – man who adored her despite her extra pounds. The moral of the story, says Marina, is to love yourself and make the very best of yourself (of which more later, apparently). According to Marina, if you're carrying under ten extra pounds, you can absolutely forget about it, because no one will notice. If you're between ten and fifty pounds over your ideal weight, you might want to think about a diet and exercise plan, but you don't have to. Learning to love your body and dressing to flatter it can be just as effective.

The permed redhead, who introduces herself as Karen, says, in a voice so frail it is barely audible, that her baggage is chronic shyness. She is so fearful of having to engage in conversation with people, let alone a relationship, that she usually avoids social interaction altogether. Never short of an inspiring example to suit any requirement, Marina tells us about a chronically shy woman who drew strength from amateur acting classes and insists that Karen is already halfway to burying her shyness baggage as a consequence of merely having turned up at the Savoy this evening. Upon hearing this news, I swear Karen begins to stand just a little taller.

The evening is drawing to a close, and Marina spends the last of it spelling out what we all have to do before the next seminar. She gives us three tasks, which I dutifully scribble down on the back of the notes we've been handed:

1. Planning: write all of our own baggage on a piece of paper and bury it somewhere. Literally.
2. Product and Packaging: organise own re-branding/repackaging session. See extensive notes in take-home pack.
3. Prospecting: take some test runs with some duck decoys. Three if possible.

The duck decoy business is the bit that initially goes over my head, until Marina explains that this is merely a matter of arranging dates with three men whom we would not ordinarily think of as our type. Men whom we might even reject outright as completely counter to type. The point of this exercise, apparently, is to open our minds to new sorts of people, and even new sides of ourselves, and to remind ourselves that a book should never be judged by its cover. Who knows, says Marina in conclusion, you might even discover that one of your duck decoys is the real thing!

On the tube journey home I find myself squashed into a seat next to an overweight city type, slumped half asleep in his seat with his head lolling forwards at regular intervals. Various of his body parts are oozing over the armrest and into my space, forcing me to lean away from him and uncomfortably close to one half of a couple who appear to be under the impression that no one else can actually hear the wet, smacking noises their lips are making as they snog under the bright fluorescent lights of the carriage.

I feel a vibration inside my bag, and fish my phone out to find a text from Mel, whom I had studiously avoided on leaving the Savoy.

Wasnt that a hoot. Caroline person a bit scary tho. Cant wait 2 tell u wot I heard. Call me 2morrow.

Hoot is not the word I would have chosen. Amusing, often toe-curlingly embarrassing, sometimes touching, occasionally uplifting. These are more like the words I would choose. I feel conflicted in a way I hadn't anticipated, and definitely don't like, and I can see my commitment to giving up on Marina's programme after two seminars weakening, if not disappearing altogether. Much as I want to remain disconnected from the whole experience, an ironic bystander doing her duty in the name of good copy, I'm not sure I'll be able to manage it. It's not that I need something like this to help me find the right person. It's not as if I would ever take it seriously myself. But there are all these other people involved, four of whom I feel I know, if just a little. Giving up on the whole thing, or, worse, standing aloof from it, would smack of capriciousness and disloyalty.

Clearly, there's nothing to do but get on with my homework and keep up a bloody good front.

Part 2

Chapter 11
A Burial

We are all three munching our way through bowls of Cheerios when Millie announces that she doesn't want to go to school. When I ask why, she tells me yet another tale of her suffering at the hands of a group of seven-year-old girls. Yesterday they apparently left her to take the blame for leaving all the netballs rolling around the playground in the rain, and Miss Penwith, the P.E. teacher, swallowed their story unquestioningly. Millie was distraught. It was not just the telling off by Miss Penwith. Worse, though she can't fully articulate it now, was the betrayal by the other girls.

What is it about her, I know she is wondering, that invites this kind of nastiness? Is it her nature or theirs that is to blame? In moments of weakness I wonder these things too. But most of the time I am certain that the problem lies in the group, and the cruel dynamic that seems to be being bred there.

I don't want to be an interfering mother, but I vow to see the headmistress if anything like this should recur. In the meantime, I tell Millie that if she knows she did nothing wrong then that is what is important. People will see the truth in the end. Where do we get these platitudes from, I wonder? Is there anything in the adult world that has shown them to be true, or are we just building up a horrible disappointment for our children to face in the days following their twenty-first birthdays?

I persuade Millie to go to school by promising that I will leave work early to collect her, and that she and I will have a special girls' afternoon while Jill looks after Jack. (It is only when I say these two names in quick succession that I wish I had chosen a babysitter with a name like Carmen.) At Millie's request, this will involve a trip to WH Smith to purchase a new pencil case (bright pink being the desired hue), followed by hot chocolate and banana cake at Mortons.

It's at times like these that my sacrifice of glamour, glitter and free lipstick samples is rewarded. For the idea of taking an afternoon off to be with Millie would have been unthinkable at Chanel. Even if I might have been able to engineer it by lying – saying I was going out to do a store check at Harvey Nichols for instance – the sheer volume of work awaiting me that evening, not to mention the weight of the guilt greeting me the following morning, would make the whole outing insufferable. I did try it once. A spontaneous afternoon off to take Jack to Tumbletots was ruined by the sound of my mobile ringing constantly and my own resulting snappishness.

At Cottage Garden Foods it is not nearly so difficult to be human. That's not to say that you can afford to tell the truth all the time. And certainly, if Anna Wyatt is hot on your tail for some particular reason, you will find it difficult to escape. But most of the time things just don't happen that fast in the marmalade game, so one afternoon playing hooky can pass without consequence.

All I have to do today is write a short diary entry ('meeting with J.M. at T.S.') that gives me lots of flexibility for invention should any questions be asked, and leave a message on my phone saying that I am in meeting and will return all calls in the morning.

This I do, having spent the morning reworking the profit forecasts for Pure Gold – Thin Cut to my satisfaction. I collect Millie and Jack from school, deposit Jack at home with Jill, and embark on my outing with Millie. Much to my surprise she chooses the turquoise pencil case, and opts for the chocolate cake over the banana. I wonder if my change of life programme is somehow rubbing off on her.

We don't discuss the netballs, or the girls at school, but stick to happy topics like *The Lost Princess*, which we plan to see at the weekend, and the rabbit that I plan to buy her for her eighth birthday. Millie seems cheered by our short excursion. For me it is a welcome break from thoughts about what lies ahead that evening.

I've decided that tonight is as good a night as any to get my baggage burying over with. It's got to be done, as I'll surely be asked about it at the next seminar, and I'm not one hundred per cent confident of my ability to make up something plausible.

The last time I tried to bury something in the garden was when Jack and Millie both had veruccas. After I complained that none of the usual potions were getting rid of the little blighters, someone told me about an old Chinese remedy, consisting of placing a fresh piece of raw meat (beef, pork, chicken – anything would do, apparently) on the verucca, inside a sock, and leaving it there overnight on each of five consecutive nights. Each morning you were required to bury the used piece of meat in the garden, preferably under some life-affirming plant.

I followed this advice to the letter. Millie was disgusted by the whole process, but Jack found its slimy aspects absolutely to his liking. I have to say I was with Millie on this one. But I persevered. On day six I inspected Jack and Millie's feet, expecting them to be clear. There they were. Two veruccas, as large as they'd been the previous week only slightly soggier. Two weeks later I told a chiropodist about the whole episode and he just shook his head in disbelief. 'I can't believe the kind of rubbish people fall for these days,' he said, obviously failing to make the connection between 'me' and 'people who fall for rubbish'. He promised me the veruccas would disappear all by themselves if I just left them. And two months later they did.

I am hoping that Marina's baggage-burying exercise will be more successful. I haven't yet written my baggage list, and think it may take some time. I know I must have a decent stretch of time alone to do it properly, so my goal is to get both Jack and Millie to bed early. This I accomplish by making tea into a pyjama party, to which we all come in our nightwear, me included. We sit together in the kitchen sipping hot chocolate and eating peanut butter toast, Millie in her short-sleeved Barbie nightie (far too flimsy for early March really), Jack in an old pair of Spiderman pyjamas handed down from Ollie, teamed with cowboy hat, and me in my favourite pair of blue and white flannels. We all watch half an hour of *Jurassic Park II*, I turn the clock ahead by half an hour as a precaution, and they go off happily to bed. Jack only appears at the top of the stairs twice: once to ask if he can sleep with his holster and chaps over his pyjamas (no) and the second time to ask if I can give him one more kiss (oh all right).

Then I sit down to face the monumental task of listing everything that is wrong with my life and will render me unprepared for meeting the man of my dreams.

After an hour staring at the page, punctuated by the occasional stroll around the kitchen to stimulate my thinking, I have come up with nothing. You see, I don't think I'm too fat. I'm maybe seven or eight pounds heavier than would be ideal if I were appearing in public in a bikini. I wouldn't mind being thinner but I don't obsess about it. I don't think it qualifies as baggage.

And I don't think I'm ugly. I'm no Jennifer Lopez, but I know I'm presentable, and there have been times in my life when people have actually called me pretty. The light, the make-up and the mood would have to be right, but it is not beyond the realms of possibility that someone might call me that again.

I don't think I'm stupid, or unworthy, or any of the other things Marina Boyd supposes might constitute my problem. I don't really have any baggage, I think, sitting down in front of the page again, this time with a glass of wine to aid flow of thought.

Except for one thing.

My husband left me.

My husband left me because he didn't want to be married any more. He left me having once told me that we would be together for ever. He left me with two beautiful children whose eyes remind me of him, and of the fact that we will never raise them together, in the family I grew up believing it was my unquestionable destiny to be part of.

It is this that makes it so difficult to cook cheesy pasta for Millie in the kitchen with David standing beside me. In the life I had always imagined for myself, the cooking of meals for children, with husband nearby, somehow represented the core of family life. And for a few years it was. We cooked and ate together. And laughed and played and argued. And we will never do that again.

What's been harder? I've often asked myself. Disassembling, piece by piece, all the love I felt for David? Wiping his touch from my memory? Instructing my heart not to turn somersaults at the sound of his voice? Arming my body against the presence of his? Or accepting that our little family is for ever broken? Perhaps it's all the same kind of hard.

I take the pen and write on the blank sheet: *David left me. The man I loved left me.*

I pause, before writing: *I will never raise my children with their father again. We will never be a family.*

I then go off to my bedroom in search of a shoebox. I take the picture of David and me with Jack and Millie off the dresser and out of its frame and put it into the shoebox. Then I go downstairs again, retrieve my coat and sneakers from the hallway and walk back to the kitchen. I fold the piece of paper with my baggage on it, dropping it into the shoebox on top of the picture. I open the door to our tiny South London garden, trowel in hand, and gasp as the unusually cold March air stings my lungs.

This will not be easy, I know. The ground is still frozen. And a shoebox is rather too large. It takes me twenty minutes to hack out a decent sized hole under the camellia bush but eventually I manage it. I place the box in the ground, and start piling the dirt back in on top of it.

And then they come. Torrents of them. The tears roll down my cheeks and drop into the hole; the digging might have been easier if I had cried first. I know I make a strange sight. A crazy woman in blue and white flannel pyjamas and sneakers, kneeling weeping on the ground in the middle of a late-winter night. But for the time being I cannot stop.

When my eyes are dryer and I have shovelled the remaining soil back into the hole, I stand and turn to face the house. Millie is standing at her bedroom window, staring at me with an expression that is impossible to read in the darkness. How long has she been watching me? Was I crying that loudly? Or is it that sixth sense of hers the midwife talked about? For a minute I feel I have betrayed her, and want to turn and uncover the box.

But I can't. I know I can't. There's only one thing to do, and that's to go back into the house and tell her I was laying out pellets to stop the foxes eating my camellias.

*

I do have other pictures of David with me and the children. Lots of them. But they are tucked away in photo albums at the bottom of the hall cupboard.

That part of my life isn't lost for ever. I'm just not going to have it on display any more.

Chapter 12
Prepackaging

Although at times I was forced to hide the fact, I was always a good student. From about the age of eight, I was the type to sit down and do my homework the minute I got home from school, before I watched TV. If my parents ever had to remind me to do my homework, I can't remember it. Even at university my essays were always handed in on time. Only once did I have to pull an all-nighter to get an essay finished, whereas my housemates regularly appeared at the breakfast table with bags and dark circles under their eyes, having worked on essays until dawn and galloped over to campus to hand them in before collapsing back into bed.

So it's difficult for me to see a list of homework tasks and ignore them. With baggage buried last night, I turn my attention to the rebranding and packaging meeting I'm supposed to organise for myself. Thanks to a quick phone call to Mel, during which she regaled me with stories she'd heard on Tuesday evening and promised me that the cheque for £1000 was in the post, I have at least decided who should attend. The Branding Ally Committee will consist of three women and a man, handpicked to provide honest yet balanced feedback.

Clara (as chairperson, naturally): selected because she never lets anyone get away with anything, and will therefore drive the group to produce something of use to me.

Lisa: trusted colleague – witness to my work persona; also single, so knows exactly what it feels like to want to sit around in tracksuit bottoms drinking Chablis with girlfriends despite this being sure-fire route to eternal spinsterhood.

Sara: married with two small children, therefore knows what it feels like to have three extra rolls hanging over low-slung jeans and weariness akin to that of amateur hiker crawling out of Grand Canyon without aid of donkey. Every day.

And, finally, George: because he must see a lot of women making a lot of mistakes; also because he has an impeccable sense of style.

I realise that George is a bit of a risk, having on occasion devastated people with his frankness. I remember a rather short, overweight young girl who came in one day while George was finishing off my hair. George asked her what she was thinking of having done, to which she replied that she'd like a choppy, chin-length bob. 'Oh no, no, no, dahling,' he pronounced. 'Your face is much too fat for that. You'll have to have something else.' The girl stood up, red faced and tearful, and marched out of the salon. I'm hoping George will be gentler with me.

The notes suggest that one of my packaging advisors should be a straight man. A former boyfriend perhaps. I'm really not sure I can pull this one off. I read about this American woman who went back to all her old boyfriends to ask them what they had thought of her and why they'd broken up. The result was an awful lot of bitter feedback she'd have been better off not hearing, and the breakdown of her marriage.

Ex-boyfriends and husbands are definitely out. So which men does that leave? There are work colleagues, like Daniel two desks over, or Paul Delaney at the agency, but letting them in on my secret rebranding exercise would be unprofessional, not to mention awkward. There is my brother, I suppose, but I'm not sure he'd be much use. He is the world's most non-judgmental person, and seems to think I am a knockout who works in advertising. Try as I will, I can't come up with a suitable straight man, so three women and a gay Chilean hairdresser will have to do. Mel will also have to attend, of course, but purely as an observer.

I've still not resolved my quandary as to what elaborate excuse to fabricate for the meeting. Clara and Mel are already in on the secret about the magazine article, but Sarah, Lisa and George are still innocents, and perhaps they should remain that way. As you might expect, Marina is unequivocal about this. In the notes we've been handed, she suggests something along the lines of:

Nancy, I so admire the way you dress and carry yourself. I hope you won't mind if I ask you something personal.

This is the year I am going to find a partner to spend my life with. Before I start, I want to make sure that I look as good as I possibly can and I would love for you to help me identify some changes that I might need to make.

I consider this option carefully, before scripting an email to Lisa.

From: ally.james@cottage.garden.foods.co.uk
To: lisa.gibbons@cottage.garden.foods.co.uk

Lisa,

I have this friend who is thinking of changing careers and becoming a lifestyle coach and I've agreed to be her guinea pig next Friday evening. Apparently she needs me to be someone in need of feedback on hair, make-up, clothes, personal habits – that sort of thing. She also needs some people to give me this feedback so she can practise her 'facilitation' techniques. You know the type of thing I mean. Could you do me a huge favour and come over? I can promise vast quantities of pinot and my mother's secret chutney recipe in return.

I then forward the email to Clara:

From: ally.james@cottage.garden.foods.co.uk
To: clara.wilson@PetersandYoung.com

Need help desperately. See below. You've not met them before, so should be quite easy to pretend you would rather be poor woman's Carole Caplin scraping together meagre living than successful management consultant earning six-figure salary with respectable firm.

Please don't let me down.

Clara doesn't respond for three hours. When she does she makes me feel like a small child.

From: clara.wilson@Petersandyoung.com
To: ally.james@cottage.garden.foods.co.uk

Anything for you, honey. But am of opinion that you are being a little feeble. Remember, self-improvement in name of finding man suitable as escort to expensive restaurants and swanky hotels in Venice is nothing to be ashamed of. People do it all the time, hence huge popularity of Trinny & Susannah.

P.S. Judging by way am feeling of late, may soon need to consult life coach rather than play one. (Kidding. Am not that desperate yet.)

Clara is probably right. I am being feeble. But it's too late now. The lie is out there, and must be repeated. I pick up the phone and call George.

'Hi, it's Ally James here. Can I speak to George, please?'

'Oh, certainly, or I can make an appointment for you?' says Emma, the receptionist and occasional hair-washer for everyone in the salon except George.

'Actually, I'd rather speak to George if you don't mind.'

'Fine,' says Emma, putting me on hold. George materialises in seconds. He can't be very busy.

'Hello, dahling. What ees the matter?' he says, his voice

heavy with concern. 'Don't you like your new haircut?'

'Oh, no, no. It's perfect,' I say. 'It's just that I need a favour from you.' I then give George the same rigmarole that I have given Lisa, except that we have to dwell on the concept of a life coach for a while because George isn't sure what it is. When we have cleared that up, he is effusively willing.

'Well, eet sounds like the most marvellous fun. I can't wait. Shall I bring anything?'

'Just yourself, George. I'll provide the rest. About eight all right?'

'Perfect, dahling. I'll see you then.'

The call to Sara is easy. She always jumps at the chance of a night out without Charles, it being far easier to leave the house with him in charge of tea, bath and bed than to try to justify the costs of a babysitter and organise one. By two thirty in the afternoon everyone has agreed to come and I am feeling quite proud of myself, despite Clara's telling off. I am enjoying a brief wallow in self-satisfaction at having organised my own meeting when the phone rings and summons me to another I'd rather not attend.

'Mrs James? Hello, it's Mrs Davis here, from the school.' I'm always called Mrs James by the school, though James is my maiden name, not something I picked up at the altar. The English don't cope particularly well with the idea of a Ms Anything, despite the fact of it now being a box on every official form we are asked to complete.

'Oh, Hello. Is everything all right?' I defy any mother not to stiffen momentarily on receipt of a phone call from her child's school. Either there will have been some ghastly accident requiring an immediate journey to casualty, or you will be asked to help escort twenty five-year-olds on a one-day outing to the science museum.

'Don't worry,' says Mrs Davis, leading me to believe that this call is science museum related. 'It's just that there has been a small incident at the school that I thought you should know about.'

'Really, what's that?' I ask warily.

'Mrs James, it's Millie. It seems that some of the other girls have soiled her gym kit. It seems they have put a squashed banana and some chewing gum and honey inside it, and I'm afraid a lot of it is ruined. I'm awfully sorry.'

Mrs Davis and I both know that we are not sorry about the ruined gym clothes. The issue here is Millie, and the humiliation she must have experienced on taking out her sticky, stinking gym kit, and knowing that people she ought to call friends were the ones who'd trashed it. The issue is these girls in her class, and why they are so intent on traumatising Millie on what I now see is an almost daily basis.

'Well, that's pretty serious. I'd better come in, hadn't I?' I say sombrely.

'Yes, that would be a good idea. Can you make it any time this week? Say, after school today for instance?'

I peer at my diary, noting an hour's briefing by the PR agency and a scheduled conference call with the chaps in the factory to discuss progress on the clumping issue. I quickly decide to skip the former and delegate the latter.

'Yes. I can make that. I'll leave now,' I say.

I tell my PA Philippa that an emergency has arisen, and

ask her if she could please make my excuses to the PR firm and ask the junior brand manager, Nicki, to take my four p.m. call. Philippa is glad to help, being the sort of person who blossoms at the hint of a drama requiring her intervention.

A meeting designed to help make me more attractive to potential partners now feels all wrong. While I have been organising it, someone I love more than life itself (someone who really is my number one priority, Marina. Are you listening?) has been bullied and belittled and made to feel she hasn't a friend on this earth. And like most things that happen to my children, it is probably, somehow, my fault.

Chapter 13
The Rescue

Last year the school hosted a seminar about building children's self-esteem. Having read so many scaremongering headlines insisting that children of divorced parents suffer low self-esteem, I was probably over-sensitive about the whole subject. It seemed to me that self-esteem would be hard enough to nourish without throwing a parental split into the mix. I wasn't exactly sure what esteem was, but I was certain that, in the modern age, it would be deemed essential, vulnerable and precariously dependent upon the actions of we poor misguided parents.

The evening turned out to be enlightening and entertaining – apart from a couple of intensely irritating interventions by two mothers who clearly saw themselves as having cracked the challenge of parenting in its entirety, never mind the self-esteem bit. (You know the type. The Professional Mother. She invariably has a gaggle of children – two would never be enough – and exudes a noisy confidence about the way she is raising them. There is nothing about parenting on which she doesn't have an opinion – an opinion shared in a tone so casually smug you would happily thump her in front of the head and the entire PTA. It is a mistake to think she is always a homemaker, because she isn't. The Professional Mother who's chief executive or city banker on the side is arguably the worst offender.)

I learned a lot about self-esteem that night. One thing I remember clearly is being told that we should support our children, but never rescue them. Supporting them in dealing with a problem builds their self-confidence; rescuing them renders them fearful and dependent. Mrs Davis has obviously remembered this rule as well, because she pronounces it to me as I sit across from her on a slightly wobbly chair with a worn brown seat in her office. Her head appears to be framed by the giant patch of dingy, flaking paint on the wall behind it.

Mrs Davis's view on the gym bag incident is that we should give Millie better 'coping strategies' to enable her to withstand the 'unwanted attention' of the 'stronger and more assertive' girls in her class. She acknowledges that Millie's class is 'particularly difficult, seeming to be more rife with nastiness' than she would expect. She also, by the way, has some helpful suggestions for the removal of banana and honey stains. She has nothing to say about chewing gum.

I listen to Mrs Davis and consider accepting her recommended line of action, but find myself unable to summon the required respect for her authority. Instead, I give her my take on the matter, which is that Millie's class seems to contain a disproportionate number of troublesome bullies who appear to be able to perpetrate small acts of torture on a weekly basis without any consequences. To my knowledge, their parents have not even been called about the gym kit smearing incident, or indeed any others involving Millie. I cite them all: blasphemous phone messages from anonymous but easily identified callers; repeated exclusion from play; framing for hairclip theft; framing for netball ruination; and finally this.

'I'm sorry you feel that way, Mrs James. You have to understand that bullies are generally insecure individuals themselves. They need our support if they are to learn appropriate behaviours,' she says with a calmness that infuriates me.

'So let me get this straight,' I say, doing an imitation of calm through clenched teeth. 'Millie is persecuted on a weekly – sometimes twice weekly – basis by a bunch of girls you acknowledge to be bullies in a class you say is "rife with nastiness". But you want me to help Millie to help herself so that you don't have to confront these girls or their parents. Have I got that right?'

'Mrs James, I don't think that is what I said. I merely think that the best way to help Millie is to help her help herself. She needs us to help her to be more assertive.'

I've never heard the word 'help' uttered so often by someone so obviously hell-bent on not providing it. This woman is so lacking in imagination and genuine empathy that she is reduced to living life by numbers. I've never liked her.

Sod it. If there were ever a situation requiring a parental rescue mission, this is it.

'Well, thank you for those insights, Mrs Davis. I'll be writing to you shortly about withdrawing Millie from the school. In the meantime, I would appreciate it if you could contact the parents of the girls responsible for this latest mess to notify them of their share of the cost of replacing Millie's gym kit.'

I stand up purposefully, knocking the wobbly brown chair to the ground in the process. I decline to pick it up. That parents are offered such a filthy, uncomfortable relic to sit on is an insult I am glad to avenge.

'The trainers were from John Lewis and cost £20,' I add sharply as I walk out the door.

I am just in time to collect Jack and Millie at the gates. Millie is dragging her blue gym bag; I can see a dark patch where the banana has started to seep through. Millie and Jack are surprised and delighted to see me. Jill is just surprised. 'What's wrong?' she asks. 'Did you think I'd forget them?'

'Of course not,' I reply. Then, kneeling to hug Millie, I say, 'I just wanted to come to tell my special girl that I love her and that I don't give two hoots about her filthy gym kit. She won't be needing it for much longer anyway.'

Chapter 14
Prospecting

I might have made a mistake. Hazlecroft, where Jack and Millie go to school now, is one of just two decent schools in the area. Both schools are reputedly full to bursting, with long waiting lists. In a fit of parental righteousness I have effectively stranded Millie in academic no-man's-land.

I call Clara, who reassures me that I've done the right thing. 'What else could you do, Ally? The woman clearly has a heart of stone – except where future young offenders are concerned – and the judgement of a wallaby. She would never have done anything about this problem, and you'd have had to haul Millie out of there sooner or later.'

Then I call David, who is somewhat less sympathetic.

'Jesus, Ally. How could you do that? What if the other

school won't have her? We'll probably end up having to pay for private education. You'll just have to go back and apologise. Tell Mrs Whats her name you'd like to give it another chance.'

If it were only my pride at stake, I might be able to crawl back to Mrs Davis swallowing it. But it isn't. Millie's happiness, and, dare I say it, her self-esteem are what's at stake. And I am as certain as I've ever been about anything in my life that if she stays in that place, with that head and those girls, she will wither. Jack seems fine now, but it's probably only a matter of time before he starts to feel the impact of leadership that's wetter than a machine full of shirts before the spin cycle.

Today I've set myself the task of persuading St George's to take both Millie and Jack. Or, rather, I've set myself the task of launching the lengthy campaign I suspect will be required to obtain them places. The hurdles I expect to have to deal with along the way include being told that the catchment area has been redrawn and we now live just outside it, and that the school is full and has a waiting list of three hundred. But I refuse to be daunted. If fifty phone calls is what it takes, fifty is how many I shall make. I'll treat it like a marketing campaign. If it can work for marmalade – and for finding a husband – it can work to secure my children's academic future.

Prepared as I am for a lengthy crusade, you can imagine my surprise when the head of St George's, Celia Harris, tells me over the phone that, yes, they happen to have two places as a family has just this week informed her that they are moving away from the area. She does need to offer the places to a few other families on the waiting list first, but should be able to let me know the outcome by early next week.

I hang up the phone feeling torn between optimism and mild despair, and, searching for something to distract myself, I decide to call Nick and tell him I'd be happy to hear from Alan after all.

The thing that has turned me around is the duck decoy exercise, the one that's supposed to 'show you that there is more to someone than meets the eye'. Of course I know there's more to people – and everything else – than meets the eye. I must have repeated this mantra to Jack and Millie a thousand times, with the same persistence that I apply to telling them to say please and thank you. You do these things in good faith as a parent, knowing that one day, perhaps when they are eight or nine but certainly by the time they are twenty, they are going to say 'thank you' to someone completely unprompted, and you will be able to congratulate yourself on having raised a civilised human being.

But however much I know that there is more to people than meets the eye, I must confess I've never applied the theory to men. I've never dated anyone I didn't fancy immediately. And I haven't strayed from type since the age of twenty-one. Before that, I had no idea what was my type, and I went out with all kinds of boys, just for the fun of it. There were a few disasters, but I suppose they all served a purpose: helping me figure out what my type was.

And that type was dark, slim, not too tall. A little mysterious. Exotic even. Not average. Definitely not average.

Like David. And before him Eddie. Eddie turned out not to be so exotic in the end. In fact, he ended up being far more average than any of the guys my friends were going out with – a graphic designer with long hair and soulful eyes who secretly wore socks to bed. But David, he was the real thing.

So I've decided to go on three dates with men who are absolutely not like David. Three men who are not my type. I haven't yet come up with the third name, but I know who the first two are going to be.

'Nick, hi, it's me,' I say.

'Ally, hi. Listen, I got your email on Tuesday. I've been waiting to call Alan, but I was just about to.'

'Well, that's why I'm calling actually. I've sort of changed my mind. I think I was just feeling slightly stressed by everything. Millie's having trouble with bullies at school and I've hauled her out. Now I have to wait and see if she'll get a place somewhere else. But then I thought, it's only a date, right? I mean, he doesn't expect anything does he?' This is a euphemism for 'will he want to sleep with me immediately after the pudding wine?' but I have to be gentle with my brother.

'Oh. No, of course not. He's a really nice guy. It will be fun. It can't hurt, can it?' he says.

'OK then. You can give him my number. Tell him I'll look forward to his call.'

'Righto, kiddo. I'll get right on it. So how do you think the school thing will work out?' he adds.

'So far so good. There's a place at St George's. If I hound the head enough I might just get it.'

'Good stuff,' he says supportively. 'You always were a

person who could get what you wanted when you set your mind to it.'

I was?

My next duck decoy is a stroke of genius. Not him, but the idea of him.

Before Christmas I noticed that all the lights in the front hall and sitting room were flickering. When I mentioned it to Nick he gave me his considered (and probably correct) opinion that it must all be down to faulty transformers.

'What's a transformer?' I'd asked, hoping it was something I might be able to replace with a new one from B&Q without too much effort.

'It's the thing that controls the dimmers for the lights. They are very temperamental and they don't last very long. You'll need an electrician to look at it.'

Oh, damn.

'Do you want me to see if I know anyone in your area?' he'd added, ever helpful.

'That would be great,' I'd said. 'I wouldn't know a quality electrician if I fell over him.'

Two days later Nick emailed me the name and number of a reliable and reasonable electrician: Gary Hamilton, of Hamilton and Sons. Gary turned up with his father, Bob, and they repaired my transformers for a mere £75. I remember taking them each a cup of coffee as they stood pondering a mass of coloured wires dangling from an open wall socket. Gary turned to me as he took his coffee with a ring-free hand, and gave me a truly beautiful, inviting smile. Not the kind of smile you dish out if you are happily involved with someone else. Gary is my man.

He's a perfect duck decoy. All I require of a duck is that he have a little something that I recognise as my type, and in Gary's case it's his smile. The rest of him is so far from what I think of as my type that he is probably a better duck than Alan. He's an electrician, ergo probably not exotic. I'd bet my life on the fact that he doesn't read books. He'll be an avid football fan who spends every other weekend travelling the length of the country to watch his team.

Of course, he's never going to ask me out, so I will have to ask him. But even this is all right. According to Marina, it's OK to break the femininity rule once and ask someone out. All I have to do now is dream up an electrical problem for him to come and fix.

I start wandering around the house trying to identify said problem. I don't have to look very hard. I soon realise that this house is an electrical disgrace. The extractor fan above the stove hasn't worked for months; the washing machine is plugged into a socket about ten feet from where it sits because the socket immediately behind it doesn't seem to emit electricity; and there must be two or three malfunctioning ceiling lights (some of them dangling down from wires in imitation of cheap ceiling decorations) in each room of the house. They are the kind of ceiling lights with bulbs that are impossible to change without a degree in astrophysics and the dexterity of a heart surgeon, so I will probably need an electrician to fix the lot. The challenge will not be finding Gary enough to do, but shortening his job list to a length I can afford.

I decide that I can live without a functional fan (I've

never really had a problem with the fumes from boiling pasta and peas rising unchecked to the ceiling) and continue to put up with the washing machine power lead stretched across the length of the utility room. So it will be the lights, which have, I now realise, been driving me quietly crazy.

I call the number on the card that Bob gave me months ago: 'Hello, this is Bob of Hamilton and Sons. Gary and I are on a job or on the phone right now, but please leave a message and we'll try to fit you in.'

'Hello, hi, this is Ally James,' I say after the beep, in a voice I'm certain is a dead giveaway of my ulterior motives. 'You did a job for me a couple of months ago, in Rosemere Road. Well, there are a couple of other things that I need sorting out, so I'd appreciate it if you could call me back. Thanks.'

Damn. I forgot to leave my number, and they may not have it. They didn't strike me as electricians with a quality record-keeping system.

'Hi, this is Ally James again. Sorry, forgot to leave my number. It's 0208 623 5657. Thanks.'

There. With two of my three duck decoys practically in the bag, all I have to do is wait. And do the Tesco shop. Car keys and black bin bag in hand, ready to be deposited outside, I am momentarily delayed by a call from Philippa, who needs to arrange a conference call with Paul Delaney for two o'clock this afternoon.

Isn't it supposed to be the client who decides when the meetings are, at her convenience? I think.

'Yes, of course I can make it,' I say, knowing that it will mean forgoing the planned trip to the gym before school pick-up time. Again.

I walk out the door and dump the bin bag in the dustbin, which is so full I can't press the lid down. If I'm lucky, the dustbin men will collect it before too long. If I'm not, the foxes will get there first and scatter the rubbish all over the road, but aligned closely enough with my front door for it to identify me as the person responsible for clearing it up.

Still concerned about a potential mid-afternoon rubbish clear-up, I glance back at the bin as I step on to the pavement, and bump straight into the poor unfortunate person who happens to be passing by at the time. The impact knocks my bag to the ground, and sends me tumbling back against the brick wall. I mutter profanities under my breath, but I know it's my fault so I can't actually direct them at anyone else. All I can do is pick up my bag with a pretence of good grace. But I'm not quick enough, so the passer-by does it for me. As he hands me the bag, I recognise him immediately as the man with the pushchair. Only today he is pushchair free. He is also charming, rushing to apologise when both he and I know that I was the klutz who wasn't looking where she was going.

'Are you all right?' he asks in the unmistakable tones of the American South. 'That was quite a thud. I'm really sorry.' He's gently cupping my elbow as if to prop me up.

'No, no. It was my fault. Not looking where I was going, as usual,' I say, rolling my eyes.

'Your bag's a little marked, I'm afraid. There's a big wet patch here where it fell.'

'Oh, you're right. Never mind. It's an old bag, and it will recover.'

I avert my eyes from his, which are a soft grey-green

and oozing sympathy and concern. He drops his hand from my elbow, which is a shame as I was rather enjoying it. My stomach dips a little, as if I've just gone over the first hump of the flume at Legoland.

I don't know what makes me so brave. Perhaps it's having made the call to Gary this morning, knowing full well that it was nothing to do with faulty electrics but part of a master plan. Perhaps it's just a general hangover from all of Marina's assertion-boosting exhortations.

'Actually, I think I've seen you walking along here before. With your little girl,' I say.

'Yeah,' he replies, smiling warmly. A lovely crease appears on the right side of his face, giving his smile a sort of lopsidedness. 'That's Grace. I take her to nursery every morning so I can get some work done. I'm on my way to pick her up.'

Aha. Nursery. Work. He's either living on his own with Grace or is house-husband to a powerful-main-bread-winner sort of wife. I can't see his ring finger, which in any case is wholly unreliable as an indicator of partnership status.

'Anyway, I'd better get going,' he says. I can't think of what else to say to hold him here so I just smile and say thanks.

As I stand by my car fumbling with my keys I watch him walk up the street and disappear around the corner. He's taller than I usually go for, and his hair's a dirty blond. Could he be my third duck?

Or might he not be a duck at all?

Chapter 15
Make-Up

This being my weekend with the kids, I've not arranged to go out this evening and I have half a thought to spend it sticking pins into home-made voodoo dolls of the parents I'm up against for the places at St George's. Once that's done, I'm going to do some early planning for the packaging meeting next Friday. Marina insists that before getting feedback from other people it's important to do a sort of self-evaluation. I've got the seminar notes propped up in the Perspex recipe-book holder my mother gave me last Christmas, and am stealing glances at them as I prepare sausages and mash for Jack and Millie.

I've read this section once before but I figure it will help to remind myself of the details. First on the list is clothes, which apparently must not be: too baggy or too tight; too sexy or too conservative; too busy; too fashionable (so no Vivienne Westwood then?); too black (not even a Max Mara sweater?); or too businesslike. Needless to say, the tracksuit bottoms with the holes in them are forbidden, even for trips to the post office.

I realise that self-evaluation may be more difficult than I'd anticipated. I don't think I'm breaking any of these rules, but I can't be a hundred per cent sure. After all, one person's fashion-forward statement is another's so-last-year-it's-destined-for-Oxfam. I may have to wait until next Friday for a final verdict

I turn the page (always tricky when the papers are in one of these Perspex things), accidentally flicking a blob of mashed potato on to the page (thereby defeating the purpose of the Perspex thing, which is designed to eliminate such culinary mishaps and maintain one's cookbooks in pristine condition). As I wipe away the mashed potato I spot an edict that I must have missed on the first reading.

> *ALWAYS wear an underwired, push-up bra: after thirty you almost certainly need it.*

I hate underwired bras. I discovered long ago that I have an unusually low tolerance for pieces of wire digging into my ribs all day. About three years ago I also discovered that my boobs had lost much of their perkiness. But my solution was never going to be the underwired bra. I opted instead for a marvel called the Uplifter from M&S, a plain white and unashamedly unadorned little Lycra and cotton construction that works wonders on the bosom of the woman over thirty-five who doesn't think metal and flesh should ever be in close proximity, and who favours a pressing and hoisting action over all that pushing and shoving.

But you would never call it sexy. It's not hideous either; more like nondescript. I have a feeling that nondescript is never going to suffice for Marina, and that the three Uplifters in my underwear drawer will have to be temporarily cast aside in favour of a ludicrously uncomfortable construction of wire, silk and lace.

I skip over the next section, which is on hair. Having opted not to cut my hair short I've already satisfied Marina's criteria in this department. There is a paragraph on colour, but I refuse to believe that mine isn't right, being a lovingly created blend of four different shades of blonde, painstakingly applied every eight weeks by a genius wielding a brush and tinfoil.

I'm about to turn to the section on make-up and serve up the sausages when the phone jolts me out of my state of hair complacency. I'm not so involved in the contemplation of my possible shortcomings that I don't feel a certain nervousness in picking it up. Will it be Gary about the lights, or Alan with a dinner invitation?

'Hello, is that Ally?' he says, in his well-bred intonation.

'Yes, this is she,' I say, as if I haven't been expecting this call all day.

'Hello there. It's Alan, you remember from Nick and Kate's?' says Alan. I'm sure I detect a small gulp at the tail end of this declaration.

'Oh yes. Of course I remember. How are you?' I reply.

'Well. Very well. How are you?'

'Cooking sausages actually, but very well,' I say. I want to be polite, but at the same time I don't want him to think this conversation can go on for ever. I've got children to feed, and, besides, I'd rather just do the duck decoy thing without a long telephonic preamble.

'Oh, sorry. I'll be quick then. Don't want those sausages to burn!' There's a pause while he waits for me to chuckle, or gathers his courage for the words to come, I'm not sure which. 'I so enjoyed meeting you and I was just wondering if you'd like to go out to dinner sometime. I was thinking about next week.'

There. He's said it. I have got to hand it to him: no audible indications of gulping this time.

'That would be lovely,' I say. 'I could do Wednesday next week.' A weekday is infinitely preferable for a duck decoy sort of date, being laden with far fewer expectations than a Friday or Saturday. I know that Wednesday precedes my repackaging on Friday, but I don't suppose this matters in the case of a date with someone I already know isn't my type. Anyway, he didn't seem put off by the way I looked last Sunday; and he's not going to get even the slightest whiff of my Uplifter so there's no need to worry on that front.

'Wonderful. Shall I pick you up or do you want to meet somewhere?'

Definitely meet somewhere. 'Oh, I think it would be easier to meet in the middle, don't you?' I say.

'So how about Bluebird at eight o'clock? I did their fireplaces so they are always pretty good about finding me a table.' I don't think he has said this to impress me with his table pulling power. I think he is the sort of man who's fastidious about details, like which kind of fire grate goes with which kind of mantelpiece, and whether or not a popular restaurant on the King's Road will have a table available on a Wednesday evening.

'Great. I'll see you then,' I say, being unable to summon up the warmer and more encouraging. 'I'll look forward to it'. Bluebird will be perfect. Busy, bustling, not too intimate. Far enough from both his place and my place to prevent the suggestion of coffee at anyone's place.

'Bye then. I'll look forward to it,' he says, hanging up.

Gary Hamilton doesn't phone. Of course, an electrician isn't going to call after six o'clock on a Friday, or indeed any time over a weekend (unless he is an industrious six-days-a-week kind of tradesman). But that doesn't stop me jumping every time the phone rings. The first two calls are from Kitchens Direct (do I want a free estimate for a new kitchen, and the chance to win £5000 worth of cabinets?) and Thames Water (could you describe your most recent encounter with our customer services team?). The third time it's a call from my mother. She catches me with one eye on *Friends* and the other on Marina's list of the most frequent make-up mistakes.

'Hello, darling,' she says. My mother's voice is the vocal embodiment of a warm embrace.

'Hi, Mum. I've been meaning to call you. How are you?'

She and I talk for about ten minutes about nothing very much. I don't tell her about the Millie situation as it would only worry her, and what's the point in that if the whole thing might be resolved on Monday? I definitely don't tell her about the Proactive Partnership Program, but I do mention the dinner with Alan next week. She has hated seeing me cope alone, and harbours a thinly veiled desire to see me happily settled down again. If she thinks I am at least in the company of eligible men every once in a while she will sleep more easily.

Mum and Dad were shell-shocked when I told them David had left. If divorce hadn't been part of my rosy picture of my future, it had never even been deemed to be within the realms of the possible by them. Married almost four decades, they'd just assumed I would repeat the pattern. Unlike a few girlfriends, whom I now remember dropping hints about David's roving eye, Mum and Dad never saw anything negative about David. Or if they did, they never shared it with me. Their adoration of him and faith in our future was all part of their optimistic, non-judgemental view of the world. When I was younger their unwillingness to criticise, to stomp their feet and make a fuss, used to drive me crazy. Sometimes I wonder if I'd have been better off with a little parental scepticism, or even some heavy-handed and strongly resented interference, right about the time David and I decided to get married. I just might have listened to them.

Even now they don't judge. They, like me, have decided that David must remain a figure of admiration for Jack and Millie, so there has never been so much as a 'what about that naughty scoundrel then?'. They just call me every few days, and turn up whenever invited, offering perfect cups of tea and babysitting without strings. Like a one-woman clippings department, Mum sends me articles featuring marmalade recipes and advertisements for competitors' marmalade brands, lovingly clipped from *Woman's Weekly* or *Ladies' Home Journal*, much in the same way she used to send me all manner of cosmetics-related bumf. I don't have the heart to tell her that the agency sends me a comprehensive stack of ads and articles on a daily basis. Her efforts are not totally wasted, in any case: about a year ago she taped a radio discussion with regional marmalade connoisseurs that no one else had spotted in advance. It arrived on my desk with a label marked *Marmalade Mch/03, from Mum*. It was horribly scratchy and barely audible – she must have taped it by pushing her old tape recorder right up against the radio – but it was worth listening to for the priceless quotes from a marmalade aficionado living in the Yorkshire Dales. We actually used one of them in the series of ads we ran in the summer.

By the time I've finished talking to my mother *Friends* has ended, so the list of make-up mistakes now gets my full attention. Marina's top five offences (in ascending order of severity I presume) are:

1. Lipstick that's too bright
2. Caked foundation
3. Smudged eye-liner
4. Mascara that clumps on your lashes.
5. Pale, ill-defined eyes

My initial thought is that I've seen far worse sins than these five. What about those women in their forties who still wear pale-blue shiny creme eye-shadow? Or women whose pressed-powder blusher has been applied like two streaks of war paint across the cheeks? And then there is the unforgivable misapplication of lip-liner, which on some people sits like a thin line of putty around the contours of pale, dry lips.

Set against infractions like these, a couple of ill-defined eyes hardly seem worth commenting on. Caked foundation is, I have to admit, pretty awful. But the occasional bit of smudged eyeliner and a few clumps of mascara? It's practically impossible to purchase a mascara that doesn't clump these days; even Chanel's best at £24.95 goes a little sticky within a month of being opened.

I feel on reasonably safe ground after reading this list. I don't wear foundation or eye-liner, and I wipe away any mascara clumps with a tissue the minute I spot them. My lipgloss is transparent with just a hint of pink, so I can't see how it could offend anyone or clash with my skin tone. The worst you could say about me is that I don't really accentuate my eyes. I don't do much with them at all. I've been applying the exact same swoop of teal-blue pencil under my bottom lashes for almost fifteen years, and can count on the fingers of one hand the occasions when I might have stretched to eye-shadow.

Perhaps this is the issue. Not that I consistently make any horrific make-up blunders, but that my make-up is nondescript, the make-up equivalent of my Uplifter. I've never really thought about it before, even during all those years I was trying to convince other people to buy chic cosmetic bags full of expensive make-up, and I've certainly never sought a professional opinion. But now that I do think about it, I suppose it would make sense to change the routine I've had for a decade and a half. A thirty-seven-year-old face is, it goes without saying, not twenty any more.

I wonder if Clara and Lisa have been secretly wishing I'd liven up a bit, experiment a little more? Do they think my make-up is frumpy? Will this all be revealed to me next Friday, along with a hitherto unmentioned distaste for my choices in jeans, sweaters and accessories? Although I'm confident that no one is going to come up with anything truly shocking (along the lines of *I've been meaning to tell you – you have this jowl thing going on that you need to get fixed*) I am beginning to feel a little apprehensive about what I might have let myself in for. It's entirely possible that I've been making a whole host of low-level mistakes for years; things that taken in isolation aren't all that bad, but the sum total of which is a look that is just a little sad.

Suddenly I'm fourteen again. I'm sitting in a cinema with my three best friends, and the three boys we've come with are seated immediately behind us. It's a sort of a group date – we couldn't even tell you which girl is supposed to be with which boy. The lights have not yet been dimmed so we are chatting in hushed voices (though not quite hushed enough as I recall; neighbouring cinemagoers are fidgeting and casting disapproving glances in our direction). The boys are leaning over the backs of our seats, and we are swivelled around to half face them. I've worn my best jumper and pale-blue corduroys, and my hair is freshly washed, with a pale-blue clip sweeping up the fringe I'm trying to grow out. I think I look pretty good.

Then one of the boys (I can't even recall which one, or whether I was particularly interested in him) says to me, 'What are those dark circles under your eyes? You should get something done about that.' There's a short silence, while we all take in what he has said, and then he realises he might have said something a little inappropriate, a little cruel even, so he lets out a sort of strangled giggle. I respond with a casual shrug of my shoulders.

'Oh, I know,' I say, emphasising the word *know* to convey collusion. 'I just get them when I'm really tired. I was up really late last night.'

The embarrassing moment is eclipsed by a chorus of *me toos*, and we all recount the reasons we stayed up daringly late the previous night. I have my own story, about a sleepover with Sally Winscott, during which we stayed up until two a.m. watching *The Exorcist*. In actual fact we'd been asleep by eleven, but my dark circles needed a good excuse for their existence.

I don't think the boy's comment had any lasting effect on our outing. Pretty soon the movie started, and we girls turned around and began watching. Two hours later when the credits were rolling everyone had forgotten that a gauche teenage boy (undoubtedly with spots and a few dark circles of his own) had said something that had made me want to be swallowed up by a folding cinema seat.

Everyone except me. I've never really forgotten it. From that day forward, a tube of under-eye cover-up cream has been a staple of my make-up bag. I absolutely never allow myself to run out.

Chapter 16
Duck Shoot

Saturday morning is crisp and sunny, with a crystal blue sky. It's the kind of sky you get in really cold places like the Swiss Alps or the Canadian Rockies, but that you only ever see about three times during an entire English winter. With reckless abandon (I'm still in my pyjamas) I fling open the shutters to let the full glory of the day into my room. I'm amazed not to have been woken at first light by Jack, so I pad across the hall in search of him. I find him sitting on the floor beside his bed arranging a battle between groups of tiny cowboy and Indian figures, his own cowboy hat tipped slightly forward. An Indian in spectacular head-dress is unceremoniously flung across the room by what looks to be an American cavalry soldier, with Jack providing the soundtrack. 'This town's not big enough for the both of us', followed by 'ughhh, ahhh'.

I decide not to interrupt, and look in on Millie instead. She's curled up in bed reading.

'What's that you're reading, Mill?' I ask.

'*Pony in the Paddock*. It's really good,' she says, smiling.

'What, better than *Puppies in the Pantry*?' I bend down to kiss her.

''Bout the same,' she says, dropping her eyes back down to her book.

Clearly I'm surplus to requirements this morning. How marvellous. I head back to my bedroom intent on crawling back into bed with my own book. This moment of peace may not last long so I'll have to be quick if I'm to make the most of it. Deciding that the sight of me in blue flannels might be a bit much for Mrs Lockhart across the street, I first go to the window to pull the shutters across the bottom half of the window.

And there he is again. Pushchair man. He's pushing his little girl, Grace, in the same direction he was headed yesterday morning. He can't possibly be taking her to nursery on a Saturday. So where is he going so early?

The park. The park is in that direction. Perhaps he's headed for the park. On his own. Without the mother of Grace or anything resembling a substitute for company.

In a moment of seminar-inspired initiative I decide to take Jack and Millie out to the park as well. I pull on my knickers and jeans, shouting at the children to hurry up because we're going to the park for breakfast. What to wear on top? A sweatshirt won't do, or will it? What is the right look, exactly, for a carefully engineered coincidental meeting in the park? After a few minutes standing topless in front of my dressing table, all the while shouting at the children to hurry up, I opt for a pale-grey long-sleeved T-shirt with a deep-pink V-neck on top.

Millie wanders into the room in her nightie, clearly having paid no attention to my frantic urgings for her to get ready.

'Why are we going to the park now, Mummy?' It's a reasonable question.

'Because it's a fantastic day for the first time in ages, and I thought it would be fun to have hot chocolate and muffins under that big tree near the climbing frame. Don't you think?'

Millie considers this proposition. I'm not entirely sure she's buying it.

'What do you think, Millie?' I try again.

'OK. I'll get ready,' she says, turning and walking back to her room to dress. In the meantime, Jack bounds into the room wearing his jeans and holster, but, as yet, no shirt.

'Yippee. We're going to the park!' he yelps.

'That's right. But you'd better hurry or we'll miss the sunshine. Quickly, go and find a shirt and sweater.'

Jack and Millie are both pretty quick to get dressed, but it's torture waiting for Jack to decide between his two pairs of trainers.

'Do you think the blue or the white today, Mummy?'

'Jack, it doesn't matter. Oh, all right . . . the blue would be best,' I say irritably. 'Come on, or all the muffins will be eaten.'

We rush out the door, Millie dragging her pink skipping rope, Jack hugging his orange-striped Tigger rugby ball. Thank goodness the sun is so warm, as I've not paid much attention to outer garments.

We take a slight detour to pick up two hot chocolates, a skinny cappuccino and three blueberry muffins at Starbucks. By the time we arrive at the park I am breathless with anticipation, and my stomach feels as though an entire school of goldfish is swimming around inside it. I can't see anyone. Of course, you wouldn't expect to see a park full of people at eight thirty on a Saturday morning, even a very sunny one, but I had convinced myself that this is where my pushchair man was headed.

We make our way over to the sprawling apple tree by the pond, which is, happily for Jack, directly in front of a large multi-tiered wooden climbing frame. Frame is a terrible understatement for such a substantial edifice. It's more like a fort, complete with slides and poles, and every sort of ladder imaginable. Jack rushes up one of the slides to get to the top, urging Millie to follow him, and leaving his hot chocolate to go cold on the bench where I've parked myself. Millie takes a couple of sips, followed by a bite of her muffin, but then the lure of the fort is too strong even for her and she is gone.

Then I spot him. I can just see the top of his head above the highest part of the wall around the sandpit. It keeps disappearing then reappearing, as if he is periodically leaning forward to dig a hole or turn a bucket upside down. What a relief. I'd have felt so foolish if this whole escapade had been in vain. All I have to do now is enjoy my cappuccino and the sunshine and wait until he notices me.

My coffee is about half finished when he climbs out of

the sandpit and looks around the park, shielding his eyes from the sun. He notices me immediately, I can tell. But he's too far away for a nonchalant greeting, so he drops his hand and turns and says something to Grace, who is still playing in the sand. After a few seconds, Grace emerges with her bucket and spade, and begins to toddle towards the climbing frame, followed by her father. She is far more sensibly dressed for early March than my own children, sporting a big woolly sweater and a little striped hat with a bobble.

I wave and laugh at Jack and Millie just for something to do. I realise it would have been far easier to convey a sense of relaxed indifference if I'd brought a newspaper. A newspaper would also have served as a prop – Marina's seventh P. Marina recommends taking a prop – something that could invite comment or questions from interesting people – along on outings whenever possible. On the other hand, Marina also says you should sometimes sit in restaurants and on park benches without anything at all to read, as this will make you appear more open to conversation. Clearly there are nuances to the whole question of reading-material-as-prop that I haven't quite grasped yet. But it's all pretty academic today, because I'm sitting newspaper-less on the park bench when Pushchair Man sits down beside me.

'Hello again,' he says cheerfully in his lovely soft drawl. 'I thought I was the only poor sucker who had to be out at the park before nine.'

'Clearly not,' I reply, smiling. 'Millie and Jack couldn't wait to get here once they saw the sun.' I'm praying neither of the children blows my cover by running over and demanding why I've dragged them here. 'What's your excuse?'

'Ah, this is a regular event for me. Grace just doesn't sleep. She wakes up at five every day and by seven thirty we are going a little stir crazy so we often head out, usually in this direction. Sometimes, if I'm lucky, she falls asleep on the way and I can head back and catch a few minutes, sleep on the sofa before the day starts properly.'

There is no mention of a 'we' in any of this, I notice. I'm pondering the range of possible explanations (including the distinct possibility that his wife is the type who refuses to take part in her fair share of the early morning torture readily dished out by toddlers) when he obliges me by providing one.

'Ever since my wife died Grace has been all over the place. I don't have the heart to be tough on her, so I just go along with it. I'm not really sure that it's the right thing to do, if I'm honest.'

There is so much to respond to in these words that I don't know where to begin. When did she die? How did she die? How do you cope? My God, your wife died and your child is barely three.

'I'm sure that you're doing whatever is right for her at the time,' I offer inadequately, after what feels like an interminable silence.

Then I really am devoid of inspiration. Intimacy has been thrust upon me without any warning whatsoever. The worst I'd been expecting to deal with was a divorce from which he might not be fully recovered. No, to be honest, the worst I'd been expecting was the discovery that Grace's mother was waiting at home with a pot of hot coffee and some freshly warmed pains au chocolat. I certainly wasn't prepared for a tragedy of this magnitude. Clearly, this would not be a suitable duck decoy.

'I'm really sorry,' I say after a time. 'About your wife.'

'Thank you,' he says. 'It's been just over a year now, so we're starting to settle down. Of course, it's going to take a lot longer than that for us both to get over it, but at least there's some semblance of normality most days.'

His eyes are soft, but not tearful, his look thoughtful rather than forlorn. You might say that his eyes are set close together and his face a little long, but his features all pull together into something that's quite lovely. I think it's that deep smile crease on one side that does it. His dark-blond hair, which is longer than it should be, has been tousled by the intermittent gusts of light March wind, and a couple of strands are falling across his right eye. I can't decide whether this makes him look a mess or dishevelled in a Ralph Lauren poster-boy kind of a way.

Jack runs up and begins tugging at my arm, instantly dispelling the air of solemnity that had begun to envelop us. There is simply no opportunity for extended bouts of self-pity when children are around, as I well remember.

'Mum, Mum, can we play rugby?' he demands.

This is something of a small disaster. I am truly hopeless with a rugby ball. I can kick a soccer ball quite respectably, and even manage to bowl a cricket ball within a reasonable distance of the wicket, but there is something about the queer, pointed-egg shape of a rugby ball that turns any ball thrown by me into something downward-spiralling and pathetic. Jack always forgets this. He begs me to throw to him, only to barrage me with accusations of ineptitude a few moments later.

Still, it must be done. I allow myself to be pulled up from the bench, then turn towards Grace's father (it now seems starkly inappropriate that I don't know his name), raising my eyebrows like The Cat in the Hat and smiling one of those lopsided, tightlipped smiles that doubles as a mock grimace and is the mark of minor, everyday parental suffering endured in good spirits.

My rugby ball throws are as humiliating as I'd feared they'd be, but luckily Grace's father's attention is directed elsewhere; he seems to have lost sight of Grace. He gets up and wanders around to the other side of the climbing frame, where he presumably finds her, because he doesn't re-emerge wearing a panicked expression. I'm grateful for the few minutes of unobserved practice this gives me; Jack has already begun to sigh and grumble about my inability to throw the ball at a height that he can reach.

When Grace's father does reappear he shouts, 'Hey, would you like me to throw you a few?' to which Jack responds by immediately turning towards him beaming irrepressibly. I'm left standing like a lemon behind Jack, but neither of them seems to notice. I take the opportunity to go in search of Millie before Grace's father asks me if I'd like to join in.

I find Millie sitting with Grace in the two-storey playhouse that marks one end of the climbing frame. Grace is showing Millie the contents of her pouch-shaped bag, which appear to include a couple of Polly Pockets, two twenty pence pieces and several coloured beads from a broken necklace. Millie is dolling out the appropriate 'oohs' and 'ahs' as she examines each item. She gives me a wink – which is actually more of a double eye scrunch – and a smile that says *isn't she sweet?*

I've been standing watching them for a few minutes when Jack comes hurtling breathlessly around the corner, rugby ball in hand.

'Mummy, Tom is a great rugby player. He does really good throws, and they don't even play rugby in America! Please don't come back, will you? I want to play some more.'

Then he's gone. Back to join the All England Squad no doubt.

Children really are quite useful sometimes. If it weren't for Jack I'd probably have left the park still thinking of Tom as Grace's Father, or Pushchair Man. Or Tom and I would have had to endure some sort of awkward mutual introduction, complete with handshake. Jack has probably told Tom my name, so now we can skip all that.

I wait another five minutes beside Millie and Grace before wandering back around to the other side of the climbing frame to join Tom and Jack. I figure five minutes is a decent amount of time: to Jack it will still feel as if I've not been long enough, but Tom might be getting bored. I stroll up to them just as Jack dives for a ball Tom has thrown a few feet to his left. Now, if I'd thrown that ball he'd have stood still, fixed to the spot, and shouted at me for my inaccuracy.

'Thank you so much for doing this,' I say to Tom. 'Jack loves it, and I'm just not good enough for him.' I figure I may as well come clean on this; he's probably noticed anyway, or Jack will have told him.

'No problem. Your Millie is looking after Grace, which is great for me. It's nice to be able to play boy games sometimes – playing make-believe with those little Polly Pocket things can get quite tedious after a while.'

Don't I know it. I've always found little girls' doll-related games mind-numbingly boring. It wouldn't be so bad if they played them quietly in a corner somewhere. But they always want you to take an active role. *Mummy, you be the blonde one and I'll be the brunette. First you say you want me to come over, then I say no I can't I'm busy cleaning my house, then you say please because you have a new puppy to show me, then I say* . . . and so on. Thankfully, Millie seems to have grown out of this sort of play, and Jack never requests any participation in the elaborate scenes he creates for his cowboys and Indians. He's quite happy to play goodie and baddie simultaneously.

'Ohh, aren't they awful?' I groan. 'You'll be pleased to learn that it's quite a short-lived phase.'

'That's a relief,' he says. He's standing about two feet away from me now, and Jack is just beside him, looking at me with furrowed brow. I will have ruined his life, of course. *Mummy, today my life is terrible*, he said once. I am always astonished to hear someone so young express such lugubrious sentiments.

'Much as I'd like to throw the ball all day, I guess I'd better get going. I'm hoping Grace will now be tired enough to nap a little.' Tom sighs. Is that his reluctance I can sense, or mine?

'Yeah, we're going to get going soon too,' I say casually. 'Things to do.'

'Anyway, it was nice to meet you. It's Ally isn't it?' Good

old Jack. I wonder if he told him David doesn't live with us any more as well.

'That's right. Nice to meet you, too. Might see you here again at the crack of dawn!'

I watch him as he fetches Grace and plonks her into the pushchair. It has occurred to me that we could all walk home together. After all, we must live reasonably close to one another or I'd not have seen him passing my house so often. But I'm not sure I'm ready for a walk home. That's an awful lot of conversation to have, and I haven't fully absorbed our earlier exchange. I'm getting conflicting signals from different parts of myself, and it might take me a while to figure out which ones are the ones to follow. So I tell Jack and Millie they can have ten more minutes and let Tom and Grace leave ahead of us.

Chapter 17
Progress Report

It's Monday. This morning I told Philippa to stand guard for a call from Celia Harris and to put her through to me no matter what. It's eleven a.m. and I've heard nothing, which makes me nervous. Surely all that business of assembly and staff meetings has been concluded by now? Surely she could have found a minute to put me out of my misery.

I'm also annoyed with myself for only leaving my home number on Hamilton and Sons' answering machine. I should have left my work number as well. I'm just contemplating leaving them another message when Nicki appears at my desk brandishing what looks like the draft promotion plan for Seville Sunset. It takes me a second or two to tell whether she's about to alert me to a disaster requiring a week to sort out, or lighten my mood with some good news. Based on the flourish with which she places the plan on my desk, and the proud tilt of her chin, I decide it's the latter.

'Well, that's the last retailer on board,' she says in a cocksure tone. 'And, you'll never guess who's agreed to provide a quote for the celebrity-snips print campaign for Pure Gold.'

'Who?' I ask obligingly. I am actually very keen to know. The celebrity-snips campaign has so far proved to be a bit of headache. We'd all been so enthusiastic about the concept of getting different celebrities to wax lyrical about marmalade, sort of like a grocery version of the 'who was your favourite teacher?' campaign run by the Department of Education a couple of years ago. They managed to get Sting and Juliet Stephenson; so far all we have managed is a lukewarm commitment from Trevor Fishman, the celebrity weatherman.

'Rachel Ireland!' she exclaims.

'What? For the fee we were offering, or several hundred thousand pounds?'

'For the normal fee! Can you believe it? It turns out she's an incredible marmalade fan. Eats it every day for breakfast, and even takes it with her to hotels in America. She so loves the idea of preserving the tradition of quality marmalade that she jumped at the chance. She also liked the sort of homespun, organic sound of Cottage Garden Foods.'

Cottage Garden Foods is not Robinson's it's true. But it is far from the small, village-based enterprise its name evokes. We have a factory, and professional marketing people and, thanks to Frank Peterson in finance, a strong bottom-line focus. But if Rachel Ireland thinks we sound homespun and organic I'm not going to disabuse her of her opinion.

'Nicki, that is stupendous news,' I say. 'Now it will all be plain sailing. Who wouldn't want to sign up once they know Rachel's involved?'

'Exactly. I thought you'd be pleased.' Nicki is beaming. 'Now for something a little more mundane. Anna says have you organised that trip to Valencia? You know, the "bonding" thing,' she says, making bendy-bunny-ear movements with two fingers from each hand.

'Oh, God no. I've been putting it off,' I say, slumping back into my chair. It's funny how business trips to glamorous places lose all of their allure when you have children. When you're a single parent they're even worse. There's so much organisation involved, and so much, well, absence.

I've been thinking of sending Nicki, though strictly speaking she's far too junior. There's no question, though: she would enjoy it far more than I would.

Or would she? Valancia means Spain, which means Spaniards. Men of middling height with dark hair and olive skin – just my type. Isn't this the kind of opportunity Marina would say must never, under any circumstances, be turned down? Can I really risk sending my assistant off to the orange groves to have her return recounting lurid tales of her affair with a swarthy Spaniard she happens to meet in the hotel bar when she's there?

'Would you like me to go?' offers Nicki. That does it.

'No, no. That's really kind of you, but historically this

sort of thing has always been done at my level. You know how they are, they might take offence if we don't send someone they see as senior enough. Ridiculous, I know.'

Nicki looks disappointed, and I feel like a fraud. I'm on the verge of suggesting that she go with me, but I stop myself just in time. *Old way of thinking: always go places with other people so you have someone to talk to. Proactive Partnership Program thinking: go everywhere alone to maximise opportunities to meet new people.*

'Oh, OK,' Nicki concedes. 'When shall I say you're going?'

'Don't worry. I'll fix something with Philippa. Just tell Anna it will be within the next month,' I say.

Nicki nods and walks back to her desk at the other side of the room, her shoulders drooping with resentment.

Marina's seminars had better deliver results, because they're in real danger of winning me some enemies.

'It's Celia Harris for you. Do you want to take it?' asks Philippa, poking her head into the meeting room where I am seated with Nicki and Paul Delaney going over some new ideas for the Seville Sunset promotion.

'Oh, yes. I have to,' I say, jumping up from my seat in a way that I realise reeks of anxiety. 'Will you excuse me for a moment? This call is one I've been waiting for.'

I take the call at my desk. 'Hello, this is Ally James.'

'Hello, Mrs James. It's Celia Harris here. From St George's.'

'Oh, yes, hello. Thank you for calling.'

'Well, I said I would let you know whether or not I can offer Millie and Jack the places in reception and year four,' she says before pausing. For God's sake, get on with it. What's the answer?

'Well, I'm delighted to say that I can offer you the places. Would you like to think about it for a day or so?' she concludes.

I'm whooping silently into the receiver. 'No, no. I don't need to think about it. We'll take them. Absolutely no question.'

'Well that's excellent news. I'll send you the appropriate paperwork, and a letter outlining how the school operates, and where to buy the uniform and so on. In the meantime, you should probably think about starting them here after the Easter break. Would that suit?'

'Yes, yes. That sounds very sensible. Thank you so much.'

'It's a pleasure. I'm sure Millie will be happy here. I'll personally look out to see that she is. Goodbye, Mrs James.'

'Goodbye. Thank you again.'

I can hardly believe my good fortune. David will never believe that I've pulled this off. Places at good schools in London are so prized that I'm frankly flabbergasted that I've managed to secure two of them within a week of first deciding to try. It must be my time. Things are definitely beginning to go my way.

I fidget through much of the rest of the meeting with Nicki and Paul. The new idea for the ad is better, but still not good enough in my view. The nauseating sarong-clad couple and the marmalade jars swinging above the bar have been eliminated. But the beach and the sunset are still there, this time with a family frolicking in the foreground.

I can't help feeling it's all a bit obvious, and off the mark at the same time. Shouldn't we be trying to tap into people's more basic feelings about marmalade? I'm sure there needs to be some toast and a cup of coffee somewhere in the shot at least.

After the meeting I feel like celebrating my St George's coup so I suggest to Lisa that we go to Papa Ciccia's for lunch. But just as I'm unhooking my coat from the coat-stand just outside Anna's office, she swivels round in her chair and catches my eye with an intensity that cannot be accidental. Has she got a rear-view mirror attached to the top of her PC for God's sake?

'Ally, I'm glad I caught you. Can I have a quick word?'

'Oh, sure.' I stand just inside her office, uncertain as to whether it's a stand-up kind of a word that Anna wants, or the full-blown, pull-up-a-chair-and-listen-carefully-to-what-I-have to-say variety.

'Please come in and sit down. And shut the door.'

I shut the door and sit down in front of Anna's desk, now almost certain that I'm about to be the beneficiary of some sort of bollocking.

'Ally, I know I don't have to tell you how important this new product launch is.'

This statement is not rhetorical, so I oblige by saying that of course I'm aware how important the launch of this new product is.

Anna continues, wearing one of her stern smiles. 'This is the first jam product we've launched since I took over here, and we've been given a good budget, so we need to make the most of it. At the same time, we can't afford to let the other products slip. We need to keep up production and sales for all of them, especially Fine Cut, which as you know is something of a cash cow. On top of this I have to say that, with your experience, I do rather count on you to lead the others by example.'

And?

'And that's an awful lot to do, Ally. Especially when you're only working four days a week.' (How does she manage to make this sound as if I'm on semi-permanent sick leave?) 'It requires a great deal of commitment. I just want to make sure that we are all aware of that.'

I'm used to Anna making slightly obtuse statements like this. Some management coach must have told her that it's better to make vague statements containing the word 'we' and allow people to draw conclusions for themselves than to tell them exactly what to do. Me, I'd much rather have clear direction, so I usually ask for it.

'Anna, is there something I've done that suggests to you that I don't have the necessary commitment? Because if there is I'm sure there's a misunderstanding.'

'I simply need to know that you are on top of things. No, let me put it another way. I'd like to see some fire in your belly. And over the past couple of weeks I've noticed a certain level of, shall we say, distraction. I'm sure it's temporary.'

A flush rises to my cheeks. It's part shame and part anger. I wonder whether my two afternoons playing hookey were noticed last week. Or whether Nicki has complained to Anna that I'm not giving her enough time. Maybe my distinct lack of enthusiasm for marmalade is becoming blatantly obvious. Or perhaps that weasel who fancies himself the next head of marketing has been making snide comments about the 'working mothers in the department not pulling their weight'. Any and all of these are possibilities.

One thing I will say for Anna. She's not one for long drawn-out discussions, and she doesn't seek to prolong the pain. She's made her point, and now her body language – fixed smile, hands already reaching for the phone on the corner of her desk – tells me it's time for me to go. As I rise from her desk I give her the reassurance she's looking for.

'Anna, I may have been distracted by some personal matters in the past couple of weeks, but I can assure you that I am as committed to this job as ever. And the launch plans for Seville Sunset are going very well. You won't be disappointed. In anything.'

Anna nods. 'Glad to hear it.' What she really means is 'I'll be watching you'.

You know, most of the time, I bumble along thinking that it's just about doable to work and mother at the same time. That motherhood needn't impinge on a career and vice-versa. But in fact that's only true when things are going smoothly in both camps. If a crisis, even a minor one, erupts in either, you're pretty much stuffed. It's just not possible to cater properly to the needs of a daughter who's troubled at school *and* care immensely and passionately about the sodding ad campaign for a sodding marmalade.

At times like these, commitment has to be faked, and I'll have to think of some much cleverer ways to fake it.

The lunch at Papa Ciccia's isn't such a celebration after all, for me or for Lisa.

'It's Mike,' she says in between mouthfuls of tortellini. 'We've finally called it a day.'

'Oh, Lisa, I'm so sorry. What happened?' Lisa has been seeing Mike for close to a year. At the beginning she thought he was the 'The One', but the past year seems to have been one long exercise in disillusionment.

'Don't be,' she says bravely, pushing her dark hair behind her ears and taking a deep breath. 'It's not like I didn't know this day would have to come. After all, there's only so long you can go out with a guy who refuses to introduce you to his mother.'

The biggest sticking point in Mike and Lisa's relationship has not been sex or money, but his mother. In the year they have been together, Mike has refused to let Lisa near his mother. In the beginning he made up elaborate excuses involving long trips abroad (his mother's) and important meetings (his), requiring the cancellation of dinners and lunches, but later on he just came straight out with it. He wasn't ready to let Lisa meet his mother because he wasn't sure she would measure up to Emma (Mike's previous girlfriend) in his mother's eyes. Ever since then Lisa has been turning somersaults in her effort to become someone who would measure up to Emma, but so far no invitation to a lunch with Mother has been forthcoming.

Lisa's sister once suggested that perhaps Mike's reluctance to instigate a mother–girlfriend rendezvous was a sign of deeper troubles – such as the fact that Mike might still be in love with Emma, for instance. Lisa seems to have come round to this view of things. Not only does she see his references to Emma as unhealthy, but she finds his constant deference to his mother just plain weird. I've met Mike only twice, but I have to say 'weird' did come to mind on both occasions. You can detect something closed and tight and obsessive about Mike even over a handshake.

To be honest, I'm not sure what Lisa has been doing with him. She's bright and pretty, and not yet at the panic-inducing age when women are encouraged to take the best thing that comes along. What, exactly, that age is I'm not sure, but it seems to be somewhere between thirty-five and forty, depending on the woman. Lisa is a mere thirty-one.

'I did it, in the end,' she continues. 'I told him we were finished on Sunday. It was finally clear to me that we were going absolutely nowhere, and that I have wasted far too much of my life trying to become all the things he wants me to be. And he couldn't even extend me the courtesy of telling me what those things were, except to say that they vaguely added up to someone like Emma.'

'You're right. You are so much better off being free of him,' I say, keen to boost her resolve. There must be no backsliding on this one. 'Thank God you never moved in with him.'

'Well, there was never any danger of that, was there?' she scoffs. 'What if Mummy had wanted to visit? He'd have had to hide me behind the shower curtain.'

She will be fine, I think; she's laughing and it's only three days since the split.

'Anyway, I've had it with mysterious, introspective types,' she declares. 'The next one is going to be an open-hearted jock. I won't complain about sweaty socks under the sofa, or Saturdays spent watching sports on TV, but the first sign of a weird hang-up and he'll be history.'

'Here, here,' I say as we clink glasses of sparkling water.

'Now,' says Lisa. 'Tell me more about this thing you're hosting next Friday, which, by the way, I'd love to come to.'

I should have foreseen this. You can't expect to drop an enormous untruth without being forced to follow it up with a few more.

'Oh, yeah. I'm just trying to help out this friend. She's not sure she wants to go into the whole life-coaching thing, but she's been advised that the best way to find out is to give it a whirl. So I volunteered. It will all be very light hearted, but I do need you to tell the truth – just so Clara can see the sort of thing she'll be dealing with.'

'Oh, I'll tell the truth all right,' says Lisa with a mischievous smile. This lunch has really cheered her up. Mike, his mother and Emma seem a million miles away. 'I'll tell you that turquoise Prada bag of yours does nothing for you so you'll have to give it to me.'

If my Prada bag is all that comes in for criticism I'll be lucky. The Prada is the best thing in my wardrobe, having been purchased pre-divorce when I felt richer and my job demanded that I look stylish at all times. Since then my clothes budget has been halved and visits to Jigsaw and Whistles are permitted only in the sales. It's the same for the children; the Mini Boden catalogue goes into the recycling box the minute it arrives, and Millie now waxes lyrical about George at Asda, where a pretty summer dress can be had for £4.

Secure in the knowledge that Anna thinks she has my number, I spend the afternoon being committed and focused. I am rewarded with Andy's report that we are finally making progress on the zest-clumping problem, which is good news as production has been halved this month and we're beginning to get calls from irate retailers about store stock-outs. Returned batches of Pure Gold are beginning to pile up in the warehouse. We'll need to think of some way of pacifying the retailers next month.

At about four thirty I allow myself a couple of personal calls. First I call David to gloat a little. I get his machine, so I leave a message that I think conveys modesty in triumph. Then I text Clara, who responds immediately with the message *Fantastic. U r superwoman after all.*

My final call is to the Hamiltons. I figure it will be too late to return their call when I get home, so decide to seize the moment. I ring half expecting to get a machine, but find myself talking to a person instead.

'Hello, Gary speaking. How can I help?'

Christ, what do I say now? I've forgotten. Oh yes. 'Hello, it's Ally James again. I was wondering if you got my message. It's mainly my overhead lights that need attention.'

'Oh, yeah, sure. Sorry, I was meaning to get back to you but I've had a lot on.' So he hadn't returned my call from Friday. Perhaps his smile wasn't quite the invitation I'd taken it for.

'That's all right,' I say. 'Can you fit me in this week, say Friday morning?'

'Let me just see.' A minute's pause, accompanied by much rustling of paper at the other end of the phone. 'Yeah, that looks OK. Shall I come early, about eight o'clock?'

I can't possibly have him come when the children are

there to witness my dissolute forwardness. And, besides, I've got the school run to do at eight thirty. 'Actually, could you make it about eleven?'

'Should be OK. I'll call you if I'm running late. It sometimes happens on a Friday, what with all the traffic and everything. See you then.'

I put the phone down and sit back in my chair. Looking ahead at my week I feel dizzied by its complexity. There's Alan on Wednesday, Gary on Friday and a potentially life-changing makeover on Friday night. And in between all this I'll probably spot Tom again and have to decide whether to pursue him as a duck or the real thing. Or not pursue him at all. I haven't had a week so full of prospects in years. And that's saying nothing about the pressure I'm now under to demonstrate superhuman levels of love for the marketing of marmalade.

By the time next week's seminar rolls around, I'll have accomplished so much I'll put the others to shame. Surely no one else will have made so much progress in just a week.

I decide to email Mel and boast about my achievements.

From: ally.james@cottage.garden.foods.co.uk
To: mel.atkinson@me.com

Mel
Thought you might want a progress report for your notes. So far am stellar pupil. Have arranged two test runs with suitable ducks, organised branding party (do not be late), and buried baggage under camellias. Turned out there wasn't much of it, but what there was was pretty heavy.

Am looking forward to receiving cheque. Want to spend it with me at Harvey Nicks on Saturday?

From: mel.atkinson@me.com
To: ally.james@cottage.garden.foods.co.uk

Great stuff. But don't get carried away. Do not, repeat NOT want friend like Caroline.

Harvey Nicks at noon sounds great. Dom working anyhow.

Chapter 18
Bluebird

Sitting in the taxi on my way to the Bluebird I'm convinced that this is among the most stupid things I've ever done. What is possibly to be gained from going out with a man I have no interest in, and no intention of ever seeing again? I know a book shouldn't be judged by its cover. And on one level this is just homework, something I've been asked to do in the interests of my future romantic life and report back on in ten days' time. But on another level it's cruel. It will only prolong my discomfort and Alan's suffering. Besides which, I ought to be spending this evening boning up on interesting facts about marmalade for tomorrow's segment on Radio Five.

It's something of a coup that I've managed to wangle myself a guest spot. Fresh from my telling-off by Anna I decided to put some real muscle into our efforts to secure promotional opportunities for the campaign, so Nicki and I spent an entire morning on the phone. By an amazing stroke of good fortune, someone from Frank Cooper's had just pulled out of Thursday afternoon's *Food of the Week* show, which normally features things like the history of the suet pudding, or a hundred and one uses for the pistachio nut, but will, tomorrow, celebrate National Marmalade Day. The show's producers think I'm the answer to their panic-induced prayers. What they don't know is that they may be the answer to mine.

For tonight I've chosen an outfit that I hope flatters without being inviting. Long jean skirt, flat suede boots, white blouse with long flowing sleeves and my Uplifter reassuringly holding me up underneath. The sleeves of this blouse have proven to be something of a liability in the past, dangling stylishly beyond the wrists in a way that prevents the carrying out of any practical tasks. Definitely not things to be worn next to a gas stove, but probably just about all right for sitting at a restaurant table, so long as there is no soup involved.

When I've checked my coat, I walk into the bar area to see Alan already seated on a sofa. He waves to me, and then stands up with his hands in his pockets and starts shifting uncomfortably from foot to foot as he waits for me to reach him. When I arrive there's an uncomfortable moment reminiscent of Charles and Diana on the polo pitch as he tries to give me a kiss on the cheek but ends up breathing in my ear.

'Hi. You got here all right,' he says.

'Yes, no problem at all. Traffic wasn't too bad.' What

would we Londoners do, I wonder, without the conversation-starters obligingly furnished by the state of the traffic?

We sit down at opposite ends of the sofa but turned towards one another. Within seconds a waiter appears and I order a white wine. Alan already has a beer on the go.

The next ten minutes are a bit of a blur. These sorts of introductory conversations at the start of dates always are. (Listen to me, talking like a woman who goes out on first dates every other night of the week.) We do a bit more on the traffic, touch on the weather, and establish whether or not we are both busy at work; we are just prevented from descent into the hell of a conversation about the latest news headlines by the sight of a waiter, who wishes to take us to our table.

After we've been seated at our table for a few minutes, Alan seems to loosen up a little. It's as if all that waiting, for me and then our table, was preventing him from getting on with enjoying the evening. Perhaps he'd been worried that we'd be given a table adjacent to the swinging kitchen doors, thus discrediting his prior claim to some sort of special status based on his connections with the fireplaces.

Alan chooses lobster bisque followed by the duck (funny that). The bisque is obviously out of the question for me, so I opt for a goat's cheese salad followed by swordfish. The room is heaving, and extremely noisy, as I'd hoped it would be. This is the perfect atmosphere for a date that isn't really.

We spend a while talking about my work and how I got into it. (Alan, it turns out, is more of a jam man.) Then Alan tells me how he stumbled upon his passion for fireplaces while apprenticing in the family antiques business. He proceeded to sink all of an inheritance from his grandmother into his first shop, an investment that, judging by his various addresses, has paid off handsomely.

By the time the duck and the swordfish have arrived, we've moved on to children. Beyond what I learned at Nick and Kate's a couple of weeks ago, I know very little about them except their names and ages: Georgia and Bella, aged thirteen and eleven. Now, as Alan talks about them – their passion for horses, Georgia's first disco, Bella's long-awaited captaincy of the netball team being thwarted by a broken wrist – he seems to come alive, one muscle at a time. With each story, the waving of the arms gets slightly more untamed, the smile wider and more unabashed.

This man really adores his children, I think. They are everything to him. Despite my better judgement, I can't resist taking the conversation into emotional territory.

'Alan, do you miss them? Seeing them every day, I mean?'

It's as if I've uncorked a champagne bottle. 'My God yes!' he exclaims. 'It's the worst part of the divorce. You know, Elizabeth didn't work so people always assumed that she was the one who did everything for the girls. All the practical stuff and all the nurturing stuff, too. I remember some people came to the house for lunch and they saw all these big leather photo albums lined up on our bookshelves. They took one down and it happened to be a sort of story about Georgia's eighth year, with funny quotes and birthday cards stuck in between the photos. And one of these people said something like "bet your Mummy worked hard on this" and the girls just said "No, Daddy does all this with us". I do. I did. It nearly kills me not to be able to do it every day.'

Then he goes quiet. 'You know, it was horrible when my marriage broke up. But when I look back I can see where it went wrong. Now I'm actually relieved to be free of the tension and the arguments. But I find it really hard to let go of the family thing.'

Here is a man who would probably never say 'I just don't want to be married any more', even if he fell out of love with you. A lot of men would be perfectly happy to be newly ensconced in a chic little bachelor flat off Eaton Square while their ex-wives deal with the kitchen of life, but he's not one of them. In a lot of ways he's a perfect catch. Kind, loving, successful entrepreneur, not unattractive. So why is it I can't bring myself to look at him with anything other than warmth, and a mild sense of solidarity arising out of our shared experience?

I could tell him how much I miss the family thing too, but I feel the need to lighten the mood, so I opt for a jovial remark instead.

'Just think, though, Alan. At least there's a good chance you won't have to be there when Georgia brings home her first boyfriend and he turns out to be a spotty, insolent and wholly unsuitable fifteen-year-old with no academic prospects whatsoever. You could be spared that.'

Alan takes the cue to lighten up, and we both bemoan our futures as parents of teenage girls. Then I launch into a story about my own father's horror upon meeting my first ever boyfriend, a wannabe guitarist called Ben. We pass the remaining hour of the meal on this level, floating safely on the surface of all the shared agony, angst and sympathy we might have delved into.

I am relieved when Alan takes the bill unhesitatingly. Not because I wouldn't have been perfectly happy to pay my share, but because that way we avoid all the uncomfortable waiting and shuffling and debating about how much tip to leave that inevitably accompanies the splitting of a bill.

We emerge from Bluebird into the March drizzle, and Alan starts to look left and right for a taxi he can put me into. Miraculously, and defying the truism that taxis seem to go into hiding when it rains, one pulls up in front of us almost immediately.

Then Alan does something that takes me completely by surprise. There I am expecting another spot of amateurish breathing in my ear when he takes me by the shoulders (causing my uplifter to shift uncomfortably up my ribs) and plants a firm, not dispassionate kiss on my lips.

'Ally, you are really quite a girl. I'd love to see you again. I'll call you.'

I mumble something about having had a lovely time and collapse into the back of the taxi. As the taxi spins itself round and heads off towards the suburbs, he stands on the curb for a moment, then hails his own taxi and heads off towards Eaton Place and his two-bedroom flat.

Damn, damn, damn. What do I do now, Marina? I'm horribly out of practice at this. It's easy enough to get rid of a man you despise, but not one you quite like but have no romantic feelings for. How can I possibly say no when he calls and asks me out to the theatre or the movies? How can I possibly go, knowing that each evening spent with him will take us one step closer to the ultimate excruciating, ego-bruising rejection followed by well-intentioned but interfering calls from my brother?

If the rest of the ducks turn out to be this much trouble I'm going to have to seriously reconsider this whole business of relaunching my love life.

Chapter 19
The History of Marmalade

* Eating marmalade on toast with a cup of tea a modern habit.
* Until 1700, a bowl of ale with some toast floating in it considered the most warming start to the day. Then came the tea revolution, and toast with tea.
* Most people think marmalade invented by Janet Keiller. Wrong. Hails from Portugal.
* First appeared in England and Scotland in wooden boxes, a solid sugary substance made from quinces. Fifteenth century. Keillers didn't invent, but did commercialise. Nineteenth century.
* Fortnum & Mason: nineteen different marmalades; Sainsbury's: twenty; Waitrose: fifteen.
* English enthusiasm for marmalade in its full

variety and mouth-watering delectability apparently unquenchable.

I've picked up bits and pieces of this during my eighteen months at the Cottage Garden Food Company. The rest has come from a small treasure by C. Anne Wilson called *The Book of Marmalade*, which I rushed out to purchase as soon as I found out about the Radio Five guest spot, having scoured the internet for the reading lists recommended by marmalade-related sites (of which there are many hundreds, by the way). I rose at five a.m. to get some prep done before Jack and Millie woke up, and have spent the rest of the day reading furiously between meetings and phone calls. I'm damned if I'm going to allow myself to look a fool within earshot of hundreds of thousands of Radio Five devotees; and I'm damned if I'm going to let Anna go on thinking that I'm marketing's equivalent of a drifter, someone who just turns up for work every day but doesn't give a stuff for her product. If I can fake my commitment to a marketing plan for landing a husband I can certainly simulate the air of a passionate marmalade expert.

Actually, the whole experience has been something of a surprise to me. I'd not known there was so much to know, for a start. And I'd forgotten how much fun it can be to try to get to grips with something new. Like a challenge, or a test.

My fellow guests on the show are Hilary Jessop, curator of the food section in the current exhibit of Edwardian Life at the V&A, Penny Alsthrop, a woman from the West Country renowned for her marmalade concoctions, including a (reputedly) very special Marmalade Queen Pudding, and Frederick Thomas, a Paddington Bear enthusiast and collector. We are all seated round a table in the studio waiting for the show to air, our bulky headsets giving us the appearance of aliens. I've done one radio interview before (a snippet about new blusher colours during London Fashion Week while I was at Chanel) but that was a long time ago so I'm nervous today. So is Frederick Thomas, who keeps adjusting his headgear and staring rather wild eyed at the technical paraphernalia behind me. Penny Alsthrop, on the other hand, is leaning back in her chair with her legs fully extended, as if in wait for tea with her next-door neighbour rather than an interview on a radio show with half a million listeners.

We all tense up a little as we hear the countdown to airtime, then our host, Danny Gray, kicks off with his introduction. (*You'll never guess what just happened to me on the way in . . . Wasn't that a great show yesterday? . . . My guests today are . . .*) I listen attentively to this, suspecting that he's going to turn to me with the first question. I am, after all, the generalist in the group, and it makes sense to give a broad picture of marmalade before moving on to the finer details, like how on earth Paddington Bear first came across marmalade in darkest Peru of all places.

'So here we are, on March tenth, which in case you hadn't realised, listeners, has been National Marmalade Day since 1995. Ally James, why March the tenth? Why not June the fifth, for example?'

I clear my throat, which is exactly what I'd not wanted to do. Radio pros never have to clear their throats; they just launch casually in without even taking a deep breath.

'March tenth 1995 was chosen because it marked the five hundredth anniversary of the earliest port record of the arrival of Portuguese marmalade in Britain in 1495. Marmalade had probably been coming in for some time before that in small quantities, but unnoticed by customs men.' God, I sound as stiff as the chair back I'm resting against, and about as interesting.

'Wait a minute, Ally. I thought we English invented marmalade. Isn't that true?'

'Well, actually it's not. The earliest port records indicate that marmalade, which was originally made from quinces, or marmelos in Portuguese, came from Portugal. A book published in the sixteenth century tells of the Moors of North Africa teaching the Portuguese to gobble up marmelada, so it seems that Arab food and customs were the original source of the confection in Portugal.'

'What a shame. There I was thinking the English – or at the very least the Scots – had given the world a great gift,' says Danny, still looking at me. It's clear I'm supposed to respond to this statement too. I wonder if the other guests are getting irritated by my apparent dominance of the first few minutes of the show.

'Well, you're not entirely wrong,' I say, my voice loosening up now. 'The most famous story about marmalade links it with the Scottish: Mary Queen of Scots was supposedly given some to combat her seasickness on the crossing from Calais to Scotland in 1561. And Janet Keiller of Dundee was one of the first, as far as we know, to make chunky marmalade from Seville oranges, which is like the marmalade we know today. The Scots, by the way, also transferred marmalade to a new mealtime position:

whereas it used to be served as a sweet food at the end of dinner, the Scots began serving it at breakfast time in the early eighteenth century.'

Then I'm off the hook for a bit, while Danny turns to Hilary to establish whether the Edwardians really were as keen on their marmalade as we've read. They were, apparently; Hilary recounts that when marmalade was in its heyday in the Edwardian era, Wilkin of Tiptree issued price-lists describing no fewer than twenty-seven marmalades. Queen Victoria's granddaughters, the Queen of Russia and the Queen of Greece, allegedly had supplies sent from Wilkin of Tiptree in Essex. And Frank Cooper's company in Oxford still has marmalade that was taken on Scott's expedition to the North Pole in 1911, discovered in perfect condition in 1980.

Hilary is then asked to give a couple of examples of Edwardian marmalade recipes before Danny turns to Frederick and asks him to recount the more humorous of the references to marmalade in Michael Bond's Paddington stories. I'm pleased when he mentions the time when Paddington goes to the theatre and drops all his marmalade sandwiches on to the people in the stalls below his box, as this is a personal favourite of Millie's.

Then Danny puts Frederick on the spot by asking him how a bear from Peru would have come across marmalade, which, he says, doesn't sound like a staple of the South American diet. Frederick looks momentarily stunned. After all, he's an expert on Paddington, not marmalade. When a look of panic begins to take over his face, I can't resist jumping in.

'Actually, Danny, the South Americans probably caught

the marmalade habit from their colonisers, the Spanish and the Portuguese. And in the nineteenth century there was quite a famous quince marmalade factory in Cuba, which is after all not too far from Peru.'

Frederick looks grateful. Hilary, on the other hand, looks somewhat miffed. She'd probably read that part of *The Book of Marmalade* too. Penny just looks impatient; she's not yet had a chance to speak.

When Penny does get her chance, it proves difficult to shut her up. As she recounts every last detail of her recipe, as well as the story of how she came upon it in the first place, I can see that Danny is desperate for a way out. There are some people that just don't pick up on conversational cues, even on radio shows, and Penny is one of them. In the end, Danny is forced to cut her off quite abruptly, and quickly turns to me with a question before she can get started again.

'Ally!' he shouts eagerly. 'Can you convince our listeners why they should all go out and buy a jar of marmalade today, this National Marmalade Day. I mean, what's so special about an orange preserve with little bits in it?'

I've thought about this one, so I'm glad he's asked me.

'Well, Danny, Noel Coward once said "Wit ought to be a glorious treat, like caviar. Never spread it about like marmalade", implying that marmalade was something other than a glorious treat itself. But I think he was wrong. To me marmalade is far from ordinary. It's mysterious, sumptuous, scintillating and amusing all at once, which is surely the reason that it pops up so often in popular culture. Think of Lady Marmalade (whom you could accuse of many things, but never dullness), and the sixties pop group Marmalade, who had a number one hit with the Beatles' "Ob-La-Di-Ob-La-Da", not to mention the famous breakfast scene in Hammer's *The Curse of Frankenstein* which inspired the naming of *Pass the Marmalade*, the website devoted to the celebration of British horror films.'

Danny doesn't yet look bored, so I carry on. 'Marmalade is so many things. It's an agent of fantasy and hallucination – think of those marmalade skies – and a cure for all sorts of ills, with a reputation as a stomachic, and a cure for coughs and colds. And I bet you didn't know that it's an aphrodisiac: Mary used it to try to help her conceive a child with Philip of Spain in the 1500s. Is there any other food about which you could say all this? Noel Coward aside, we British, at least, appreciate marmalade for the marvellous thing it is.'

'Well, what more can we say?' effuses Danny. 'I can see that you people at Cottage Garden Foods certainly love your marmalade, as do all my other guests here today. I think they might have inspired me as well. I'm off to find a bit of toast and marmalade to have with my cup tea. In the meantime, thanks to all my guests for an enlightening half-hour.'

I'm quite pleased with my little speech, and I can tell Danny is, too. It summed up the show rather nicely, saving him the trouble. He gives me a friendly wink and a wave as I take off my headphones and leave the studio with the others.

And as I leave I'm thinking about two things. First (and it's the first time this has crossed my mind) I think how lucky I am to be working with a product with such a fascinating history and such a hold over the hearts and breakfast tables of the British people. How much better to spend one's days dreaming up ways of keeping the great marmalade tradition alive, or worrying about how to de-clump marmalade zest for that matter, than designing packaging for yet another blusher at £21.99. Today, at least, I don't feel like a product manager working for a boring food company off the M4. I feel more like someone with a genuine stake in a splendid tradition.

And the second thing I'm thinking is: I wonder if Danny Gray is married.

Chapter 20
Lighting

Last night, after I got home from work, Jack and Millie and I went shopping for new school shoes. I don't know why, but this is something I've never been able to delegate. I don't mind if Jill has to buy socks for them, or the odd birthday present for a party they have to attend, but school shoes are somehow different. School shoes, jeans, nice little sweaters – these are things a mother should buy with her children, aren't they? It's not just that Jill has suspect taste (which, unfortunately, she has) but that whatever the merits of the taste, it should be mine.

When we got home there was a message from Anna Wyatt congratulating me on my performance on Danny Gray's show. She described it as inspired; said she'd had no idea there was so much to know about marmalade, or that I knew so much. Said I'd really put Cottage Garden Foods on the map, and wouldn't Frank Cooper's and Robinson's be steaming. There was also a message from Alan, thanking me for a nice evening and promising to call me again.

If I didn't have so much else on my mind I would probably sit quietly gloating about Anna's message and worrying about Alan's. But I've quite a day ahead. I plan to buy all the uniform for Jack and Millie's new school. Then I've got to plan for this evening's packaging and branding party, the prospect of which fills me with a peculiar combination of dread and curiosity. But more imminent and frightening than even this, I have an electrician coming at 11 a.m.

On the face of it, Gary is an ideal duck. But this morning I'm far from sure that using him for a practice run is a good idea. I know so little about him. He's not like Alan, who is connected with my brother and therefore highly unlikely to be a nutcase or a trainspotter. But what do I know about Gary except that he has a sexy smile and a knack with transformers?

Millie could sense my apprehension this morning. It would have been hard for her not to sense it, because I did that most unforgivable of unforgivable things. I shouted at her. No, despite being fully aware of all the research showing that shouting at children damages their self-esteem and kills off neural pathways a dozen at a time, I screamed at her. About spilled orange juice.

Here's a brief description of the scene so you can see just how unreasonable I was: I ask Millie to please move her orange juice away from the edge of her cereal bowl or she will surely knock it over; Millie persists in keeping her orange juice next to her cereal bowl, and promptly knocks it over; I stand up from the table in a fit of temper and tell her how stupid it was, and that she should have listened to me in the first place; I mop up the orange juice with kitchen roll, which of course disintegrates in my hand because, whatever they tell you to the contrary on TV, kitchen roll is useless when it comes to absorbing spills of more than a teaspoonful; I am so incensed that the kitchen roll isn't working and that the juice is now running over the edge of the table and on to my pale leather handbag that, in response to Millie's statement that 'it's only orange juice, and I didn't mean to', I say to her (wait for it): 'Not only was that a stupid thing to do BUT YOU ALWAYS DO IT. YOU ARE SO CLUMSY.'

As any good mother knows, this kind of statement breaks every rule in the parenting handbook: (1) Never shout. It means you have lost control of the situation. (2) Never hurl insults at your children, using such inflammatory and defamatory words as 'stupid' or 'clumsy'. (3) Never say 'always'. If you tell your child they always do something, it will become a self-fulfilling prophecy. Instead, focus on the isolated incident at hand, and criticise the behaviour not the person.

I know all this. Everyone knows all this. Do they, like me, know it even as they are shouting and hurling insults and saying the word 'always'? Are they better than me at stopping themselves before the shouted insult rises to their lips, and saying instead, and in a calm tone of voice: 'Well, that was a bit silly, darling. But never mind. At least it will help you to remember not to put your orange juice so close to your cereal bowl next time.' I'm sure they are, so within minutes, perhaps even seconds of my outburst, I am filled with guilt. I drop the ineffectual kitchen roll into the bin and walk round the table to give Millie a hug. She, of course, wants nothing to do with me. I lost control of the situation when I shouted, but now I've really lost control because I'm apologising for my terrible behaviour and begging her forgiveness. And all in full view of Jack, who has watched the whole incident open-mouthed and no doubt had a few of his own neural pathways damaged in the process.

I made an extra effort to be calm on the way to school, even managing to remain unruffled when Jack walked straight through a muddy puddle in his new school shoes. But Millie didn't thaw until we got to the school gates, at which point she relented and gave me a hug. That's the glory of young children, and the saving grace of the less-than-perfect parent, I suppose. No matter how horrible you are to them, they usually forgive you. They just can't seem to sustain their anger, such is their desire to see you in a positive light.

It was indeed only orange juice, but the whole incident left me feeling unsettled and full of remorse. I knew my flare-up was the side-effect of the tension I was feeling: a sort of giddy satisfaction at something having gone very right at work combined with nervous anticipation of the meeting with Gary, which, let's face it, could easily go very wrong. So I stood in the shower and made promises to myself: I will not allow my own feelings about work (and future visits from duck decoys) to spill over into life with the children; I will count to ten before I shout; in the event of absolutely having to shout, I will do so without ever using the words *stupid* and *clumsy*, or, for that matter, *bad* and *horrid*.

Now here I sit in the kitchen at ten to eleven, as if in wait for a visit from the Crown Prince of Prussia. I've even blowdried my hair, which I rarely do on a Friday. I've also been mapping out possible routes to the request for a date with Gary, trying to settle on one that will seem uncontrived.

The doorbell rings and I can muse on the problem no longer. I walk to the door, mussing up my hair a little as I go (it wouldn't do to look as if I've just brushed it). When I open the door I am greeted by Gary's wide smile. It's still sexy.

'Hiya. Here for the lights,' he announces.

'Oh, great,' I say, managing to sound surprised, as if this whole thing had slipped my mind.

Gary comes into the house, stomping his boots on the mat to shake off the dust. He stands there waiting for directions from me, a stepladder slung over his shoulder.

'So, where do you want me to start?' he prompts.

'Well, there are ceiling lights in every room that don't work. I'm not sure whether it's just the bulbs that need changing, or whether there are some malfunctioning transformers somewhere,' I say, rather proud of my grasp of the technical vocabulary. 'Whatever the case I need your help as I can't change these light bulbs anyway!' I laugh.

'Can't say I blame you. Those little clips on the lights are bastards to remove, and even worse to put back.' His voice reminds me of someone but I can't put my finger on it.

'So, do you want to start up or down?' I ask.

'How about up at the top?' he asks. Now I know why he sounds familiar. His voice is very Johnny Vaughan. Smooth and knowing, with just a hint of a hard edge.

I walk upstairs ahead of him, hoping my bum doesn't look too big from his vantage point. We head to my bedroom, which looks extremely respectable, the knickers, bras and wet towels having been stuffed into drawers and linen baskets, and the pile of books and assorted birthday cards, loose photos and used tissues that usually clutter the bedside table having been shoved into the closet.

Gary flicks the light switch on and off to get a sense of where the trouble lies in this room, then sets up his stepladder at the end of the bed.

'Right, I'll leave you to it', I say breezily. Then, being fully aware that the real purpose of today's visit is for me to develop some sort of rapport with him so that I can ask him out, I add, 'Would you like a coffee?'

'Cheers. That would be great. One sugar please,' he says, flashing another one of his irresistible smiles before lifting his head to face the ceiling, where he is already struggling with the removal of one of the bastard clips.

As I'm making the coffee I'm desperately searching for a ruse that will enable me to spend some time talking to Gary. Coffee isn't enough. There's got to be a reason for me to stay there with him and have a conversation.

I make two cups of coffee and head upstairs, where I discover Gary is getting through the lights at an alarming rate. He's already in Millie's room. Quick, think fast.

'Do you mind if I stay in here while you work?' I venture. 'I was about to start sorting out Millie's drawers.'

'Fine with me,' Gary replies, stepping down from his

ladder to move it along under the next faulty light. 'By the way, so far it looks like just a light-bulb problem.'

'Oh, good,' I say, pulling out Millie's middle drawer, which is, happily, quite a mess. Thank goodness I didn't get around to it when I was doing the closets last weekend.

We pass the next minute or two in silence, me occupied by the removal of heaps of T-shirts and sweaters from Millie's drawer, Gary by the unbending of a bent light-bulb clip with a pair of pliers. I'm sure he's going to move on to Jack's room and then downstairs without our having made any conversation at all when he says something that can only be described as a gift.

'So isn't your husband any good at this sort of thing then?' he asks, indicating the ceiling lights with a flick of his head.

'Well, actually, we're divorced,' I say. Then, anxious not to let this opportunity slip away, 'I've found that after two years of living on my own, I've got quite good at things plumbing related, but electrical stuff is beyond me. I'm a desk-job person, you see, not very good with my hands.' Now if that isn't an invitation for him to delve into the details of what I do for a living I don't know what is.

'Really, what do you do then?' he asks, stopping to look down from the height of his ladder.

'I'm a product manager for Cottage Garden Foods. I manage their marmalade business. So if you ever want any marmalade, you know who to come to.' I sit in quiet contempt of my cringe-making words. If he ever wants any marmalade he's going to go to Sainsbury's, isn't he?

'Really? Well, I'll remember that. I happen to love marmalade for breakfast,' he says.

'Really? I bet you're a coarse-cut man, right? You know, it's a proven fact that men prefer their marmalade with large chunks in it. Scott took it to the Antarctic, and Hillary hauled it all the way to the top of Everest.'

And then we are off, rambling through the usual discourse about thin versus thick, orange versus grapefruit. I make him laugh with a couple of Paddington anecdotes I heard yesterday, and before I know it he's stopped unbending clips and screwing in bulbs and is seated on the bottom step of his ladder laughing as if I'm Bob Monkhouse. For the second time this week I'm full of gratitude for the presence of marmalade in my life.

Eventually my stories come to a natural end, and it's clear Gary's going to have to move on to another room. I must stay and finish sorting Millie's drawer; for the life of me I can't think of a plausible excuse to leave this task unfinished and take up another one in Jack's room.

'Anyway, I'll move on to the next room,' Gary announces, folding up his ladder. 'But I'll have to get that marmalade recipe from you later.'

I finish Millie's drawer and head downstairs to the kitchen, where I pretend to sift through a pile of bills. A few minutes later I can hear Gary descending with his stepladder and toolbox and setting up for work in the sitting room. He's finished that and the hallway in no time, and pretty soon all there is left is the kitchen. I glance up and notice that there's only one light-bulb hanging down, clip-less, in here. He'll be finished and on the road again in less than three minutes if I don't do something.

When he comes into the kitchen I point to the extractor

fan above the oven, all thoughts of pecuniary restraint flying out the window. 'You know, I forgot to mention that the extractor fan has been broken for ages and it's driving me crazy. Would you have time to look at that, too?'

Gary glances at his watch, then says, 'Yeah. Should do.'

After he's fixed the single light in the kitchen I watch him twisting and bending to get a good look at the underside of the extractor fan. The bottom of his sweatshirt lifts up slightly to reveal a slip of flesh around his lower back. There is no fat there. Not even the slightest sign of a love handle.

I decide that a bold move is in order. It's now or never.

'So, Gary, do you do this sort of thing at home. Does your wife expect you to spend all your weekends fixing things?'

Then the answer I've been waiting for. 'Actually, I don't have a wife. I live on my own. But I do pretty much all my own DIY and electrical work.'

'Ohh, and without anyone to make you cups of coffee,' I say, hardly able to believe my own incorrigible flirtatiousness. I'd like to see Francesca match this. I haven't done anything this obvious since I called up Sonny Simpson in year seven and played the song 'Sonny' into the receiver.

Gary can hardly believe it either. He stops what he's doing and turns around to face me. Through another of his wide, alluring smiles he replies, 'Yeah, it's a shame, isn't it. I could really do with someone to make me cups of coffee.'

I've seen this in movies. Two people standing with their eyes locked into each other as if time and the rest of the world don't exist. And it's happening now. This is obviously how it's done. I honestly believe that if I wanted to have this man right here on my kitchen floor I could. But I don't. As Marina says, I'm not looking for casual sex. I'm looking for a partner. And this is only a duck decoy after all, if a very beautiful one.

I tear my eyes away from Gary's and move back behind the table, where I resume the aimless rearranging of my bills. I know what's going to happen in a few minutes when Gary has finished with the fan. I would almost bet my life on it.

And, sure enough, it does. As I see Gary to the door, having paid his bill, he turns and puts his ladder down, then says, 'Listen, I don't mean to sound forward or anything, but would you fancy going out sometime? We could have dinner next Friday if you're free.'

Bingo. I have just set my sights on someone and corralled them into asking me out. How wonderful is that? I haven't felt so, well, powerful, in a long time. Perhaps Marina Boyd is really on to something. Perhaps the whole duck decoy has less to do with broadening your horizons and teaching you not to judge books by their covers, than getting you to sample the heady experience of playing the game again. And discovering that you're actually not bad at it.

Chapter 21
The Interview

For much of the afternoon I've been half expecting to bump into Tom. It's strange not to have seen him at all this week, given that I spotted him at least twice last week I wonder if he's changed his pattern. Or perhaps he's gone away somewhere. With Grace being so young he won't be bound by school-term dates like we parents of school-age children.

Fresh from my triumph this morning, I'm sure that if I did see Tom I'd manage to find a way to ask him out, or to induce him to ask me. But without a sighting I'm pretty helpless. I've no idea of his last name or address, so I can hardly call him or stake out his home. And another accidental early morning meeting in the park will be out of the question this weekend since Millie and Jack will be with David. It's beginning to look as though we should have walked home with them last week after all. Now there's a lesson, probably one that's buried in Marina's notes somewhere. Never pass up an opportunity for a conversation with someone, whether duck decoy or bona fide dating material, for you never know when that opportunity will arise again.

Since last weekend I've decided that Tom might be a suitable duck candidate after all. The news about his wife was very sad, but it shouldn't mean he's out of bounds completely. He might still be on the edge of a grieving process, but maybe a harmless dinner or two would be just what he needs.

But all this is pretty academic unless I bump into him again. In the meantime I just have to get on with things. David will be here in half an hour to collect Jack and Millie, and soon after that, five of my friends are coming round for a bit of packaging and branding.

Millie is packing her own bag. She's decided that her tiny suitcase on wheels with the Little Mermaid on the front is beneath her now that she is almost eight. So she's asked me to lend her one of mine. She's busy stuffing half the contents of her room into it. Ever since I told her that she'll be changing schools after half-term she's had something of a confident, take-charge air about her. I'm sure she'll be trembling on the day she starts, but for now the whole thing seems to have given her a boost. I've not heard a thing from her about any of the other girls being horrible. Either they've given up, knowing they are soon to lose their victim, or she doesn't care any more.

I wish Jack were packing his own case, but he isn't. He's

sitting on the floor of his room in his underpants, crashing trucks together. It isn't enough to own several large vehicles and move them around on the floor as if on a motorway. The thrill lies in the sound of them smashing together in a miniature simulated road accident. Are all little boys like this? Where does this desire to test the effects of a collision come from? The same place as the instinct to turn a stick or a banana into a gun?

'Hey, Jack. We'd better start getting ready or you won't be ready when Daddy comes.'

'When will he be here?' He asks this without averting his eyes from the road accident.

'In about half an hour. That's not very long. Now let's decide what you're going to take.' Then begins the predictable debate about which clothes he'll take with him. If it were up to him, he'd wear his jeans and cowboy attire all weekend. But that's not acceptable to David. The case must contain at least one outfit suitable for a lunch with other people and an outing to the movies. It's not that David minds the cowboy gear, in moderation, but that he thinks we shouldn't indulge the constant sporting of it. I think this has more to do with David's acute aesthetic sensibility than any theories about what is or isn't good for children.

At six thirty the doorbell rings, and Millie runs to the door to open it. David is standing there, alone. No Chantal. I wonder if she's in the car, or waiting at his flat, where they are spending the weekend.

'Hi, Ally. How are you?' He looks a little tired, as if he's been on a twenty-four-hour shoot.

'Hi. Fine. How are you?' I reciprocate.

'Fine thanks.' He yawns widely. 'Sorry, just been really busy this week. Hope the kids are in a sympathetic mood,' he says, then grins.

After hugging David, Millie has gone off in search of her (or rather my) bag, and Jack can now be seen bumping his suitcase down the stairs. It is white and bright green, with a picture of Buzz Lightyear emblazoned on the front.

'Hi, Dad. I've packed my trucks for us to play with,' he announces enthusiastically.

'Great. I'll look forward to that.' David has come into the house now and is standing at the foot of the stairs. He turns to me. 'So what have you got planned this weekend?'

'Oh, not much really. I've a few friends coming round this evening.' And then the lie. 'And I'm going out to dinner with someone tomorrow night. Otherwise, just domestic catch-up really.'

I've never done that before. All the times I've stood here knowing that David was fresh from seeing some other woman, or about to fall into bed with one, and it never occurred to me to fabricate a love interest of my own, just to save face. Suddenly it seems the most natural thing in the world. It's not even a real lie. I may not be going out with anyone tomorrow night, but I do have a date with Gary next Friday, and I did just have dinner with Alan. It would be fair to say that I am going out with men. Two different ones in the space of less than two weeks; a third if I can possibly manage it. David is looking at me curiously. I wonder if I am radiating something, like a confidence he doesn't like, perhaps. The thought fills me with a self-satisfied warmth. Or perhaps it's just that I have something on my nose. I give it a surreptitious wipe with the tip of my finger just in case.

Millie re-emerges with her bag and stands beside Jack looking eager. I've been waiting for her to express her customary concern about my being abandoned to a lonely weekend, but so far she's said nothing. Could it be that I am emitting some kind of inappropriate glee at the prospect of two days on my own? Or is it my self-congratulatory frame of mind and newly acquired sense of power that's coming across?

'Right then. Let's go!' says David. 'We've got pizza to have now, and tomorrow is movie night.'

They make a comic sight, all trying to squeeze through the front door together, jostling with unruly suitcases and provoking a precarious wobble from the little potted bay tree on the front step. It's true. I'm not really sorry to see them go. Something's come alive in me this week, something completely unconnected with family, home and hearth. I can't put my finger on it, exactly, but it isn't at all unpleasant, and I'm not going to discourage it.

Mel is the first to arrive. We've planned it this way so that she can quiz me on my impressions of the past ten days before everyone else gets here. She's sitting at the kitchen table now, pen in hand, while I attempt the creation of home-made salsa from some tomatoes and mango. Fresh limes are also required, but I neglected to put them on my shopping list so the remains of the lime cordial bottle will have to suffice.

'So, let's start at the beginning. Tell me what you thought about the seminar itself? Did you hate it? Did you want to crawl under your chair? Wallop Marina Boyd with her own microphone perhaps?'

'Well . . .' I pause, trying to remember the exact sequence of the thoughts and emotions I was experiencing a week ago last Tuesday. 'I think I did hate it at first. Or maybe hate is too strong a word. But I was convinced that I was above it, that I would find it quite appalling. And I went into the room with all of my sceptical armour on. More like an observer really. A bit like you.'

'Right. And then what?' urges Mel.

'And then I think I realised that the people in the room weren't freaks. They looked more or less like your normal, average group of women. Like a cross-section of the people you might see at the supermarket, or the school gates.'

'Wait a minute,' interrupts Mel. 'You're telling me you didn't spot the horror in the fishnet tights and the red boots? Or the one with all that orange foundation? And what about that Caroline woman, the one who's given up all pretence of living a real life so that she can hunt down a husband on a full-time basis?'

'Oh, I know. There were few extreme sorts. People you know are never going to be your best friends. But for the most part I thought they were quite normal.'

'Right, so what next. What did you think then?' Mel sits back with her glass of wine in her hand, waiting for the pearls to drop from my mouth.

'Well, I listened to what Marina had to say, and I think I didn't take it in at first. It sounded a little contrived to me. I really can't stand all that stuff about the eight Ps – all that marketing terminology. And I found the whole business of sitting in the small group talking about how committed we were to the course to be truly painful. I wasn't ready for that at all. But the next bit I was sort of taken in by.'

'Which bit was that?' Mel is sitting up straighter now, with pen poised.

'The bit about burying your baggage. It made sense to me that you can't move on in life until you've fully accepted the things that are getting in the way, or eradicated them. Whatever. And, you know, I came home and tried that baggage-burying exercise the very next night.'

'Yeah, so you said. I thought you were joking.' Mel is incredulous. I don't know what she was expecting. She knows I'm someone who has to do something properly once I'm committed to it. Surely that's why she picked me for her little charade.

'Well, I wasn't,' I say, squeezing the last of the mango juice from the flesh around the stone. 'I actually put David in a box – David and the whole idea of us being a family, all that romantic, idealistic stuff – and went outside and buried it. I felt really, really sad. So sad that I cried for at least ten minutes, which is saying something because it was bloody freezing that night. But I also felt relieved. Like I'd made a decision, or got rid of something.'

'Wow. All that from digging a hole and burying a box?'

'I guess so. Anyway, then I decided to get going on the rest of the homework. You remember our instructions? We were supposed to organise this party – which, as you can see, I did – and organise three practice dates with inappropriate men. Duck decoys, she calls them.'

'Yeah. I thought you were joking about that, too.' Mel is clearly stunned by my conscientiousness.

'Nope. Perfectly serious. I went out with this friend of my brother's, whom I'd originally said no to. He's forty-two, with two girls. Nice bloke but not my type. Then – and you'll never believe this – I invited an electrician round under the pretence of needing him to fix my lights, and I flirted shamelessly until he asked me out. We're going out next Friday.' My sense of triumph is undisguised.

'That's shocking!' Mel exclaims.

'Wait, it gets better.' I'm having a really good time now. I can't remember the last time I had stories like this to tell Mel and Clara. Have I ever had stories like this to tell?

'At one point, we were standing here in the kitchen, about ten feet apart, just staring at each other. And there was this tension, a sort of heat, just like you see in films when two perfect strangers are about to hurl themselves at one another.'

'It's called lust, Ally. You didn't did you?'

'No. I restrained myself. I wasn't about to have sex with someone I hardly knew on my kitchen floor before noon on a Friday. But it sure was a great feeling.'

'My God, Ally. I don't knew whether to congratulate you or be ashamed for you.' I can tell by her expression that she is not ashamed. This is a funny tightrope we women insist on walking where sex is concerned – enveloping the telling of our sexual desires and exploits in the good girl's modesty.

'And, you know, the best feeling was not all that desire swilling around between us, but the knowledge that I had made it happen. I felt like I'd been let loose from something. I think that for the past two years I've been so focused on keeping my depleted little family going that I've been keeping everything all tightly wrapped up, in case anyone should come in and mess it all up. I'm sure I must have been sending off smoke signals that spelled *Stay away. Not interested.*'

Mel smiles a self-satisfied smile. Is this something she's been wanting to tell me for some time?

'Brilliant. So what about the third duck person?'

'The third one I haven't managed to snare yet. But I have one in mind, a lovely American who I've bumped into a few times around here. I actually engineered one of our encounters last Saturday – saw him walking along towards the park and practically dragged Jack and Millie there. I'm not sure about him – he's still recovering from the loss of his wife and he must be pretty raw. But one date wouldn't hurt. Trouble is, I haven't seen him again since our accidental park meeting.'

'Hell of a result, Ally,' says Mel, sipping gingerly from her almost empty glass and offering the bottle to me. 'I am so impressed.'

'And I haven't even been rebranded yet. Imagine what I'll be able to accomplish then?'

'And don't forget the telemarketing. There will be no stopping you once she gets you going on that next week!'

'Don't remind me,' I groan, suddenly remembering the parts of Marina's programme of action that most repel me. A spot of successful flirting might have given me a high, but I'm certain I'm not up to the challenge of creating direct mail and telemarketing campaigns for myself. That might be the stage when Marina and I are forced to part company.

'Anyway,' says Mel. 'I have some news of my own. Are you sitting comfortably?'

'I am now,' I say, plonking myself opposite her.

'I'm pregnant!' she squeals, with a girlish hunch of her shoulders.

I leap from my chair and round the table to give her a hug. Mel's eyes are already moist, and it proves to be catching.

This is stunning news. Mel has never really expressed a burning desire for children. She and Dom love their slightly dishevelled, bohemian life so much, going to out of the way music clubs until late at night, sleeping in until late on weekends, taking weekend breaks at a moment's notice. They always said they might have children someday, but with Dom being so relaxed and Mel so frenetic and disorganised it just never seemed that someday would arrive. And now it has.

'Yeah, just when I've decided to get all ambitious and fight for an editor's job. I've always had great timing,' she says, but her disgruntlement is transparently shallow. She is clearly thrilled.

Mel and I stand holding each other for a minute. Then a realisation comes over both of us, and we say simultaneously, 'Don't tell Clara.'

Chapter 22
Branding Ally

Mel, Lisa, Sara and George are all seated in my sitting room, sampling my home-made salsa and the store-bought hummus when Clara comes into the room. My plan had been to introduce Clara as the life coach in training, but suddenly I don't see the point. If I can send out predatory signals to an electrician I've met only once before, I can surely handle the ridicule and outrage that could result from my telling the truth about this evening.

'Clara, this is George, Lisa, Sara, and of course you know Mel. Everyone, this is Clara, one of my oldest friends.'

Everyone raises glasses to Clara, who takes a seat on the faux-suede pouf by the fireplace. Then I take a deep breath and continue.

'Clara is a successful management consultant with

absolutely no desire to become a life coach. As a matter of fact, I've brought you all here under false pretences. The truth is, I'm taking part in a series of seminars that are supposed to help me find a great man, and I'm required to hold an evening like this to sort of repackage and rebrand me in readiness for the whole exercise. The woman who runs these seminars believes in applying business principles to the search for romance.'

George looks startled. I feel badly that I've forced him to get to grips with a newfangled concept like life coaching only to deny him the pleasure of experiencing it first hand. Now he's being asked to take in the fact that there are business-like courses for women who want to find husbands. I rush to reassure him.

'Actually, George, you are part of the reason I decided to attend these seminars. Do you remember when you told me about Francesca, the client who's taken her romantic life into her own hands? Who refuses to let life pass her by? Well, when Mel here asked me if I'd attend these seminars and allow her to write about my experience for her magazine, I remembered your Francesca and thought *why not?* Why not help Mel get her story and maybe learn a few things along the way?'

'Well, I for one am relieved you've come clean,' says Clara. 'I'm not sure I'd have been capable of keeping up appearances beyond the first half-hour.'

'My goodness, Ally. You little liar. I should wash your mouth out with hair dye for this!' scolds George. He's over the initial shock of the deception and on the way to enjoying this with his usual spiritedness.

'You are one brave woman, Ally,' says Sara. 'I saw a

Channel Four documentary about these sorts of seminars. They are scary!'

It's only Lisa who's holding back now. She's squinting at me from the other side of the room.

'So, Lisa, what do you think? Are you game to help me and Mel?'

Lisa leaves an uncomfortable gap before responding. 'Well, of course I'll help, if that's what you want. But to be honest I find the whole thing laughable. Why would you need a course, or a book or anything else for that matter, to find yourself a decent man? The whole thing is nonsense. And the idea of changing yourself for the sake of a man is just repugnant.'

She's never been one to pull her punches, Lisa. Unless, of course, you count remaining silent and compliant for a year while her boyfriend finds new excuses to hide her from his mother.

'I know it is. I know. That's exactly what I thought. But I'm more relaxed about it now. Believe it or not, some of what this woman has to say makes sense, and I've found it useful. The rest of the stuff we'll just have fun with for the sake of Mel's article. Right, Mel?'

'Right. Only you're all sworn to secrecy about who Ally really is. We're going to use the pseudonym Francesca,' she says, smiling at George.

'Wonderful,' purrs George.

Mel gets up and starts offering round the salsa and chips while I refill empty glasses. Lisa's disapproval is almost palpable, but I'm hoping she'll be carried along by the others' enthusiasm. She'll soon see that it's only a bit of harmless fun.

Clara then hands out the notes I faxed her earlier in the week when I was still intending to position her as the one in charge. The first page of the notes contains guidelines about what, exactly, is in the frame for a repackaging session. The list is pretty daunting, even for me, who's seen it before. It contains twenty-five items, including make-up, jewellery, clothing (formal and casual wear), perfume and posture. Even my breath and laugh are up for grabs. Lord knows where we will start. Or who will have the courage to start.

I'm suddenly reminded that I'm the one who needs the courage. With all the excitement of the past week, and the chat with Mel, I've managed to ignore the fact that I'm due to come in for something of a drubbing this evening. I might even get my feelings hurt. I console myself with the thought that it will be better to be told about my glaring faults now than to continue on blissfully unaware of them for another twenty years.

George, God bless him, starts us off. 'You know I theenk you are perfect, Ally. Een almost every way. I find eet very hard to tell you to change anytheeng.'

But. There is a big but coming.

'But,' he continues, 'I theenk you could use a stronger scent. Or more of the one you use. I hardly ever smell perfume on you, and I am standing preety close.'

What a relief. If we'd started out with a revelation about halitosis I'm not sure I'd have coped. But too little perfume? That I can handle. I could even say to George that the reason he can't smell my perfume is because his senses have been dulled by daily exposure to hairspray fumes.

I'm unsure as to what to do next. Clearly there is a

need for some sort of facilitator for this session after all, and I glance at Clara imploringly. She picks up the baton, in her usual take-charge manner.

'So, does anyone else agree with George? Could Ally do more with her perfume? Or do with more perfume?'

The others give the impression of deep thought, then Sara says, 'Well, I'm not one to talk. I always smell like baby spew. But now that you mention it, I've never noticed any perfume on Ally. I don't think it would hurt. Charles always notices when I smell nice, and I always mean to put perfume on. But I usually forget.'

I've worn Chanel Number 19 for fifteen years. I've tried others perfumes – the Kenzos, and Josephs and Poisons – but always found them cloying. Chanel is light and delicate and pretty, Number 19 even more than Number 5 or Coco. I'm not willing to give it up. But I will consider indulging in the eau de parfum instead of the less expensive eau de toilette if greater impact is required.

'Good. I like that idea,' I announce. I want them to know I am open to suggestions. There's nothing worse than someone who asks for feedback then sulks upon receipt of it.

Clara, having been redesignated chairperson, tries to keep the conversation flowing. 'So, any feedback from anyone else?'

Again, Sara pipes up. She's really entering into this. Perhaps she's like this done to her next.

'Well, again, I'm really not one to talk, because I hang around in old tracksuit bottoms and T-shirts all the time. But then again I'm not trying to meet Mr Right. So I would say, Ally, that perhaps you need to invest in some really nice new casual wear. Tracksuit bottoms are fine, but what about something with a bit of an edge? And a pair of those DKNY trainers with the stripes? I just think it would help if you looked a little jazzed up even when you're being a slob.'

She's right, of course. She and I occasionally go for long pseudo-aerobic walks on the common (a large part of the aerobic aspect consisting of our constant chatter), and I inevitably put on my oldest clothes. I've tended to reserve what little there is of my clothes budget for work wear and smart weekend wear like my Max Mara sweater. But now that I have £1000 to spend, I really should splurge on some nice sloppy wear.

'Yup. I like that idea too,' I say to everyone. 'Those blue horrors are going straight in the bin after you all leave.' I'm a makeover party dream. Has there ever been anyone so amenable to constructive criticism?

'And you know what?' says Mel, who I'd thought wasn't supposed to be a participant in this process. 'I would try to lose that half-stone you keep moaning about. You are pretty damn good for thirty-seven, Ally, and if you weren't going out there dating again I would say don't bother. But those extra pounds tend to sit right on the stomach, just above the jeans. Believe me, I know from experience. And you just don't want to have to worry about them when you contemplate flinging your clothes off and making love with some near stranger on the kitchen floor.'

I shoot her a look that says I'm going to tip the salsa bowl over her head if she says any more. I don't want everyone to know about my kitchen-lust experience, least of all George. I know he's in favour of courageous flirting, but unrestrained licentiousness? Definitely not. Not even the idea of it.

Luckily, the others just laugh, as if the idea is a preposterous one. Sarah interjects, effectively putting a stop to Mel's mischief. 'I know what you mean. I've got at least five pounds sitting there. Probably ten. I'll join you in trying to lose them, Ally. We can keep each other on the straight and narrow.'

'God, it's such a cliché, isn't it?' I groan. 'Want to meet man? Lose weight. Surely that can't be the answer.'

'It may not be the answer, honey, but it sure can't hurt,' drawls Clara. 'It's just one less thing to worry about.' Easy for her to say. She never gains an ounce; then again, I've never seen her eat a biscuit.

I will try to shift the pounds, but I refuse to go to Weight Watchers. Between Marina's seminars and Weight Watchers meetings I'd be in grave danger of support-group overload.

'What about make-up?' I ask, changing tack. 'The other day I realised that I've been applying my eye make-up in exactly the same way for over a decade. Is there something revolutionary that I'm missing?'

'Ooh. Yes. Yes. I bought some make-up from Mac the other day and they gave me a sort of mini-eye makeover. Let me show you.' Mel takes her make-up bag out of her fringed satchel and instructs me to sit up with my head back. She then proceeds to brush a complex combination of pinks and browns on to my eyelids, and finishes by holding up her make-up mirror for me to assess the results. Everyone else gathers round, and I feel a little like a patient in ER.

'What do you think?'

There isn't a smudge of teal-blue eye pencil in sight, which makes me feel a little insecure. And the eyes don't, at first, look like mine. But I have to admit I like the overall effect.

'I think you must have walked out of there with over a hundred quid's worth of stuff is what I think. They saw you coming. But I do like it. Perhaps I'll spend some of your £1000 on eye shadows tomorrow.'

Now Clara decides that a change of pace is in order. 'Tell you what,' she says. 'Why don't we do that Trinny and Susannah thing where we go through your closet and throw out all the things we think look awful on you?'

And that is how six adults end up sprawled around my bedroom amidst piles of clothes. George looks surprisingly at home, considering he's the only male in the room. He's lying propped up on one elbow on my bed wearing an enormous pink feathered hat that I wore to Ascot ten years ago, and tossing clothes into various piles as Clara hands them to him. There are a few outfits I have to try on, but most can be kept or discarded based on the impression they create on the hanger.

Even Lisa is having fun. She's wearing the offending track-suit bottoms around her neck like a scarf, and must be well into her fourth glass of wine. As I'm pulling on a beige corduroy jacket for inspection, she raises her glass and calls everyone to attention.

'I've one more idea for you, Ally, and I hope you won't take it the wrong way,' she says. 'Do you know what I've noticed? I've noticed that you carry around this sort of armour. You're a little bristly with men. You probably don't mean to be. And sometimes they might be complete tossers, in which case you are certainly justified. But the rest of the time it might help if you just softened up a little. I think that might make more difference than all this wardrobe revamping.'

I glance at Mel, who returns my look with the same one she gave me in the kitchen earlier in the evening. So this is something everyone has been wanting to tell me.

Loosen up. Lighten up. Open up. Flirt for God's sake. How is it that it took a choreographed makeover and three bottles of wine for them to tell me?

I really should have planned this more thoughtfully. We've moved on from repackaging and come downstairs to commence the rebranding part of the agenda, which is by far the most difficult, but the pickled state they're all in makes any kind of sensible outcome look highly unlikely. Mel is giddy despite having nursed a single glass of wine for the whole evening. (My guess is it's all part of her plan to throw Clara off the scent of her news.) Lisa is reading out from the second page of the notes, and it's all the others can do to keep themselves from choking on their laughter.

'It says here that we need to list all of Ally's characteristics, and select the three that best describe her and will be most appealing to other people. Now listen to the examples. Are you ready?' Lisa looks up into faces that are gagging in anticipation.

'Here's a good one, apparently: "Outgoing, spirited, nurse". And here's how NOT to define your brand: "Freckly, temperamental, travel agent". Or "sensual, adventurous, babe" – too forward, apparently. Makes people think you're up for one-night stands.'

'For goodness sake, what ees the purpose of thees brand thing?' asks George.

'Wait. Wait. I can tell you that,' shouts Lisa. 'It's supposed to be a quick way for us to describe Ally to people we think might be interested in meeting her, and a way for her to describe herself when she registers for all those computer dating services. Then there's the blurb she needs for her flyer.'

Ah, yes. I'd forgotten about these. I know they are lurking in seminar two, a set of hurdles I'm quite sure I won't manage to clear. George is a little confused ('What is this thing, a flyer?'), and Sara is just incredulous ('What? To leave in pubs and restaurants and stuff?').

With the notes in her hand, Lisa is irrepressible. 'Listen to these,' she says in disbelief. 'How about "intellectual, Presbyterian, nurse". Or "witty, Scottish, teacher". I reckon if I were a bloke forced to choose between these two I'd run to the outer Hebrides.'

'So what am I? "On the short side, shabbily dressed, with half a stone to lose"?' I venture.

'Or, "frosty single mother with orange-preserve obsession",' jokes Mel.

'No, no. What about this? "Bossy" – well, you are, a bit – "sex starved, with suspect standards of household cleanliness". Well, look at this, Ally. You should be ashamed,' says Sara, holding up a food-encrusted sock she's found under a sofa cushion.

We're really on a roll with this. It's far easier, and more

fun, to dream up ghastly personal brands than something that you could actually say with a straight face. We spend another fifteen minutes like this, batting cringe-making descriptions of me back and forth between us. By this time it's eleven thirty and we are all pretty tired. I'm just thinking we will have to call it a night, leaving me without any brand at all, when I remember something I have stashed away upstairs.

'Wait here,' I say, as if anyone is capable of moving quickly at this stage.

In the top drawer of my dresser, I find what I'm looking for. It's a Mother's Day card made by Millie last year. On the front there's a hand-drawn picture of me, dressed in a blue mini-skirt and pink ankle boots and looking rather skinnier than I do in real life. Underneath the picture it says *My mummy*.

I open the card to read Millie's hand-written inscription. It is almost as I'd remembered it.

To my mummy. You are pretty and nice and funny. And sometimes very clever. (I remember now. This card was made three days after I'd managed to help Millie construct a log cabin for her history project. It had lolly sticks for sides and a roof made of Shreddies, glued on with sugar icing.)

Is that me? Could I live with that as a brand?

It seems to me that it's as good as any we're going to come up with. The descriptors are a trifle bland, but anything more interesting inevitably comes across as false and self-congratulatory, or lays itself open to misinterpretation. Take *attractive*, for instance. Doesn't that immediately say *not pretty enough, quite plain in fact*? Or the word *ambitious*, which cries out *ballbreaker*? *Loyal*? Means you'll never get rid of her. *Fun loving?* Sounds intensely annoying. Hearing someone described like that would make you long instead for someone morose but interesting.

Even *clever* is over the top, and will have to be jettisoned. I'll stick with *nice, pretty and funny*, however bland it is. I take the card downstairs, where I find Lisa asleep and the others singing along to a Jamie Cullam CD that Mel has put on.

'I've got it,' I announce to those who are awake. 'Look at this.' I thrust Millie's card into Sara's hands.

'To my mummy. You are pretty, and nice and funny. And sometimes very clever,' Sara reads out from the card.

'That's perfect,' says Clara, yawning and reaching for her bag.

'Great. That'll do nicely. Just drop the clever bit, which is a bit pompous,' says Mel.

This evening has clearly run its course. There's only so long you can expect people to remain focused on you, after all. They've all been good sports. Now they clearly want to go home. It's not as if any of them is going to pay attention to my brand. They'll say the same things about me that they always have. If they happen to be upset with me they'll say something less flattering. There's nothing I can do about that.

The more important thing, it seems to me, is that I am actually quite nice, and, on a good day, bordering on pretty. I'm not much good at telling jokes, but I know I can be amusing when the mood strikes me. That's not a bad brand to have. I should be quite a catch.

*

When the others have gone, Clara and I are left slumped on the sofa waiting for her taxi. She's ordered a black cab on her account as usual (minicabs give her the creeps), which means she has to wait longer.

She has seemed quite cheerful tonight relative to the last few times we've spoken. Perhaps the ridiculousness of it all has taken her mind off things.

I tell her everything I told Mel earlier, about the burial and Alan and Gary and Tom. 'So what do you think, Clara? Do you suppose I've gone mad?' I ask, half expecting her to say yes.

'You really want to know what I think?' she says with a heavy sigh. 'I wish a few marketing methods could do for me what they seem to be doing for you. If only getting pregnant were about making a few bold moves and changing a few superficial things about myself. Wouldn't that be grand?'

Grand indeed.

Chapter 23
Busted

I have a confession to make. I love Busted. I often pinch Millie's CD and put it on while I'm cooking. I love their upbeat sound and all that leaping about with guitars, perhaps because it reminds me of the bands I grew up dancing to in school gymnasiums. Come to think of it, Busted is exactly what my first boyfriend Ben was probably aspiring to, and what I must have thought he was. I can see now that he was horribly short of the mark.

That isn't the real confession. The real confession is that listening to Busted stirs in me simultaneous feelings of motherly pride and teenage sexual longing. The other night I was watching them being interviewed by Jonathon Ross, sitting there fresh faced and innocent in a way that only eighteen-year-old boys can be. I felt like their mother or their aunt, beaming in admiration of their talent and their unaffected natures.

Then they played their new hit single and I turned to jelly. Charlie leaned into the microphone and sang something about a hot uniform and I felt a wave of something like desire. I say 'like desire' because it isn't real, even when you're experiencing it. It's a bit like a fantasy, or a memory. A remembered desire, dug up from parts of yourself long forgotten. And always dulled by the knowledge that you'd be proud to be their mother (something that never once occurs to you when you are actually sixteen and quivering in the presence of a band).

Is this what happens when you're thirty-seven and a mother? When you're almost past it but not quite? I read an article about grown women with a passion for boy bands. One woman had a shrine to Westlife in her kitchen. Another follows the band around on tour. Both were dubbed 'embarrassing' by their teenage daughters. I'm not that bad. But I'm not beyond being able to appreciate what the fuss is all about.

Busted is currently blaring from a loudspeaker that must be just outside the cramped changing room in which I am working my way through three hooks dripping with sportswear. Listening to 'You Said No' when I've spent the better part of the morning peering out between the shutters to see if I can spot Tom walking by, it occurs to me that I am behaving somewhat like a sixteen-year-old.

There was no sighting. Not at seven thirty, when I thought he might be heading out to the park to shake off the effects of an early morning waking by Grace; not at eight thirty, when I thought he might be coming back with Grace asleep in the pushchair. And not during the next two hours, when I'd hoped he might happen by my front door on the way to pick up groceries or a newspaper. Of course, I was only been able to peep out of the window intermittently; I couldn't stand there on permanent guard with a pair of binoculars. So it's entirely possible that he walked by while I was making a cup of tea, or staring at the sales forecast for one of our clear jellied marmalades that I was supposed to be reworking.

'How do they look? Are you going to come out and show me?' Mel shouts through the changing-room door.

I open the door a crack. 'Just a second. I'm almost ready.'

A few seconds later I emerge, wearing a pale pink tracksuit, the top of which is beautifully fitted at the waist, like something J-Lo would wear with a pair of rose-tinted sunglasses.

Unfortunately the bottoms are low slung to the point of indecency. They reveal not just the tops of my knickers, but an enormous expanse of white Lycra. I'm not sure they even make knickers small enough to remain hidden in trousers like these. Surely even the tiniest thong would be peeping out over the top of the waistband (which, sitting a good five inches below the waist, does not deserve its appellation).

'Oh God. Those will never do!' Mel doubles over with laughter. 'I saw a young girl in a pair like that the other day. Her entire backside was showing, and I just thought get over yourself.'

'So it's not just that I'm thirty-seven and carrying a redundant half stone?'

'No, Ally. It's not. Try on the other things.'

I return obediently to my cubbyhole and retrieve another tracksuit from its hanger. This one is pale blue with a white stripe down the side of the leg and, on first inspection, somewhat more decent. When I open the changing room door Mel claps her hand to her mouth and exclaims, 'That's perfect! It is so you I will not allow you to walk out without it. Now all you need is the perfect white T-shirt to go underneath.'

Mel goes in search of a white T-shirt while I try on the next pair of trousers. I'm not sure what these are, exactly. They're not tracksuit bottoms, but they're not ordinary trousers either. They're some sort of hybrid that I think looks rather marvellous, and must surely satisfy Sara's criteria for smart sloppy wear. I'm wearing them when Mel returns with three T-shirts. She stands looking at me studiously with her index finger pressed over her lips and nose.

'I like these. They're a bit tight, but when you shake off those extra pounds they'll be perfect. I think you should get them,' she pronounces.

Thus concludes our shopping trip. We pay for two T-shirts, the pale-blue tracksuit and the black smart-sloppy trousers, all of which brings the total of my expenditure to £715. Before coming to this department we managed to dispense with £565 through the purchase of a very special pair of DKNY trainers (beige and white with a red stripe on one side, £70), a pair of butter-coloured imitation Todd slip-ons (£65), a fantastic belted trench (£155), some Mac eye shadows (£65), a bottle of Chanel Number 19 eau de parfum (£120!) and three new underwired bras (fuchsia, flowered and black (£90, but a good deal cheaper than at Rigby and Peller)). I've decided that the rest of my £1000 must be saved for another day. You never know what I may be required to do after next week's seminar.

Mel and I grab a late lunch in the Fifth Floor Café, during which she eats very obviously for two and attempts to prise out of me a few last insights for her first article, the copy for which will be due next week. I've shared almost everything with her already, so I haven't much to offer besides a comment on Friday night's branding party.

'I really enjoyed that. I was expecting it to be really uncomfortable, you know. But it was fun. And I did need a bit of a kick up the arse to make me bother to go out and get some new clothes – and to lose that half-stone.'

'I think everyone else enjoyed it too,' says Mel, nodding her head. 'Even Lisa. Is she always that scary?'

'Well she's pretty opinionated, but she's not generally that harsh about it.' I consider Lisa for a minute, trying to fathom why she's had such a violent initial reaction to the event. Why would she care so much?

And then it dawns on me. We touched a nerve. Lisa has just broken up with Mike, and she's probably wondering how, and if, she's going to go out there again and find her Mr Right. She knows she's going to have to start all over again, making an effort, even changing some things to please a man. The thought of it probably fills her with horror. And the possibility that it might not be good enough to just amble along hoping to bump into someone, that she might be required to be proactive in the manner specified by the Proactive Partnership Program, is too awful to contemplate.

I say all this to Mel, who nods vehemently. 'That's really good. Fascinating. Can I put it in the article, if I change the names?'

'Don't you dare. Lisa will read it and know immediately we're talking about her. It's not fair. I may have signed up for this but she didn't.'

Mel looks disappointed, but she doesn't fight back. She's a journalist with integrity, after all.

I manage to finish the sales forecast on Sunday morning, then make a trip to the gym for the first time in about three weeks. I figure exercising the seven pounds off will be easier than starving myself. Wearing my new blue track-suit bottoms and white T-shirt (which I know is really for hanging around in a park rather than for actual sweat-inducing exercise) I feel pretty good on the Stairmaster, but it's still boring.

While I'm out Alan calls again. This time he asks me to return his call, which rather perturbs me. I decide not to do it right away, and instead, spend the rest of Sunday moving between kitchen (for cups of tea and Diet Cokes only) and sofa, reading an Anne Tyler novel and watching a rerun of *Casablanca*. I'm used to these types of solitary days. When I was younger I remember being terrified by them. Even if all I was going to do was loll around, I wanted to loll around with somebody else. But I've grown out of this morbid fear of aloneness, partly out of necessity. A single mother doesn't have much option. On the weekends she spends without her children she can hardly expect all her friends to drop their families to spend days at the spa or watching old films with her. I'm lucky enough that neither Clara nor Mel have yet had children so have time to do things like shop and lunch at Harvey Nicks with me every once in a while.

In the middle of the afternoon I hear the beep of a text. It's from Lisa. *There's this guy I'd call a nosepicking, fascist, dimwit. Interested?* She's obviously fully recovered from her fit of disgust and moved on to wholehearted ridicule. I text her back: *Sorry, only interested in nosepicking fascists if also intelligent and rich.*

At about six I hear voices outside, a little way down the street, and know that Jack and Millie are home. I make it to the door before they've even rung the bell, and stand watching them as they ready their suitcases for the short walk to the house, Jack pulling up the handle and bending down to check that the wheels are straight, Millie pulling my sack on to her shoulder and bending over under its weight.

I give them both hugs as they walk in the door, and everything seems perfectly normal until David says, 'Any chance of a beer? I'm parched.'

I'm so staggered by this that my voice breaks a little on answering. 'Oh, sure. I'll just check that I have some. You might have to make do with a cup of tea.'

Jack and Millie rush upstairs to inspect their rooms, and David and I go into the kitchen. It turns out that I do have some beer. Three bottles. I offer one to David, and decide to have one myself. As I'm pouring mine into a glass I'm running through all the possibilities that could have led David to ask to come in. The one I settle on is that he's got something important to tell me, something that can't be said over the phone. He's going to tell me that he and Chantal are getting married, isn't he? I feel a swilling sensation in my stomach, and I'm glad I've had little else besides Diet Coke this afternoon.

I summon up the courage to turn round and go over to the table, but I can't face actually sitting opposite him so I stand with my bum leaning against the end of the counter next to the table. The newly replaced ceiling light is shining directly down on his head like a spotlight. I attempt a casual smile, before saying, 'So?'

'Sooo, the kids were great this weekend. Really great. Millie seems much happier. I wanted to tell you that I think it's great what you're doing, moving schools. I didn't think you would pull it off but you have.'

Oh for God's sake. Get on with it. Put me out of my misery.

'Yes, well I hope it works out. I think it will. Anything has to be better than what she had to endure at Hazlecroft. And to be honest I've not been that impressed with the school anyway. Even for Jack. They don't seem to be able to take account of individual personalities, to understand that a five-year-old boy like him might have a little trouble buckling down to number work, might need a little extra encouragement.'

I'm rambling a bit, because much as I want David to get the torture over with I don't want to deal with the news. So I have mixed feelings when he begins to tell me about the weekend, what they all did, what they ate, what they said that made him laugh. Any pleasure I might take from the stories is shrouded by the fear of what's coming next.

What comes next is indeed something to fear, but it isn't the thing I'd expected.

'So anyway,' he says, leaning forward and planting his beer bottle on the table. 'I was thinking that it might be nice for us all to get together, as a family, sometime. I know it's your weekend next week, but maybe we could all have Sunday lunch together. What do you think?'

Lunch next Sunday? Together? What's going on?

'Oh. I guess that would be fine. The kids would probably like it. You don't think they'd be a bit confused?'

'Of course not. Surely other divorced parents get together with their kids every once in a while. It's a perfectly civilised thing to do.'

Of course it is. I'm being oversensitive. Perhaps David is trying to drag us into a new mature phase of our divorce, one in which we can become friends of sorts for the sake of our children's well-being. I can go along with that.

After David has left and Jack has gone to bed, Millie and I lie on her bed reading. She doesn't really need me to read to her any more, but every now and again I like to do it. I usually read her something completely different from the book she has on the go, something gentle or magical and much more suited to a five-year-old. Tonight it's *Room on the Broom*. But before I've even get to the bit about the truly magnificent new broom with a nest for the bird and a shower for the frog, Millie rolls over on one side and draws Pooh Bear into her arms. I lean down to kiss her, resting my lips on her cheeks for a long moment.

Just as I'm switching off the light at the door her voice rises from the pillow.

'Mummy?'

'Yes, sweetheart. What is it?'

'Daddy says he and Chantal aren't going to see each other any more.'

I put my own feelings about this news to one side for a minute. 'And how do you feel about that, Mill?'

'Fine. It's OK. She was nice but not that nice. Daddy says you're way nicer.'

What the hell is going on?

Chapter 24
Star Pupil

The first person I spot as I am ejected from the fast moving revolving doors at the Savoy is Angie. She's wearing another twin-set, pale green this time, and smiling widely as she stands waiting for me. When I reach her, she raises her shoulders in a little shrug and stretches out her grin as if to say 'Isn't this exciting?'

'Isn't this exciting?'

'It is a bit,' I say. And I'm not being dishonest. Last night I had difficulty falling asleep, and put it down to anticipation. I'm not quite sure what it is I'm looking forward to – seeing Angie and Claudia again and hearing how they've fared, gleaning a few more gems from Marina. Or perhaps just the quietly satisfying experience of sitting listening to Marina go over last week's tips and knowing that I've not done too badly with them. Like the satisfaction drawn from being one of the few in the class who'd actually done the assignment on female role models in Shakespeare.

This evening is also a welcome diversion from thoughts of David. His behaviour on Sunday has me thoroughly alarmed and confused. It's so contrary to the pattern we've established. So out of the blue. It's not that his breaking up with Chantal is so shocking – after all it's only one in a long line up of break-ups, even if his and Chantal's relationship had looked more substantial than its predecessors. But he's never suggested Sunday lunch after a break-up before. And Millie's never come out with anything remotely resembling 'Daddy thinks you're nicer than her'. Has she made it up, or did he really say that? If he really said it, why? Why stir up all those confusing feelings in the children? A child whose romantic sensibilities have been heightened by repeated exposure to *Beauty and the Beast* and *Pocahontas* is bound to misinterpret something like this.

Angie and I make our way into the Wessex Room, which is already bubbling over with noise and activity. Women are grouped together in the aisles and at the sides of the room, in twos, threes and fours, some whispering conspiratorially, others giggling aloud. There are a few women sitting quietly in seats, but not many. I spot one in black stirrup trousers with white stilettos who's clearly not yet had an opportunity to organise her repackaging party.

Angie and I decide on seats in the middle, about row ten. Just as we are about to sit down Claudia taps me on the shoulder.

'Hello, Ally,' she says in her husky voice.

I turn to face her and she kisses me on both cheeks. Not an insipid double-cheeked air kiss, but one with genuine, Southern European warmth. I notice that she's wearing jeans again, but this time with a perfect, crisp white shirt and brown leather belt. Was there ever a sexier woman than this?

'Claudia, hi. How've you been?'

'Really well, and you?'

'Fine. More than fine actually. I've had quite a good couple of weeks.'

'Really, do tell?'

I'd like to tell, but just at that moment someone tries to squeeze past us to get to the other side of the room, and then Marina's assistant is at the microphone saying 'Ladies, would you please take your seats'.

Angie, Claudia and I sit down next to one another. I can't see Louise or Katherine or Nancy, but I'm sure they're here somewhere. The scary enthusiast, Caroline, is sitting in the first row, and two rows behind her I can see Mel's favourite, the one in the fishnet tights and red boots. Mel herself is of course nowhere to be seen; she wasn't allowed to come and will have to rely entirely on my interpretation of the evening.

A sparkling Marina comes to the podium dressed in a long, cream silk skirt and blouse, her blonde hair pulled back into a neat ponytail to reveal an extremely significant looking gold necklace. She is greeted by even more rapturous applause than two weeks ago, if that is possible. She stands looking around the room for half a minute, waiting for the applause to die down. When it doesn't, she gives us her signature hand signal.

'Hello, ladies. How are you tonight?'

A chorus of 'fines' rises from the audience. I'm slightly surprised to find that my voice is among them; for someone historically so uncomfortable with things done in herds, I seem to be taking to this rather naturally.

'Well I'm so glad to hear that,' says Marina. 'And I had a feeling I would hear it, because people are usually feeling pretty good after the first seminar. That seminar will, I hope, have opened up your minds to new possibilities, and new ways of fulfilling them. It will have shown you that you have nothing to fear. That you *can* take your love life into your own hands.' Marina pauses dramatically and looks around that room. I swear she settles her gaze upon me for longer than the nanosecond she grants other people.

'Last time we learned about the first four Ps of the Proactive Partnership Program. First, the importance of planning – which is all about making this a priority and getting rid of your baggage; second, the importance of the product – that's you – and understanding how to brand it; third, packaging, which is really just about making the best of yourself; and, finally, practice! Getting out there, experimenting, expanding your ideas about what is your type. Tonight we're going to cover the next three Ps: promotion, place and props. But first, I want to hear all about how you all got on, as, I'm sure, do the friends you have made here.'

The room is momentarily filled with the hum of exchanged asides. Then Marina gives us our instructions. 'What I'd like to do now,' she begins, 'is to ask a few brave women, who think they've had a good two weeks, to stand up and tell us about it. Then I'd like us all to split into small groups much as we did last time, and exchange stories with one another. Success stories and the other type too. That way we can help those who are struggling more than others. Now, who has a good story to tell? It doesn't have to be perfect. I'm not expecting you all to have checked off all of the first four Ps. All I'm looking for is a little progress, perhaps on one or two of them.'

We all look around us, wondering who is going to volunteer. Then begins a silence that gets more excruciating by the second. Marina is looking left and right trying to encourage someone to come forward. Claudia elbows me in the ribs and whispers, 'You said you'd had a good couple of weeks.' I ignore her. I feel pretty good about what I've done in the past two weeks, but I'd rather share it in a small group than a large one.

But it's too late. Marina, who clearly has eyes like a hawk, has spotted the rib elbowing and, desperate as she is for a volunteer, has decided that I'm to be it.

'You, the blonde woman in the middle. You look like you'd like to tell your story.'

Bugger. Perhaps if I just sit here she'll realise that she has made a mistake.

'Would you like to come up here and stand with me?'

No, I would not. But I do. I inch my way along my row and out to the aisle, then begin what seems like an unbearably long walk to the podium, aware that all eyes are upon me. I'm wishing I'd worn something more striking, with heels, rather than this straight-from-work look of grey trouser suit with flat black boots.

When I reach Marina she stretches out her arms as if to pull me towards her. In fact, she just takes my right hand and squeezes it. She must be trying to take the edge of my imminent mortification.

'So, you are?'

'Ally James.'

'Hello, Ally. So good to meet you. Can you tell us how the past two weeks have been for you? Have you had any luck, any great experiences, any revelations?'

Staring at the sea of expectant faces in front of me I'm wishing I was making a presentation about the different production processes deployed in the making of fine-cut and coarse-cut. Or doing another stint on Danny Gray's *Food of the Week* show. Or even single-handedly stuffing three hundred jam jars with trinkets for a tombola stall. Anything would be better than this.

'Don't be shy, Ally. I could tell you had something to say to us. Please don't worry about it.'

Now I'm starting to feel like a five-year-old child who's volunteered for show-and-tell then, once at the head of the classroom with the prized object in her hands, found the challenge of speaking aloud in front of fifteen other five-year-olds all too much. Get a grip, woman.

'Sorry,' I say. Always a bad start, that. Solidifies the image of ineptitude that has already crept into the audience's minds. 'I have to admit that I was somewhat sceptical when I came here last time. I just wasn't sure that this sort of thing would work for me.' I stop myself from making disparaging remarks about the eight Ps, which I think are contrived, and the concept of promoting oneself, which I'm sure I'm going to find laughable.

'But after the seminar I decided just to give it a go. To do the things you'd suggested. I guess I saw it as a bit of a challenge. I started by burying my baggage in the garden, and I was amazed how good this felt.'

'Tell us, Ally, what exactly was your baggage. We'd all love to hear,' interrupts Marina.

Oh, hell. Here we go. 'Well, I'm divorced. And I think I'd been hanging on to the idea of my ex, and the whole notion of keeping that family unit intact. Not that I wanted to get back together with him. That wasn't it really. But at the same time I didn't want to let him go. And I realised I just didn't want to let go of the possibility of having that perfect family.'

The low hum of deep sighs and sympathetic 'ahs' disperses the silence in the room, communicating understanding and egging me on.

'So, anyway, I took a picture of that perfect family and put in a box and got rid of it. Silly, isn't it?' Of course I know Marina won't think it silly. She invented the whole idea. But there is something silly about it that has to be acknowledged.

Marina ignores my remark and encourages me to continue with a barely perceptible nod of her head. It's a subtle gesture, much like the gently waving arms.

'Anyway, I felt better after that. It probably sounds trite, but I felt as if I'd made some sort of decision. So I went ahead and organised my branding party, which turned out to be laugh. My friends gave me some good feedback; one of them said that I'd been communicating hostility somehow, and that I needed to change that.'

'Good, good,' says Marina, turning then to the audience. 'Do you see, ladies? Packaging isn't just about what we wear or how we do our hair. It's about body language, too. Go on, Ally.'

'Well, there's not much more actually. Except that I did organise two out of three of those practice-run dates you suggested. I went out with one man I'd turned down before. He wasn't my type and I knew I didn't fancy him, but I went.'

'And what did you learn from that, Ally?' She doesn't let up, this woman. She's determined to draw every last drop of insight from my stories in case no one else volunteers.

'I'm not sure really. That he liked me. That I am likeable, I suppose.' This must be the right answer, because Marina is nodding her head and smiling meaningfully.

I press on. 'Then I did something I still can't believe I've done. I called up an electrician that I remembered being quite nice, and made an appointment for him to come and fix all the broken lights in my house. And while he was there I flirted like I've never flirted before. I made it so obvious that I was interested that he couldn't possibly mistake my intentions. I had expected to have to go all the way and ask him out, but in the end he asked me. We're going out this coming Friday.'

A spontaneous cheer erupts from the audience, and Marina has her hands pressed firmly together, pointing upwards against her lips, not in prayer, but in glee. When the cheering and clapping subside, Marina turns to the group, presumably to summarise the learning points from my story. She'd better be going to sum up, because there isn't any more. I've no intention of talking about lust under the extractor fan.

'That, dear ladies, is what I call success. By being proactive, and putting herself out there, Ally has discovered some things. Some very valuable things. That she can move on. That she is likeable. That she can flirt, with results. And besides all of this, she'll soon have had two dates in two weeks. That alone is good for the soul. Far better than sitting home eating Pot Noodles in front of the TV. Thank you, Ally, for sharing this with us. Now, would anyone else like to tell their story?'

Thus dismissed, I walk back down the aisle towards my seat. I notice that the audience is now awash with raised hands. Now everyone wants to testify. As I press past the others in my row and sit down, both Angie and Claudia lean in and squeeze my arms. 'Well done you,' says Angie. 'I wish I'd accomplished as much. You're a bit of an inspiration.'

An inspiration? Oh God, don't make me that, please. Don't make me the inspiration for a room full of single women so desperate to change their lives they've paid £500 for a series of lessons on how to do it. I'm very happy to make my own quiet progress, but I don't want to be anybody's inspiration.

Marina ends up having to take three volunteers rather than the one she's asked for, so eager and insistent are the arms waving in the air. With my ordeal over, I can sit back and enjoy other people's tales from the front. One woman, Christina, tells us how she went out with a duck decoy and discovered that she actually likes him a lot. They're planning another date this weekend. Then a woman with short red hair cut in a bob has us in stitches with her description of her branding and packaging evening. Apparently her friends pulled no punches, and she emerged from the evening with a to-do list three pages long, about which she seems delighted. It's not until she sits down that I realise that she was once the chronically shy Karen with the shoulder-length red perm.

I'm half expecting Caroline to rush up there to tell us about her success. But she doesn't materialise. Either she's a very private person or she's not had much luck, which would be pretty sad considering she's sacrificed her job for the cause. The last story is in fact rather sad, from a woman who was halfway through burying her baggage when she realised she wasn't ready to do it, and had to dig up her box again. Marina gives her a hug and tells her she's done the right thing: there's no point in forcing matters before they are ready to be resolved. Take your time. Try again next week.

As we are listening, Claudia leans towards me and says, 'I'm afraid I haven't done any of this. I never got that far. But I did sleep with someone in my shiatsu class.' She giggles at my surprised expression. 'I'll tell you during the break,' she promises.

The break can hardly come fast enough. Angie and I huddle together to listen to Claudia. At the last minute we are joined by Louise, who looks rather nice in a fitted black sweater-dress. The rust suit appears to have been ditched.

'So . . . ?' I say, lest Claudia have a last-minute attack of discretion.

'So, there is this man in my shiatsu class. I've been noticing him for some time. Anyway, the past two times I've been, I noticed he was sort of, looking at me, you know? I could feel it, through my spine. And instead of pretending it wasn't happening, I started looking back.' She pauses to take a sip of her wine.

'And then what?' asks Angie.

'And then we had a drink in the juice bar after the class, and went on to dinner, and back to my flat, and . . . and that was that.'

'And what's he like?' asks Angie. 'Is he a suitable duck thingy?

'I don't care if he's a duck or a fucking partridge. All I know is he's gorgeous, twenty-five and the best sex I've ever had.'

There is a sharp intake of breath from Louise. She's probably remembered Marina's advice not to sleep with a man on the first date. Or perhaps she's wishing she could have sex like that. Come to think of it, given that she told us she's never had a relationship, she could be wishing she could just have sex, full stop.

'Oh my God,' gasps Angie. 'That is amazing. Will you see him again?'

'I've seen him every night since,' says Claudia. 'This is my first night off.'

You see. I wondered what a woman like her needed with a course like this, and I was right. Claudia could have reeled in this shiatsu Adonis without ever setting foot in this place. I'm honestly surprised she'd not managed it before. And she is just the sort that could carry off a proper relationship with a twenty-five-year-old.

'So, I guess you won't be coming here again?' I say.

'Oh, I probably will. Keep me focused. And, besides, I can't abandon all of you mid programme!'

Louise is staring at Claudia admiringly. Claudia returns her stare with a smile, then asks, 'And how are you, Louise? You look well.'

Louise stands a little taller, to show off her dress. 'Yes, this is new. A friend told me to buy it. She threw out half my clothes and told me to buy some new ones *before* I lose weight. But I've done something better than that. Nothing like you, Claudia. I could never. But something.'

'What? Tell us,' I say encouragingly.

'I've moved out of my mother's house. I haven't found a flat yet, but I'm staying with another PA from work until I do. You know what I discovered? My biggest baggage wasn't my weight – though obviously that's a problem. It was feeling like a little girl, still living with my mum. And feeling responsible for keeping her company. I decided just to get rid of that, and moved out. Mum was pretty shocked.'

We all mutter 'Good for you' and 'Congratulations' as if Louise has just bedded several shiatsu instructors in quick succession. She is clearly delighted with what she's accomplished. Looking at her and Claudia together you'd be hard pressed to say who was emitting the brighter glow.

On Wednesday morning I call Mel to update her. I can hear her furiously tapping at the keys of her laptop as I'm talking.

'You're kidding? Twenty-five years old? Good fucking on 'er.'

'Hmm. Brilliant isn't it? Everyone seemed to have something to say. Except poor Angie, who just stood there smiling sweetly and being supportive, as she does. When I asked her how things were going she didn't seem to want to talk about it. Kept deflecting the questions elsewhere.'

'Maybe she's found herself a nineteen-year-old but is too embarrassed to say.'

'Possibly. But, anyway, now the really hard part begins. Marina taught us all about self-promotion last night. And place. You'll never guess what our assignments are this week.'

'Go on then. Shock me.'

'First, we have to design a direct mail flyer for ourselves. More on that later. Then we have to start telemarketing, by ringing five people and asking them to introduce us to someone special. And lastly, because you know she likes to do things in threes, we're supposed to make a place plan.'

'What's that?'

'It's a plan to help you change your patterns of activity, try out new places, in order to improve your chances of meeting different sorts of men and getting out of whatever rut you're in. It could be something as simple as shopping at Waitrose instead of Tesco.'

'Well, that doesn't sound too bad,' says Mel.

'No. The bad news is the part about the online dating sites. Our place plans are supposed to feature at least one "visit" to an online dating site, where we're supposed to post our brand descriptor and perhaps even a digital version of our flyer.'

'Fucking hell. You can't do that, Ally.'

'I know I bloody well can't. But it looks as if I might have to if I'm to keep up my end of the bargain. Anyway, don't you go breaking out in a cold sweat just as the going gets tough. Remember who I'm doing this for.'

'You're right. Listen, I'll help you. I'll ask around about dating sites, find out which ones are the best. The most civilised. I bet there are loads of people who you'd never suspect using them. In the meantime, you'd better get a move on. It's already Wednesday, which means you've only got two and half days to get ready for your date with Mr Electric Bollocks.'

Chapter 25
Calling All Mums

My impending launch into cyberspace has given me an idea. Maybe there's a website that could help Clara. Maybe mumsworld.com could help her. Its chatroom must be full of mothers who had difficulty getting pregnant at first, maybe even of women trying to get pregnant for the first time.

Clara's doctors have apparently not been able to come up with any definitive explanation as to why she and Jonathon are not having any success. There is nothing very obviously wrong with either of them. No substandard sperm count or slow-swimming sperm for him. No history of endometriosis for her. *Probably just a case of old eggs* was the best the doctor had to offer. If Clara's reluctant to go the IVF route, I'll be damned if I know what to tell her.

I had no trouble getting pregnant the first time (obviously), and Jack was conceived practically within minutes of David's saying to me, 'Shall we make another baby then'.

Clara is never going to visit a chatroom of her own volition. Buying self-help books (for other people) is one thing; conversing with strangers (who, for all you know, could be mad, immoral or otherwise unsuited to advise you) about personal matters is another. But mumsworld convinced me that chatroom conversations don't have to be that scary. You can always ignore the more outlandish responses.

Thinking that a little meddling is justified, I post a question to mumsworld. I have to renew my membership first as it has lapsed.

> *Dear mums,*
>
> *A very dear friend of mine is experiencing great difficulty getting pregnant. She is 38 but deemed very healthy, and the doctors can find nothing wrong with either her or her husband. They have been trying for over a year, and she is desperate.*
>
> *Can anyone offer any good advice?*

By the end of the day on Thursday (my God, these mumsworld women are efficient) there are sixteen replies to my posting. There's a lot of advice about having sex at the right time of the month, in the right position, and even in the right room of the house (one that's been feng shuied being the best option). There's stuff about eating the right foods and taking the right vitamins, and an entire posting about how to have a boy by controlling your thought patterns. It's all well intentioned but unlikely to be persuasive to someone like Clara. Except for one down near the bottom, which sounds as if it might have been written explicitly for her.

Dear friend,

Three years ago I found myself in your friend's position, only I was already forty so it was really bad news. I was working fourteen hours a day in investment banking, getting on a plane several times a week. My husband and I barely had sex, let alone at the right time of the day or month. Eventually someone said to me, how much do you want this baby? Because if you really want it, you have to make it a priority. Your body is telling you it's too stressed out to do all that it's doing and make a baby at the same time, so you have to make a decision.

So I did. I made a decision that I would get myself out of the rat race for a while and focus on enjoying life and trying to have a baby. It was a huge decision for us, and meant a lot of financial sacrifices. But I knew that if I didn't give it my best shot I would never know what might have happened. I didn't want to live with that kind of regret all my life.

I am now back at work, though not in investment banking. And I have an eighteen-month-old daughter. I'm not saying your friend will definitely be this lucky. But she might. And she deserves to give herself a shot.

Alice

Just below Alice's posting is another by someone called Monica, insisting that the key to conception lies in hanging upside down for two hours after having sex. Like I said, you have to be prepared to pick and choose when you venture into a chatroom.

Perhaps Alice and Jonathon have been comparing notes. Perhaps they are even both right. Maybe Clara is subconsciously running from a baby by continuing to structure her life in such a way that getting pregnant is an impossibility. Both biological and practical.

But how do you tell a woman who's spent the best part of the last seventeen years nurturing professional success that she needs to pull out of the competition in order to become a mother? (Even worse, how do you tell her this may involve the sacrifice of the Joseph suits, Prada handbags and Ferragamo shoes she's come to see as wardrobe staples?) Clara always insists that there's no other way to do her job than the way she does it (long hours, lots of travel, playing the PowerPoint wankers at their own game). There's no way she's going to be receptive to someone telling her to slow down for a while. The messenger won't just be shot but hung, drawn and quartered.

There has to be another way to encourage Clara to try something new. I can't think what it might be right now, but I'm sure it will come to me.

Chapter 26
Tide Pool Creatures

Question: What do I have in common with crabs, anemones and barnacles?

Answer: All of us are spineless.

Alan caught me on the hop last night. Asked me if I'd like to go to the theatre the week after next. Not knowing how to say *No*, I said *Yes*.

Now, if my brother were a marine biologist, I wouldn't be in this mess.

Chapter 27
Something Exotic

'H-A-T. What does that say, Jack? Spell out the letters first then say them all together.'

Friday is not supposed to be a work day, but it has ended up as one. Paul Delaney is very excited about the new campaign he and his team have developed, and insists it can't wait until the following week. So I'm heading into work for two hours, just as soon as I've got the children off to school. The blockage is Jack, whose reading we are attempting to do in the car outside the school gates. Millie is sitting in the back seat reading her own book while I try to inveigle Jack into reading the last half of his.

Jack examines the page with a screwed up face. 'H-A-T. Hop!' he shouts.

'Come on, Jack. You're not trying! How can H-A-T make

hop? Concentrate. Let's try this one.' I point at another word.

'C-A-R. Caaarruh. Carrot!'

I can't take any more of this. I shall probably strangle him if we don't stop. Is mine the only child in reception who is failing to grasp the point of phonics?

'That's enough,' I snap, slamming the book shut. Then, remembering the orange juice incident and my guilt about neural pathway damage, I soften a little. 'You did very well, Jack. We can do some more later.' (Shouting at children kills neural pathways, but praise apparently encourages them to sprout like fury.) In his reading record book I quickly scribble a note to his teacher. *Mrs Lindhurst, Jack not fully able to concentrate today. Can we please try this book again tonight*. There. At least she'll know I've tried.

'OK, you two. Let's go.' We all get out of the car and head into the school, Millie continuing to read her book as she makes her way to the steps. I'm sure that's part of what's made her a target here, a place in which this sort of quiet, unparticipating studiousness is not viewed positively. Brash confidence and energetic engagement are what are required here. Still, there's no point in dwelling on that now, with just three weeks remaining at the school.

Three weeks remaining at the school! That means three weeks until Easter break and the spring fête and the tombola jars, about which I've done absolutely nothing. I meant to send around a short note to the mothers in Millie's class asking them all to make up a few jars, or at the very least collar a few of the ones I know in the playground. But the whole thing somehow slipped off my radar screen. I don't think it has slipped off Ellie

Masterson's, because she's sidling up to me now with a slightly accusing look on her face.

'Ally, Helen tells me you're in charge of jam jars. Is that true?'

'Yes. Yes it is.'

'Oh good. I took the liberty of making up a dozen.' Ellie hands me a plastic carrier bag clanking with jars. 'Have you had many others?'

Has she sniffed out my inadequacy? I wonder. Has Helen Chambers put her up to this, to encourage me to get a move on?

'No, not many. I mean, a few. From the people I've managed to ask. But I really must get round to asking everyone else. Thanks for these. I'm very grateful. And they look so beautiful!' I say, peering into the bag.

Ellie's jars are bright and colourful, having been filled with tiny matchbox cars and little shiny beads and all manner of things designed to appeal to children under seven. Each jar has been lovingly covered in a little circle of green and white checked fabric tied with a ribbon. What a thing to have to live up to.

On the train I scribble the word *tombola* in enormous black letters across an entire page of my diary, lest I forget the damn thing again. Then I mull over the planned trip to Valencia for my bonding exercise with the suppliers, which has proved to be more of a headache than I'd even expected. The date that works for me is the week just before Easter, but that's not convenient for the growers. It's also a slight problem for Mum and Dad, who are being counted on to babysit. Dad has a long-standing commitment to a four-ball with some old work colleagues; Mum has an appointment with a specialist about her bad hip. Both have offered to rearrange things for me (such is the depth of their selflessness) but I know how long specialist appointments take to get, and how funny a bunch of seventy-year-olds are likely to get if their tee-off time is messed around with. So I am making alternative arrangements for the first day of my expected three-day absence (consisting of calls to David, Mel and Clara in that order) and have told Mum and Dad to get here when they can on day two.

Jill isn't a viable solution because she doesn't do overnights. She's got a funny thing (her description, not mine) about sleeping in her own bed at night. Apparently, she and her husband didn't spend a night apart in twenty years, and she isn't about to desert the marital bed even now that he's been dead seven years. And she did forewarn me when I hired her as an after-school sitter two years ago, so I can hardly move the goalposts now. She's so precious to me in so many ways – it's practically impossible to find someone to cover the inconvenient hours of three to seven, four days a week, for a start – that I can forgive her eccentricities. I figure a fifty-year-old widow whose only hobby is the weekly replenishment of her teddy bear collection is entitled to a few, so long as she's kind to my children and doesn't let me down.

I walk into my meeting ten minutes late, to find Nicki, Paul Delaney and two junior agency staff huddled over something at one end of the conference table. They all look up as I enter, then Nicki beckons to me.

'Ally, quick. I think you're going to love this.'

Laid out on the table are three sheets of A2 card, each

one with a mock-up on it. The sunset and beach from Paul's earlier efforts are still in evidence in the first drawing. Only the beach isn't some white-sanded Bahamian paradise, but an English beach, with flat brown sand and pebbles. And instead of a vaguely stomach-churning shot of a couple cooing under some marmalade jars at a sea-front bar, there is a picture of a bear eating marmalade from a jar with his hands. It's Paddington Bear, in his floppy red hat, sitting on a decrepit-looking suitcase covered in stickers. The caption says *Seville Sunset. Good enough to tempt a bear to an English beach*.

I look up from the picture at four expectant faces. Only Nicki's is confident. Paul has the look of a rabbit who's expecting a fox to leap from the undergrowth at any moment.

'It's Paddington Bear,' I say unnecessarily. 'Good idea.'

Paul can hardly wait to fill me in on just how good an idea it is. 'Great, isn't it? When I heard you on the radio last week I thought "that's it!" All that stuff you reminded us of – about marmalade's fascinating history, and the famous people who've loved it in the past – just seemed too good to waste. And perfect for launching a new and different marmalade. Look at the next two.'

I look down at the table at the second picture, which I can now see is of Mary Queen of Scots on a ship bed, being spoonfed marmalade by a toothless sailor, with a tawny orange sunset just visible through the porthole. The caption reads *Seville Sunset. If only it had been around when Mary needed it*. The third picture is of King Henry VIII being presented with a jar of marmalade, with a caption reading *Seville Sunset. Good enough to present to a king*. In this one, the sun is setting into the hills behind his throne. I now see that all three shots have a second, smaller caption across the bottom of the page: *Marmalade. A Great British Tradition*.

'What do you think?' asks Paul eagerly. He's not overly cool, Paul. Could do with a little of that icy arrogance practised by so many agency people.

'I think it's brilliant.' And I do. I think the campaign could do with some fine-tuning, but it's pretty good. And a damn sight better than the ones that preceded it. Marmalade and its history are exotic enough; we don't need to shout about it with vulgar references to lovers and Mauritian sunsets.

Paul punches the air, and Nicki claps her hands together. The other two aren't sure what to do, but since this is clearly a celebratory moment, they allow slim smiles to creep on to their faces.

We spend the next hour or so talking about the campaign in more detail. Should the captions read exactly like this, or would different words be better? Can we be sure that people will recognise the historical figures, or do we need to be more obvious? Do we need to place a potted version of the story behind the picture in the corner of each advertisement, or on the opposite page, just in case people don't get it?

But, basically, we are there. We have the idea. The rest is all about execution, and that's the job of Paul and his two trusty sidekicks, who are at present both furiously scribbling notes. I lean back in my chair for a minute to take a breather from the intense discussion. And while I'm at it I say a silent but heartfelt thank you to C. Anne Wilson.

Unbelievably, intermingled with my gratitude to C. Anne is a trace of appreciation for Anna, who, whatever else you might say about her, helped to jolt me out of that professional no-man's-land I've been wallowing in for more than a year now. Wasn't she really only telling me something my father told me a thousand times when I was growing up, and which I must often have greeted with rolling eyes and scornful sighs but somehow absorbed? If something's worth doing, it's worth doing well.

Neither Anna Wyatt nor C. Anne Wilson are much use, though, when you're trying to decide on an outfit for a date with an electrician with whom you've exchanged inappropriate innuendo. According to the message left by Gary on my machine this afternoon, we're to meet at the Sparrow first, then go on to a local Italian he's been to before. That sounds like jeans and a shirt to me. But which shirt? The choice will be crucial. In a dialogue with myself that sounds as if it's been taken straight from Marina's notes, I determine that it must neither be too tight nor too loose, too low cut nor too matronly, too plain (not trying hard enough) nor too fancy (trying way too hard).

I have nothing at all in my wardrobe that meets all of these criteria. With time running short I opt for my Max Mara V-neck with a white lace camisole peeping out of the top rather than the white shirt or high-necked T-shirt I usually wear underneath it. I've ditched the uplifter in favour of my newly purchased floral number.

I descend to the sitting room, where Jill (who does do evenings if not nights) is sitting watching *Changing Rooms* with Millie. Jack is lying on the floor moving toy soldiers into formation. Millie looks up as I enter the room, and manages to prick my precarious self-confidence in one fell swoop.

'Mummy, are you still going out? You don't look very dressed up.'

'Yes, I'm going out, but just to a pub so I don't have to dress up. But do I look nice? I've done my eyes, see,' I say, bending down for her to inspect my shimmery brown and pink eye shadow, painstakingly applied with a technique I hope resembles the one Mel used on me last week.

'Ooh yes. That's pretty,' she says. 'And you smell nice.'

'Good. Now please be good for Jill. Bed at eight for you, Jack, and eight thirty for you, Millie. Jill, I won't be too late.'

Jill has already told me I mustn't be late as she's driving to Swanage for an antique-bear exhibit early in the morning, something for which I'm quite grateful. A firm deadline will prevent me getting carried away, having one too many drinks and doing something I'm sure to regret.

The Sparrow is a five-minute walk away. Approaching it I have an overwhelming desire to turn and run in the other direction. This is not something I'm used to doing. This isn't even something I'm sure I want to be doing. It seemed like a good idea last week, and when I was recounting my triumph at the seminar, but now the prospect of walking alone into a pub to meet someone I know nothing about except that he's very likely not my type seems like madness. Right now, I'd so much rather be at home watching other people going on nerve-racking dates in *Friends*.

What stops me from actually turning round at the door

and running back home I'm not entirely sure. But I know what stops me from leaving once I'm inside. Because I spot him immediately, slouched alluringly in a corner seat opposite a beer. My breath is taken away, as they say, partly by the mere sight of him, waiting for me, and partly by the memory of those sensations I felt last week in my kitchen. All that heat, and tension. That knotted stomach. And this is all before we've exchanged a word. Steady, girl.

Gary sees me walking across the pub and gets up from his seat. 'Hiya,' he says, kissing me on one cheek and moving along his seat to make room for me. Now I'm really in trouble, I think. There's not even a table to protect me from myself.

He doesn't seem nervous. He's obviously not overcome by inappropriate emotions or uncontrollable urges. Perhaps he's used to this sort of thing. Or perhaps I misread the signs last week, and he just doesn't fancy me that much.

He asks me what I'd like to drink then orders it and turns towards me, lifting one knee and resting it at an angle on the padded bench. 'So, how are the lights holding up?' he asks. The way his eyes are twinkling, you'd think he was asking me how I like my new vibrator.

I didn't misread the signs.

'Pretty well, I think. At least none has fallen out on to my head so far.'

'That's good. I always like to do a good job.'

Then silence. Where do we go from here? We have to start pretty much at the beginning, create some sort of context for this evening. I opt for the banal but workmanlike enquiry about his day.

'So, did you have a busy day today. Rushing around, lots of jobs?'

'Nah. Not too bad. Had a couple of other things to do this morning so I only did one or two electrical jobs. With my dad.'

The mention of Dad gives me the straw I've been grasping for.

'Do you get on well with your dad? I mean, is it difficult working together?'

'Nah. He's a really easygoing bloke. We get on really well. I work as much as I like really. No pressure.'

So he's a laid-back type. Doesn't like to work too hard. Likes to come and go. If he were genuine long-term partner material that would be a strike against him, but as it is it's quite appealing.

'What about your parents? Do you get on well with them?' he asks. How is it that two people over the age of thirty have started off an evening talking about their parents? It's as if we're trying to steer ourselves on to safe ground, away from the quicksand we glimpsed last week.

'My parents are great actually. They've been so supportive of me in the past two years, and, well, all my life really. Almost anything I do is fine with them. And they help as much as they can. But they are both almost seventy, so there's a limit.'

'My mum died a long time ago,' he announces. 'So it's just me and my dad and my brother now.'

'Oh, I'm sorry. Your brother – what's he like?'

Now that we are on to family the possibilities are endless. I hear about Gary's brother (a painter and decorator, also unmarried) and he hears about Nick and Kate and the boys, and Jack and Millie. We stay on this topic for what must be half an hour, our primal impulses simmering gently in the background. By the time this conversation has finished and I'm into my second (very large) glass of wine I've discovered that he is thirty-two. In my present state this worries me less than it thrills me.

At some point during out conversation Gary slips his arm along the back of the bench, and moves a few inches closer to me. I'm suddenly acutely aware of his arm there, tantalisingly close to my shoulder. Then, unexpectedly, he leans in towards me, and I'm sure he's going to kiss me, right here under the bright lights of the Sparrow surrounded by tables full of lads drinking their way towards an inevitable curry.

Instead of kissing me he just whispers, 'I'm getting hungry? Are you?' I'm enfeebled by anticipation.

I'm not hungry for an Italian but I make all the right noises and we leave the Sparrow. Gary places his hand at the small of my back and ushers me out on to the street and towards Giovanni's, a favourite of his that he's sure I will love. A few seconds into the short walk he takes my hand. It's all too fast, I know, but at the same time there's something natural, even inevitable about it. Giovanni's is small, cramped even. The tables are small, too, so that as we sit down at ours, in the corner near the window, I lean in and nearly set my hair alight on the candle that's burning in the middle. Our knees are within millimetres of touching under the table, and there will be no need to lean in to be heard. We can't get any closer. If this is all part of a plan, it's a very good one. It would never have worked for the dinner with Alan, but it's working wonders tonight.

I'm vaguely aware of ordering seafood linguine with a side salad. As it happens I barely make a dent in it, so distracted am I by our conversation. It turns out that Gary is a Hemingway fan, and has read every one of his novels and every biography ever written about him. (I give myself a mental rap on the knuckles for earlier having branded him a likely illiterate.) When we've finished with Ernest we move on to nonsense. Just flirtatious inanities and lots of laughter. And all the while I'm staring at his chocolate-brown eyes and the lock of jet hair that keeps falling across his forehead, and imagining the bare spot above his jeans that I glimpsed last week. And basking in his engaging smile. He has one tooth that overlaps another in the top row and lends his expression a certain mischeviousness.

Later I will realise that the dark eyes and hair remind me of David. But I don't realise this now. I'm too wrapped up in the heady experience of being adored over a red and white checked tablecloth, in full, if dim and candlelit, view of twenty-five fellow diners.

The waiter clears away my half-finished linguine and Gary's empty mussel shells and we both start twirling our red wine glasses around self-consciously. Then, just as I can see the waiter returning with a pudding menu out of the corner of my eye, Gary lifts my chin with one finger and kisses me. The first kiss is polite and gentle. The second one is not. When I look up the waiter has vanished. We are obviously not going to need pudding.

I'm hoping for another kiss like the second one when Gary whispers something that sounds like 'I've got a secret to tell you'.

'Go on. Tell me,' I say. What's he going to tell me? More

silly, sexy nonsense? That he was attracted to me all those months ago when he first came to the house with his father?

'I'm not just a boring electrician, you know. I have another job. Something much more interesting.'

Where is this going, I wonder. We're way beyond discussing the job thing. My curiosity is piqued.

'Do you want to know what it is?'

'OK . . .' I say, smiling.

'I run an exotic dance company. I audition exotic dancers for clubs. That's what I was doing for most of today. Most of the time the girls come to audition in bikinis, suspenders, tassels, that sort of thing. But today there was one in a nurse's uniform. And you know what I was thinking all day? I'd love to see you in that nurse's uniform.'

Then he kisses me again. An even less polite kiss than the last time. So impolite in fact that I nearly choke.

'How about it? Will you do that for me sometime?' he says after retrieving his tongue from my throat.

Like puddles in the glaring sun, my desire has evaporated. I'm not the dressing-up type. And I've always been vaguely repelled by the thought of men who are. In the space of a minute and a half Gary has managed to eradicate a week's worth of pent-up voracity and annihilate the potency of two perfectly good kisses.

I don't let on to Gary just how much of a turn-off his exotic dance company and the nurse's uniform idea are to me. I joke with him as we pay the bill, keeping things light. Nurse's uniform? I'd be better as an air hostess, don't you think? No, I can't have coffee at his place because

I have to get home to Jill. Bear convention. Sure, we can do dinner again, but I'm very busy over the next few weeks. Very.

I think he's a little shocked by the abrupt end to what was such a promising evening. When we reach my house, instead of allowing him to give me the tongue treatment again, I press my fingers to my lips, then to his, and disappear through my front door shouting 'Thanks for dinner'.

Perhaps I'm highly unusual. Perhaps other women go along with his ideas because he's so attractive. Perhaps other women find his sideline in tassels intriguing. Something to add spice to their relationship.

I'm disappointed, but my disappointment is dulled by relief at being back inside my little house, knowing I'm going up to my bedroom alone to sleep in a pair of flannels. Tonight has taught me a lesson; the very lesson that Marina intended me to learn, as it happens. You really should never judge a book by its cover. Exotic comes in all kinds of packages, and exotic isn't always what you want.

Chapter 28
Shopping

I've had enough of ducks. They are all right, up to a point. And they've served some sort of purpose for me, I suppose. I feel differently from the way I did two weeks ago, as if I've thrown off the covers and decided to get out of bed after two and a half years in a half slumber.

But in the end the ducks are too much trouble. Going out with people you know from the start are not your type can backfire on you. Now I have Alan calling twice a week and will probably find myself being stalked by a man wielding a nurse's uniform. I don't have the stamina to try all this again on a third target, so I plan to give up on the duck decoy idea while I'm ahead.

It will be safer to stick to the parts of Marina's programme of activities that I can control. Like the place plan. I can choose where I'm going to go, and with whom I will make eye contact when I'm there. I might carry a prop, but if someone I don't like expresses interest in it I'll cut them dead. There will be no more of this nonsense about trying people on for size and stretching my boundaries. From now on, it's only sure bets for me.

First on today's agenda is the weekly shop, which is what Millie, Jack and I are currently driving towards. I normally shop at Tesco, but in the interests of trying out new places we're driving to Waitrose. It's a bit further and quite a lot more expensive, but once won't hurt. I despise shopping with children in tow, but today I have no choice. I've bribed them with a promise that they will both be entitled to choose three items for the shopping cart, regardless of how unhealthy an option they represent.

Waitrose is buzzing, even at nine thirty a.m. Clearly Waitrose shoppers are the types who need to get their shopping out of the way before going on to do more interesting things. I've shopped here in the past, but I'd forgotten about its greatest asset: it carries Skippy peanut butter, which Clara introduced me to and I now rate as the only peanut butter worth eating. There are some things we British don't do a quarter as well as the Americans, and peanut butter is one of them.

We are shopping for the week, but we are also shopping for Sunday lunch with David. So I'm having enormous trouble thinking about quantities. This isn't an unusual problem when you're a single parent who only has to feed the whole family on alternate weekends. Your shopping is completely without rhythm. Some weeks you're buying family sized roast chickens and large bags of turkey dinosaurs and jammy dodgers in anticipation of weekends with two small children and their friends, the next week you're hunting down single servings of cream cheese and small salad bags like other singletons. This week, with both the children and David to cater for, I'm finding myself temporarily overwhelmed by the task.

Just to add to the confusion, Jack, who has declined to sit in the trolley and is wandering perilously close to its front wheel instead, chooses this moment, when I'm trying to decide between lamb and chicken, to ask me a pressing question.

'Mum, do you know where all the pooh goes when it leaves the loo?'

'What? Oh, no, I don't.' I have a feeling he's going to tell me.

'I'll tell you. It goes out of a big, ginormous pipe and drives – like if we were driving to the beach – it drives all the way to the sea and goes into the sea. And that's why the sea is so dirty.'

'Hmm. I'm sure it gets cleaned up before it gets into the sea, Jack,' I say, peering at the chickens in an effort to find one with some actual meat on it.

'No it doesn't! It doesn't!' Occasionally he gets like this if you disagree with something he's claiming to have learned at school. It's usually best to back down.

'Goodness. Well that's a big problem isn't it?' Then I go for the interception. 'Now, Jack, what veggies shall we have tomorrow when Daddy comes to lunch?'

'Why is Daddy coming to lunch?' interjects Millie, who has so far been an angel, helpfully running to the ends of aisles to pick up a bottle of ketchup or a bag of rice.

'Because we thought it would be nice to spend some time together as a family for a change.'

That's right, isn't it?

'We are still a family, even if Daddy and I don't live together any more.'

That's right, too, I suppose. Please, please don't anyone ask me why Daddy and I aren't living together any more. Not again.

'Oh.' Millie is working hard to absorb this information. 'Will we do it every week?'

'I don't think so, honey. Perhaps every now and again.'

I then send both children off in search of their vegetables of choice. In the meantime, I go in search of peanut butter in the condiments aisle, noticing with some satisfaction that Cottage Garden Food's marmalade brands have the same shelf space as both Frank Cooper's and the premium brand with the French name. Millie returns with a head of broccoli and some carrots. Jack comes back with a large object that looks a little like an oversized artichoke.

'Jack, I'm not sure I know how to cook that.'

'But, Mummy, you said we could choose anything we wanted. This looks interesting.'

'You're right. Put it in,' I say resignedly. We are almost at the end of the expedition and we haven't had a major breakdown or tantrum yet, so I must count myself lucky. Stopping to pick up some wine, Diet Cokes and apple juice on the way, we head to one of the checkout counters.

I'm in luck, as I've pushed my trolley up to a checkout at which there is already a keen looking packer standing waiting with several open plastic bags. 'Would you like me to load the items on, or pack them into bags, madam?'

Gosh. I've never been aware of such an option. 'I'll load them on, thanks. You can put them into bags.'

And thus we commence. When the trolley is half empty, Jack insists on standing in it to help unload the remaining items, and it takes every ounce of my reserve to prevent myself from screaming at him when he stands on the organic vine tomatoes. I'm distracted from the observation of any further mishaps by the sight of the packer's expression as he picks up the items at the other end of the counter and places them purposefully into plastic bags; it veers between mild amusement and outright disapproval. He's classified me as a shopper with a cluttered mind and a poor sense of organisation, I can tell. I've had dairy mixed up with fresh fruit, and raw meat sitting alongside cereal boxes in my trolley. And the bread has clearly been sitting at the bottom of it all, directly under the bags of flour, because all three loaves have been squashed into a warped V-shape.

With the last of the items on the counter and Jack now having moved to the other end to assist the officious packer, I begin the search for my debit card, which has found a hiding place amidst the dozens of receipts I have stashed in my wallet. I finally locate the card and vow to do a major clear-out of my wallet when I get home. Then I look up and across at the next counter, and there he is.

Tom is loading food items on to the counter as Grace sits eating a digestive biscuit in the trolley. I'm completely taken aback by the sight of him. Luckily, Millie intervenes.

'Mummy, there's Grace! Look.'

'Oh yes, so it is.'

Millie waves at Grace, who waves back, leading Tom to turn around to see who she's waving at. He sees Millie first, then his eyes find me and he grins widely. Not the fixed grin of someone who's wondering how they can escape without being drawn into a long conversation, but a grin that says he's genuinely pleased to see me.

'How are you?' he says over the head of the checkout girl in front of me.

'Glad this is over,' I say.

'Me too,' he replies.

My groceries are all bagged up now and I'm going through the payment routine, getting my car park ticket stamped, stuffing my card back into my already over-stuffed wallet. All the while I'm talking myself through my next move. Will I wait while he finishes paying or will that be too obvious? Can I find an excuse to stall us here – perhaps by searching for some item of food to keep Jack quiet?

Then I remember that I'm through with ducks, and think that perhaps I ought just to wave and disappear nonchalantly. But that feels wrong. There's an opportunity here, and for some reason I think it must not be missed.

So I move the trolley into the aisle at the end of the counter and begin to linger with purpose. 'Jack, would you like one of those chocolate biscuits you chose?'

'Ooh yes,' he shouts, jumping up and down.

'Me too,' says Millie.

I begin rooting around amongst the bags, genuinely unsure as to which one contains the chocolate biscuits. Sure enough, the effort takes long enough for Tom to finish paying and steer his trolley towards us. Who needs to carry a prop when you have children, I think.

'I've never seen you here before,' says Tom. 'Usually you spot the same old faces every week.'

'I used to shop here, actually,' I say mendaciously. 'Then I decided to try Tesco, but I might come back here occasionally just for a change. They do a great line in chocolate biscuits.' I point at Jack, whose appears to have sprouted a second pair of lips, large and chocolate covered, within seconds of getting hold of a biscuit.

Tom laughs and turns to indicate Grace, who is working her way through another biscuit. 'That's why I stick to digestives.'

Millie starts tickling Grace, then pretends to steal her biscuit. Tom and I stand watching the two of them. I wonder if he is just enjoying the moment, or searching, like me, for a way to prolong it.

Obviously, it was the former. 'Well, I'll see you around,' he says suddenly.

'Oh, yes. See you. Maybe at the park.' I hope that didn't sound too desperate.

Tom grins and wheels Grace away towards the exit. I engage myself in restacking the bags in the trolley so that the top few won't fall off when we walk through the car park, trying to pretend (for whom? it occurs to me) that I'm unconcerned about Tom's quick departure and apparent lack of interest.

It's probably for the best anyway. Definitely for the best. I've no time for any more ducks, and he's probably not ready to be anything else. Someone who lost their wife just a year ago is not going to be in any emotional shape to deal with someone new. Someone who's barely recovered from her own loss. He would be comparing all the time, and I'm sure I'd never measure up. His wife was probably perfect. Pretty and kind, and probably clever too.

I don't really need that, do I?

Chapter 29
Main Squeeze

I used to cook Sunday lunch all the time. Roast pork with crackling. Lamb with rosemary and garlic. Toad in the hole. I've done the lot. But it never reduced me to the blithering wreck I am today. And this is just a roast chicken.

Millie has helped with the broccoli and carrots and the crumble mixture for the top of the apples. Jack's monstrous artichoke thingy sits untouched on the windowsill. The disastrous bit is the potatoes, which I've parboiled to the point of disintegration. They will make awful mashers. I'm contemplating running out to the Somerfield at the petrol station to see if they sell any of those frozen roast potatoes, but in the end I decide to just peel another batch and start again. This I do while Jack and Millie set the table and I eye up the bottle of white wine on the counter, which I plan to open as soon as would be deemed respectable. I figure eleven forty-five will be just on the right side of borderline proper.

When the big hand hits the nine I dive at the bottle like the proverbial man in the desert. The first two sips have a marvellously steadying effect, of which I'm immediately glad. I need to be calm and unruffled when David arrives; everything must seem relaxed and pleasant for Jack and Millie. (I realise that this is asking a lot, given that all across the country, perfect unbroken families will be arguing over the preparation of the roast, and more than a few people will be storming off to the pub to cool down.)

At the sound of the doorbell I find myself standing rigid and fixed to my spot in front of the second batch of boiling potatoes. Using the excuse of needing to watch them carefully so as not to over-boil them again, I send Millie to answer the door, something my paranoia about lurking strangers normally disallows.

'It's OK. I know it will be Daddy,' I reassure her.

From the kitchen I can hear Millie's squeals of delight as David enters, followed by the sound of Jack's simulated gunfire. Jack loves to greet people by shooting them. It's a sign of affection.

All three of them walk into the kitchen together, Jack in one of David's arms, Millie hanging on to the other. Millie is lit up like a Christmas tree, and I'm struck by what an enormous thing this must be for her. The two people she loves most in the world, having lunch together. I hope she's not seeing it as a sign of great things to come, but I have a feeling she might be.

'Hi, Ally,' says David. 'Smells good.'

'Hi. Should do. Jack and Millie have been working hard. You should see the crumble.'

'Really? Have you two been helping Mummy? That's great.'

'Wine?' I raise my glass questioningly.

'Sure. Why not?' he says, plonking Jack down and moving over to the back doors to look out over the minute garden, which is a mess. The bad thing about early spring is that everything starts growing like fury before you've even contemplated getting to grips with it.

'Garden looks nice,' he says.

'Stop it. I haven't had much time.'

'No, no. I'm serious. It looks nice.'

Who is he trying to kid? Is he trying out some new line in flattery, complimenting me on my domestic achievements?

There's only so long you can stare at a garden that's fifteen feet square and overrun by early spring weeds and bedraggled daffodils. So, once I've drained the potatoes and left them to cool, we move into the sitting room. Jack and Millie want to play cards before lunch. We settle on Snap for the sake of Jack, which disappoints Millie. She's learned to play rummy and wants to show David.

'You and I will play rummy later, Mill,' he says, tousling her hair.

Snap fills the room with noise and prevents David and me from having to talk too much. Jack fills in whatever silences exist with questions and stories that seem to emerge from nowhere but are perfectly in context to him.

'Dad, do you think darkest Peru would be a good place to go hunting for bears?'

'Not sure, Jack. Why?'

'Because when I'm older, say seventeen, I want to go hunting with you. For bears. We could stop off in cowboy land and buy some proper guns.'

'And where's cowboy land?' David enquires.

'You know. Mexico. Or Nexus.'

'You mean Texas.'

'Yeah, Texas. Can we go, Dad? When I'm seventeen?'

'Sounds like a great idea,' agrees David. Seventeen is a long way off, and hopefully Jack won't be interested in guns or bears when it arrives.

David and I exchange a glance over Jack's head, and David stifles a smile. This is what I've missed. This very thing. There's nothing quite so wonderful as sharing amazement and amusement at one's offspring with the other parent of those offspring. Nothing. I'd thought I would never experience it again. But maybe there's hope for David and me. Maybe we can evolve our divorce into something that can accommodate shared experiences like this.

After the game of Snap we all busy ourselves with last-minute lunch preparations. David mashes the potatoes – the one culinary task at which he is actually quite adept – while I carve the chicken and attempt to make gravy. It doesn't taste quite right, so I splash in another glass of white wine for good measure before refilling our wine-glasses. Millie puts the napkins on the table and lights a candle while Jack readies himself for the meal by placing his guns on either side of his plate.

The conversation over lunch is mostly child centred, which is fine with me. Millie tells David how much she is looking forward to her new school, to which statement Jack protests that he doesn't see why he should have to go to school at all. Then we talk about the impending arrival of Millie's rabbit. Her birthday is just a month away, so I'm reminded that I must get my skates on. Do you have to order rabbits, or can you expect to just walk into a pet shop and find the perfect one? Jack asks when he will be allowed to have a pet. A gerbil is what he has in mind.

'I don't like gerbils, Jack,' I say. 'The tails give me the creeps. What about a hamster?'

'No, Harry has a gerbil,' says Jack, digging in.

'Cowboys don't have gerbils, Jack,' says David helpfully. 'Hamsters are more of a cowboy thing.'

'Oh,' says Jack, sinking into deep thought. I'm surprised by David. His usual approach is more heavy handed. He says no and that's it; the children are expected to accept it. This imaginative persuasiveness is new.

We decide that we are all too full to eat the crumble straightaway, so Jack and Millie are excused and run into the sitting room to watch *Chitty Chitty Bang Bang*, which I've hired for the occasion. This was the movie they settled on as a compromise between *Parent Trap* (Millie's choice) and *The Magnificent Seven* (Jack's). I was quick to discourage *Parent Trap* on this occasion; a story of divorced parents whose love affair is rekindled by the machinations of their daughters would make uncomfortable viewing today.

Sitting at the table alone, David and I are momentarily quiet. As ever loathing a gaping silence, and relying on wine-induced confidence to carry me through, I ask David about Chantal.

'So, Millie tells me you're not going to see Chantal any more.'

'Oh, did she? Yeah. That's true. Just didn't work out. Seeing her with the children was a big step, and it put everything in perspective I guess. She's not the woman I thought she was.'

'And what kind of woman was that?'

I don't really want to know, so I'm glad when he deflects my question. 'Anyway, you seem really well. How are things?'

'I am well, actually. Work is going really well now. We've got a good campaign coming out and I'm just much happier with the whole idea of working for Cottage Garden Foods than I was a year ago. I think I've come round to the idea that marmalade isn't so bad after all. I'm not even sure I'd want to be back in the glamour industry.'

'Hey, Charles told me he heard you on the radio. Said you were pretty impressive.' This is Charles of Sara and Charles, who we used to see as a couple.

'I don't know about that, but it was fun. Anyway, I'm kind of determined to enjoy work a bit more. Otherwise it sort of colours everything else. And everything else is pretty good really. We're all fine.'

'Happy?' he says. The question pierces like a skewer.

'Happy? Yes. I guess I am.'

'Good,' he says, but his face betrays something that looks to me like regret. Or have I imagined it?

'Shall we eat our crumble in the sitting room, and watch the movie with the kids?' I ask, anxious to escape the disturbing undercurrents in this room.

'Sure. That would be great,' he says, downing the last of the wine in his glass. 'Any more where this came from?'

There is, and I pour him some before dishing our four servings of crumble and ice-cream. We both carry these through to the sitting room, where Jack is staring wide eyed as the magic car makes its first flight. We end up sitting at either end of the sofa, with the children squashed between us, all of us trying to eat apple crumble without elbowing the life out of anyone else or dropping ice-cream on to our laps.

We pass the next hour and a half like this. It's raining outside, so no one suggests a walk or a bike ride. About halfway through the movie David and Jack both break out into laughter while Millie and I sit straight faced. I look over at David, expecting him to be transfixed by the screen, but instead our eyes lock together. His soulful brown eyes, the ones I once told Mel were deeper and more luscious than a bowl of melted Dairy Milk, are staring at me. They linger for a few moments and there's nothing remotely accidental about it. When I look away we both carry on as before, being alternately amused and irritated by Dick Van Dyke. But we both know that David meant something by that look and that it has changed things.

After the movie David keeps his promise to Millie, and they play rummy for a while. I'm happy to tidy the kitchen because it gives me some time to clear my head a little and helps dispel the leftover effects of all the wine. I return to the sitting room just as David is rising from his kneeling position in front of the coffee table.

'I'd better get going. Got some prep to do for a shoot in the morning,' he says.

'OK. It was nice to see you, wasn't it, guys?' I say, turning to Jack and Millie.

They both agree that it was, and give David hugs. Then I walk him out into the hall. He shrugs on the jacket he's left hanging over the banister, a beaten-up brown leather thing I've always loved.

When he's opened the door and I think I'm about to see the last of him, he turns around and places his hand on my upper arm and gives it a squeeze. He's not touched me for two years, so the effect is the same as if he's pulled me towards him and pressed my hips to his. I can hardly speak. I don't speak. He smiles and says goodbye and I stand and watch him go.

When he's out of sight and I'm shutting the door I look down and see a slim white envelope. It must have been shoved through the letter box this afternoon. I pick it up and open it to find a hand-written note.

Ally,

Thought it would be nice to get together for coffee or something. Will you call me?

Tom

0208 947 8891

I exhale noisily, suddenly aware that I've been holding my breath. I don't know if I'm delirious with happiness or terrified. Is it possible to be both? None of this is supposed to be happening. I'd not anticipated any of it, and now it's all happening at once.

And there I was thinking that all that lay ahead of me was a series of unwanted dinners with a fireplace aficionado and continuous propositioning by someone with a nurse fetish.

Part 3

Chapter 30
Pep Talk

There's nothing more certain to engender weight loss than stress and lovesickness. I seem to be suffering from a peculiar combination of the two, and have shed four pounds in the past week, most of which has disappeared since Friday. Visceral sensations associated with intense libidinousness, followed by enormous surprise and thwarted hopes: two pounds; worry about impending lunch with ex: one pound; shock at receiving loving gaze and arm squeeze from ex, followed by astonishment at discovery of note from man earlier pronounced *not interested*: one pound. Then there's the fact that I left nearly all of my linguine untouched on Friday.

Of course, stress is far too strong a word for what I've experienced this past week. A heightened sense of both excitement and trepidation in the face of the new freneticism that seems to have taken over my life would be more accurate. And new-found love isn't quite right either. I've felt the faintest stirrings of an old love, and the hint of something like a new crush. But the combination of all of this is pretty potent, and means I most definitely won't be needing Weight Watchers.

There's so much going on in my head and my life right now that I don't know how I'd cope with another half-dozen dating opportunities. Which is why I've been revisiting Mel's email all morning but doing nothing about it. She's sent me the names of the top three online dating sites, as recommended by people she trusts. There's one I recognise from its frequent appearance in my inbox: UsTogether.com. The two others are FindYourMatch.com and PerfectPartnership.com. I wouldn't know how to choose between them on the basis of any rational criteria, so I opt for PerfectPartnership.com because it starts with a P, and there's a certain symmetry to that.

Just before lunch I log on to Perfect Partnership and begin the lengthy registration process. I know it's probably breaking some sort of rule to use my work PC for this, but it feels safer somehow. Anyway, I plan to de-register just as soon as I've given it enough of a fair shake for Mel to be able to report on it. I've spent most of *Me*'s £1000, so I feel obligated to keep up the appearance of a Program devotee at least.

I'm stumped at the first hurdle, being unable to fill in the box marked USER NAME. You're not supposed to use your own name, for obvious reasons, so most people seem to choose pseudonyms that communicate one of three things: funny, cute, or outrageously suggestive. My branding party has left me ill equipped for this, as nothing we came up with seems suitable as a shorthand reference to me. So I fall back on an old faithful and type 'Francesca' into the box.

I then fill in all the routine boxes covering age, height, hair colour, occupation and so on, before finding myself confronted with an intimidating white space into which I am supposed to type a fifty-word summary of myself. I suppose this would be the perfect opportunity to attach a digital version of my flyer, but I don't have one and am not likely ever to create one. So I'm forced to write something from scratch. My first attempt is so dull even I am tempted to lie down while reading it. It makes something like *intellectual, catholic, dental hygienist* look appealing.

> *I'm Francesca, a thirty-seven-year-old single mother with two young children. I work in marketing, and my hobbies are cooking, horse-riding and skiing. I am fit and healthy, and enjoy working out. I also enjoy going to the theatre and eating out; my favourite foods are Japanese and Italian.*

I've taken huge license with the hobbies. The last time I skied I was twenty-eight; these days the only things I seem to cook are fish fingers and sausages, interspersed with the occasional roast for guests – I certainly don't spend my evening poring over cookery books dreaming up menu combinations – and horse-riding, while once a passion, is something I manage to do about twice a year. Anyway, who has time for hobbies when they're working and looking after two children? Surely the best people can manage is doing something they enjoy, and that can't be classified as either work or childcare, very occasionally.

Perhaps the secret is to say less. Or to underplay your qualities and accomplishments. That way you weed out all the earnest types, and the ones looking for a trophy date. I try again.

Francesca. Cleans up reasonably well. Daughter thinks am quite clever at least. No time for hobbies as have two children and job, but would one day love to spend winters skiing and summers riding horses. Would like to be accomplished cook, but daily exposure to nursery food and severe weekday time shortage have dulled once promising talents.

That's better. Anyone who responds to that will have to be halfway decent. There's not the slightest indication of attainment, and no hint of any intimate action on offer. It should serve my purposes perfectly. I enter my credit card details and press the send button with crossed fingers.

For lunch I decide to make do with a quick sandwich from Emilia's Café so that I can spend the time running errands. The most crucial one on the list is a trip to Dixons to find out why all my photos are dingy and indecipherable. I know it must be something to do with the indoor/outdoor settings, or the night-flash option, but I can't for the life of me figure out how to rectify the problem.

The helpful chap on the small digital appliances counter, who is identified by his nametag as Don, informs me that, yes, I've erroneously been taking indoor photos with the outdoor/night-time option activated. But there is more. Apparently I've got my resolution all wrong. Resolution? Yes, it needs to be at 240 rather than 125. Ahh. Would you like me to change it for you? Yes please, I'd be grateful.

As Don fiddles with the resolution he compliments me on my camera. 'This is a beaut,' he says. 'My brother has one. He lives in Canada now. Sends me the most spectacular photos of the Rockies and all that.'

'Canada? How wonderful,' I respond politely.

'Yeah. Loves it there. He used to live here, but he met this Canadian girl and that was that. Been there seven years. He met her on the internet, you know.'

All these years I've never actually known anyone who even availed themselves of internet dating sites. And now here I am, fresh from sending in my own profile, and the first person I get talking to actually knows someone for whom the internet resulted in happy ever after.

'Really?' I say. 'That's amazing. How did that work then?'

'They just got connected through one of those chatrooms, and started writing to one another. Then after about two months she invited him out there. He knew it was a big risk. I mean he'd never met her or anything, only seen a picture. But he went. Says it was the best thing he's ever done.' My new friend hands me back my adjusted camera with a small flourish and a wide smile that forces his cheeks into two pink balls that press up against his round, steel-framed glasses. 'Doesn't always work out like that, though, does it? It's a pretty risky business. I'm divorced five years, but it's certainly not something I'd want to do.'

'No. Me neither,' I say, placing the camera in my bag. 'Anyway, thanks a lot for fixing this. My photo albums would have been filled with sinister-looking pictures otherwise.'

'Pleasure. Any time. I'm always here.'

Don's words are ringing in my ears as I leave the shop. Internet dating might have worked miracles for Don's brother, but there's no denying its riskiness. It's too late to retract my registration now, but that doesn't mean I actually have to respond to any of the messages I receive. The delete button could prove to be the handiest dating tool I've yet deployed.

Anyway, who really needs internet dating sites when there are people like Don who are willing to enter into conversation over the counter of an electrical goods shop? It's seemed to me over the past few weeks that the world is full of people like that. If you were interested in a man like Don you would have no trouble engineering a date with him. All you'd have to do would be to turn up at Dixons with a faulty appliance once a week and he'd soon get the hint. Or if yours is the Starbucks type it wouldn't be difficult to meet him there. I've noticed the same bloke sitting at the window counter of the local Starbucks every morning for three weeks now as we drive to school. He's clearly got a routine, and if you adopted the same one you'd probably find yourself sharing his apple and cinnamon muffin within two weeks.

There really is no shortage of ways to meet men. But meeting a man with that magic, one you can fall in love with? That's a different matter. And all the dating sites in cyberspace can't really help with that, can they?

After work, and once the kids are in bed, I settle down on the sofa with the phone in hand to try to muster the courage to call Tom's number. I'm not sure why I'm finding it so difficult. It's only coffee after all. And I know something about him – a whole lot more than I knew about Gary when I agreed to go to dinner with him. Perhaps it's the tone of voice that's the obstruction here. Mine, that is. Am I supposed to be cheerful and light, like the friendly neighbour who's going to support him through a difficult time, offering to babysit Grace when he needs a break? Or am I to speak in the tones of someone who wouldn't mind being a romantic distraction for him as he works his way back to normality? Would I want to be that person? Surely, if I'm not the supportive neighbour there's nothing else I could be. He's not about to properly fall for someone when he's so raw from loss.

In the end I decide I'm making far too much of the whole business. I'll put to use my neutral tone. Friendly but slightly detached. Waiting to see what happens. I'm halfway through dialling his number when the phone rings in my hand.

'Hello.'

'Hello, Ally?' says a familiar woman's voice.

'Yes. It's Ally.'

'Ally, it's Angie here. From the Savoy.'

'Angie! How lovely to hear from you. How are you?'

'Well, not so great to tell you the truth. That's why I'm calling. I thought you might be able to help me sort things out. You seem to have the knack of everything.'

'I don't know about that. But I'll try. What's the matter?'

'Oh, I don't know really. It's just that I can't seem to get on with anything. I leave those seminars all fired up, but when it comes to actually doing anything I'm supposed to I just seem to clam up. I managed that baggage business, but the rest? I've done nothing.'

'Angie, you shouldn't be so hard on yourself. The pace that Marina sets is pretty challenging, and it's probably got more to do with her touring timetable than what works for her punters. I'm sure you can do things at whatever pace suits you.'

'But what if it never suits me? What if I just never manage to do anything?'

'Well that's not very likely. You spent £500. You'd never allow yourself to waste it completely. Anyway, what do you think is stopping you?'

There's a heavy pause before Angie responds. 'I'm terrified. Terrified of making a fool of myself. Terrified of calling people up for those stupid duck thingies and having them turn me down. Terrified of asking people what they think I need to change in case they say everything. And I just keep thinking: maybe things are fine the way they are. Why mess them up?'

Whoa. There's a lot of unburied baggage here. 'Angie, I completely understand why you're afraid of all these things. Were they on that list you buried?'

'No. I didn't know about all this then. The biggest thing on the list was something my husband always used to tell me. About me being, you know, not particularly adventurous.'

I think I know the kind of adventure she means. 'Well, adventurous isn't all it's cracked up to be. But the thing is, Angie, if all this fear is what's really holding you back – fear of change, fear of rejection – maybe you need to write down all these things you're afraid of, on a new list, and bury them in a really deep hole. And then maybe you should write yourself another list, with all the good things that could come out of this. And keep that one on your fridge or in your handbag. Take it out whenever you have to do something, just to remind yourself.'

'That's a good idea,' she says. I can hear her mulling it over.

'So, what do you think might go on your good list?' I ask, wary of allowing any conversational lulls to serve as the wellsprings of new fears. 'Companionship? Someone to make you cups of tea in bed? Someone to kiss the tips of your fingers? Someone to take the rubbish out?'

'I'm not sure really. All of that sounds pretty good!'

'Well, if nothing specific comes to mind, maybe it's a feeling you need to keep in mind. You know what I would do? I would imagine your favourite romantic scene in your favourite movie, and just describe it on a piece of paper. And every time you feel you can't do something, read that piece of paper and remember all the things you love about that scene, how it makes you feel, what it makes you wish about your own life. Maybe that will help. Because you've got to have something fabulous worth shooting for.'

'*An Officer and a Gentleman*!' she says instantly. 'That scene where he rides up on his bike and walks into the factory and carries her out. Then when she's in his arms she takes his hat off and puts it on her head. Remember that?'

'There. You see! That will be you. You've just got to hold that picture in your mind? It'll make all this nonsense worthwhile.'

'But that could never be me. Richard Gere isn't going

to ride up and swoop me away from the construction office.'

'No, but your own Richard Gere is. For God's sake, Deborah Whatshername worked in a factory where she probably had to wear one of those hairnet things all day. You sitting in one of your lovely sweaters with your charming telephone manner is five-star glamour compared to that.'

Angie laughs. 'You think?'

'Of course. Now, when you hang up the phone, I want you to write down all those fears you told me about and put them in a box and bury them outside. Spit on the list as you put it inside the box, just for good measure. Then I want you to go straight out and rent *An Officer and a Gentleman*, and watch your favourite scenes until they're imprinted on your memory. Then tomorrow try just doing one thing differently. Maybe make one call to someone who might be a duck candidate, or to someone who might know a good duck. That's all. Will you do that?'

'If you say so,' she says, laughing again. 'Thank you so much for talking to me, Ally. It's really helped.'

'Pleasure. I know just how you feel, I really do. We're all a bit terrified. And for what it's worth, I think you can skip the packaging party. I think you're great just the way you are. You're pretty, and warm, and full of life. What more could a man ask for?'

I didn't mean to be an inspiration, but what else could I do?

Chapter 31
Perfect Partnership

If I'd known what happens when you register with an online dating site I'd never have complained about all the Viagra messages in my inbox every morning. The sex-enhancement industry has nothing on the dating industry. When I log on to PerfectPartnership and open my personalised mailbox I have one hundred and fifty messages. I feel like Bruce Almighty confronted with prayer overload.

The messages are from people like Keen in Kedleston and Hot Sauce, as well as plain old Barry and Len. I can't face opening all of them, or indeed any of them, and only go to Barry's out of some peculiar combination of curiosity and dread. His message is titled *I'm a horse lover too*, and he says:

Dear Francesca, I so loved reading your introduction yesterday. I'm a horse lover and a skier too. Both give me such a sense of freedom. Perhaps that's why you love them too. You sound like a woman with a free and loving spirit. I would love to get to know you better. We could soar together. Tell me more.

From a fellow free spirit, Barry.

If free spirit was what my introductory paragraph communicated there must be some sort of dating site equivalent of Morse code I'm not aware of. I thought I was painting a picture of a mildly harassed but quite nice semi-suburban mum. I thought I was managing expectations in the interest of keeping the responses to a reasonable number. Instead, I appear to have conceived an image redolent of Daryl Hannah in *Splash*. When I go to Hot Sauce's message I realise the image must also contain elements of Sharon Stone in *Basic Instinct*.

The idea of you on a horse makes me hot. No time to cook? I'll cook for you. I promise not to disappoint. I always cook with lots of sauce.
Awaiting an invitation to dine.

Hot Sauce

Knowing that Mel will delight in seeing the results of my first and last dating site adventure, I copy and send the two messages to her. Then, terrified that Nicki or Anna Wyatt will suddenly appear at my desk, I delete them both.

I'm about to click on the next one hundred and forty-eight messages and avail myself of the *delete all* function, when something catches my eye. It's a message from someone called *M*, titled simply *Hello*.

Hello Francesca,

I'm also raising a child on my own, since my wife died. Not easy is it? Not easy to forget what you shared with your spouse either. But someone told me it's time to start moving on, so that's what I'm doing. Yours is the first message I've seen that made me think 'there's a real person, someone I could talk to'. Thought I would let you know that. Good luck.

M

No invitation to ride naked and bareback with my hair blowing freely in the wind. No offer to smother my body in hot sauce. No invitation of any kind, in fact. How clever. How mysterious. I decide to keep this one for a while. The rest have to go, and quickly.

Seeing M's message reminds me that I never called Tom. By the time I got off the phone with Angie I'd lost all vestiges of the courage I'd had, as if I'd poured all of it into Angie without first checking that I'd sufficient reserves of it for myself.

The humming third floor of Cottage Garden Foods is no place to make a call like this so I go in search of a cappuccino with my mobile in hand. Once outside the building I find a seat on the wall surrounding the small courtyard fountain, and dial Tom's number. It's ten a.m., so Grace should be at nursery, and he should be . . . doing what? I have no idea what he does. I just hope it has nothing to do with exotic dancers.

'Hello, Tom here.'

'Tom,' I say in a strangled voice. 'It's Ally. From the park. And from Waitrose.' For God's sake. He doesn't need a rundown of the local amenities.

'Hi, Ally. Thanks for calling. I wasn't sure you would. It was a bit weird leaving a note, but I wasn't sure how else to get hold of you.'

Gosh, he really is so warm and unaffected. No sign of any posing or game playing.

'Well, you could always have tried knocking me to the ground again,' I say.

'That's true. I'll remember that. Anyway, what do you think? Would you like to have coffee, or maybe grab a bite one evening. It would be really nice to have a friend in the neighbourhood.'

A friend in the neighbourhood. At least that makes things clearer.

'That would be lovely,' I say. 'When were you thinking?'

'Oh, anytime really. What about Friday morning. Are you working?'

'No. No I'm not. I have most Fridays off. Lets meet at Suzette's, across from Starbucks. Coffee's nicer there and it's less frenetic.'

'Great. About ten then?'

'Ten's good. See you then.'

I don't get up from the wall immediately, but sit staring at the mobile in my hands. Right at this moment I'm feeling a little like Angie, paralysed by fear. Only, unlike her, I can't really articulate the cause of my fear. Am I afraid I'll fall for Tom and he won't be interested in anything more than a coffee mate? Or, is it the thought of getting involved with someone whose heart is bound to be shrouded in grief that's worrying me? Or maybe my fear has nothing to do with Tom at all.

I manage to snap myself out of my confused meditation to go in search of coffee when the phone rings. David's name pops up in the window.

'Hi, David.'

'Hi, have I caught you at a bad time?' he says.

'No. It's fine. I'm just doing a coffee run,' I say. 'What's up? Have you got a problem this weekend?'

'No, not exactly. Not a problem. It's just that I was thinking of taking Jack and Millie down to the coast, and wondered if you'd like to go with us.'

Would I like to go away for the weekend with my ex-husband and our children? To the coast? Is he mad?

'Why?' is the best I can manage.

'Why? Because it would be nice, don't you think? The kids would love it.'

'No, David. Why? Why now? What is going on?'

There is a pause, perhaps while David tries to understand why, why now, what is going on.

'Ally, I just suddenly wanted to do this. I miss you. I miss what we had. I just want you to go to the coast with us. Is that so bad?'

If Sunday's arm squeeze had dredged up a visceral reaction I'd thought cleverly extirpated, these words of David's are enough to knock me backwards. In fact they do. I wobble precariously as I try to sit down on the wall surrounding the fountain and its pool full of copper.

'David, I don't know. I just don't know.'

'Come on, Al. What harm could it do?'

A lot.

'All right. OK.'

It's true. I really am spineless. I can't say no to the theatre with a man I'm not attracted to, and I can't say no to a weekend with a man I shouldn't be attracted to. I can see nothing but trouble four days ahead, but I'm powerless to prevent myself from hurtling towards it. What is that thing they say about Elizabeth Taylor? That her eighth marriage represented the triumph of optimism over experience? Yes, quite.

At the end of the day I'm exhausted. Exhausted not, as I ought to be, by worries over the impending Seville Sunset launch, or the fact that the Pure Gold numbers are atrocious. Exhausted by thinking about David's call, over and over again. And by the constant deletion of messages from my PerfectPartnership inbox. I'm wading through the last of them, vowing never to use the internet again, when Lisa pops up at my side.

'Hi,' she says. The fact that she is whispering is a dead giveaway she's not about to fill me in on the launch plans for the new redcurrant and onion chutney.

'Hi,' I whisper back, trying not to sound selfishly preoccupied by my own affairs, which I can see now are spiralling out of control.

'You'll never guess what,' she says.

I won't, of course. Who would ever guess that within two weeks of breaking up with her long-term boyfriend, Lisa has met the love of her life? Who would ever guess that she would meet him while sitting at home, or, worse, in her mother's home, sipping Earl Grey tea? At home, which is a fucking four-letter word where you're never going to meet anyone? Who would ever have predicted that Lisa, who summarily dismissed the idea of using marketing techniques to snag a man, would end up snagging one she adores, while the person using all the smart techniques nearly drowns in a sea of emails from cybersex wannabes before catapulting herself into the abyss of a no-hope dalliance with her ex-husband and an equally fruitless role as one-woman support group for a recent widower.

And my brother says I'm the kind of person who could always get what she wanted.

Chapter 32
Decision

Lisa has known Matthew for much of her life. He is, quite literally, the boy next door. His family and her family used to do Sunday lunches and wet country weekends together when Lisa was small, and as the children grew up they would bump into each other at sixteenth and eighteenth birthday parties. Then Matthew went away to university, several gap years, and a stint working in New York, and Lisa was forced to forget about him. She would hear of him very occasionally through her mother, and once came close to bumping into him when he dropped in on her parents the night before their annual Guy Fawkes party.

Then, two weekends ago, fresh from acquiring a stinking hangover at my house, Lisa is sitting in her parents' farm-house kitchen near Petworth, no doubt preparing to douse wounds still raw from her break-up with Mike in a healthy dose of maternal sympathy and home cooking, when her mother announces that Matthew called during the week and will be dropping by for tea. At the time, which is noon, Lisa is sitting in her oldest jeans and shirt with unwashed hair, feeling grey and looking green. But with three hours' warning she manages to summon some colour into her cheeks and some shine to her hair. Matthew comes for tea, and stays for dinner and the night. Lisa's old room is across the hall from the guest room where Matthew is sleeping, which makes it remarkably easy to consummate the escalating fancy-fest in which the two of them have been engaged throughout tea, supper and two excruciating hours of Scrabble with Lisa's parents.

The next day, like teenagers carrying on under the gaze of disapproving parents, they find themselves surreptitiously holding hands under the tablecloth or sneaking kisses behind the hedgerow. Lisa's parents are apparently mildly curious as to why Matthew has stayed Saturday night and now all of Sunday, but they're happy to have him there, and seem to buy the story of the call on his mobile cancelling the lunch he was supposed to attend in London. When Sunday evening arrives, the two new lovers decide to take the train up to London together, no doubt inflicting their newly discovered passion upon every other person unfortunate enough to have booked themselves on to the six ten from Petworth to Waterloo.

This is the full version of the story Lisa began telling me late Tuesday afternoon. It's not actually that different from the version she told me the first time, but infatuation seems to have addled her brain so she's having trouble remembering which bits she's told me before. Or perhaps it's just that she gets pleasure from recounting the details, again and again, as if it's a way of living through what was clearly a seminal twenty-four hours.

'And you don't think your parents suspected anything?' I ask dubiously.

'Well, they might have by the end. But my mother is remarkably insensitive to stuff like that. She's far too busy worrying about things like fertilising the back paddock, or winning at Scrabble. Which she did, of course. I was putting down all kinds of low-point nonsense because I couldn't concentrate.'

'But they know now, surely?'

'No, not really. We've been up here the whole time. And, to be honest, we've been together so much I've not had much chance to talk to anyone. Did you notice I wasn't here for three days of last week?'

This is the second time in two weeks that I've heard about two people being so head-over-heels in love that they can't prise themselves apart for a single evening. I'm getting rather tired of it. Now that I think about it, I didn't see much of Lisa last week, but I must have been so preoccupied with my own dilemmas that I failed to investigate why.

'You're right. I did wonder.'

'Just couldn't face it. So I took three days' holiday. There wasn't much going on, so no one seemed to mind. And it was worth it.'

I really don't want to know why it was worth it. Last week I might have been in the mood to hear every last detail, but this week I'm feeling rather fragile.

'Anyway, what about you? How are things?' asks Lisa,

making a futile attempt to suppress the joyous glow radiating from her every pore for a minute or two.

It's lunchtime on Wednesday and we are sitting over two bowls of tomato pasta in Papa Ciccia's. It's as good a place as any to sound Lisa out on my dilemma, I suppose. I'm not sure she'll be able to conjure up the required empathy from the midst of her understandable self-absorption, but it's worth a try.

'You know, since that Friday night you were at my house, a lot has happened.'

'Really, like what?'

'Well, to cut a long story short, David came over for lunch, looked at me in a funny way, then asked me to go away with him and the kids this weekend. That's the main thing. I said yes but I don't know if I should go. Then there's this guy I've been sort of bumping into all over the place. I didn't think he was interested, but he's asked me to meet him on Friday. I don't know if he wants to be friends, or if he's interested in something else.'

'Slow down. That's a lot all at once. Let's do the David thing first. Why does he want you to go?'

'That's just it. I'm not really sure. He said he misses what we had. But I don't know.'

'Of course he misses what you had! He fucked it up royally!'

'I know he did. But what if he's being genuine? What if he's learned a lesson and really wants to try again? Don't I owe it to the kids to try?'

'Or, what if he's not learned his lesson but he's just feeling nostalgic and horny. What if he quite fancies a little comfort love to soothe him through his post-Charmaine phase?'

'Chantal. It's Chantal,' I say defensively.

'Whatever. What if it's that, Ally? You have to consider that, because it's a possibility, and you do not want to go there.'

'I don't think even David is selfish enough to enter into something for those reasons if he doesn't think there's a reasonable chance there's something in it. He wouldn't do that to the children.'

'Wouldn't he? Maybe he's not thinking as clearly as you. You always said he was a romantic.'

It's funny how Lisa can be so brutally analytical about other people's personal quandaries when she's always been so feeble about her own. Now her assertions have the added authority afforded by her apparent conviction that she is party to the inception of the perfect relationship.

I don't know what to say to Lisa, so I start twisting another forkful of pasta round in my spoon and say nothing. She's probably right. I know that. But if there's the slightest chance she's wrong, don't I owe it to myself and to Jack and Millie to find out?

I never got to hear Lisa's opinion on the Tom dilemma. That's all right. As dilemmas go, it's not yet much of one. But David and the weekend, that's a dilemma to be reckoned with. I've said I'll go, but there are two days remaining in which I can change my mind.

The person I really want to ask about it is Millie. I'm not about to ask her if she thinks David might just be feeling nostalgic and horny, but I'd love to know how she might perceive the whole idea of us all going away together. But tonight may not be the ideal time to bring it up, as she's overcome with emotion at the idea of a mid-week sleepover. Her friend Charlotte from two streets over is coming to stay the night while her parents travel to Bath for some sort of overnight business event. Millie is beside herself with preparations. We've already made up a bed on the floor beside Millie's and she's now surrounding it with cuddly toys to make Charlotte feel at home.

On second thought, perhaps with Millie so preoccupied and happy, now could be the perfect time to mention the weekend.

'Millie, has Daddy mentioned that he's taking you away to the seaside this weekend?'

'Yes. He told me last week,' she says, lovingly placing her Angelina Ballerina on the pillow.

'And did he mention that I might go with you?'

'No,' she says, looking up at me.

'Oh. Well, I was thinking of perhaps going with you. I love the seaside and it seems a shame for you all to enjoy it without me. What would you think about that?'

Millie sits back on her heels and thinks. 'Where would we all sleep?' She's smart, this one. Gets straight to the heart of matters.

'I think you and Jack would share a room, Daddy would have a room, and I would have another room.'

Then another question that perforates the protective ambiguity I'm trying to maintain. 'Does that mean you and Daddy are getting back together?'

'No, honey. It doesn't mean that. It means that Daddy and I are friends, and we both love spending time with you and Jack, so sometimes we might spend it together. Like when we had lunch last weekend. Does that make sense?'

Millie looks disappointed. When do they stop hoping for reconciliation, I wonder. Someone once told me that her son didn't stop asking if she and her ex-husband would get back together until he was fifteen and her ex had a baby with his new wife. I blame the wretched *Parent Trap*.

'What do you think, Millie? Would you like me to go or would you prefer me to stay home and you go with Daddy.'

'I think you should go too,' she says. 'We'll all have a nice time.' At this moment the expression in her eyes seems more like that of a sage old woman than a seven-year-old girl.

'OK then. I'll go with you.' I kiss the top of her head and leave her there, making a space for Brown Bear between Angelina and Pooh.

Chapter 33
Coffee

It's funny how things that loom large in your life at a particular moment can seem inconsequential in retrospect. The first time you ever have to stand up in front of fifty people and give a coherent speech you think you're going to collapse into the overhead projector before you've managed to utter three sentences. Five years and several dozen speaking engagements later, you really can't recall what all the fuss was about. Even the horrors of childbirth are thus glossed over. You can quite happily describe them in clinical fashion to the newly pregnant woman who asks 'what's it really like?' but, in all honesty, you can't really remember what they feel like.

I'm not even looking back on Friday yet but already it's lost the air of importance I'd attached to it earlier in the week. Preparations – mental and otherwise – for the weekend with David and the children have dwarfed any sense of trepidation I might have had about the coffee with Tom. Compared to the possibilities represented by a weekend away with my ex-husband, a cappuccino with an attractive neighbourhood friend who may or may not be interested in me now seems almost a trifling event.

All the same, there's a swirling sensation in my stomach when I see Tom sitting at a small round table in the far corner of Suzette's, just in front of the speciality cake display. At first I don't recognize him, then I realise he's cut his hair. Very short, into one of those cuts that sticks artfully up and out in all kinds of places. Gone are the longish dirty-blond wisps that fell over his eyes in the wind, which is something of a disappointment.

He doesn't see me approach the table, but looks up from a pad he's scribbling on just as I sit down.

'Oh God. Sorry. I was so preoccupied I didn't see you come in,' he apologises, immediately turning his pad face down on the table and placing his coffee cup on top of it. 'Can I get you a coffee?'

'That would be great. A skinny cappuccino please.'

Tom goes up to the counter to order my coffee. He is shooed away by the woman behind the counter, who is obviously going to bring my coffee when it's ready. Within thirty seconds, Tom is back sitting in front of me.

We go through the ritual *how are yous* and *fine thank yous*, which at this stage mean absolutely nothing to either of us, we've so little knowledge of what might be going on in each other's lives that might make them fine or otherwise. Then I point to the pad under Tom's cup.

'What's that you were working on?' I ask. The question's a bit prying but I'm not in the mood for a morning full of inanities.

'Oh, just some ideas for a script that's giving me some trouble.'

'A script? Is that what you do?'

'Yeah. Most of the time. I've not done much for a year because of Grace, and everything, but I'm trying to get back into it. Once you get out of the flow it's quite hard.'

'That's fascinating,' I say. 'What kinds of things do you normally do?'

'TV stuff mostly. A real mix. Do you remember that comedy-drama series *Little Feet*? That was mine. And I did a police drama the year before. They love us Americans over here – so long as we know which rules to follow and which ones to break.'

'Hmm. Makes my job look a little dull,' I joke.

'And what is that?' he says, leaning forward and smiling.

'Marmalade. I market marmalade.'

'No kidding? Well what's so dull about that? The world needs good marmalade,' he says, still smiling.

'Anyway,' I say, anxious to steer the conversation away from marmalade this time. Somehow it seems such a trivial topic when I know there are others we need to get out of the way. 'How long have you and Grace lived around here?'

'For three years. Jenny – she was my wife – and I moved here from Fulham just before Grace was born. You think that after you lose someone you're going to want to run away to a new life, to get away from all the things that remind you of them, but it wasn't like that for me. I wanted to stay where it felt like home, especially for Grace. I was so lonely for a while that if I hadn't been able to walk past the same familiar buildings I might have lost it.'

'It must have been awful for you,' I say. 'How did she die?'

'Lymphoma. She was gone in six months, so we didn't really have much time. She was thirty-three.'

His grey-green eyes are looking directly into mine. I return his gaze and smile sympathetically. Then we sit for a moment or two and don't say anything. I realise, to my surprise, that this feels perfectly natural. There's no awkwardness this time, and no need to bury the silence in platitudes. When I do speak it is not out of any panic-induced desire to fill the space, but because I want to know more.

'And how have you coped, with Grace and work and everything? Do you have help?'

'Sure,' he says. 'My parents live in Maryland, but Jenny's parents have been good. And her sister tries hard, but she lives in Norwich so it's not easy for her to be practically helpful. But I can't complain. Anyway, I just have to get on with it really. I'm lucky I've a job that I can do from home a lot. Now I just have to produce something for the first time in a year before I go bankrupt!' There's a pause before he says, 'Anyway, tell me about you. Marmalade can't be all there is to you. All I know is that you and your husband aren't together. Jack told me that in the park.'

'Children are useful, aren't they? Say all the things we'd rather not. It's true. David and I are divorced.'

'Is that difficult?'

What I can't quite fathom is how Tom and I have leaped

past niceties like where did you go to school and how did you become a scriptwriter, or even how long have you been divorced, and straight to 'is that difficult?'. But, like the silence a few moments ago, it feels perfectly natural. In fact, there hardly seems any point in any other sort of discourse.

'It was very difficult. Less so now, but still not easy.' Now there's an understatement. 'I can't compare it to losing someone to an illness, but it is a form of death I suppose. The death of the life you had together, and the life you hoped for. Does that sound too sentimental?'

'Not at all,' he says. 'Sentimental's good.' There's that smile again. Wide and warm. Like maple syrup as it oozes across a pancake.

'But I think we're getting there. The children have adjusted, in the best way they can, and David and I seem to be embarking on a new phase of our divorce that looks a little like friendship.' These last words stick to the roof of my mouth, and I take a sip from my coffee to disguise a deceit I feel must be apparent to everyone in Suzette's.

'Kids are amazing, aren't they? You're so afraid they'll break when awful things happen, but they seem to find things to hang on to. I'm not saying Grace hasn't suffered, because she has. And I'm sure there's plenty more of that in store. But they have this way of surviving on a day-to-day level. Don't you think?'

'You're right,' I say. Then we engage in one of our comfortable silences. The silence is so comfortable that it emboldens me.

'Tom, can I ask you a question? Why did you ask me to meet you here?'

'Honestly?'

'Honestly.' I'm preparing myself for an answer about friends in the neighbourhood, and people you can talk to. But I know now the answer I want.

'I thought there was this connection. Each time I saw you it got stronger. So I thought what the hell.'

'What, even over the Waitrose trolleys?' I say with attempted jocularity.

'Especially over the Waitrose trolleys. That was the worst. I ran from that one. Part of me thinks I can't be doing this.'

Yes, I know. Part of me thinks I can't be doing this either.

'Anyway,' he goes on. 'Tell me if I'm wrong. I can take it. I've been through a hell of a lot worse.'

At five o'clock this evening I will be driving to the coast with my ex-husband and our two children, towards what I'm not entirely sure. We could find ourselves making mature, platonic sandcastles on the beach, or dipping our toes into dangerous waters I'll regret having ventured towards. But Tom's not wrong.

'No, you're not wrong,' I say.

Chapter 34
Dangerous Waters

Tom and I made arrangements to see one another on Monday evening. He first suggested Saturday, to which I mumbled something about taking the kids to see my parents. Then he suggested Tuesday, to which I replied that I had a dinner with a couple of key retailers. I didn't like having to perjure myself so early on but coming clean about the impending weekend away with my ex-husband followed by a seminar with a relationship guru would have surely strangled the tiny stems of the relationship that we're nurturing here. So we settle on Monday evening. A movie and dinner.

I spent most of the rest of Friday washing and packing. In between washing and packing I managed to run off a rather desperate note to the mothers of Millie's class, pleading with them to support the jam jar effort and apologising for the horribly short notice. After distributing the note (rather sheepishly) in the schoolyard, I whisked Jack and Millie back home for a quick snack before David arrived.

Jack has been apoplectic with excitement. He was adamant that he was going to wear his wetsuit in the car, and it was only the prospect of being unable to wee at the side of the road that made him opt for jeans in the end. But he remained insistent on keeping the wetsuit close to hand, so it now sits on top of his suitcase, waiting to be packed into the car.

We are taking my car because it's bigger than David's. So David, who never has been very good at public transport, arrives by taxi. He seems uneasy as we load the bags into the car. Either he's preoccupied by work or he's regretting having suggested this little excursion. Who am I kidding? It's not a little excursion at all. Looking at it now from my stance behind a boot heaving with bags and fishing nets, I can see that it's a journey of monumental consequences.

Cornwall was always a favoured destination for us, but it's too far for a two-day trip so we're headed for Barton-on-Sea, which is just a two-hour drive taking us through the pony-filled moors of the New Forest. It feels mightily strange to find myself in the driver's seat next to David again, and even odder to hear us all playing I-spy on the M3. I'm not a huge fan of car games, preferring those moments when each passenger sinks into their own private reverie or gets absorbed by their book tape and stares out of the window. After about forty-five minutes on the road, it's something of a relief when Jack announces that he's had enough of counting red cars and puts on his earphones.

Millie and Jack are snapped out of their daydreams when we spot the first foal nibbling grass at the side of the road, with its mother standing protectively behind it. It is a dazzling sight, I have to admit. Wild ponies dotting the heather-sheathed moors in the fading sunlight of early spring.

'Mummy, look at that one. She has two babies!' Millie is overcome by awe.

'And over there, behind the tree, I can see another one!' shouts Jack.

Then follow the inevitable questions about why we can't take one home with us if, after all, they don't belong to anyone. Could we not put them up at the end of the garden, or, if that isn't big enough, at the end of Mrs Jackson's garden, which is a corner plot and therefore much larger? We could take them to the park for walks, and tie them to the poles of the climbing frame when they need to eat grass, offers Jack helpfully.

We are still talking about the possibilities of keeping ponies on Rosemere Road as we pull into the hotel car park. The hotel is a small, family-run enterprise that David discovered through a friend (which friend I don't want to know). Its white paint is cracked and flaking in places, and the wisteria adorning its front has a slightly bedraggled air, but it is sweet. Perfect for a weekend with the kids; anything grander would only have resulted in forty-eight hours' worth of precautionary admonishments for Jack.

David unloads the bags while I register our arrival with the owners, a Mr and Mrs Jessop. It's immediately clear that Mrs Jessop runs the show; Mr Jessop seems to hover ineffectually like Basil Fawlty, then knocks over the full umbrella stand with one of our bags. Mrs Jessop ushers in the first of what I anticipate to be a great many awkward moments when she says 'My what a lovely family you are' immediately after handing me and David the keys to our separate rooms. She seems far too nice to be fishing for dirt, but I can tell she's bemused by the setup.

The doors to our rooms are in a little triangle in one wing of the seventeen-room building. It takes us a little while to get settled in, partly because Jack and Millie insist on exploring every inch of the three rooms as they unpack, and on counting the little tablets of Toblerone and packets of shortbread biscuits in the baskets on top of the televisions. So we make it to the dining room just minutes before the kitchen closes. Jack and Millie aren't clamouring for food, which probably has something to do with the two large bags of crisps and the family-sized packet of wine gums that were consumed on the journey. I'm not that hungry either, but I'm glad of the ritual of the meal, which will help mask my opening-night nerves.

At this late hour, the chef is apparently unwilling to prepare any of the more interesting items on the menu but is happy to whisk us up four omelettes with chips and a tomato salad. That's good enough for all of us. Jack will only pick at his food in any case, and both of them will be drooping before long.

We don't talk about much of anything except the weekend plans, which we decide will include several trips to the beach, a visit to Highcliffe Castle and an outing to the motor museum at Beaulieu. Jack is particularly keen on the motor museum idea, but the castle also has its appeal, there being the distinct possibility that he will encounter a real live knight in the grounds.

All the while, David and I are operating like acquaintances, all our warmth and intimacy being directed at the children, mere politeness reserved for our own interchanges. There is no sign of a look like the one exchanged in the middle of *Chitty Chitty Bang Bang*, and no repeat of the arm squeeze. Still, as the meal progresses I feel more comfortable than uncomfortable, which is saying something after two years in which we've hardly been in the same room together. A strange sort of fatalism about the weekend seems to overtake me round about ice-cream time. A very Doris Day-ish *que sera sera*.

Here's what it is: I realise I'm not desperate. I'm not desperate for him to love me, like I was when he first left and at so many moments after that. I'm not desperate for him to touch me again, or for him not to. I feel, at this moment, and with an undoubtedly false sense of self-assurance, that I could probably survive almost any of these eventualities. I don't know if this comes from two years of working at becoming whole again, or the far simpler fact of Tom.

Before long we are all ready for bed. Millie and Jack have a short squabble about who's going to sleep on which side of the bed, but their hearts aren't really in it so it is quickly resolved. I tuck them up into the lumpy double bed, pulling the faded orange flowered eiderdown up to their chins, and reassure them that both David and I will be sleeping right next door with our doors unlocked. We kiss them goodnight, then find ourselves standing outside their room, each of us gripping the handle of the door to our own room ready to escape the impending tricky moment with grace.

'Night then,' he says.

'Night. See you in the morning.' I smile.

And that is that.

You wouldn't expect perfect weather on an English beach in late March, and we don't get it. We sit huddled over our enormous sandcastle, David and I turning our faces greedily towards the sun every time a ray sneaks through the cloud cover. When it does, you'd swear it was mid July in the Riviera. Then it's gone again, leaving us shivering in its wake. The sporadic bursts of light rain just add to the variety.

This morning there was none of this fickleness, just drizzle and grey skies. So we opted to visit Highcliffe Castle and hoped for better weather in the afternoon. The brochure described the attraction as 'the most important remaining example of Romantic and Picturesque architecture', which got David's juices flowing. Unfortunately, years of under-investment under council ownership and the rows of bungalows that have been allowed to creep up to the castle walls have robbed the once great building of much of its allure. We lasted less than an hour, much of which was spent with Jack shouting 'Knight Stuart, I know you're here somewhere', every time he turned a corner.

Still, the castle's romantic style furnishes plenty of inspiration for the afternoon's sandcastle construction effort. Millie carves lace-like detail into the sides of one tower with a stick, while Jack, suitably clad in his wetsuit, attempts to fill the moat. David's job is overall design, mine the collection of multicoloured rocks to sit atop the walls.

At no point during the afternoon am I completely convinced that David will end up in my bed. Not as we kneel side by side placing rocks on turrets under Millie's considered direction; not when we all sit huddled under an umbrella with our picnic, waiting for a particularly forceful shower to pass; not during our pathetic attempt at family rounders. Not even when the children are in bed and David suggests a late-evening stroll in the hotel grounds, during which he confesses to have tired of finding himself with women like Chantal.

I don't know it until a few minutes after we've said our goodnights and I open the door of my room to find David leaning against the doorframe, his grey T-shirt having worked its way loose from the top of his jeans. He just stares at me without smiling or speaking. Then he reaches out and pulls me towards him, and gives me the gentlest of kisses on the tip of my nose.

Well, would you be able to resist that?

I'd love to say that we fall asleep in each other's arms, but I hardly sleep a wink, so conscious am I of needing to get David safely back into his room before the children wake up. But he does sleep, and I watch him. When he is facing away from me I study his hair, still thick and wavy, but shorter than it used to be. And his shoulders, broad and smooth skinned, and glowing slightly in the narrow stream of moonlight that has slipped in through a gap in the curtains. When he is facing me I contemplate the rhythm of his chest, and the movement of his eyes under his lids.

And that flimsy sense of calm and self-possession I'd felt the previous evening vanishes. I think, with astonishment, how easy it would be to slip back into loving him. How easy to let him back into my life.

And what a waste of time digging that hole under the camellia bush turned out to be.

Chapter 35
Straddling Two Horses

'You're straddling two horses and you're in danger of doing the splits,' admonished Clara when I told her. Mel was less condemning. 'Hell of a result if you ask me,' she said. The journalist in her probably revels in the twist it could add to her story.

Me, I'm in something of a state, and have been from the minute David's lips made contact with my nose. It's all been quite well disguised, since I was forced to camouflage my inner turmoil in the outer garb of parental contentment through a visit to the motor museum, a pub lunch and a three-hour car journey on Sunday. I felt a little like Lisa, carrying on under her parents' noses. Only the carrying-on has been mostly in my head; David and I were the model of discretion, only allowing ourselves one kiss behind a nineteenth-century tram and the gentle brushing of our fingers as we passed the road map between us in the car. When we arrived home he didn't even come inside, I think for fear that the bed just upstairs would prove to be a temptation neither of us would have the resolve to resist. And we absolutely can't go there. Not yet.

On Monday night, as I waited for Tom to arrive, I alternated between bemusement and self-condemnation. Because I wanted to see Tom. I really did. But I wondered how that could possibly be, when in the back of my mind, even as I was helping Millie with the last of her long division, I was thinking of David. The way he looked before he came into my room, his eyes hinting at the thing that was to follow. And the thing that followed.

I take some comfort from the fact that I stopped thinking about David the minute Tom turned up. I'm not sure what that says about me, but it must be something positive. If I can forget about David for four hours and experience a rush of adrenalin when my arm accidentally brushes against someone else's in the cinema then surely all is not lost. It means I'm not about to jettison more than two years of self-affirming recovery to risk everything again for a man who loves women. At least not with undue haste.

There's nothing not to like about Tom. Even his haircut has grown on me. The thing I like best about him is the total absence of any coy evasiveness, any macho posturing. A kind of unequivocal quality. This isn't dull, but challenging. Because it makes you wonder how anyone could ever live up to that level of ingenuousness.

Just as you have leg men and bottom men, you have smile women. And I'm one of them. Someone's smile can turn me off in an instant or reel me in like an angler with a tug on his line. David's smile is confident and sexy, and has always been hard for me to resist. Mr Electric Bollocks has a naughty, twinkling smile that he has no problem living up to, I can now see. Tom's smile is not like either of these. It's warm and intense, and you get the feeling there's a lot behind it.

After a whole evening being smiled at by Tom I'm not sure of much except that I want more of it. Even if I am intimidated by the memory of his wife – a GP of all things, and a good mother. I asked to see her picture just to get the whole thing out of the way, and she was exactly as I'd imagined her. Dark hair, an unaffected face, pretty but not made up. I felt reassured by the dark hair. At least he's not doing a Boris Becker or a Rod Stewart, looking for an exact replica of the one that got away.

We didn't talk about Jenny all evening. In fact, we didn't talk about her for more than a few minutes, and only at my instigation. The rest of the time we talked about me and the kids, about why I left Chanel and how he got into scriptwriting. (We rather gloss over the whole topic of David, my not being in the ideal position to talk about how I've put him behind me.) And we laugh. Because behind Tom's intense smile is a quietly wicked sense of humour that takes you by surprise every time.

Our first kiss was tentative. Both of us were holding back, so there was nothing greedy about it. I guess you would say it was a kiss that grew on us. When our lips parted he looked down at me and smiled shyly, and I reached up and traced that captivating crease in his cheek with my finger.

So I came home from Barton-on-Sea in a mess, and I'm still in a mess. Having canvassed opinions from Clara and Mel, I'm not really any the wiser as to what I should do now. The thought of adding further confusion to the pot by taking on the last of Marina's tasks at tonight's seminar fills me with dismay. I'm in serious need of some good advice, not another list of things to do.

I haven't used a chatroom for myself since I turned to mumsworld to reassure myself that I wasn't some sort of failure as a mother just because I would rather stand and roll two dozen rum babas or clean out the oven than sit on the floor for hours at a time playing games with my small children. I'm not sure it's right to turn to one now, except that I just don't know anyone else who could answer the questions I want the answers to. I don't know any widowers besides Tom, and I can't ask him.

Dear M,

Thanks for replying to my posting. Yours was the first reply I had that made me think 'this person is human'. I also thought, this person is friendly, and probably wouldn't mind dishing out some advice, human to human. Would you mind that? Even if it meant there was nothing in it for you?

Yours truly,

Francesca

Dear Francesca,

A lot of people have given me a lot of advice over the past year, and I've been desperately grateful for some of it.

How could I deprive you of same? In any case, I'm not sure I want there to be anything in it for me. Remember, I was put up to this.

Yours truly,

M

Dear M,

Here's the situation. Am divorced, but ex is making amorous advances. That's one issue. You probably can't help with that one. Other issue is that have met lovely man who lost his wife last year. He says we have a connection. Is that possible? Or am I in danger of being used as human tissue for tears?

Gratefully,

F

Dear F

Did lovely man love his wife?

M

Dear M,

Haven't asked him that directly, but general impression is yes. General impression is of lovely sensitive man who did all right things and suffered from very bad luck. Question is: can a man who loved someone wholeheartedly ever really love someone else that way?

Ever faithfully,

F

Dear F,

Do you know what people say to their first child when they have the second? They say that our hearts expand when we have another child. That we have more love to give. I'm hoping it's the same with spouses. Just because we loved someone and they die, or we divorced them, doesn't mean we've less love to give someone else. And loving the new person doesn't mean we're being disloyal to the old one. Can you imagine thinking that loving your second child meant that you loved your first one less? Impossible, right? Perhaps that's the answer. Sure hope so.

Fondly,

M

Dear M,

Food for thought. The thing that worries me is, when is the right time to start again? Do you think there is such a thing as too soon? Am I destined to be transition person? If so, not interested. Might be transition person for ex-husband, which is bad enough.

Would you be ready to meet someone now? Could you experience a connection with someone else a year after losing the person you loved?

Yours,

F

Dear F,

Just recently met someone. So far feels right, but can't say am not wary. Trying not to think too much about it. Does that answer your question?

You sound nice. Pity.

Fondly as ever,

M

Chapter 36
Too Many Hearts

Sitting in Tuesday's seminar, the last of the series, I could be in a Brazilian rainforest for all that I am absorbing. Marina is on particularly effusive form tonight. We're on to the final P – perseverance – having heard a half a dozen stories of the successful conquering of place, promotion and props. I tune back in to see Marina holding up a flyer made by someone called Kelly. Her brand is *adventurous*, *sporty*, *loving*, and she's got a picture representing each of these aspects of her brand on the cover of her flyer. Inside is a heartfelt plea to her friends to introduce her to people they think would like her brand.

Angie digs me in the ribs and whispers, 'That's a step too far, don't you think?' She's probably desperate for me to agree, being worried that if I tell her I've had five hundred copies of my own flyer printed she'll feel compelled to follow my example.

'Absolutely,' I say. 'Couldn't bring myself to embrace that particular P.'

The break can't come too quickly for me. My whirling head can't focus on Marina's assiduous guidance, and I'm feeling far too self-involved to properly care about the progress of any of the other hundred and forty-nine women in the room, except perhaps for Angie, Claudia and Louise.

Angie is the first to speak when we gather with our wineglasses. 'Ally, I have to thank you for what you said the other night.'

'Well, I'm glad it helped. But I don't remember saying anything terribly insightful,' I say. 'You knew all that stuff. Sometimes it just helps when someone else says it.'

'Well, whatever you said, it got me going. I did what you said. I even carry this around with me now.' She holds up a small magazine clipping she's retrieved from her bag. When I look more closely I see that it's actually the inside cover of a video, with a picture of Richard Gere walking out of the factory with Debra Winger in his arms. The others wear perplexed expressions until Angie explains.

'So anyway,' Angie continues, 'I actually made a phone call. Called up my friend Della and asked her if she could think of anyone to introduce me to. At first she said she couldn't, that I'd already met everyone she knew. But two days later she rang back and said would I be game on to meet the brother of her husband's football mate. She just remembered that he's broken up with someone. So we're going out this weekend. How's that for progress? First date in four years!'

'Angie, that's great,' gushes Louise. 'Just as soon as I lose some weight I'm going to do what you did. For now I'm having the best time living with my friend. If I'd known it would be this great I'd have moved out years ago.'

Then a voice says, 'Why wait until you've lost weight, Louise? You know what I think about that.' Marina is suddenly standing in a little circle, in between Angie and Louise. She looks earnestly at Louise as if to emphasise that hers was not a rhetorical question.

'I don't know really,' stutters Louise. 'I think it's just that I don't really want to fall for a man who'll fall for me as a fat woman and expect me to stay that way. You know, one of those blokes who prefers fat women? I don't want one of those. It will end up being just another trap, and I'm sick of being trapped.'

That's the sanest articulation of a rationale I've ever heard, and I hope Marina gives Louise her due. She cocks her head to one side and considers Louise for a second, before saying, 'That's good, Louise. That's a very positive way of looking at it. You'll go out there when you're ready. Just don't forget what you've learned here. I hope you'll count on all the friends you've made to remind you.'

We all brace ourselves for the weight of the responsibility Marina has just thrust upon us. Claudia is looking uncomfortable; she's probably worried that Marina will turn to her to ask her what positive steps she's taken to find herself a proper partner. I know from her whispered asides that her action plan thus far has consisted of little other than a nightly shag with her shiatsu dreamboat. Personally, I think that if they're still shagging every night after a month there's got to be something to the relationship, and Marina might just be impressed. But Claudia's not up for sharing this. She mutters something about needing a tissue and excuses herself. So Marina turns to me.

'And you, Ally? How are you doing? I was so thrilled to hear your story last time.'

At this point I know I have a choice, albeit one I have to make quickly. I can smile and say that everything's fine, and hope Marina moves on to another group. Or I can share my dilemma with her, Louise and Angie. But the choice is taken from me because Marina has an inbuilt sonic radar system, and she's picked up some signals she thinks are worth exploring.

'Now, come on, Ally. You look a little troubled? What is it? Share it with us.'

So I do. I stand in the middle of the Wessex Room underneath an enormous three-tier chandelier monopolising Marina's time for at least fifteen minutes. She is so engrossed by my story that she shoos away her assistant when she comes to give her the five-minutes-to-airtime signal.

I can tell that she is most thrilled by the fact that her duck decoy and place plan exercises have resulted in the coming to fruition of a real live opportunity. She can even see some value in the Gary episode, though she's quick to point out that duck decoys work best when they aren't people for whom we feel inappropriate levels of physical attraction. She's also genuinely interested in the dilemma that's resulted from all of this, but not, in the end, much help in resolving it.

'In the end, Ally, none of the P's can help you make a choice. You can take a horse to water, as they say. You need to listen to your heart to know which relationship you should bet on.'

If only it were that easy. The trouble is, it's not just my heart we're talking about. There's David's heart, and whether he's really capable of giving it. There's Tom's heart, and the question of whether it has been so broken that anyone trying to fill Jenny's shoes could only ever come a poor second. And there are three tiny hearts involved, two of which I know could never withstand a false start.

One thing's for sure. My heart's not in this any more. Marina is right about one thing. Nothing I learn here tonight, and none of the tricks of the dating trade, can help me. They're an irrelevance now. So when, at the end, we are all asked to stand up and link arms and pledge to support each other (as I always knew we would be) I feel a bit like a fraud. I've no intention of forming a self-directed support group to carry on the good work we've all started here, or indeed persevering with the techniques Marina has carefully spelled out in our notes.

I will miss Angie, Claudia and Louise, though. And we may even stay in touch. I'm not happy going away not knowing whether Angie's rendezvous with the friend of her friend's brother (or was it her husband's friend's brother?) will work out. I'd love to see Louise settle into her new independent life, and lose the two stone she's set as her target weight-loss. And I'll not rest unless I hear the outcome of the Claudia story. I think her twenty-five-year-old would be mad to let her go, and I hope he's smart enough to see that.

As we go our separate ways from the Savoy I wonder what they're all thinking about me. Would they just be curious to see how things work out? Or would they will me in one direction or another? They've all been good listeners, but none offered a surefire route out of my impasse. The best that anyone had to say was that I should just relax and see how things work out. How useful is that?

Pretty useful, as it happens.

Chapter 37
Another Burial

Important, verging on earth-shattering phone calls on Wednesday: mine to Alan, explaining that I can't go out with him because I'm involved with someone else (two of them, in fact); Tom's to me, asking whether we can see each other this weekend; David's to me, in which he tells me he thinks he might be in love with me still, or again – might; and mine to Strand Hair Design, during which I intend to book an appointment for a full head of highlights with George, but discover that he has died.

I am incredulous, and my first words betray me. 'No. You're not serious?' As if anyone would joke about something like this.

'It's true, my darlin',' says Grant, the owner of the salon. 'He died last night. A heart attack.'

'A heart attack? But he was always so slim and fit. And he didn't smoke.'

'I know. They think it might have been the asthma. He was actually in the hospital at the time. He was in there for food poisoning again. Cooked himself another chicken.'

George got food poisoning every time he cooked for himself, which is why he took most of his meals at a bistro close to his flat. He had his own table there, a free half-bottle of wine with every meal, and many friends among the steady flow of regular customers.

'My God. I can't believe it. What a terrible, terrible thing. You must be devastated,' I say to Grant.

'It's a big loss. A huge loss. I haven't really taken it in myself.'

'How is his son?' I ask. George has a twenty-two-year-old son, a budding film director.

'Taking it hard, as you can imagine. But he's a strong kid. A really great kid. He's asked for donations to Asthma for Children instead of flowers at the house or the funeral.'

The funeral is on Saturday morning. David agrees to have the children, and I go alone. By the time I walk into the church there are at least two hundred people there, a lot of them women. George's clients, their beautifully cut suits and tasteful little hats worn as a final homage to a man who believed in small luxuries. Cashmere sweaters, bottles of Moët, a single fresh red rose in each vase in the salon. A good perfume perfectly applied.

Like me, many of these people will have been seeing George for ten or twenty years. That's a lot of conversation. More than you might have with any other of your friends or family. There aren't many other people with whom I've spent three or four uninterrupted hours every six weeks, engaged in a form of therapy. Therapy-light – in which you are invited to unload your every thought, distasteful or otherwise, about the latest news and celebrity gossip, and laugh about your own or George's recent adventures, mishaps and dilemmas. Not every stylist is up to that kind of relationship, but George was.

Many of the women here will have seen each other at their worst, as had George. Not many women's looks bear close inspection when their hair is wrapped in a hundred squares of tinfoil, or their face is bare and exposed after a vigorous wash and comb out. But no one seems to mind. For a place that's all about improving what you look like, there's remarkably little vanity about.

I find myself a seat at the end of a pew next to a woman and her daughter whom I recognise from the salon. The woman drove down from Nottingham once a month to have George cut her hair, such was her devotion. Her daughter, Elena, has magnificent thick dark hair cut to fall in gentle waves on her shoulders. She used to time her own visits to George to coincide with her mother's so they could spend time together, but also so that Elena could stock up on the expensive shampoos, conditioners and texturisers that she couldn't afford on her own salary.

It's difficult to remain dry eyed during the service and few do. The hymns are beautifully chosen, and an old friend of George sings a haunting solo. But most moving is the tribute paid George by his son Damian, a young man who has been forced to rise to the occasion at a cruelly young age. And rise to the occasion he does, lifting our spirits as he reminds us of the enormity of our loss.

'First of all, I have to apologise,' he begins. 'If you're wondering where that strong smell of cologne is coming from . . .' He glances behind him at his father's coffin, eliciting smiles and then low laughter from the congregation. We all exhale heavily, our relief palpable.

Damian goes on to recount many tales we've all heard, and a few we haven't. Those who are new to the salon are perhaps surprised to learn that George was once a top model, dancing at Studio 54 with glamourous types like Bianca Jagger. Glamour. Understated elegance. These were words you would naturally associate with George. But he was more than just a man with a cashmere habit. He had real decisiveness and strength, which was never more in evidence than when he thwarted the attempted theft of his Rolex by swinging a hairdryer around by its cord and bashing the armed thug on the temple while everyone else cowered behind the chairs of the salon.

After the service, the courtyard of the restaurant where we are all gathered is humming with people sharing stories about George. Grant, who's known George for fifteen years, looks lost. He keeps muttering 'A huge loss. Such a loss' in his clipped Scottish accent. Grant was the steadying counterpart to George's volatility and flamboyance, but they shared a wicked sense of humour. If you were ever in the mood to just sit, you could listen to the banter between the two of them over the clip-clip of scissors and steady hum of hairdryers. Today, Grant and Damian huddle together for much of the gathering, perhaps in recognition that it is they who will feel George's absence the most acutely.

I don't know many people here, just the dozen or so I've happened to coincide with in the salon over the years. I chat with Elena and her mother, Carole, for a while, then find myself commiserating with an elegant woman with ash-blonde hair held in a neat ponytail by a tortoise-shell clip. She looks to be in her late forties, and is wearing the most gorgeous fitted black suit I've ever seen.

'Terrible. Don't know how we will all cope, do you?' she says, shaking her head before taking a sip from her wine-glass.

'I know. It's quite unreal, isn't it? Hard to take in,' I say.

'Do you want to know what I loved most about him?' she volunteers. 'He made me feel marvellous. Even when my life was shit, he made me feel beautiful and special. When I first got divorced, I used to book an appointment with him every week, just so I could come and see him. And he always said to me, "Francesca, you are going to be happy again. You will find another man who will adore you. You'll see."'

I can hardly believe I'm standing opposite the woman whose name I've pinched. A woman who, in a funny way, was partly responsible for the rejuvenation of my own romantic life, or for the mess I'm in, depending on how you look at it. But it makes perfect sense. Of course she would be here.

Funerals are feeling factories, inspiring immediate familiarity. So I say, 'George really admired you. He told me he loved the way you embraced life after your divorce, didn't sit around feeling sorry for yourself.'

'Did he now? Well let me tell you, dear, there was plenty

of feeling sorry for myself at the beginning, but he helped me to snap out of it. But what was he doing telling people stories about me?' She smiles mischievously, as if she doesn't really mind the fact that she's been discussed at length.

'He thought it might help me. I'm divorced myself, you see, and I was asking him whether he knew any women who were doing better than me at starting over again. You know, getting out there with some fight in them.'

At this news Francesca says 'Come, come' and steers me towards a small round table, taking two full wineglasses from a passing tray as she goes. We sit at this table for the next hour, oblivious to the conversation around us. Francesca tells me all about her marriage to a wealthy polo pony-owning businessman who left her for his secretary. (*So predictable it's sad, don't you think?*) She tells me about feeling miserable and worthless and unattractive. And about all the mistakes she made as she started seeing men again, and the tremendous fun she had making them.

'It was all worth it,' she says. 'Because I found out a lot about myself along the way, and realised I'd been married to the wrong man in the first place. I vowed to find the right one before my fiftieth birthday.'

'And have you?' I ask.

'I'm getting close,' she says smiling. 'Very close indeed. I think I might have found him, he just doesn't know it yet.' She winks at me, then adds, 'I turn fifty at the end of the year. So wish me luck.' She winks again and raises her glass. I raise mine to meet it.

'What's he like? The one you've set your sights on?' I'm not just making idle conversation; for some reason I'm dying to know the answer.

'Oh, he's just lovely. Not perfect, you understand. Not even someone I would have looked twice at ten years ago. But I think I've grown up a lot. I feel ready for a man like him. Honest and straight. None of those silly games. That's so sexy, don't you think?'

I consider Francesca's words as I watch her pop a quail's egg into her mouth.

'You may be right,' I say.

Chapter 38
Lists

Marina thinks lists are a good thing. She says they bring definition to the indefinable, and there's nothing so indefinable as love. I could use a spot of definition right now, so I make a few lists of my own.

Things I loved about David:

Milk chocolate eyes. Eyes that you can sink into.
Provocative self-confidence. Bordering on arrogance but v. sexy.
Shoulders.
Mouth.
Hair. Just long enough so your hands could get lost in it.
Brilliant with images.

That he called me clever and determined and liked it when I argued.
Perfect height for me.
His romanticism. That he thrust himself into our marriage like a huge adventure.
That he loves Jack and Millie and they adore him.
That he was useless at most mundane domestic tasks, but would surprise you with his brilliance at something complicated.
Surprises, in general.
The way he looks when he's leaning against a doorframe in a loose grey T-shirt, not saying a word.

Things to (maybe) love about Tom:

Lovely grey-green eyes. Sad and smiling all at once.
Honest but not maudlin. Can talk about his wife but without falling apart. Where does that kind of strength come from?
Lovely warm smile. Maple syrup kind of smile. And that line on one side of his mouth when he smiles.
Very funny. Lovely laugh.
Stomach?
Delicious voice. Am sucker for a Southern drawl.
Brilliant with words.
That he could announce something like 'we have a connection' in the broad daylight of a coffee shop, without the safety net of alcohol or darkness.
Tall enough to pick me up like R. Gere
Honest. Straight.
Good father. Takes Grace to park at crack of dawn. Knows enough to take supply of digestives to Waitrose.
Also good at surprises. Note through letter box v. surprising. Coffee shop confession also v. surprising

The way I feel when he touches me accidentally in the cinema, or on purpose when he picks me up from the pavement.

Reasons not to love David again:

Big risk. Does he mean it? Can a leopard ever change his spots? Why now? Already buried under camellia. Too late?

Reasons not to keep seeing Tom:

Big risk. Probably not ready to love someone yet. Might be transition person. Might be person he wants to make life with Grace easier. (But he's not that sort of person, surely?)

Reasons must make decision:

Not fair to string along two men. Is it?

If sleep with Tom, will really not be fair to string along two men. Will it?

Reasons to wait and see:

How can possibly decide now, when known Tom such short time?

Probably will not sleep with Tom any time soon, so still have time before become wicked two-timing trollop.

Surely will soon receive a sign?

Well, that wasn't much help.

Chapter 39
Splits

The trip to Valencia is incredibly poorly timed. George's funeral and my state of mind are not the ideal backdrop to a three-day meeting in the orange groves, however pleasant that might sound to someone else.

I'm not miserable, you understand. In fact, I'm giddy with excitement much of the time. Like a girl who's suddenly discovered she's the belle of the ball, and is whizzing from one dancing partner to another while her friends watch in jealous disbelief. I'm loving the attention, and the thrill of being thrilled by someone again. If only there weren't two someones involved.

David and I spent Sunday night together, him sneaking back home before dawn. Every fibre of my body told me this was wrong: the children were in the house and might have woken up; we were in our former marital bed, which will confuse matters horribly; things will surely get too cosy if we carry on like this, which will definitely confuse matters horribly. But after writing out my list of all the reasons I'd loved David, I found myself even less capable of steeling myself against them. All the stuff about risk I was somehow able to ignore.

To make matters worse, the night before the day of my departure for Spain, I crossed the line between confused woman taking reasonable steps to figure out her feelings for two people, and wicked two-timing trollop. It turns out that making the list of all the things I like about Tom made him more irresistible as well. To the list I am now forced to add: nice stomach after all; gracious lover; great kisser. Really great kisser.

I hadn't planned for this to happen either. But I hadn't seen Tom for a week, and when he learned that I would be away for three days he suggested he come over for one drink, leaving Grace to be looked after by a babysitter. When the drink was over and we were standing at my front door, a kiss goodnight turned quickly to a kind of undignified and desperate ravenousness. This time he kissed me unhesitatingly, as if he'd given himself permission. I said, 'Stay', to which he replied by picking me up, wrapping my legs around his hips and moving towards the stairs – at which moment I had a quick flash of Angie with Richard Gere that made me smile. I said, 'Not up there. The children,' and pointed towards the sitting room, where we collapsed on to the sofa. From that moment on I wasn't thinking altogether clearly, and at some point I stopped thinking altogether, but I do remember remarking to myself about the stroke of luck involved in having opted for the fuchsia bra.

We ended the evening lying on the floor wrapped in a blanket from the back of the sofa, laughing in whispers lest our voices occasion the appearance of a small person at the door. He said, 'This is incredible to me. You have no idea.' And I thought, actually, I might. When it was quite late, and my face was still tingling in all the places he'd just kissed it, he said, 'Could you do me a favour and stop kissing me or I'm never going to leave. And I have to leave.' I sat on the sofa with the blanket wrapped around me and watched him get dressed. Then I walked him back to the door, and he said, 'Let's try that good-night thing again. See if it works this time,' before creeping back home to explain to the babysitter why he'd been two hours longer than planned, and on a school night too.

A couple of days in Valencia will give things a chance to cool down. At the very least, it will keep me away from both of them, and give me some space to think about what I'm doing. And I must think about it. Now that I've crossed the line, I can't just carry on. Francesca might approve of it, but George never would. When I call Clara from the airport, she definitely doesn't.

'What did I tell you about straddling two horses, honey?' she asks exasperatedly. 'I knew you'd end up doing the splits. You've got to sort yourself out.' Any minute now she'll be running out to the bookshop to dig out some advice manual like *Choosing Between Two Lovers*. or *Knowing Your Own Heart*.

'It's not that easy, Clara,' I say. 'It's not like I planned any of it. If Mel hadn't got me involved in that Proactive

Partnership thing I'd never be in this situation because I'd never have met Tom. David would probably not have reappeared on the scene either, come to think of it. I'm sure it was his subconscious fear of my starting to get away that spurred him to action.'

Clara starts to say something. 'Doesn't that tell you . . .', but my mobile dies mid sentence and I don't catch it all. I have to go to the gate in any case. As I walk towards it I check the time and see that it's almost three. Almost time for the complicated set of childcare arrangements I've made to kick in. David has volunteered to take over from Jill after tea and spend the night, thereby absolving Mel of that responsibility. (Here's what I meant about cosy. It's amazing how cooperative your ex-husband suddenly becomes when there's sex involved again.) Then Mum and Dad arrive tomorrow, for two days. They'll play back-up to Jill at teatime, and do solo duty overnight. The children should get more attention that I could ever give them if I were at home alone with them.

During the flight I'm wondering how such a good girl could have ended up in such an appalling situation. There's the not knowing what to do. That's bad enough. But there's also the doubt about what I've done. In retrospect, I can see that there were better ways to handle every situation in which I found myself. Ex-husband suggests weekend away? Say no, and suggest a few cautious dinners instead. Ex-husband stands at door of hotel room looking unspeakably alluring? No question. Shut door immediately, with ex on other side. Nice-looking man from neighbourhood suggests coffee, then evening out? Say must sort out confused relationship with ex first, please. Nice-looking man from neighbourhood proves to be more interesting and more gorgeous than first anticipated? Don't, whatever you do, then sleep with ex-husband in quaint wisteria-clad hotel, and again in former marital bed. Don't, whatever you do, compound sins by then sleeping with new man later in same week.

It's as if all my good judgement flew the coop one night when I wasn't looking. Lisa said I ought to unbutton myself and open up a little, but I'm sure she didn't mean this. I've become so unbuttoned I'm in danger of unravelling. My agitation is such that not only am I shedding ounces by the minute, I have become oblivious to the perils of turbulance. At one point just before our descent I look around me to see my fellow passengers gripping their arm-rests and seeking out reassurance on the faces of the air stewards, and I realise that most of the swooping and bumping in the air currents must have passed me by; my stomach has been doing double-flips for days all of its own accord and it's a state I've grown accustomed to.

Walking out of the airport into the balmy April air I feel a fragile sense of calm descend over me. I'm quite sure it's temporary, but I'll take it all the same. I scan the line of black-trouser-clad, dark-haired drivers leaning against their limousines and taxis, searching for a sign that says 'Señora James'. My driver spots me just as I spot his sign, and hurries towards me.

'Señora James?'

'Yes. Hello.'

'Please, let me to take your bag. Señor Rico will to meet you at the hotel.'

Señor Rico is a liaison officer with the main packing house used by Cottage Garden Foods. I've met him once before, when I first started in the business. His job will be to welcome me, see that all my needs are catered for and escort me on a round robin tour of the major growers in the area. These friendly visits from product managers and buyers must be among the easiest aspects of his job. He doesn't yet know that we've a contract to discuss, but as we'll probably do this in a lively tapas bar, even that shouldn't be too painful for anyone.

The drive from the airport takes us first through a few miles of dry, barren-looking fields, but it isn't long before we are surrounded by rows of flowering almond trees and acres of orange trees. The blend of early summer evening warmth and almond blossom is intoxicating. I open my window and hold my face up to the breeze and the last warming rays of the waning sun. By the time we arrive at the hotel, and Señor Rico appears at my door to open it, I'm as close to mellow as my inner deliberations will allow.

Señor Rico, having anticipated that I might be tired after a day's work and a flight, has considerately left some space in my itinerary. After settling me into my hotel, he says a polite goodbye and confirms that he'll collect me the following morning. So the evening is mine, to do with as I wish. All I really wish is a gin and tonic in a long bath and a quiet dinner during which I won't be required to speak.

My room is dark and cool. Everything is white except the terracotta floor tiles and the single multicoloured rug at the end of the bed. I open the shutters and the doors to reveal a minute balcony overlooking a courtyard. A single branch of an almond tree is drooping over one corner of the balcony, partly obscuring the view of the courtyard and the other rooms. Outside, the air is cooling but the light is still bright. It's that peaceful, unobtrusive brightness of early evening, the brightness of a day that's lost its edge.

I go into the bathroom to run myself a bath, then lie down on the bed and pick up the phone. It's too late to speak to Jack and Millie but I can find out how they are. David sounds tired when he answers the phone.

'Hi, it's Ally. I thought I'd check in and see how everything is going.'

'Great. Kids are great. I'm managing fine. Still remember where the saucepans are. How are you?'

'A little tired, but fine. I'm not really required for duty until the morning so I'll probably have a quiet dinner and go to bed.'

'Sounds good. I'm keeping our bed warm for you.'

Something about the presumption behind the words 'our bed' irks me.

'David, for the past two years it's been my bed. I'm not sure I'm quite ready to call it our bed, just like that.'

'Well, you seemed pretty ready when you were in it with me a few nights ago.'

'That's different. You know that. That's me being caught up in the moment, forgetting about everything that's happened. But those things have happened, and I can't pretend they haven't.'

'I know they happened, Ally. And I'm sorry. But they are in the past. Out of my system.'

'What about my system?'

'Come on, Al. Don't go all funny and cold on me. You bring out the best in me. I need you.'

I know something soft and conciliatory is in order, but I can't summon it up.

'Anyway, we can't resolve all this on the phone. I have to go to dinner now.'

'Ally, do you still love me or not? Because I got the impression you did.'

'David, I'll probably always love you. That doesn't mean it's easy for me to do this. Or possible for me to do this.'

'If you still love me, that's all that counts, Ally.'

Lying in the bath with my gin and tonic, I'm agitated when I should be relaxing. Is it all that counts, the fact that I still love David? Surely other things count, too. Like the fact that he was once prepared to trade what we had for two years hopping in and out of bed with other women. And the fact that his coming back is not just a matter between him and me, but something that will affect Jack and Millie. We can't make another mistake. There's no suck it and see option for us.

And, surely, the question of whether or not he still loves me, surely that counts too. And shouldn't he be hoping I love him too, not assuming my bed is ours again with so little effort on his part? I forgot to ask him about that. So when I'm out of the bath, I pick up the phone again. This time it sounds like I might have actually woken him up.

'Hi. It's me again. Did I wake you?'

'Just dozing. What's up?'

'I was just wondering what you meant earlier when you said you needed me.'

He laughs. 'You're a funny one. Why the seriousness all of a sudden?'

'I just want to know, that's all.'

'I meant just what I said. I don't think I want that life any more. I need a different sort of life. I want what we had. I felt like I was coming home when we spent that day together, and I liked it.'

'How do I know you won't change your mind again?'

'I won't, Al. You won't let me. I know I can count on you to protect me from myself.'

He laughs, but I don't think it's very funny.

I sit at my table for one, sipping rioja and picking at my paella. The dining room is full, but happily no one is paying any attention to me. There is one other person dining alone, a not unhandsome man, probably here on business as well. It amuses me to think that a few weeks ago I'd anticipated seeing someone like him here and using some sort of Marina-recommended prop or trick of body language to try to meet him. Tonight there couldn't be anything further from my mind. I could have sent Nicki on this trip after all, for all the scouting I'm doing.

I leave half of my paella and decline dessert. (There goes another half-pound.) I'm not calm enough to sit here and relish the atmosphere and the solitude, so decide to go upstairs and try to distract myself with a book. But the book doesn't work either, so I open up my laptop and log into my PerfectPartnership mailbox. The metres of unanswered emails don't bother me any more. I know I can just delete the lot in one swoop when I want to. I'm not here to read, but to write.

Dear M

I find myself in a state of unrest. Now getting dangerously close to being seriously involved with two men. Ex and lovely man just met. Am torn: is it best to do right thing? Give broken marriage another chance. Give children back their father – which is also, by the way, the easiest thing and v. tempting. Or should I take a chance on new thing, with all its possibilities?

Yours,

F

I wait for a few minutes then check the inbox to see if he has replied. But there's nothing. I leave the laptop unattended to get undressed, then check it again. Still nothing. He's obviously got better things to do late at night than sit and wait for an opportunity to give advice to someone he's never met. The better things probably have to do with the blossoming love interest he wrote about last time. Good luck to him.

So I go to bed without a reply. There's no reply in the morning either, so I depart for my day's touring none the wiser. Wearing light trousers and shirt, my new butter-coloured loafers and a large wide-brimmed hat, I slip into Señor Rico's open-topped car feeling ever so slightly Grace Kelly. The hat is, it soon becomes obvious, totally impractical, ideally needing to be held in place by a couple of Hobie Cat tarpaulins. As there don't appear to be any of these to hand, I am forced to ditch the hat and retrieve the less glamorous but far easier to contain baseball cap from my bag.

Señor Rico's packing house deals with over three

thousand growers in the region. I can't think that they are all charming and amiable, but the ones he takes me to meet today certainly are. My favourite is Angelo Recatala, a man with two young daughters who runs a twelve-hectare farm with his two brothers. His farm is among the smaller ones we visit, but he is so passionate about it that you can't fail to be drawn in. In halting English that I can just barely understand, he talks me through the pruning in January and February, the careful watching during the summer, and the harvesting in September. I exaggerate my fascination with the new drip-irrigation system he has installed so as not to dampen his fervour.

Señor Recatala's wife announces a lunch of *jamón de bellota* and *parrillada de verduras*, which turn out to be a rich, dark ham and grilled vegetables. Plates of other delicacies keep arriving at the table – enormous king prawns in garlic and fried squid with black and white mayonaise. I gulp it all down eagerly, along with several glasses of home-made wine. It's the first meal I've eaten in its entirety, and with any real enjoyment, in over a week.

We bid farewell to Señor Recatala and drive to another, much larger farm. It's a new supplier for us, so desperate to please. There is slick machinery everywhere, and the drip-irrigation system of which Señor Recatala was so proud has been in place here for years. The complex is heaving with people rushing to and fro. It's like a sped-up version of the Recatala farm, but not without its charms.

I'm warmed by the beauty of the landscape and the spirit of the people, and worn out by the relentless pace of the day. But David and Tom and my persisting dilemma still punctuate my thoughts. I catch myself looking at people but not really seeing them, or tuning into conversations half a minute too late. Even during the lively dinner with Señor Rico and his colleagues that follows the farm tours, my mind wanders a little.

When I'm back in my room after dinner I log on to PerfectPartnership.com to see if M has replied. He has.

Dear F

Is it possible that the right thing might also be the new thing?

M

I type in my reply.

Dear M,

Meaning?

I'm anticipating having to wait until the morning for M's reply, so I'm astonished when I come back from brushing my teeth to find he's already sent it.

Dear F

Meaning that what's right has to be right for you. Does ex want to come back for right reasons?

Fondly,

M

Dear M,

Says he needs me. Says he misses our life together. Says I'll protect him from himself (himself being the one with a former penchant for romantic variety).

Dear F,

Doesn't sound right to me. Sounds convenient.

Dear M,

Touché.

But question about readiness of new man remains. Perhaps he too is under illusion that I will protect him from himself. Perhaps he wants me just to fill hole left by death of wife.

Dear F,

Let me tell you something about that hole. There's no easy way of filling it. There's not even an illusion about filling it. Not with casual nonsense anyway. The best you can hope for from your average light liaison is the papering over of the hole. The hole is so big that only the real thing could ever hope to fill it again. So you might find that your new man's a very good judge of the real thing, and that the thing he feels for you is it.

Dear M,

How will I know for sure?

Dear F,

Ask him. What have you got to lose? What if he said he can't go back to the way he was before now that he's met you? What if he told you all the things he loved about you? Then you'd know he wasn't looking to paper over that hole, but to fill it right up.

Wouldn't that be nice?

Goodnight.

M

I don't think there's anything I can say to that, so I log off and get into bed. But even the cool cotton sheets and the smell of jasmine wafting up from the courtyard can't lull me to sleep. After lying staring at the ceiling for a while, I switch on the light and pick up the phone again.

It's one in the morning in England but Tom sounds wide awake. 'Ally, are you back?'

'No. I'm still in Spain. I just wanted to hear your voice.'

There are two ways this can go. There will be a silent, awkward rejection of my confession, or a warm embrace of it.

'Tell me about it. I've been waiting to hear your voice for two days. I miss you. How crazy is that? I was managing perfectly well without you until two weeks ago, but now I feel like I spend every waking minute waiting to see you.'

'Tom, the night before I left . . .'

'I know. That was probably too fast, and we should slow down a little.'

'No, it wasn't too fast for me. But isn't it too fast for you? Shouldn't you be testing the waters a little, finding your feet? You know, doing a little casual dating or something.' Please don't let him say this is his idea of casual dating.

'I'm not the casual-dating type. Never have been,' he says. 'I really want this.'

What? To protect him from himself or from his past? Or to paper over a hole?

'Why? Why do you want it, Tom?'

'Why? Because now that I've let you in I can't just forget about you and go back to the way I was. It would be like another kind of bereavement. I can't promise anything,

Ally. I can't promise things will work out. But I can promise that I want them to. Is that good enough?'

'Hmm. It's not bad as promises go,' I say, chewing my lip.

'You've done something to me, Ally. I don't know, maybe it's the extraordinary way you have of throwing a rugby ball. Or the way you get all animated when you talk about the great marmalade tradition – and, incidentally, I hate the stuff. Or the way you are so gorgeous with your kids. And the way it feels when I kiss you. The whole fucking lot. But especially the last part. Is that good enough to go on?'

Yup.

Chapter 40
Welcome Home

Halfway through my second morning touring with Señor Rico, he turns to me and asks, 'Señora James. You are all right? Something it is not right?'

'Sorry? Oh, no, everything is fine. I'm just a little distracted.'

'You are sure? Because we can perhaps change the itinerary for the last afternoon if you would prefer.'

'No, it's perfect. Please carry on.'

It's no wonder I'm distracted, with all the questions that are whirring round in my head. Does David really know what he wants? What did he mean last night? Did I believe Tom when he said he wanted things to work out? Can I trust the leap of my heart when he said it? But most troubling of all: what am I going to do about all this?

But I've decided one thing at least. I've decided that, strictly speaking, I'm not a wicked two-timing trollop after all. True, I slept with David, then I slept with Tom. But I'm not going to sleep with either of them again until everything has been sorted out. So, strictly speaking, there's been no overlap.

The day can't pass quickly enough for me. I suspect that I'm somewhat harsher than I might have been during our late-afternoon contract discussions; I'm so intent on making the six o'clock fight to Heathrow that I'm not prepared to allow us to meander through the clauses at a leisurely pace, and I'm even less inclined to give way on one lest it invite dawdling over the rest.

Desperate as I am to get home, I'm loath to leave the sweet, balmy air and the genial company. Two days here has been intensely refreshing, even if I have had to spend much of it cooing over state of the art irrigation systems and chopping facilities. I can't expect to be greeted by such sumptuous weather in England, and will very likely face a taxi ride home in the rain.

But I'm wrong. England is experiencing one of those tantalising bursts of summer in early April – a sure sign that we're in for rain and cold during May. I emerge from the terminal and step into early evening air that has something of the feel of Valencia; only the almond blossom and the lines of olive-skinned drivers slouched against their taxis are missing.

As my taxi pulls up in front of the house I see Mum's face peeking out through an opening in the shutters. Then before I've even paid the driver she is standing beside me while Dad is wrestling my suitcase up the front step. The way Mum fusses over me you'd think I'd been backpacking solo through Nepal for six months rather than being wined and dined in sunny lands just a two-hour flight away.

'Darling, would you like a cup of tea?' she asks, smiling as she watches Jack and Millie rushing in for a hug.

Mum's cups of tea are not to be spurned, such is the thought and method that goes into the making of them. Boil fresh water (too little oxygen in the reboiled stuff); warm pot for one minute; throw in three bags (in my pot at least); wait four and half minutes; don't stir! (causes stewing). I never bother making tea for them when they visit because I always get it wrong and I can't bear to watch their polite but strained expressions as they swallow.

'Please,' I say, then, 'How are my two angels? I've missed you both.' I have, in a funny way, though it's fair to say my mind has been on other things. When I'm away from them for more than a day my body experiences a sort of subconscious longing for them. More than two days away and the quiet longing becomes a persistent, irrepressible ache. There's something so completely unnatural about not being the last one to see them before they go to sleep, not knowing what they've had to eat, or what's made them happy or angry during their day.

Dad has been reading to them in the sitting room, but they want me to finish the story. It's one of Jack's favourites, about a small boy who goes on midnight adventures involving tow trucks, midnight turkeys and great vats of treasure. Her usual affable self, Millie listens as if it were *The Princess and the Pea*. Just as I near the end I'm handed my perfect cup of tea, which I have some trouble sipping with a child tucked under each arm.

Millie says will I tell her about Spain, so I tell her the bits I think she will like. Then Jack rushes off to fetch the atlas so I can show him where, exactly, I've been. As we are poring over a two-page spread of southern Spain Millie makes an announcement.

'Mummy, you got flowers.'

'Flowers? Where?' I want to say 'from whom' but the heat rising through my throat won't allow me to.

'They're in the kitchen,' says Mum. 'They were dropped off this morning while we were on our way to school. We found them on the doorstep.'

'I'll get them!' shouts Jack, running to the kitchen. He returns with a small basket full of snowdrops and lillies. There's a blue envelope protruding from one side. Jack takes the card and hands it to me, his eyes wide with expectancy.

'We've had a lot of trouble preventing certain little people from opening the card,' says Dad. He winks and tips his head towards Jack, but I can tell he's as keen to know the identity of the sender as Jack is.

There's no signature, and the inscription is a little mysterious. *Missed You xox*. But I think I know who they are from.

No one else can read the card, but my cheeks redden and a shy smile creeps on to my face. I feel as though I've been caught at something.

'Who is it, Mummy?' asks Millie. Does she hope it's David, I wonder.

'It's Grace's daddy. You remember him? That nice man who played rugby with you, Jack.'

Jack looks puzzled. 'Why did he send you flowers?' he asks scornfully.

Mum comes to the rescue. 'That, my darlings, is none of our business. Come on, let Mummy go upstairs and get changed, and I'll take you two to brush your teeth.' And with that she shuffles them off upstairs, leaving Dad to clear his throat awkwardly and bury his head in his paper.

I get up and give him a kiss on the forehead, then say, 'I'm going up to change. Back in a minute.' As I'm walking out into the hall he says, without looking up from his paper, 'Hope he's a nice chap, love.'

Going away always means a bedtime routine that takes at least an hour longer than usual when you get back. Three more stories, several extra hugs, dozens of important thoughts that must be expressed. This is as true tonight as after any other time I've been away. It's funny, but the same isn't true of the times they leave me to go away with David. It's only when you make the choice to leave them that you have to pay.

By the time I come back downstairs it's almost nine and Mum and Dad are watching the news. I sit down on the sofa beside Mum and she says, 'I assumed you'd eat on the plane, darling, but I'll make you something if you like.'

'No, no. I'm fine,' I say.

Then we talk about their two days with the children, pausing to watch a particularly amusing news clip of George Bush spluttering his way through a press conference of which he appears to have lost control. Mum tells me how great she thinks Jill is, and wonders at how helpful David seems to have been. All the while I'm wondering whether my shallow breathing and jumping heart are evident to them both. Surely Mum can see the ridiculously fast rise and fall of my chest beneath my shirt.

Eventually I can't stand it any more. 'Would you consider it really rude of me if I went out for an hour or so? There's something I have to do.'

My father looks bewildered, but Mum doesn't hesitate. 'Of course not, darling. You go. We have all weekend together.'

And this is how I end up running along the three streets that separate my house from his. I don't think about what I'm wearing, or whether my hair is a mess. I just run. When I reach his door I can see that the lights are still on. But Grace will be asleep, so I knock rather than ring the doorbell. When he opens the door he gives me that slow, oozing smile. The one that starts with a trickle but ends up everywhere.

'Well, look who's here. The intrepid explorer.'

'I didn't want to wait until tomorrow. I hope that's OK.'

'Oh, I think I can just about live with it. Come here.' He pulls me inside and wraps his arms round me, then kisses me very gently.

'I wanted to come and tell you something.'

'OK. Let me get you a drink and you can tell me,' he says, not looking the least bit worried about what I'm going to say. He picks me up just like the other night and carries me through to the kitchen, where he sits me on the counter and stands against it with his hands on my thighs.

'You know on the phone, when you told me all those lovely things? It sort of took me by surprise and I didn't have a chance to tell you anything.'

'Yeah. It didn't go unnoticed,' he says lightly.

'Well I'm going to tell you now. All the things I love. First, there's this,' I say, tracing his smile line with my finger.

The line deepens as his smile widens.

'Another thing I love is that you know to take a supply of digestive biscuits for Grace when you go to Waitrose.'

'You're gonna have to explain that one to me sometime,' he says, standing back and giving me a quizzical look.

'And there's the way you threw that rugby ball with Jack, and the fact that you could say something bold and scary like "I think we have a connection" in the middle of a coffee shop in broad daylight when we'd only just met. I love that.'

Then he kisses me and I say, 'And, of course, there's the fact that you're a great kisser. A really great kisser.' Then I remember what really prompted me to run over here in the first place. 'And you send flowers. Thank you. They are lovely.'

Tom leans back again with a puzzled look on his face. 'Flowers?'

'The lilies and snowdrops you had sent to the house.' A chill runs down my insides as it occurs to me that I might have made a mistake.

'Ally, I'd love to take credit for the flowers, but I'm afraid I can't. They must be from your other lover.'

I know that in response to this statement I'm supposed to say don't be silly there is no other lover they must be from the neighbour whose cat I looked after, or from the fellow at work who's become somewhat obsessed with me, or from my boss, Anna Wyatt, to congratulate me for my brilliance of late. But instead I sit in front of him with my mouth slightly agape. I never was very good at lying under extreme pressure.

Tom's face darkens a little. 'Ally, am I in competition with someone?'

The thing is, I bet when he was younger the prospect of being in competition with another bloke for some girl's affections wouldn't have bothered him at all. I bet he won most of his competitions in any case. But now, after all he's been through, losing Jenny, being on his own, being afraid of not finding someone else then even more afraid when it seems he might have found them, a competition is probably not the scenario he's hoped for.

'No. Not exactly. Things are just, um, complicated.'

'How complicated?' He removes his hands from my thighs. He's not gone cold, exactly. He's not even really angry yet. He's just creating some distance, which I can't blame him for. But it scares me a little.

'It's my ex-husband David. Let's just say he's been showing more interest in me lately. I think he might have been the one who sent the flowers.'

Of course he was the one who sent the flowers. Only wishful thinking could have convinced me it was Tom. David has always been a flower kind of guy. Romantic gestures to make up for bad behaviour and all that.

'I thought you'd been divorced over two years! I thought you said he'd been with so many other women you couldn't count them. Why is he suddenly showing interest?'

I don't really know the right answer to this question, but I have my suspicions. I bury my head in my hands trying to decide what to tell Tom.

'Tom, I'm not really sure why. He says he regrets what

happened and misses the life we had. I think it might also have frightened him to see me finally moving on with my life. When I decided to get out and find someone else I guess that was something of a shock to him. It doesn't mean his feelings are genuine. And it doesn't mean that I necessarily want him back.'

Necessarily was a mistake. But Tom doesn't pick up on it. He's too focused on the previous sentence. The one about my deciding to go out and find someone.

'Whoa. What do you mean you decided to go out and find someone? How, exactly, do you do that? Am I the result of some sort of project or something?'

Did I set out to find someone? It's only been six weeks since Mel asked me to help her with her article, but somehow, in that time, everything has become confused in my mind. One minute I'm having to be dragged kicking and screaming to a seminar full of single women at the Savoy, the next I'm burying baggage and engineering dates and signing up for dating websites. And chasing handsome strangers to the park. What has happened to me? How did I end up here?

And is it such a bad place to be really?

'Don't make it sound so alarming. It's not what you think.'

Might it be worse?

'I just meant that in the past two years I haven't really been open to a relationship. In fact I've probably subconsciously rejected the idea of one. Then something changed and I decided it was time. It just happens that I met you soon after that, and then David started making all these weird overtures.'

Tom's face has softened a little, the alarm gone from

his eyes. 'So you just sort of decided you were ready for a change and then, bingo, you met me. Just like that?'

Yes, just like that, give or take a few details. Does he really need to know the details? Would he be more incensed to hear about the details now, or to find out about them later and know that I'd misled him? Assuming there is a later, that is.

'Sort of,' I say. Then I plunge in, for better or worse. 'My friend Mel asked me to attend a series of seminars for women who want to find husbands or partners or whatever. She's a journalist and she needed someone to write about. So I agreed. Very reluctantly, I have to tell you. And I went along to these seminars, and I followed my instructions, and that's how I met you. And I suspect David saw all this happening and was intrigued.'

The cloud descends upon Tom's face again. It's much darker this time.

'So you go on a course and you follow some instructions and you meet me? What the fuck were the instructions for Christ's sake? Accidentally bump into vulnerable widower in children's playground and make him fall for you?'

Well, yes, if you want to put it like that. For all Marina's smooth talking and charm and her elaborately alliterated marketing patter, that's what it essentially boils down to. You manage your situation so that you have more chance of accidentally meeting someone who's right for you. According to Marina you could hit the jackpot within the year, or, in my case, six weeks. Immersed as I've been in the whole thing, none of it looks so bad to me, but I can see why it looks bad to Tom. He's not been where I've been for the past six weeks.

'Well, yes and no. I mean I'd seen you before, and then we met just outside the house. Remember? Then one day I just decided to follow you when I saw you walking past the window. Then I was hoping to bump into you again but I didn't, until I tried shopping at Waitrose instead of Tesco, where I normally shop, and there you were. Is that so awful? Really?'

I can see that he thinks this is awful. Really awful. If I put myself in his shoes I might think it was awful too. There he was thinking serendipity has been watching over him, that somehow he's been incredibly lucky to meet someone he feels connected to, and now I'm telling him that, no, actually, it was all part of some grand scheme. Someone else's scheme.

'And your ex? What's his name again? David? Where does he fit into all this now? Did you have a plan for reeling him in, too?'

God he's making me sound terrible. Like some sort of cold-hearted, manipulative freak. Like that woman from *Fatal Attraction*. Surely that's not what I am?

'You know, Ally, this is all a bit much for me right now. I don't really understand it, but it doesn't sound good to me. First you tell me you might be sort of involved with your ex, because that is what it sounds like to me, then you tell me you've had this whole thing planned from the beginning, like some sort of bizarre dating challenge. It's just too weird for me. Not what I expected.'

I look down at my feet dangling aimlessly below the counter, so I don't see the expression on his face when he says, 'I think you'd better leave.'

So this is what it's come down to. All of Marina's advice.

All the Ps and the camaraderie and well-intentioned enthusiasm at the Savoy. In the end, it all falls to pieces because the minute someone discovers you found them with the help of all these shenanigans they drop you like a hot potato. Of course they drop you. Who in their right mind wants to be with a woman who's been so intent on finding them that she was prepared to pay £500, sit through three seminars and follow her instructions like some over-zealous sixth-former?

Tom has moved away from the counter now and is standing with his hands on his hips. His eyes, normally so soft and forgiving, are like steel. Somehow it doesn't seem appropriate to plead with him, and I'm not sure what I would plead in any case. I ease myself down from the counter and walk out of the kitchen towards the front door. When I reach it I'm hoping, though not expecting, that he will suddenly appear behind me and stop me from leaving. I wait about three seconds with my hand on the door latch for this to happen, but it doesn't. Something makes me turn and shout out the last word through the stunned silence of the hallway.

'You know, Tom, I'm sorry about the way I met you. But I'm not sorry we met. For a while there I thought I'd been amazingly lucky.'

Then I open the door and walk the three blocks home, all the while praying that my parents are in bed so I don't have to conjure up some sort of elation for their benefit. It would be so disappointing for them to see snowdrops and lilies followed so closely by such total and utter gloom.

Part 4

Chapter 41
Goodbye to All That

The weekend is a blur. Just something to be got through. I think that I'm managing to hold myself together for my parents' sake, not to mention the children's, but when my mum is hugging me goodbye she whispers, 'Things will work out. You'll see,' so I know she's been aware of my dismal spirits all along.

On Saturday I'm half expecting Tom to call or appear at my door. By Sunday I'm not expecting any more, just hoping. By Monday I'm convinced it's not going to happen. And it doesn't. A whole week goes by and I don't see him walking past my front door on the way to Grace's nursery. He must have changed his route just to avoid seeing me.

The more time passes the more excruciating

introspection I indulge in. Now it's as clear as crystal to me why Tom would be so distressed by the idea of my having ensnared him as part of my homework.

Mel says 'For God's sake, Ally. Stop beating yourself up. Why is what you did so much worse than going to one of those speed-dating things?' But it is worse, because it's not consensual. When two people meet on a speed date, objectionable as the whole thing might appear to outsiders, at least there is something honest about it. Both parties have gone into it with their eyes open. No one's being duped. But with Marina's methods it's different. All this duck decoy business, and place planning and branding – it's so one sided. What would Alan say if he knew I'd only gone out with him because I knew he wasn't my type? I'm sure he'd hate me now. Just like Tom.

Every night before I go to bed I go in to kiss the top of Jack and Millie's heads. Millie sleeps like a little princess waiting for someone to kiss her awake; ramrod straight on her back, her golden hair spread about on the pillow like Rapunzel's. I usually find Jack with the duvet thrown off, sprawled on his side with his favourite rabbit under his arm, his dark hair wet with perspiration.

Tonight, as I wipe away a bead of sweat from the bridge of Jack's nose, I catch a glimpse of David in the pout of his lips and the tilt of his cheeks. Those invisible threads that link my heart to Jack's pull tighter. I suppose I'd better get used to that. I'm always going to see David in Jack and Millie.

But as hard as I try, and I really have tried, I can't see David with me any more. It's as if, by coming back and giving me another look, he's made me see everything I didn't see clearly enough the first time.

David is beautiful and passionate and intriguing, and he has a playful, reckless boyishness about him that I used to adore. Now, I can appreciate it from afar. But I don't want to be married to it.

I don't think he can make me happy any more. Maybe we've just used up all the love we were supposed to feel for each other. Or maybe all the love we're supposed to feel is in Jack and Millie now.

David has been away on a shoot so he doesn't call me until midweek. He wants to see me Friday. Says we need to talk. I know we do. I just don't know exactly how to say the things I think I need to say. I'm hoping Clara's lucid thinking will help sort me out.

She is actually there with me when David calls. We are sipping wine on my sofa after the kids have gone to bed. It's late, and she's paid a mercy visit on her way home from a business trip to Madrid. It's a long detour from Heathrow to Notting Hill via South London, so I'm incredibly grateful.

'Was that David?' she asks when I hang up and come back into the room.

'Yup. How'd you guess?'

'Could tell by your tone of voice. You have a special voice just for him.' Then a pause. 'What are you going to do?'

'I don't exactly know. Part of me thinks I should give in, go along with him and see where it takes us. But . . .'

'But what? You know it would be wrong? Or you don't want to?'

I think hard for a minute, giving myself the opportunity to retract the thoughts I'd had the night before.

'I think – and this is hard for me to believe – that I don't want to. Not enough, anyway. You know that thing he said the other night? About getting all that nonsense out of his system? Well, I think I might have got him out of my system. I probably still love him, but I don't think I'm obsessed with the idea of loving him. For the first time I can see that maybe he wasn't my mate for life. Not really. Not like I thought. I think sleeping with him again was the best thing I could have done.'

Clara raises her eyebrows questioningly, but there's only kindness in her eyes and her lips are poised in a half-smile.

'Really, I mean it,' I say. 'Not that I didn't enjoy it, because I did. But it sort of broke the spell.'

Clara says again, 'So, what are you going to do?'

I twist my wineglass round in my fingers, staring into its depths as if some kind of answer will be found there.

'I think I'm going to tell him we can't see each other any more. Not like that, anyway.'

A flutter of panic suddenly rises up in me. God I hope that's the right thing to do. When I had Tom, or the promise of Tom to be more precise, I felt stronger. Now I don't have it and it feels like I'm flinging myself into an abyss. At the bottom of it is that woman from the *Observer*, looking as despondent as ever.

Clara looks at me with her piercing blue eyes. As if she too has seen the *Observer* woman, staring bleakly up at us, she says, 'You will find the right person some day, Ally. I just know it. I've been watching you. It's amazed me how you took this whole thing on, this challenge of Mel's, and actually made things happen. OK, so Tom may not be the man in the end – and I'm not saying he isn't by the way. But if he isn't someone else will be. At least you got out there instead of sitting here getting fat and moping. And at least you're not sinking back into the comfort of something you know isn't right just because it's available.' She takes loud gulp of her wine.

'I've decided I'm going to do just what you did.'

I look up in horror. 'But, Jonathon . . .'

'No, no. I don't mean that. I mean I'm going to take things into my own hands and stop being a victim. I want a baby. I'm going to change my life so I have the best chance of having one. Jonathon was right. We don't stand much chance of getting pregnant when I'm away three nights a week and exhausted the rest of the time. I'm going to ask for a sabbatical. Six months. Maybe longer. I'll offer to do some part-time industry research or something. If they don't like it, fuck 'em! If someone steals my clients, fuck them, too. Some things are more important.'

Clara is nearly bubbling over with exhilaration.

'Clara, I'm so proud of you. I think you're doing the right thing.'

'Yeah, so do I. I have no idea what will await me when I go back, or how on earth we'll manage on less than half our income. But I figure you can't always look for a safe landing. Sometimes maybe you have to take a risk, and give up something that feels wrong even if you might never get the thing that's right. Don't you think?'

Yes, I do think.

'And by the way, I know about Mel. I know you said she

shouldn't tell me but I'm glad she did. It hit me like a rocket through my gut then. I knew I wanted what she had so badly I'd do anything to get it.'

'Al, I can't believe you're doing this.'

I'm sitting on a sofa draped in what look like props abducted from the set of *Easy Rider*. Jack's been using the back of the sofa as a horse, and has dressed it up with a makeshift saddle (a piece of cardboard he rescued from the recycling bag), reins (four shoelaces tied together), a blanket for cold nights and a saddlebag stuffed with juice boxes and chocolate mini rolls for his imaginary journey. Under no circumstances is any of it to be moved.

David is sitting opposite me on the coffee table. He's leaning towards me and we are so close that I can smell the lunchtime beer on his breath mingled with the faint remains of soap.

'Don't think it's easy for me, because it's not. But I know in my heart that we can't start over. I don't want to start over.'

'How can you say that!' he shouts in disbelief, sitting back on the table with his hands on his knees.

Then he relents, leaning towards me again and slipping his hand under the bottom of my shirt where it finds some bare skin. I feel a familiar rush of something, but I push his hand away.

'David, don't. I love you. But I don't love you like I did.'

Sensing that the power of sex isn't going to work its magic this time, he tries another tack. The power of guilt.

'Al, don't you feel just a little compelled to try again, for the kids? We have two great kids together, and life would be better for them if we were together. We can work the other stuff out.'

'No. I don't think so. The other stuff, as you call it, it's too big. It's not just that you betrayed me. It's that I don't think I could ever really know that you wouldn't betray me again. But it's not just about that. I don't want to be the person you need to keep you on the straight and narrow, or to give you the life you miss. I don't even want to be the one you've decided you fancy quite a lot when all the rest haven't worked out. I don't want to back into a relationship, do you see? I want to be chosen.'

I've got to hand it to David. He doesn't give up easily, and when guilt doesn't work he has one more crack at sex. As we stand at the door, he pulls me towards him and slips his hand around my back and under my shirt. Then he gives me a long, searching kiss that just about breaks my will.

'You're making a mistake, Al. Think about it,' he says before walking out the door.

I think about a lot of things in the minutes after he's gone, not least of which is the fact of how awkward the weekend handovers are going to be for the next long while.

'Jesus that was hard. I don't know how I did it,' I say to Clara afterwards.

'You did the right thing, honey. Hang in there. All things pass, and that wretched self-doubt will be no exception.'

I don't call Mel, because I'm not sure she'll give me the advice I need. She's always had a soft spot for David;

combine that with her general devil-may-care, see-how-things-work-out approach to life, and she'd be all for my carrying on a highly secret, no-strings affair with David until the thing between us had truly run its course. And I don't want to hear that.

Chapter 42
Marking Time

David is avoiding me. I'm not sure if it's a tactic intended for his own protection or to win me round. He sends his friend Chris to collect Jack and Millie when it's his weekend, muttering something about how they are all going to spend the weekend together. (Chris is also divorced, with two boys.) Millie thinks it's a bit strange, but she's not alarmed. She knows Chris. Jack is overjoyed at the prospect of spending a weekend in the company of two older boys.

Not wanting to think about Tom and David, and with no seminar homework to keep me busy, I allow marmalade to fill the days. It's not too difficult, because everything is coming together. The new ad campaign for Seville Sunset is ready and the launch programme is fuller than

I could have wished for. Retailers are crying out for tasting packs and in-store promotion material. The zest-clumping problem for Pure Gold now resolved, we are making up for lost time and rectifying stock shortages by trying to shift double the normal volume of jars through the warehouse.

Anna is pleased. Thinks the Sunset print campaign is inspired. The best she's seen in a long time. I have Anna to thank for an idea that I've had. When I told her how much I enjoyed doing the research about marmalade she said, in an offhand way, 'Well you should think about doing more of it. Life's too short to not do things that you enjoy.'

I'm not sure exactly what she meant by that, but one evening I was slumped glumly in front of some mind-numbing property show when I glimpsed C. Anne Wilson's name amidst a pile of old *Vogue*s on the coffee table. I reached under the mess and pulled out *The Book of Marmalade*. Its brown and orange cover struck me as rather plain, which I hadn't noticed before. And it's really not a very weighty book at all, I thought. Considering what you could do with the topic.

And that is how I ended up marching into Anna's office with a proposal for a large, full-colour coffee-table book about marmalade. My plan was to have everything in it – historical anecdotes, recipes, full-colour spreads of marmalade sauces and puddings and orange groves, close-ups of the people whose every breath goes into the making of marmalade. A magnificent book about a magnificent tradition. Something to really put Cottage Garden Foods on the marmalade map. Something to revive marmalade in the public's imagination. And to give me a project I can really sink my teeth into.

Anna thought it was a great idea. She's volunteered an assistant to help with the copy, and agreed to a budget large enough to secure the services of a quality photographer. Now the challenge is to produce a template of sufficient quality to tempt a mainstream publisher to support the project and smooth the way into bookstores and cooking shops. Nicki is thrilled, as the project promises to lend a certain glamour to days that would otherwise be filled with budgets and agency contact reports.

So I've spent a lot of evenings on the internet, researching obscure websites, looking up the details of small UK marmalade cooperatives we can go to interview. Millie sometimes sits with me doing her own research, which consists of re-rereading the St George's prospectus and student handbook. With the Easter holidays in full flow, it's just over a week until she starts there. Her new uniform is carefully laid out on the floor underneath her desk, the socks tucked neatly into the shoes.

Jack is moving too, of course, but he seems blissfully oblivious to the fact. He's so out of tune with school as a concept that it doesn't much matter to him which one he goes to at this stage. School, any school, involves the reading of unbearably long books and the consumption of unappetising school lunches, so it's best not to give it too much unnecessary consideration.

Clara and Mel do their best to keep me chirpy. Mel has suddenly been overwhelmed by all-day nausea. ('Who was the fucker who called it morning sickness, I'd like to know?') Clara seems, I don't know, serene. She's always been a tower of strength, solid as a rock and all that, but lately she seems to have taken on an air of tranquillity as well. True to her word, she's requested a sabbatical from Peters and Young and ridden the storm of their objections (of which there were many). Now she's winding down and handing over and preparing for her new life, renting out her and Jonathon's flat and looking for something smaller for a while. She even gave two pairs of her Ferragamos to her PA when she realised that normal sized closets couldn't possibly contain her entire collection. Once she took that first step it's as if a whole new world opened up to her. Or the possibility of a whole new life.

Amidst all of this, I can just about convince myself that I'm all right. Before school broke up there was the tombola stall, for which I eventually managed to rustle up 265 spectacular looking jars and which resulted in a handsome profit of £56.40. Now, I'm so busy being inspired by Clara's new lease of life, researching remedies for Mel's morning sickness, trying to enjoy the lunches Anna suddenly wants to have with me, planning outings for the school holidays and beavering away at my spectacular book of marmalade that I almost don't have time to think about what I'm missing.

But I am missing something. And at night, lying in the middle of my queen-sized bed in the aching silence, I miss it most. What is it I miss most? What's gone?

Possibility has gone. I don't miss Marina's advice or her seminars or all the efforts I made, all that activity. But I do miss the sense of possibility I had for those few weeks. A sense that life was moving somwhere, towards a better place. And the thrill of anticipating.

But mostly I just miss him. Funny, I've not really known him long enough to miss him, but I do. What was that he said? I'd won him over? Well he'd won me over, too. It feels like I love him. All that realness, packed into such a short time. It's hard to give that up.

I know Clara is right. I know that I will, one day, meet someone. I'm not really afraid of being alone. But I hate the thought of being without him.

Chapter 43
Chorus Line

By the beginning of week three (in the calendar in my head, time is measured out in days since I was standing in his kitchen) I'm not despairing any more, not exactly. More like quietly melancholic. And resigned. Resigned to the fact that I'm not likely to see Tom again. He's not going to call, or drop by, or put another note through my door. And I don't have the heart to hang around Waitrose in the hope of running into him. What would be the point of that? He'd only take it for another manipulative stunt, and it's clear what he thinks of all that.

I know all this. Which is why it's such a shock when I peer out of my bedroom window, just like that morning all those weeks ago, and see him walking up the street towards my house with Grace in the pushchair. My heart skips a beat and my immediate reaction is to pull the shutters across the window and stand with my back to them. I've waited all this time to see him, but now I can't face it. What if he were to look up on his way by and see me standing there like some pathetic, lovesick teenager?

But that's what I am. Not pathetic perhaps. And definitely not a teenager. But lovesick. And seeing him has suddenly reminded me of just how lovesick I am. Surely I owe it to myself to try it one more time. How bad would it be if I chased him this one last time and tried to persuade him that what I did was not so terrible after all? What would it take to run down the stairs and out of my door and after him?

Not much, because I'm already dressed. Jack is playing with his plastic carwash in the kitchen, and Millie is creating a masterpiece with her rainbow art set. They could easily be left alone for the five minutes it will take me to run up the street, have my say and come back.

I sprint down the stairs, slip on the loafers that are by the front door and shout to Millie that I'm just going out into the front garden for a minute. (None of us sees anything strange in calling the five foot square repository of two dustbins and a couple of shabbily adorned window boxes a garden.) Then, breathless and with a heart that feels as though it's about to burst, I open the door and walk with a thud into a chest that turns out to be Tom's.

He's standing with his hand poised just above the doorbell. Grace is behind him in her pushchair. She leans out of it and beams at me from behind Tom's legs. After a second, he beams at me too.

'Hi there. We gotta stop doing this or someone's gonna get hurt.'

I'm momentarily speechless, but I manage something I think resembles a pleased expression.

'Well, are you gonna invite me in, or shall I head straight out to that climbing frame in the hope that you'll follow me?'

I stand back from the door and gesture for him to come in. It takes me another few seconds before I find my voice, and when I do it doesn't sound anything like the one I used to have. This one's all quiet and tentative.

'Would you like me to follow you to the park? I thought you disapproved of such behaviour?'

'Well, I've been thinking about that. A lot. And I came round here specially, to tell you what I've been thinking. If you'll let me.'

I feel my body relax, and my voicebox regain some of its strength. 'Come in then. I'll put some coffee on.'

Then I bend down to help Grace out of her pushchair. 'Millie, Jack. Tom and Grace have come for a visit.'

Millie rushes up the hallway from the kitchen, then comes to a sudden, shy halt in front of Tom and Grace.

'Mill, would you take Grace into the kitchen and share your paints with her while Tom and I have a chat?'

Millie glares at me. Her paints are brand new and precious and obviously not to be shared with an almost three-year-old.

'Or maybe you could find her those crayons of Jack's and give her some paper?' I try again.

At this suggestion, Millie manages to find her gracious hostess expression, and takes Grace by the hand. Tom and

I follow them to the kitchen, where I fill the kettle. It's only a ritual really. Just something to do. I don't want any coffee.

'I'll make that in a minute,' I say. 'Shall we go in the other room?'

'Sure, just as soon as I've said hello to my rugby pal. How're you doing, Jack?'

'Fine,' says Jack, without lifting his gaze from the red Ferrari he is pushing up the ramp of the carwash. At some point I must teach him some social graces, but now doesn't seem like the most appropriate moment.

When we reach the sitting room Tom stands in the middle of it and turns to face me with his hands on his hips. It's just like that moment in his kitchen, only without all that shock and disapproval polluting the atmosphere. He doesn't wait for me to speak, or try to fill the air with introductory pleasantries.

'Look, I wanted to come and say something,' he starts. 'That last time, I think I might have overreacted a little. I know I did. I just wasn't ready to hear all that. But then I got to thinking.'

I watch his lovely face as he pauses and tries to think what to say next and how to say it. It's a serious face, but not a hard one.

'And what I thought was that the thing between us is very new, but it's too good to throw away just like that. I've been lucky enough to have it happen to me for a second time, and I don't want to throw it away. I meant all those things I said to you. The days after I met you it felt like a light had gone on. Then you were gone and it felt dark again and I hated that.'

He closes his eyes for a brief moment and scrunches

up his face, as if the effort of saying these things has exhausted him. Then he opens his eyes and stares at me intensely. 'It feels like I love you. I do love you. Don't ask me how I know that, but I do.'

I know it's my turn to say something, but I'm a bit stunned so nothing comes out. He smiles. A wide, twinkling, beautiful smile. 'If you think about it, relationships are a bit like a good marmalade aren't they? Bitter and sweet at the same time, bright and golden but full of dark patches, mostly smooth but with the odd lumpy bit that gets stuck in your teeth. Well, the way I figure it, we've already got a real big lumpy bit out of the way, which has got to be a good thing. Should be all smooth sailing from here.'

Then a pause before he adds, scrunching up his face again, 'And if you have to work stuff out with David, I will have to live with it until you do.' Then he smiles again. 'Just tell me one thing. You were dragged to those seminars right? You didn't actually want to go?'

'God no!' I say over-anxiously. 'I hated the idea. I just got kind of carried away. But once I met you it wasn't really about that any more. I went to those places because I hoped I'd see you. I know that's kind of childish, but it isn't reprehensible, is it?'

'No. No it's not.' He smiles again and steps towards me. When he pulls me against him, the warmth of his chest is intoxicating. I can feel his breath on the top of my head and the gentle touch of his fingers behind my neck as he holds me close. Inside me, relief and joy are all mixed up together, swirling around and making me light headed. I could happily stay like this for hours, silently breathing him in, but there's something I need to make absolutely clear.

I look up. 'There's nothing to work out with David any more. I worked it out. Honestly. That doesn't mean he won't be coming round here, because he will. He's Jack and Millie's father, after all. And it doesn't mean he's totally comfortable with things yet. With just being their father, I mean. Things are still a bit raw and messy. But he'll get used to the idea. The important thing is, it's my idea.'

'Message received,' he says. He's about to kiss me when the doorbell rings. 'What a fabulous piece of timing,' he says with a pained look on his face.

I'm on my way to the door when I am affronted by a loud wail from Jack.

'I'll get the door. You go see what's up,' says Tom.

Jack has scalded his hand, having turned on the tap to refill his carwash. I run it under the cold tap then apply some antiseptic cream and give him two Club biscuits from the tin. Millie and Grace are oblivious to the whole episode, having gone out into the garden with a skipping rope. Grace, who is far too small for skipping, is standing with the rope tangled round her ankles while Millie looks on giggling.

As I walk back to the sitting room I can hear the low murmur of male voices. One is Tom's, obviously. The other is the voice of a visitor who has evidently been invited in. I realise whose voice it is before I walk into the room, but it doesn't help to assuage the acute anxiety I feel when I see him.

'David! What are you doing here?'

As uncomfortable moments go, this is pretty bad. It's bad enough for me. Perhaps it's worse for the two of them.

'That's not much of a greeting,' says David with a very small laugh.

'Sorry. It's just that I wasn't expecting you.' I glance involuntarily at Tom. David looks at me, then at Tom. I can almost see the colour draining from his face. He looks down with a heavy sigh, then starts nodding his head as if he's just understood. I can't ever remember having seen David looking awkward. At one time, perhaps two years ago, I might have taken some small pleasure in witnessing his awkwardness, but not today. Today it pains me. Part of me longs to wrap my arms round him. It just doesn't suit him not to have the upper hand.

The awkwardness is infectious. Now Tom has thrust his hands into his jeans pockets and is looking down at his feet as if he's wishing the moment to pass unnoticed.

'So, I'm guessing you two have introduced yourselves?' I say.

'Yeah,' says Tom, looking up at David.

'Hmm,' says David.' And I'm guessing my dropping in isn't all that convenient,' he says, laughing that small laugh again. It's not quite the antidote to his awkwardness that he probably hopes.

Even less convenient is the ring of the doorbell, for the second time. All three of us look at each other, then Tom says, 'For Christ's sake, it's like Grand Central Station in here,' before going out to open the door.

There's something territorial about the way Tom answers the door automatically, and I can see that David is disturbed by it. But that's nothing to what I feel when

Tom reappears, flanked closely by Gary. Gary of Hamilton and Sons, but thankfully without a nurse's uniform.

'Hiya,' he says, quickly becoming afflicted by the awkwardness that now permeates the atmosphere.

'Gary's here. Your lighting man, apparently. Are you having your lights fixed?' says Tom with knitted eyebrows. He glances up at a ceiling full of lights that appear to be in perfect working order.

Everyone looks so deadly serious, including me. And yet there is something terribly funny about this, I can see that. All we need now is for Alan to turn up, just so we could see the fruits of all my efforts arrayed before me in their full splendour. I'm tempted to laugh. I'm sure I will laugh, with Clara or Mel tomorrow. Or with Tom some time far in the future. But to even smirk now would be to risk too much.

'No. There's nothing to do here. Everything's fine now,' I say. 'But thank you for coming.'

Gary gives a wry smile and an almost imperceptible shake of his head. 'I guess I'll be going then. Doesn't look like you need me here.'

'No, not really,' I say.

'Yeah. I should go too,' says David. 'I'll see you when I pick up the kids next week, right?'

'Right.'

This time Tom stays in the room and I accompany David and Gary to the door. I can't bear to look at either of them, though I feel I owe it to David, so I grab him by the arm just before I shut the door.

'I'm sorry,' I say.

'Me too,' he fires back without turning to look.

Through the crack in the door I watch David and Gary exchanging polite goodbyes on the pavement before heading off in opposite directions. I'm not worried about Gary. I was probably nothing but another potential exotic recruit to him. But watching David walk away without his usual confident strut is almost enough to fracture me.

But I haven't got a monopoly on fracture. Tom knows all about that. He is suddenly behind me, pressing the door shut. For a minute we both stand there, me with my forehead resting on the door, him with his arms about my waist and his lips gently pressing against my hair.

'I love you too,' I say.

I can hear Jack and Millie and Grace in the garden, their playful voices mingling with the drone of an electric hedge-cutter and the faint chimes of an ice-cream van a few streets over.

And it feels right.

Epilogue

The sun is unusually strong for September. We are enjoying an Indian summer after a July and August marred by rain. I've even lathered Millie and Jack in sunscreen.

They don't really need it, though. They are playing in the darkest, most protected part of the climbing frame, the part with the pitched roof. Some sort of charade is being enacted, in which Jack is pretending to have captured Millie and Grace, who are dutifully cowering in a corner.

Tom has gone in search of coffee and I snatch a moment to sit on the bench in peace. In less than an hour I will have to be chopping and stirring and marinating in preparation for our last-day-of-summer barbeque. Pudding is sorted at least: Claudia is bringing a banoffee pie, and her Nathanial, of course.

I run through the list of what I still need to pick up at Somerfield. Wine isn't on it. We have plenty, because neither Mel nor Clara are drinking much and Dom has cut down as an expression of moral support. Mel would probably have slipped into a glass-of-wine-a-day habit by now, but with Clara as both her example and her conscience she daren't.

Clara isn't showing much (it's very early days after all), but Mel is huge. What she isn't consuming in alcohol she's making up for in other carbs. Crisps, doughnuts, Carrs water biscuits. You name it. And pickled onions, which I suppose count as vegetables at least.

Soy sauce. That was it. There are just a few dregs in the bottom of the old bottle. I reach into my bag to find the shopping list and a pen. Rummaging around, I lay my hands on several pieces of paper, none of which turns out to be the list.

I unfold the first piece of crumpled paper, recognising it immediately as the article from the June issue of *Me*. Mel's article. It's not the whole thing – somehow I've managed to misplace the first few pages. I chuckle as I reread Mel's copy, which walks a fine line between respectful and cynical.

Perhaps that was my doing. When she asked me what I thought of the whole Proactive Partnership business in the end, I couldn't decide what I thought. Picking on its most ridiculous aspects was easy. Anyone with half an ounce of sanity would have concluded that creating a brand and outlining it in a brochure is madness. But the rest, she asked me, was it really all that bad?

No, I told her. Not bad exactly. Good in some ways.

Good for galvanising people, getting them going, creating possibilities. But dangerous, I said, in the end. You have to be careful not to use too many of Marina's tactics too often or with too much vigour because, taken to their extreme, they're just a kind of maniacal manipulation by another name. And no man is going to be comfortable with that. It could end up costing you the very prize you think you've captured.

I laugh at Mel's last line. *You can pay £500 to learn how to bury your past and create your very own brand if you like, ladies. Me? I'll stick to simply following that fit specimen to the park and hope he notices me.*

Under Mel's article is the other piece of paper, which is even more crumpled and has a giant coffee stain adorning its centre. The coffee has seeped into the paper and makes reading the text difficult, but not impossible if you squint hard enough and use your imagination to fill in the gaps. The solitary M at the bottom of the text immediately identifies it as the last message I received from him and printed off with the intention of putting it somewhere safe. I must have looked at it at least twenty times in the two weeks after Tom got angry and I left his house and it looked as though I'd blown everything.

Dear Francesca

You were right to tell him everything. Honesty isn't always the best policy, but when you're dealing with something you think might be quite special, it absolutely is. If he is ready to get over Jenny, really ready, then he'll forgive all that other business. Just give him time. Don't chase him. Don't rush him. Let him realise. He's taken an enormous bashing in his life but in some ways that could make him clearer than ever about what he wants. And he sounds like the kind of guy who, if he chooses you, will choose you for good.

Actually, this wasn't M's last email to me. Feeling elated after Tom came back, I emailed M one last time.

He chose me.

And he wrote back.

Excellent choice.

That time he'd signed off with his full name, Michael Ellis, and given me his home email address, saying he'd tired of the PerfectPartnership game but would be happy to hear from me any time. Having harboured vague suspicions that M might turn out to be Tom, I was mightily relieved to discover his real identity. There would be no more uncomfortable revelations and confessions to jeopardise the beginnings of the lovely thing Tom and I had fallen into. No more lumpy bits in the marmalade. And in Michael I'd found a friend.

I can see Tom now, wandering back with two coffees. I shield my eyes from the sun and watch him. When he reaches the trio of silver birch trees about twenty yards away from me he suddenly disappears from view altogether as a beam of sunlight shoots through the tops of the trees and bursts around him. For a split second all I can see is a splash of yellow and white light punctuated by tiny silver sparkles.

Then he's there again, smiling at me and holding up two venti cappuccinos triumphantly. When he reaches me he bends down to hand me my coffee and gives me a kiss that tastes of sugar and chocolate and cappuccino foam.

And I think, this must surely be the sweetest thing on earth.

Lessons in Duck Shooting

Jayne Buxton is a consultant and spokesperson in the field of work-life balance. After her non-fiction book *Ending the Mother War* was published in 1998 she became a regular contributor to press, radio and conference discussions about working parents and workplace change. She co-founded Flametree, a specialist work-life balance consultancy and interactive web based community for working parents. She now lives in London with her husband and three children and is currently working on her next novel.